LAND ON ME

A NOVEL

MATTHEW R. CORR

QUILL HAWK PUBLISHING

First Edition: August 2021
Edited by: Alicia Dean
Cover Art by: Dessiree Perez. Illustrations copyright © 2021 by Dessiree Perez
Interior Design by: Matthew R. Corr
Printed in the United States of America
Fiction: New Adult Contemporary
Fiction: LGBT/Gay
Fiction: Coming-of-Age
**Content Warnings: Homophobia, Hate-Speech, Underage Drug and Alcohol
Use, Strong Language, Sex, Conversion Therapy, School Shooter Drill,
Violence, Suicide, Death.**
ISBN: 978-1-7351194-6-5 (Paperback)
ISBN 978-1-7351194-7-2 (Hardcover)

ALSO BY MATTHEW R. CORR

Land On Him: A Sequel

Just For The Weekend

CAMP 1985

For Andrew Norman Coit
You're still here with me, in everything I do.

———

For anyone who has ever felt like they don't fit into a societal norm.
You are still valid, and you are loved.

ONE

My ears rang. I'd heard gunshots in movies, but in real life, they are louder than you'd expect. My elbows locked and my arms shook. I wanted to drop the gun, but my entire body was frozen in place. All I could smell was the scent of hot metal emanating from the barrel of the weapon. My mouth was too dry to speak, and I could hardly swallow. I desperately wanted to reach out to make sure he was okay, but there was so much blood. It was so red, and it was coming out so quickly. I didn't want to shoot him but he wouldn't have stopped otherwise. Tears welled in my eyes. His blood was on my hands now.

——————

My phone alarm was so loud it jolted me awake every morning, making my heart race. It was like being zapped by the machine that brings you back to life after you've flatlined. All the alarms on my phone failed to wake me up, so I downloaded this app called 'Nuclear', which sounded like one of those old-time nuclear warning sirens. It did the trick every time. I twisted over, snatched my phone, and clicked the snooze button. I wasn't a morning person. I turned on my back, closing my eyes, ready to let sleep take me again.

"Landon! Get up!" My dad's voice could wake the entire neighborhood. My face scrunched.

"I'm up!" I yelled. Just because I wasn't out of bed didn't mean I wasn't up. My dad was not a fan of that philosophy.

"No, you're not. Hurry!" he shouted from downstairs.

The same conversation happened most mornings. My dad was a military vet, and he'd been waking up early most of his life. I wished it was as easy for me.

My bedroom faced the street, which meant it got all the sun in the morning. The year before I tried to convince my dad to let me get blackout curtains, but he said no, saying I'd never get out of bed. I can't say he was wrong. I stood and took a big stretch, rubbing my eyes, letting my vision focus on all the commotion outside. Fun fact: I lived across the road from my school, Madison High of Madison, Texas, or "Mad High" as it was better known. Another fun fact; we had the highest use of marijuana in the county.

I shut the curtains in fear that someone would glance up and see me standing there in my underwear, staring at them like a creep. I shuffled over to my closet like the zombie I was, grabbing the first shirt I could reach, then grabbed a pair of shorts to slip into.

I trotted down the stairs, which led into the kitchen, and yawned as I sat at the island counter, popping up onto a stool. My dad was leaning against the sink, dressed in a blue suit. He was reading his phone with an intense expression; it was usually the news. The bitter smell of coffee brewing filled the air. It was one of my favorite scents.

"You should start going to bed earlier," my dad said, placing a plate of burned toast in front of me. He wasn't much of a chef.

"That's the benefit of living across the street from the school," I said, taking a bite of the toast. It crunched and crumbled back onto the plate. "I can wake up ten minutes before class starts." I could barely finish my sentence, the toast was terribly dry. "Pass the butter, please?" I reached my hand out like a toddler asking for his bottle. My dad placed the butter dish next to me and handed me a knife before rushing to pour his coffee. I laid the butter on thick while scraping off bits of black flecks.

"How do you think practice went yesterday?"

Dad was referring to football; I was the team's running-back. It didn't help that my dad was the Superintendent of the high school and had access to any practice he could get to. Growing up an only child was great, but it also meant all the pressure to succeed was on me. Not only did he grind me on the field whenever he could, but he was always making sure my grades were the best they could be. Football was something my dad loved, he played in high school but never had the chance to pursue it after joining military school. Most of the time it felt like he was living vicariously through me.

"Practice was fine," I said unenthusiastically.

My dad sipped his coffee. "You need to work harder if you want a scholarship, Landon."

You need to work harder on your cooking skills. What adult couldn't even make toast? The blame wasn't entirely on him. My mom was the one who had done all the cooking. He'd made nothing for himself for at least fifteen years that didn't take more effort than slapping the meat and cheese between two pieces of bread. I was better off making my food, which most of the time I did. I took one last bite of toast before giving up; It tasted like eating ash, buttered ash.

"And It needs to be better than fine if you want scouts to consider you instead of Dan," Dad said.

I rolled my eyes. Dan Wilson was my best friend, quarterback, and captain of the team. That was typical of my dad. All he cared to talk about was football, scholarships, or grades with a bit of politics sprinkled on top.

I whipped out my phone and scrolled through Instagram, waiting for my dad to mention something else I needed to do. Dan had posted a picture from an hour ago of him holding a fan of $20 bills. I tapped it twice to like it and commented: 'Dooouu-ucchhheeee.'

Dad's voice took my eyes off of my phone. "Are you hearing what I'm saying?"

"Yes, Dad," I said with a sigh. "I hear you loud and clear. I'll be better." I put my phone on the table and took my plate to the sink. My dad was next to me, leaning on the counter.

"It's not about being better," he said, turning to face me. "It's about putting in the work."

I scrubbed the small plate without looking at him.

"What is it you think I'm doing, Dad?" I placed the plate into the empty drying rack with a little too much force. "Taking a nap on the field every day?"

My phone started vibrating before dad could say anything.

Lauren Calling.

I clicked the message button and started typing.

ME

Can't talk right now.

LAUREN

I'm outside, I thought we were walking in together?

ME

Sorry, I totally forgot, be out in a sec.

"Gotta go, I'll see you later," I said with my back to my dad. I slipped my phone into my pocket, rushing for the door.

"You're forgetting something!" My dad yelled out to me. I spun on my heels, seeing he was holding up my backpack. I jogged over and grabbed it, but he didn't let it go. "I know I've been hard on you," he said, looking me in the eye. "I'm trying my best. Things have been hard for me too, you know."

"I know," I mumbled, looking at the floor. My dad let go of the backpack and I received the full weight of it. "You around later?" I swung the backpack around my shoulders as I walked backward.

"Not sure yet. I have a few meetings later in the day. My campaign manager is putting a lot on our plate." he said, picking up his coffee mug.

My dad was in his first year of campaigning to become Mayor of Madison, which packed on the pressure of being the golden boy. Politics weren't my thing, so we scarcely talked about it. It was weird when I saw signs popping up around town in people's front lawns with my dad's face on them. People looked up to him, people believed in him. I was just along for the ride.

"All right, I'll see ya then," I said before whirling around out the side door.

Lauren Ramirez was waiting for me at the end of the driveway, her backpack slung over one shoulder. She looked great in jean shorts and a flowy white button-up shirt. Lauren was a few inches shorter than me, with long, brown hair kissed by the sun, giving her natural copper highlights. She completed her outfit with a pair of black-framed glasses she used as an accessory. Lauren took me by the hand and we crossed the street. I caught a whiff of her sweet floral perfume in the breeze. The school's front courtyard was filled with people, clamoring to get inside to feel the first gust of wind from the air conditioning hit their faces.

Lauren and I had been dating for almost a year. She was the president of the school's drama club and the lead in all the school plays. She was hands down the best actor at our school. Her dream was to go off to New York City to become the next big thing. My parents loved her because she was polite and pretty; they assumed we were the perfect match. My mom and dad met in college and got married soon after, I assumed they wanted a similar path for me and Lauren.

We maneuvered through the crowd easily, my vision filled with blurs of color as kids whizzed by us, heading toward the entrance and their homerooms. Then something strange caught my attention, a shirtless guy. I saw the tanned skin of his back amongst the chaos when I shifted my gaze to the right. I squinted to focus, but like a mirage, he disappeared in a blink.

Lauren squeezed my arm. "Are you looking for someone?"

"What?"

"You were just looking around so attentively like you were looking for someone."

"Oh? No, I wasn't. Sorry, I just saw something weird. What were you saying?" I tried playing it cool.

"I was asking you if you wanted to go with red for our prom outfits, or if you were feeling another color?"

"Red?" I focused on Lauren, "No. Yeah. I mean, yeah, red is a good choice. I'm ok with that." I said. She smiled in agreement as we walked through the front doors of the school. I didn't care what color we wore to prom. It felt a little early to be thinking of it anyway, as it wasn't for another couple of months. While Lauren was thinking about prom dresses, I was thinking about a guy's back muscles that may or may not have been real.

"Hey, Landon!" A familiar voice rang out. "I need that short story by Thursday, we print on Friday, you know this!" Tasha Morgan yelled as she hurried toward us. Tasha was the editor-in-chief of our school newspaper. Once a month, the *Madison*

Monthly was published and handed out to students, chronicling all the important news we all needed to know. But, it also included student works, like poems, essays, pictures, or in my case, short stories. My brain came up with some pretty wild stuff. I liked to write it and share it with others.

Writing was something I loved doing more than anything. Much more than football, even. I knew it was something I wanted as a career. But I still hadn't told my dad. He had never read anything I'd written because I'd been too nervous to show him, fearing he'd be disappointed or say that I wasn't focused enough on football.

"Hey girl," Tasha said as she gave Lauren a quick hug. "Sorry for rushing by, I have a meeting about the paper with Mr. Jones." Tasha dashed off just as quickly as she showed up.

"I'll have the story by then, I promise!" I said to Tasha, watching her bouncing curls become lost in the crowd.

Lauren looked at me. "What's this one about?"

"I'm not sure," I said. "I haven't written it yet." I chuckled a bit as Lauren leaned in for a kiss. The bell rang, and everyone pushed through the hallway. Lauren liked to hold the kiss long enough for everyone to notice. She never said it, but I knew she wanted people to think we were a perfect couple. Lauren was the opposite of me--she loved being on stage for a reason. My eyes were closed while I kissed her, as they normally were, but this time I saw the flash of that guy's shirtless back and pulled my lips away. "All right, I need to go, or else we're both going to be late."

She took a step back, did a cute wave, and trotted off.

I wiped the lip gloss from my lips and headed for my Advanced Placement Literature class, wondering if anyone had been staring at us kissing. I tried shaking the thought of this shirtless person from my brain before climbing the stairs to the second floor. AP Lit was my favorite class. I enjoyed having in-depth conversations about characters, storytelling, symbolism, and everything else that came with classic literature. Mrs. Donahue was my teacher, a tall, slender woman with tanned skin and short dark hair. She was one of the few teachers up to date on the latest fashion trends. A lot of the guys from the football team had the hots for her. I mean, she *was* beautiful, in a teacher sort of way.

My seat was in the third row, on the far right side of the class, next to the large windows. I was one of the last ones to arrive as everyone had already filled the room with noise and chatter. I sat at my desk, placing my backpack next to me. I unzipped it and took out a notebook. Just as I sat back up, my eyes caught movement from outside the window. My eyebrows scrunched as my brain processed what I was seeing.

What the...

My eyes hadn't deceived me earlier. I was seeing the same shirtless back for the second time in the courtyard. The way the sun hit him, it was as if he was lighting up the entire street. It was like God had a single light shining down on his most beautiful angel. I felt like a creep, because everything else in my world fell away, and I was locked on him. I couldn't even hear the surrounding chatter anymore. He was doing something to the half wall that separated the courtyard from the sidewalk. Cleaning it, maybe?

I couldn't see his face; his back was facing me. He was slender, with broad shoulders. I noticed his jeans were sagging a bit, showing off the band of his white underwear; every curve of muscle in his back was pure perfection. He had those hard muscles poking out of his lower back, causing indents at either side of his spine that looked like dimples pointing toward his tailbone. His shoulders looked perfectly rounded as if they were sculpted by high-tech lasers. Every time he moved his arm I caught a glimpse of hair poking out from his armpit. His triceps flexed with every swipe across the stone wall. His hair was wavy and dark brown. It was longer on top than the back. I imagined myself being able to zoom in with my eyes like a camera just so I could see every bead of sweat pushing from the pores of his tanned skin. It was almost like he was sparkling like one of those vampires from *Twilight*. The sun was beating down hard. I couldn't help but wonder why anyone would want to stay outside. The boy was a fascinating mystery to me. Who was he? Why was he there? Why was his shirtless back making me feel some type of way? I watched, desperately waiting for him to turn around so I could see his face, hoping it would stop my wandering thoughts.

"All right, everyone," Mrs. Donahue announced, pulling me out of my trance, settling the hustle and bustle of the roaring class. "Today we are going to discuss obsession, sexuality, and sexual orientation in fiction." She was known for discussing more taboo topics that other teachers were afraid to talk about. "Who are some characters you think of when I say this?" No one raised their hands or even shouted out an answer. "Come on, people, there are some pretty obvious ones."

I hesitantly raised my hand, not wanting to be the first to answer, but I felt I needed to break the ice. I glanced through the window one more time to check on Mystery Boy, but he wasn't there. I was still very unsure if he was real or if I was suffering from heatstroke.

"Yes, Landon?"

My head whipped around to the front of the class when I heard my name. I faced Mrs. Donahue, but my eyes yearned for another quick peek out the window.

"Jay Gatsby," I said with a burst of energy as if I was holding the answer in my gut for days. He was the first to pop into my head.

"Yes," Mrs. Donahue said with a smile. "Some would say that

Gatsby was quite obsessive. Accomplishing everything he could to get the seemingly off-limits girl. Not stopping until he had her. Very good! Anyone else?" She looked around the class.

Steven Mori was the next one to raise his hand. He was the most flamboyant guy in our school. He wore a lot of tight clothes, sometimes even women's clothes, eyeliner, and dyed his hair a different color every two months. Steven had a very distinct tone of voice that guys in my school could only describe as girly. He had his group of friends that didn't intermingle with mine much, except for Lauren and Tasha. I knew little about him those days other than the constant offerings he got from guys walking by him calling him fag or fairy. As much as I wanted to come to his defense, I said nothing to stop the verbal assault. I guess that made me part of the problem. Lauren was better at calling out guys like Dan about it. But guys like Dan seem to be fed by the disapproval of others.

"Barbara Covett," Steven said.

"Ah yes!" Mrs. Donahue said. "From Notes on a Scandal, perfect example!" Steven smiled and Mrs. Donahue continued. "Barbara became obsessed with a female co-worker named Sheba after falling in love with her. She became very jealous of the attention that Sheba was showing to one of their young students. Barbara began manipulating her way into Sheba's life until she finally felt comfortable enough to make a move on her."

Steven tilted his head. "So, is that how sexuality or sexual orientation comes into this?"

"Sexual orientation has a lot to do with it, which is why I tacked it onto this topic. Sometimes a person's sexual attraction can lead to obsession, even if it's a same-sex attraction. Some could say that a character with no sort of outlet to express their sexual orientation and seems isolated within it, could cause deviance to brew. It can then of course become dangerous and predatory. Just look at the principal character of Lolita. Of course, not everyone's sexual attractions lead to obsession, but it's something that can make for gripping storytelling in fiction."

I couldn't help but think of Mystery Boy throughout the discussion. Watching him, and even just the thought of him had taken me to a different place that day more than once. I had a girlfriend, yet I couldn't stop fantasizing about what Mystery Boy might look like. I didn't know at the time if I just wanted to know who he was or if I wanted something more from him. I'd be lying if I said it was my first time thinking about a shirtless guy but never like that, or for that long. Normally I'd brush it off and push it from my mind. If people found out, everyone would treat me differently. I'd be the one Dan yelled fag at, and I'd lose my best friend. It could even ruin my dad's chances of getting the votes he needed for mayor. But the tingle I felt down my stomach when I saw Mystery Boy's shiny, sweaty back made me feel both excited and confused. Maybe I was Gatsby, and Mystery Boy was my Daisy, off-limits. But I needed to shake it, enabling those thoughts could ruin everything.

TWO

"Landon Griffin!" Someone hollered my name from the back of the class. I glanced behind me, unable to put a face to the voice I heard.

"Again, excellent example," Mrs. Donahue said. I whipped my gaze back to the front of the class to catch Mrs. Donahue with a Cheshire grin. "Landon is the epitome of the word obsessed. It's even caused him to question his own sexual orientation. Mr. Griffin has a classic case of obsessive fascination. He saw a shirtless guy from behind and now he can't stop thinking about him. How can one become infatuated so quickly?"

"Maybe because he's never had a gay crush before?" Someone exclaimed from behind me. I tried to speak up, but my mouth was dry. How did everyone know?

"Maybe he has a back fetish?!" Someone yelled. I didn't recognize their voice either. I began to sweat. The walls felt like they were closing in on me and it glued me to my seat. I stared at my desk, hoping no one would notice I was still in the room.

"Does he like men, or does he like women? Because you can't like both!" Mrs. Donahue sneered as she stepped to my desk, glaring down at me. Out of nowhere, the sound of the bell thundered through me. My eyes came into focus and I took a deep breath.

"Landon, are you all right? You seemed checked out there."

I looked over my shoulder to find Mrs. Donahue standing over me. Everyone in the class was shuffling out of the room, and I realized that I had fully zoned out and became wholly numb to the rest of the class discussion.

"Wow, I'm sorry Mrs. D. I'm not sure where I went." I lied. I couldn't exactly tell her my dream had transported me to High School hell. "That won't happen again."

"It's okay." She smiled, walking around to the front of my desk. "Football isn't keeping you up too late, is it?"

"Uh, no, no. That's not it at all." That time I told the truth. I took another breath and collected my things. Steven was the last person to walk out. His bright pink hair was hard to miss. I felt the need to follow him as I started for the door.

"I'm looking forward to your next story in the *Monthly!*" Mrs. Donahue proclaimed at me before I left the room. I swiftly turned on my heels and smiled at her. I wasn't usually that standoffish, but I was still jittery from my nightmare. Mrs. Donahue was one of the biggest supporters of my writing. She was the teacher that gave me honest but constructive feedback and was the only person I trusted with my work. Mrs. D knew what she was talking about. If she liked something, I believed her, unlike my mom who used to say she loved everything. But If Mrs. D said it was shit, I believed her. If something I wrote was terrible, she would tell me positively, inspiring me to make it better. That's what a brilliant teacher does. She was a published author herself, so her feedback meant a lot to me.

I stepped into the hall, looking left and right. The traffic was heavy. Shoulder to shoulder, as teenagers swarmed to their next class, shuffling along like a hoard of zombies. A tuft of pink hair stood out from the crowd and I hurried toward it. Steven was stuffing books into his locker. I stopped and leaned against the lockers opposite him across the hall to think. I didn't want too many people seeing me talking to Steven, I didn't need the rumors circulating.

The crowd was starting to thin out. Steven grabbed a book and closed the locker heading for his class. I slowly followed behind him, searching for an opportunity to get him alone. Luckily for me, Steven stepped into the bathroom.

Perfect.

I stepped to the door, glancing left and right before I pushed through. Steven was washing his hands and noticed me in the mirror.

"Hey, Steven," I whispered.

He gave me a sharp look and surveyed me before his eyes shot back to the sink. "Um, who are you?"

My brow furrowed. "Wait, are you serious?"

"It was a joke," Steven said with a flat tone. "I know who you are, obviously. What do you want?"

"Oh... right." I let out a small, awkward laugh. "I just wanted to ask you a question, real quick."

He seemed unamused by me. ".... okay."

It was the first time we'd spoken in years.

I started to speak but my mouth felt like it was wired shut. Was I really about to ask him this? "How did you know you were gay?" I was whispering again.

"Who says I'm gay?" Steven gazed into the mirror, fixing his hair.

"Wait, you're *not* gay?" There was a small crack in my voice and one eyebrow popped up.

"Of course I am," Steven said with a giggle as he pantomimed a hair toss.

He was joking... again. With him, it was hard to tell what was a joke and what wasn't. My face relaxed again.

"Oh, good. I mean, cool." I almost forgot the point I was trying to get to. "So how did you, like, know though?"

Steven stood there and pondered. "It's hard to explain, I guess. It's just something you feel inside you? Like I've known since I was five. It just seemed normal to me. Why do you care all of a sudden? You sure as hell didn't when I first told you."

An all too familiar bolt of guilt hit my stomach as I searched my brain for an excuse, needing something good enough that my questions wouldn't get back to Lauren. "My next story has a gay character. Just trying to hear a real-life experience," I said. I needed to end the conversation before he got suspicious. "Thanks, man. That was really helpful!" I turned and walked out before he could further the conversation. I glanced back long enough to see him huff with a twisted face.

I walked to my next class, staring at the floor the entire time, holding the straps of my backpack. The bell rang again and everyone scattered into different rooms like cockroaches. I noticed a familiar back at the end of the hallway, removing a bag from a trash can. This time he was wearing a white tank top, but I recognized the bare shoulders and his short brown hair at the back of his head. My eyes widened. It was Mystery Boy again!

Before I could step closer to him, Dan tackled me through a door frame. It wasn't a full-on football field tackle, but a small tackle that pushed me into the classroom. It was enough to pull me out of my Mystery Boy trance.

"What's up, Griffin?" Dan said, slapping me on the shoulder.

Most of the football team called me by my last name. With Dan being the quarterback on the team, he didn't get to do a lot of tackling on the field, so he did it off the field. Dan was a tall, slender guy, standing at 5' 11" who had a different football jersey to wear every day of the week. He was good-looking with dark hair, shaved on the sides and pushed back and slick on top, and had more girlfriends in the past four years of high school than I could count. The football team used to keep an ongoing tally, but everyone had eventually lost count. No one could keep up with him.

"I saw you go into the bathroom after Gay-ven. You goin' over to the pink side?" Dan wrapped his arms around me, making kissing noises.

A pit formed in my stomach, I worried Dan might be the one to start a rumor. I needed to shut it down.

"Nope, just needed to take a piss." I scoffed, pushing him off of me.

"All right," Dan said, raising his hands in the air. "Don't get so defensive."

"Well, don't be such a dick." I smiled.

Dan could be rude a lot. Out of all the guys calling Steven a fag in the hallway, Dan did it the most.

"All right, gentlemen," the teacher called out to us, "sit down, please, so we can get started."

As I sat, I wondered what I would've done if Dan hadn't pushed me into class. I remember taking a step in Mystery Boy's direction, but what was I going to do once I got close to him? I was dying to see his face. I could've acted like I had something I needed to throw away before he tied the garbage bag up. That seemed like a normal thing to do. But then what? I just stare at his face? Dan might've saved me from major embarrassment.

Throughout the class, I couldn't stop making up scenarios in my head. I imagined walking by Mystery Boy pretending to talk on my phone or asking if he needed help. Or maybe say, 'hey I'm that guy who keeps staring at you from afar, my name's Landon, what's yours? And why are you taking out the trash?'

When my day ended, Lauren met me in the school's front courtyard. I usually had football practice after school, but that day we had off because of a game the next night. Usually, we had football games on Friday nights, but they pushed this particular game up to Wednesday because of impending weather for Friday.

Lauren planted a small kiss. Two guys from the football team had been watching us and hollered in our direction. I rolled my eyes, taking Lauren's hand as I walked toward my house.

My house was bright yellow. Couldn't miss it. I'm not sure whose decision it was to make it the brightest house on the block, but there it was in all its sunny glory. Living across the street from my high school made things very convenient. I didn't have to waste gas going back and forth, not that I even had a car. It sucked having to rely on my dad, or my friends to drive me around places. I couldn't just pick up and go when I wanted when I didn't feel like walking. If my dad wasn't using his car, he'd let me borrow it if I gave him an important enough reason.

"Hey, you want to go to Lucky's for some ice cream?" Lauren asked, pulling on my arm. Lucky's was our local diner. They made the best milkshakes in all of Texas.

"Yeah sure." I smiled. "Just let me put my bag down, I'll be right back."

It took me all of thirty seconds to run across the street and up my driveway. I was moving so fast I practically knocked over my dad coming out the side door.

"Whoa! Slow down killer," he said, taking me by the shoulders.

"Sorry, dad." I stepped inside, dropped my bag near the couch, and turned right around to head out the door. My dad was getting into his car when I called out for him. He stopped before climbing into the driver's seat and stared at me, waiting to hear what I had to say. I stepped to his car on the opposite side, resting my arms on the roof of his blue Ford Taurus. "I'm wondering if you'd know about something people have been talking about?"

I didn't want to tell him I was staring at Mystery Boy so I used gossip as an excuse.

"Make it quick," my dad said.

"Some kids were talking about this guy, like cleaning the wall or something." I pointed across the street at the half-wall. "Do you know anything about that?"

"Yeah, there was some graffiti there," Dad said before sitting in the driver's seat.

I hunched over, resting my arms on the open window, and looked in at him. "Okay, but like, who's the guy?"

"You don't need to concern yourself with that," Dad said, starting the engine.

"Dad, come on," I said, staring at him with too much desperation. He sighed and tapped his fingers on the steering wheel a few times before looking at me.

"He's here on community service."

"What did he do?"

"That's none of our business." Dad shifted the car into reverse.

"Wait!" I blurted out. "How old is he?"

My dad searched his memory. "Nineteen, I think? Or twenty, I don't know."

"How long is he gonna be here? At the school I mean?"

"I don't know," my dad said. "A couple of months? I just signed the papers to allow him to be here. Principle Jamison is the one working directly with the kid. Why do you care so much?"

"Just curious."

"Well, don't be," Dad said. "He is not someone I want you hanging around with. He's not like you."

"What's that supposed to mean?"

"He...you aren't... " Dad was hesitating, trying to find the right words to say. "He's a troubled kid, is what I mean. You shouldn't want to be associated with someone who has obviously broken the law. Is that understood?"

"Got it," I mumbled. I looked at the passenger seat, cycling through the other questions my mind was coming up with.

"Landon, I have a meeting to get to. Is there anything else?"

"Oh!" I said, perking up again. "Can I have a twenty? Lauren wants to go to Lucky's." My dad made a noise, sounding like the Big Bad Wolf before reaching into his pocket for his wallet. He eased off the brake and the car roll backward, forcing me to take a step back.

"Put on some sunblock, would you? You're looking a little red," Dad shouted, backing out of the driveway. "I'll see you later tonight, get your homework done!" I gave him a salute before he sped down the street.

I rushed back inside to grab the sunblock that I always kept in my bag. Being a redhead and living in Texas where the sun was always shining wasn't the best combination. Like Steven's, my hair was easy to spot in a crowd. The color was just under the tone of flaming hot Cheetos. I couldn't believe I was from Texas. With my pale skin, I was one of the few kids in my school who didn't have a tan.

I hopped into Lauren's car, sweating from being outside for eight minutes. She owned a beat-up old Volkswagen bug that used to be her mom's. The AC took a while to kick in. Lauren was sitting in the driver's seat adjusting the rear-view mirror. Her eyes swiveled over to me and she let out an abrupt laugh.

I grinned. "What?"

"You have sunscreen on your face." She smiled back.

I felt my face get warm and pulled down the visor to look in its mirror. There was a small white dollop on the side of my nose. I brushed it off and smoothed it into my hands.

A loud thud against my door made Lauren gasp. Dan was

standing there peering in through the window, appearing out of nowhere. I rolled the window down, letting more hot air in.

"Where you goin', Carrot Top?" Dan's tone was perky. Like the jerseys he wore, he also had a new ginger-related word to call me every day, most weren't very original.

"Lucky's," I said.

"Cool, I'll grab the guys and meet you there." Dan rubbed my head as if he were a dad ruffling the hair of his child. Lauren rolled her eyes. Before she had the chance to interject, Dan was halfway to his car rounding up the troops. I shrugged at Lauren. She huffed and put the car in drive.

Lauren and I got to the diner before everyone else. We took a booth at the back of the restaurant. Every tabletop had a different theme, put together like a scrapbook under the plexiglass casing. One table had a space theme with pictures of astronauts and planets. One table had a video game theme with pictures of Mario and Sonic the Hedgehog. The one we sat at was a 50s nostalgia theme, complete with pictures of Elvis Presley, old cars, even a few old ads for cigarettes and diners. They placed the menus in a rack on the table along with the mustard and ketchup bottles. We never touched the menu though because we knew it by heart. The diner smelled like a sugar factory that day.

A tall woman with stylish glasses greeted us. Her hair was cut into a short bob, dyed black and silver, wearing an apron with 'Lucky's' branded across her chest. Her long arms were covered in intricate tattoos. She even had a small rainbow flag button clipped to her apron next to a small Mexican flag.

"Hey there, my name's Steph," she said with a toothy smile. She must have been new because I'd been there a hundred times over the years and I didn't recognize her face. "Can I start y'all with something to drink?"

Lauren must have noticed the Mexican flag pin because she

ordered in Spanish. Steph smiled and she jotted down the order. After four years of Spanish classes, I still wasn't confident enough to speak the language but I understood most of it.

"I'll do a strawberry and chocolate milkshake too," I said.

Steph nodded and walked off to put in our order. I heard the bell above the front door chime and in walked Dan with four other boys from the football team. Trailing behind was Chris Wilson, Dan's younger brother, who was shorter and stockier. On the field, it was Chris' job to stop the other team from tackling Dan. Not much was different off the field, Chris was always there to back Dan up if need be. The two of them sat in our booth while the other three guys sat at an adjacent table.

Lauren and I had hardly said anything to each other when Dan struck up the conversation about the day. "So what was actually going on between you and the faggot today, Landon?"

Chris, meanwhile, looked over the menu. I glanced at Lauren, who tilted her head at me with squinted eyes.

"Just because we were in the bathroom at the same time it doesn't mean anything is going on."

Lauren peered at Dan and interjected. "Wish you wouldn't call him that. His name is Steven." Lauren knew Steven from the drama club. He made most of the costumes for the shows.

Dan rolled his eyes. "I know his name. Fag just suits him better."

"Stop being such an asshole, for once," Lauren said.

Chris shook his head, still staring at the menu. Steph walked up before the conversation went any further. The brothers ordered fries and soda.

"Fuck, she's hot," Dan said as Steph walked away. "Too bad she's a dyke."

Chris watched her too. "How do you know?"

"She just has that look," Dan said. "The tattoos, the hair, and the flag pin she's wearing." Chris nodded in agreement as Dan continued, "I bet I could turn her, she just needs the right dick, you know?"

"Wow," Lauren said in disgust. "Is there anything that comes out of your mouth that isn't offensive?"

Dan pointed a thumb at Steph. "Landon, you wouldn't bang her?"

Lauren's eyes shot to me, ready to cut my head off if I answered. I looked away, rubbing my forehead. The more Dan spoke, the more I questioned whether I wanted to continue to use the word 'friend' to describe him. It was like puberty turned him into an entitled macho man that very much differed from the person he was when we were kids.

"I wonder if she has a hot girlfriend," Chris said.

"I hope so." Dan sighed. He was practically drooling over the thought.

"Okay," Lauren said. "So it's okay for Steph to be gay because she's an attractive woman that gets you all tingly? But it's not okay for a guy to be gay because that makes him a fag?"

"It's just gross," Dan said, twisting his face. He was being a hypocrite, and it was pissing Lauren off.

Chris put up his hands in defense. "Hey, I don't care if a guy is gay."

Finally, something good to come out of this conversation.

"As long as he isn't hitting on me," Chris said.

Okay, not the best, still not terrible.

Lauren stood, agitated by the entire conversation, rolling her eyes. "Yeah, because you're every gay guy's type," she said before stomping off to the restroom. The guys just laughed her off. I told them to shut up again and shook my head at them. I whipped out my phone and texted Lauren to make sure she was all right. She texted back saying she just needed to cool off for a second.

Steph had arrived with our milkshakes and placed them on the table. "Is she okay?"

"Yeah, she's fine," Dan said, putting on his best attempt at a charming voice. "We were just talking about how I could turn you straight, how bout you and I go out sometime?" The guy had no shame.

"Turn me? Really?" Steph's eyes narrowed and she crossed her arms. "Well, to me it seems like you don't even have a dick big enough to please a woman, never mind 'turn' her. I'd have to decline seeing as I already have someone who can do things that you couldn't even wrap your fragile masculinity ass mind around on your best day." Without batting an eye, she turned on her heels and walked back to the counter. Chris and I hollered laughing, bouncing in our seats, while Dan sunk lower in his.

Through my tears of laughter, I spotted Lauren standing outside the restroom, smiling, having heard the whole conversation. Dan shut up and moved on to other topics throughout our time at the diner. Though he continued his douchebaggery when he refused to tip Steph before we left. It made me wonder what Dan would say if I told him about my feelings toward Mystery Boy. Perhaps he'd call me a faggot too and drop me like trash. I needed to keep better company.

When we left, Lauren thanked me before starting the car.

"For what?" I said, thinking it was for paying for the milkshakes.

"For not being like him," she said.

That made me smile.

THREE

I busted through the front door and threw my helmet to the ground; I was headed for my room with mud trailing the floor behind me. I had almost reached my bedroom door before my dad screamed, chasing after me.

"Where the hell was your head tonight?! There could have been scouts there! If they had seen the way you played, they would've left at halftime and not even considered your ass for a scholarship. Has everything I've taught you this season gone out the window?" I just stood there with clenched fists. "Landon, answer me!"

I couldn't take it; the best I could do was slam my door in his face and lock it. My poor thin wooden door barely kept back his loud voice. I was expecting it to crack up the middle and explode until his volume calmed, and I heard him sigh and walk away. The tension left my body as I flicked on my desk lamp and peeled off my greasy jersey and pads, dropping onto my bed. I laid there, still in my muddy pants and leg gear, staring at the ceiling.

Where was my head tonight?

The obvious answer was Mystery Boy. I spent the entire

game looking over at the stands to see if Mystery Boy might be sitting there, watching. I would do double-takes every time I noticed a guy with brown hair walking through the crowd of spectators. Catching the football was the farthest thing from my mind, and that was my most important job on the field. I couldn't focus for one damn minute. All I thought about was his sweaty back and what his face might look like and I didn't know why.

Thanks to me, we lost the game. My team would've killed me if they could see inside my mind. My entire life had been football and scholarships, and now some alleged criminal comes into my life that I couldn't stop thinking about and screws everything up? I was usually flawless on the field, I was used to getting praise from everyone after every game. Nothing had ever distracted me as much as Mystery Boy. Why was it happening now? I didn't even know him! I decided at that moment to stop obsessing over Mystery Boy. He was ruining things.

My phone dinged from across the room. I groaned, not wanting to get up yet. I could lie there forever, burying myself in pity and guilt for losing the game for the rest of the guys. When I got up, I had to search my backpack for my phone. It was a text from Lauren.

LAUREN
Hey babe, you okay?

ME
Yeah, why, what's up?

LAUREN
Oh, you just didn't say bye after the game.

ME

Sorry, I just wanted to get out of there. My head wasn't in it tonight.

LAUREN

Yeah, I think everyone noticed that. What's going on?

A couple of different answers came to mind. Like: oh nothing, just feeling too much pressure from my dad. Oh nothing, I'm pretty sure I'm failing trig. Oh nothing, I'm obsessing over a GUY I've never met.

ME

Just not feeling well.

LAUREN

Are you sick?

Another text popped in from the top of my screen from Tasha.

TASHA

Landon, the deadline is tomorrow! You haven't emailed me the story yet.

Shit. I'd forgotten to write the new story. *Thanks again, Mystery Boy.*

. . .

ME

I'll get it to you by tonight.

LAUREN

What?

ME

Shit, sorry, wrong text.

I did that a lot.

ME

I'll get it to you by tonight.

TASHA

Great, thank you.

LAUREN

Who was that for?

ME

Tasha. I forgot about my deadline. I gotta go. I need to finish this. I'll talk to you later?

LAUREN

All right.

Wait one more thing. Let's go out somewhere on Saturday? Just you and me, give us a chance to talk about what's on your mind.

ME

Sounds good. I'll see you at school tomorrow.

LAUREN

<3

I placed my phone on the desk and flipped open my laptop, clicking through to an empty word document. I took a deep breath and closed my eyes. Coming up with something would not be as easy as I hoped it would, not with my mind in so many places. I imagined myself in the world of *Harry Potter*, waving my wand in front of the computer as it magically typed the most amazing, addictive story. But I opened my eyes to white nothingness on the screen.

My phone chimed again. I picked it up, feeling annoyed by the distraction.

DAN

WTF man, what happened out there tonight?

I tossed my phone back on the desk with more force than intended. I had that quick moment of panic, wondering if I might have cracked the screen. I didn't have the patience for Dan, so I stood from my chair and walked over to my window. People were still crowded around the school post-game. I noticed Dan walking to his car with an unfamiliar girl on his left and Chris on his right. I closed my curtains before he looked up and saw me standing there shirtless.

With a huff, I plopped down on my bed again, closing my eyes. I wanted to get rid of the thoughts of Mystery Boy, but it was so hard. Flashes of his sparkling back passed through my mind again. The thought was so vivid I felt like I could smell him. It was a combination of freshly cut grass and sweat.

No! Stop.

I took a deep breath in through my nose, yearning to smell even more. I fantasized about waking up next to him on a bright sunny morning in my bed and turning him around to see what he looked like. I could feel his skin; it was soft and damp. I'd never fantasized about Lauren in my bed, or about touching her so intimately.

Different combinations of facial features came and went as if his face were a Rubik's Cube and I was trying to match everything just right. I imagined myself looking down, studying Mystery Boy's shirtless body. My hand instinctively slid under my football pants, where I could feel my lust for him growing. The thoughts were so new and exciting to me and I let them take over.

Stop thinking about him!

"Landon!" My dad burst through my bedroom door without knocking. My eyes exploded open, and I sat up in my bed faster than any human being should be able to move. My chest was rising and my heart was beating as fast as a hummingbird's.

"Dad! Jesus, I swear I locked that door!" I yelled between fits of breath.

"You know the lock comes loose if you jiggle the handle," he said. "I'm sorry, I should've knocked."

"Yes, you should have." I grabbed the pillow from behind me and covered my bare chest. "I could've been changing"... *or worse.*

"I'm sorry, I'm sorry," he said, raising his hands in defense. He took a breath, walking further into my room. He hadn't seemed to notice anything out of the ordinary, thank God. "I just wanted to say that, I shouldn't have yelled at you like that. I was going to bed, but it was bothering me too much. I had to come in and apologize."

"It's fine," I said, calming my breath. My heart slowed down to a normal rhythm again. Any arousal I had going was shut down and would stay that way for a while.

"You just seemed a little off tonight."

"I just have a lot on my mind," I said as I pushed my fingers through my buzzed hair. So much for forgetting about Mystery Boy; that lasted all of two minutes.

"Right," Dad said as he crossed his arms. "I know it may not seem like it all the time, but I'm here if you need to talk about anything." His eyes were darting around my room, looking for anything to focus on that wasn't me. There was obvious tension that was still floating through the air between us. He noticed I was still wearing my dirty football pants. "Landon, you're getting your sheets all dirty. Throw them in the hamper before you go to bed, I'll try to wash them tomorrow."

"It's ok, I can put them in tonight," I said as I swung my legs off the bed. I looked around my room and saw some other pieces of clothing scattered across the floor that I could throw in the wash as well. "You probably have a busy day tomorrow and I might not get to bed for a while anyway. I have a deadline I forgot about."

"All right, I'll let you get to it then." He turned around. "Again," he said, stopping himself in the doorframe, looking back at me. "I'm sorry I got overheated. This has been such a sudden change for me, I'm still trying to find the balance."

"I know dad," I sighed. "I am too." He gave me a half-smile, closing my door behind him.

As soon as he closed the door, my room filled with light passing through my window. Cars were leaving the school, their headlights reflecting off my house as they drove by. I pushed myself off the bed, sauntered back to my desk, and sat in front of my laptop again. I clicked my phone to check the time and saw Dan's text still there on the screen. I didn't want to respond yet. Staring at his text message, I thought about how he used to act when we were younger. He was nicer; he cared more about people. I thought about our long history as friends as I typed out some plot points. It was becoming clearer the more my fingers pressed the keys. I was going to write a story about two best friends that grew apart as they got older.

――――

SEVEN YEARS AGO.

Dan and I met on the first day of 5th grade. I was ten years old. He and his family had just moved to town from North Carolina. I sat with him at lunch one day after noticing him sitting alone, and I remember he had a cool *Ninja Turtles* lunch box that caught my eye. I liked that. Turns out he liked my *Spider-Man* lunch box. That day we traded lunchboxes and promised to sit together the next day at lunch to get them back, which we did. Then we sat together the next day and the day after that, and the day after that, until it just became automatic. We talked about everything and anything: our favorite superheroes, cartoons, action figures, bugs, sports, pizza, and video games. I realized everything I liked, he liked, too. We always made each other laugh; we were in our own little bubble, no other kid in the school could penetrate it. We were a club of two.

That year on picture day my mom made me wear a purple collared shirt, which when you were ten years old was like wearing a huge neon sign that says "please make fun of me." I pleaded with her not to send me to school wearing it. I wanted to wear a shirt with skateboards on it, but she said that wasn't the shirt you wear for picture day. I remember wearing a windbreaker for most of the day, trying to hide my embarrassment. When the teacher took my class to the gym to take the pictures, we all had to line up against the wall in alphabetical order and move one by one until we made it to the cameraman.

I was next, but with my last name being Griffin, there were still a good number of kids behind me in line who I didn't want to see me wearing a purple shirt. I decided I was going to keep my windbreaker on and make up some excuse for my mom when she saw the picture, an excuse I'd worry about later.

Confident in my decision, I strolled up to the small stool sitting in front of a dark blue background. I sat and practiced my smile while the cameraman was resetting the lights. To my surprise, my teacher popped up next to me and kneeled to eye level. "Hun, take this off," she said, pointing to my windbreaker.

"No," I said, shaking my head back and forth.

"Now come on, your mother put you in this nice collared shirt for a reason. Take it off, please."

I unzipped the jacket as slow as I could, hoping she'd change her mind and tell me to keep it on in a fit of impatience. But she was an elementary school teacher, her patience level was through the roof. She waited politely until I handed it to her. Once in hand, my teacher walked away, leaving me in plain sight of all the other kids in line to feast their eyes upon my Barney-colored polo. To make things even worse, another class came in to line up behind mine. I didn't dare glance over to see if anyone was looking. I didn't have to because I could hear the tiny giggles. It started with one or two kids, and then it spread down the line like wildfire.

"Look! He's wearing a girl color!" a voice shouted out, which was followed by more laughter. Along with pink and yellow, we all considered purple a girl's color. I felt my face go red. Kids had already been making fun of my ginger hair, but now they had another thing to make fun of me for. I'd forever be seen as the redhead with freckles who wore purple. I clenched my jaw, fighting back tears. They couldn't see me cry, too; that would just fuel the fire. More than anything, I wanted to sprout wings and fly away, busting through the roof of the gym and never coming back.

"I think he looks awesome!" a voice rang out. Those five words from someone in the newly formed line caused the laughter to go silent. I gained the courage to look over to the line of kids and saw Dan leaning out from everyone else with a thumb in the air.

I smiled, suddenly feeling a warm sensation in my stomach for him, until a boy further up in line looked back at Dan and shouted, "You're both losers!" That's when the laughter started up again. My boost in confidence shattered, I felt defeated as I looked back at the cameraman, unwilling to show my face to the crowd of devils any longer. The next second came with a flash and I was being told to move on. It should go without saying, I wasn't smiling in my school picture that year.

The next day I didn't see Dan until lunchtime, because we were in separate classes. The only time we got to interact was at lunch and recess. I sat down at a table by myself, still feeling the social pain from the day before. I assumed Dan would be too embarrassed to be seen with me now.

"Hey Landon," Dan said, smiling. I looked up from my lunch box in complete awe of him standing across the table. He was wearing an oversized, frayed purple shirt. My mouth dropped open. It looked to be an adult shirt, cut to his size with a pair of scissors. He sat in front of me and talked about what we were going to do at recess as if he wasn't making some major fashion statement. My body filled with warmth as I sat there watching him talk. My eyes darted left and right to see if anyone was staring at him, which they were, but he didn't care!

He didn't wear a purple shirt because he liked it; he wore it for me. Dan wore it to show he was on my side, that no one could infiltrate our bubble. My small brain couldn't register my emotions that day. All I felt was warmth and happiness, that's the only way I could describe it back then. My smile couldn't be shattered after that.

As our friendship grew, so did our desire to hang outside of school. Soon enough we were having sleepovers almost every weekend. We spent our nights reading comic books and playing video games way past our bedtime. Dan shared a bedroom with Chris, who was eight years old. Chris was constantly wanting to hang out with us or do what we were doing; he was Dan's little shadow.

"You're so lucky you don't have a little brother," Dan said to me before his face lit up. "We should camp outside tonight so we don't have to play with Chris!" Dan was so excited by the idea; before I could even say anything, he ran off to ask his parents if we could set up the tent in his backyard.

Once Dan's dad set up the tent for us, we got to work on the signs that said: No Little Brother Allowed. We had our flashlights and our sleeping bags, some snacks, and some action figures; we were ready for the night. It got dark fast, so we flipped on our flashlights and placed them between our sleeping bags, illuminating the Great War between Ninja Turtles and professional wrestlers.

"Hey Dan," I mumbled, not wanting to interrupt our action figure fight, but something was on my mind. Dan looked at me so I continued. "I never thanked you for what you did." Dan tilted his head with a confused look. He had forgotten about the lunch after picture day, so I had to explain further. "Coming into school wearing your dad's purple shirt that day. That was really cool."

"No problem. That's what friends do," Dan said. The way he smiled at me made me feel that rush of warmth again.

"Can I kiss you?" The words projected out of my 10-year-old mouth like vomit. My brain didn't have a second to think about what I'd said before I said it. I felt my throat hold back any words that could've come next. Time seemed to slow down.

What did I just say?

It felt excruciatingly long before Dan spoke.

"Boys aren't supposed to kiss other boys, stupid," he said, laughing it off and going back to his Ninja Turtles. I laughed, too, not giving the topic any more attention. The warmth faded at that moment, but the happiness didn't. Luckily for me, he still wanted to be my best friend after that.

———

My alarm blared, and I pushed my head up from my desk. It was 7:00 a.m. I panicked, realizing I'd fallen asleep. I clicked the trackpad of my laptop to wake it up, and I couldn't remember if I'd finished writing. Once the screen came back to life, I saw my email dashboard. I had an unread message from Tasha that just said, 'Thanks!' I slouched back in my chair; I'd made my Thursday deadline. I stayed up so late it was hard to remember what I'd even written. As I sat there slouched in my chair, pieces of my story were coming back to me and I panicked again. I knew I had written the story of Dan and I's friendship, but I couldn't remember if I changed the names, or if I left out the part about me wanting to kiss him. My heart started racing. If Tasha had already read it, then she would know my biggest secret, and even worse, if she had printed it, it could force me out of my very confused closet to face the entire school.

FOUR

I jolted out of my seat, smashing my fingers on the edge of my desk trying to reach the trackpad of my laptop. Bolts of pain shot up my forearm and I let out an agitated growl. I moved the small cursor as fast as I could to click the file. My eyes passed from left to right like a speed reader trying to win a Guinness world record and I realized I changed the names. My tired eyes slowed down to make sure I didn't miss the part about the kiss. I sighed in relief. The kiss was nowhere to be found. How could I be stupid enough to think I would add that? Even at 3:00 am that would've been an idiotic mistake. I closed my laptop, noticing my knuckles had gone red from the collision with the hardwood. I tried to shake the pain away, but now it just felt like pins and needles.

I stood and cracked my neck; I kinked it from sleeping on the desk. I peered out the window, people had already started parking their cars and filling up the front courtyard. I got closer to look for Mystery Boy and caught my reflection out of my peripheral in the mirror hanging on my closet door. I was still wearing nothing but my football pants; I looked down at myself, still caked in a few patches of mud and dirt. I needed a shower ASAP.

———

"It was good," Tasha said as she flipped through a printed copy of my short story. "There was actual heart and emotion there, you know?" Tasha's curls were held back by a red headband that day. Her dark skin was flawless, and she wore a black T-shirt that said 'QUEEN' across her chest in bold white letters. She was sitting across from me at a table in the library. When it was a free period for both of us, we liked to get together and talk about the *Monthly*.

"Really? You think so?"

"Yes." She smiled as she checked a text on her phone. "Have you been looking at any colleges for writing? I hear Columbia has a great program."

I scoffed. "Yeah right."

Tasha placed her phone on the table. Her bright red nails matched her headband. "Maybe NYU, then?"

"I feel like my dad would be devastated if I moved halfway across the country." I'd never thought about living in New York City. I'd never even been there, only seen pictures and movies. The people would be more open-minded for sure. Many people in my town thought the same way Dan did, with ignorance and fear. Tasha and Lauren were two of the few that were different. She was very outspoken about social justice and human rights. She and Lauren attended at least three women's marches across the state that year, even Steven tagged along with them. "Plus, my dad wants me to pursue football so--"

Tasha cut me off. "But what do you want?" That was a hard question for me. Tasha sat up straight and interlocked her fingers as if it were an interview.

"I don't know," I said with an awkward smirk. "I mean, I love football, but I love writing, too. I just don't think my dad would let me do it. He's worked so hard with me on the field over the years." I averted making eye contact. The library was a sea of whispers, typing fingers, and pages being turned.

"Boy, look at me," Tasha said, along with a few finger snaps in my direction. My eyes darted back to her. "Do what makes you happy, not what makes your dad happy. I wouldn't want to see your talent go to waste."

I chuckled. "You sound like Mrs. Donahue. Maybe I can do both," I said, puffing my chest out.

"How scandalous!" Tasha said as she brought her hands to her cheeks, playing along with my charade. We laughed louder, and it was met with an anonymous 'shush' from somewhere in the room. "Continue writing so that when you make it big, I can be the one to say I discovered you." I rolled my eyes at her and laughed more.

———

ONE YEAR AGO.

During my English class junior year, the teacher assigned me to write an essay about my most prized possession. I remember sitting in my room looking around at all my useless things, wracking my brain to think of an item I truly cherished. It was probably my cell phone; what teenager didn't have their phone glued to their hand at all times? But writing about it would be the dumbest Gen Z decision I could make. After twenty long minutes of empty thought, I decided to make it up. I was going to turn this true-life personal essay into pure fiction and play it off as if it were real.

I wrote an entire paper about a picture of me and my grandma dancing at a family reunion and how I had made a copy to bury with her after she passed away. None of which was true at all because one, I didn't even have a family large enough for a reunion, and two, my grandmother was still alive and well. Was it morally wrong? Yes, absolutely, but it got me an A.

During my free period, I was in the library on my laptop finishing up the essay before I had to turn it in. Unbeknownst to me, Tasha had been walking by and spotted me writing. She stopped and stared at my computer screen from behind. I was in one of my power modes, where the entire world went silent and my fingers were typing a mile a minute, I never felt her eyes on me. Tasha dropped her books on the table next to me, releasing me from the spell.

Tasha plopped in a chair. "What is this?"

My brow furrowed. "What is what?"

"This?" She pointed a blue painted nail to my computer screen. "What is this that you're writing?"

Taken aback by her assertiveness, I said, "It's an essay for my English class, why?"

"I like what I saw," Tasha said.

I turned my computer away and squinted at her. "Were you reading over my shoulder?"

"Of course. What is it about?"

"Uh," I said, unconvinced if I should tell her to go away. My school housed about a thousand kids, so I was having trouble placing her name, but I had seen her around before. "It's about my most prized possession, a picture of my grandmother and me."

Tasha bounced in her seat. "Can I read it?"

"Oh God, no."

"Oh, come on! It looked good! Why won't you let me read it?"

"It's personal, all right?" I was hoping that would send her on her way. Tasha didn't blink; she just stared at me, tapping her fingers on the table. I didn't know what else to say, I wasn't sure she would give up. I sighed and blurted out, "I made it up, okay?"

Tasha raised an eyebrow, "What?"

"This is supposed to be true, about my life, but I made it up because I couldn't think of anything," I confessed as I rubbed my forehead.

"Oh, now I have to read it," Tasha said with a growing smile. She gestured for me to pass the computer as she bounced up and down in her seat. I was confused about why she was so excited by it. I pushed the laptop over to her. She was a fast reader. I watched her eyes scroll from side to side as she enveloped my fictionalized true story. Now and then her eyebrows would scrunch or raise. "So you made this up?" I nodded. "Is your grandma even dead?"

"No," I whispered, slouching in my chair. I looked away in embarrassment.

"Oh, that's cold!" Tasha laughed her words out. "That. Is. Cold," she said again, this time clapping with each word. I wasn't sure how to respond. I assumed she didn't like it because of how hard she was laughing at it, until she said, "this is brilliant."

"What?" It surprised me. I was so confused by her.

Tasha pushed my laptop back. "I think it's great. How did you come up with this?"

"I don't know. My brain just does it and I write it down, I guess." The heat in my face disappeared.

"That's perfect! Can you write more?" She pulled her chair closer.

"What? What do you mean write more?"

"I just took over as editor for the *Madison Monthly*." Tasha's face lit up. "I've been looking for someone who can write short stories. We have way too many poems and essays and reports, it's so boring. I need something fun and new!"

"You want me to write for the *Monthly*? Seriously?" I said, flabbergasted. "No one has ever read anything I've written besides my teachers."

"The way you told that story felt so real," Tasha spoke with her hands. "The way your words flow together, it was captivating and emotional. I want to see what else you have. I want to know what else your brain can come up with."

I didn't know what to say. A brief scenario played through my head where this was all a practical joke, I would answer yes and Dan would jump out from behind the bookshelves and start laughing, calling me names. But so far there were no surprise appearances by Dan Wilson. I hesitated, glancing back and forth a few times between her and my computer screen before saying yes.

"Great!" Tasha stood from her chair. "It's Landon, right?"

"Yeah, how d'you know?"

"We had health class together freshman year."

"Of course, yeah," I said, playing it off as if I remembered her, but she saw right through me.

"I'm Tasha," she said after extending a hand. I completed her gesture, still sitting. "Well, all documents are due next Thursday and we print on Friday!" She dug through her stack of books until she found a notepad. She ripped out a page and scribbled something. "Just send it to me at this email. I'll be looking forward to it!"

"Thanks," I said. I smiled and watched her strut away.

I remember the first short story I submitted to her. It was a post-apocalyptic tale of a flesh-eating disease that took over a small Texas town. Thirty minutes after I sent it to Tasha, I had an email back from her, asking me to turn the dial down on the gore of the story. I had no problem doing it. Mad High just wasn't ready for that yet, I understood. To my surprise, the story was a hit. Many people were talking about it after the paper was passed out that morning. For someone who barely had the attention span to tolerate a book, even Dan liked it. He didn't read a single one of my stories that were published after that. One was enough for him. That first story got Mrs. Donahue's attention as well. She pulled me aside in the hallway one afternoon and praised my storytelling abilities. She asked me if I wouldn't mind if she helped me out. Since then she's read most of my stories before I've published them, helping me with formatting or editing, sometimes even story development. Football was such a team effort, but with writing, I could do something successful on my own.

———

"I'll be sure to give you full credit for discovering me." I chuckled.

Tasha pointed a red polished nail at me. "You better."

The bell rang, and we both said our goodbyes. I had dropped off a copy of my latest story on Mrs. Donahue's desk that morning. I was in her class next and was curious about what she thought of it. It wouldn't be printed until the next day, so I thought I could bounce the edits off her if needed.

"Just the man I wanted to see," Mrs. Donahue said as I walked into the classroom. Not everyone had shown up yet, so we had time to talk.

"What'd you think? Be honest."

"It felt... very personal," she said. It wasn't the response I expected. A big part of the story was about my purple shirt incident, so she wasn't wrong.

"There may have been a little non-fiction thrown in there," I said with a smile, sitting at a desk in front of hers. I wondered if anyone who read it would remember that real-life event from elementary school. If Dan took the time to read it, he'd remember. But it was safe from him since he didn't give a crap about the *Monthly*.

"It was sort of heartbreaking at the end. I was sad they couldn't stay friends after everything. It seemed like they had a fondness for each other," she said as she stood and walked over to me. She placed the story on my desk. "I made a few edits, nothing major. You're getting better at this, Landon," she said with a smile.

"Thank you!" I plucked through the pages. "I'll make sure I get this to Tasha in time for tomorrow's print."

My mind fluttered at the thought of Mystery Boy again as I walked to my next class and sat near the windows again. I hadn't seen him all day. I hadn't seen him since I glimpsed him cutting grass the morning before. My eyes flicked over to the windows; that classroom overlooked the parking lot on the side of the school, but there was no one outside. I'd hoped I would see him as if I had the power to summon him. I wondered if anyone else around the school knew him. I could ask some people? Mystery Boy could be a drug addict. Maybe I'd ask the stoner kids if they knew who he was. He could be their dealer.

After class, I was putting books away in my locker when Dan rolled up behind me and slapped me on the back. "What's up, pumpkin head?"

"It feels like you've just forgotten my name," I said, rolling my eyes.

Lauren also appeared out of the crowd and planted a kiss on my cheek. The three of us made small talk and complained about homework before Lauren brought up a much more interesting topic.

"I heard these girls in the bathroom talking about a new janitor or something? Apparently, he works outside shirtless," she said, asking Dan and me if we had heard of him. If girls were talking about him, maybe I wasn't the only one obsessed.

Dan scratched his head. "That's weird, I haven't seen him."

"Yeah, I've seen him," I interjected, closing my locker. "A couple days ago. My dad said he was here for some community service thing."

"Oh shit, wait," Dan said. "Yeah, I've heard of him. Some kids were talking about him the other day. They said he burned down his school or something and got into all this trouble. That's why they made him do community service at a school." Dan seemed confident in his statement, but the logic of what he was saying made little sense.

"The girls were saying something different in the bathroom," Lauren said as she looked back and forth between Dan and me. "They said he was here because he beat someone half to death over some drugs."

"That doesn't seem right," I said, "Wouldn't he get more than community service for doing any of that? It couldn't have been something that bad."

"I don't know, but he freaks me out. I hope I don't see him around," Lauren said, hooking her arm around mine.

"The guy shouldn't even be around kids," Dan said.

"We aren't kids," I scoffed. "And he's not that much older than us," I said with more of a defensive tone than intended.

Dan tried to call my bluff. "How do you know?"

"Because my dad told me he was like nineteen or twenty." I realized I had given away everything I'd learned about Mystery Boy. Two things, his age, and his criminal sentencing. I thought I knew more, but everything else was stuff I'd made up in my head. I yearned for more information about him; he was like a drug I wanted another hit of.

Now I knew two rumors, one of which could be true but seemed very unlikely. I knew nothing about the justice system and how they treated certain crimes. I was certain that he'd be in prison for anything violent, so I determined right then he wasn't dangerous. Which then led me to assume that he was a nice guy and that he would talk to me if I approached him. I might've been a little too optimistic. As I walked to my next class, I made a mental checklist of things to say if I ever saw him again.

FIVE

Class was over, and I stepped into the hallway of never-ending bodies. The last bell had rung and everyone was trying to escape the educated concrete walls. I doubted people would find my new story interesting once they published it in the *Monthly* the next day. I wondered if it was too dry for a high school reader. The student body that read the *Monthly* was so used to my wild, imaginative stories. I had yet to write something so true to life and personal. I sighed, not wanting to ridicule my mind with self-deprecating thoughts any longer.

Pushing through the crowds, I noticed a familiar tank top and broad shoulders, and my eyes focused. I was seeing tunnel vision. It was Mystery Boy again. He was about twenty feet ahead of me, the closest we'd ever been to each other. I wanted to see his face so desperately that it unleashed a frenzy inside of me. It seemed like the faster I moved, the more bodies got in my way and I accidentally shoulder bumped a kid, knocking his backpack off of him and spilling its contents onto the floor. I twirled around, walking backward. "Sorry!" I shouted to him, and then I spun forward in a snap. My eyes searched the crowd, I zeroed in on the shoulders again. I was gaining on him. I pushed through more bodies, but it felt like I was treading quicksand.

Mystery Boy turned a corner; he was headed for the front doors. I raced now, turning the corner myself, but a crouching girl sipping from the water fountain met me. My hip slammed into the side of her body, causing me to spin out of control. I was in a car making my last lap in the Indy 500, just to peel out and crash right before I passed the finish line. My body hit the floor, and I rolled into a pack of denim-covered legs. Before I could propel myself up, I was already being hoisted back to my feet.

"What the hell, dude," Chris said, pulling me up from under my arms.

Dan was there too. "Landon, you okay? What's up with you lately?"

I fixated my eyes on the exit. I nudged the guys aside and ran the rest of the way through the front doors. The sun was too bright to ignore as I shielded my eyes. I squinted, darting my head from left to right, hoping to spot the one guy in a tank top. But he was gone. I groaned as I bent, holding myself up on my knees, trying to catch my breath.

"Landon, what the hell was that?" Dan was behind me. Chris was close by, waiting for an answer too.

I shook my head, standing upright again. "Nothing. I was just looking for someone."

Chris shrugged. "Who?"

Dan looked at me. "Lauren?"

My eyes widened. "No," I said, and I realized I hadn't thought about Lauren in days. I had physically been around her, but even then my mind was on Mystery Boy. I felt terrible; I wasn't even thinking about my girlfriend because he'd taken priority. I wondered for a second if I should tell her.

It's too soon. What would I even say? You can't just tell your girl-

friend you've been fantasizing about someone you've never met. It would destroy her. This could all go away tomorrow.

I'd hoped the feelings and desires would've fizzled out by that point. I worried that they never would, at least maybe not until I saw Mystery Boy's face. What the hell was wrong with me? I knew I looked crazy and was worried I'd completely outed myself. I was an idiot for going after Mystery Boy but I was blinded by obsession.

———

ONE YEAR AGO.

I met Lauren during our Junior year. I was standing outside the auditorium waiting for Dan to meet me before practice. The halls were bustling with movement; waves of kids passed by, heading to their after-school activities. My eye caught a tiny boy running past me and outside to catch his bus. His backpack looked as big as he did; he could probably fit inside of it. I wondered why a boy that young was at the high school. Then another passed by me at breakneck speed. I realized they were freshmen, smirking to myself, thinking about how they seemed to get smaller and smaller every year.

As I watched the munchkins flee, someone bumped into me as they reached for the auditorium door. I scowled as I turned to face the culprit, thinking I'd say something crass. By the time I looked at the door, the person had already run inside. The doors had two slim windows above each handle. I looked inside and saw a skinny guy running toward the stage. The assailant had bright blue, messy hair. It was Steven, the only kid in school who stood out that much. I rolled my eyes; there was no point in getting into it over a bump.

A girl's voice surprised me from behind. "Are you auditioning?"

I spun around, startled by the voice being so close to me. "Uh, what?" I said as I looked her up and down. Her brown hair was pulled back in a messy bun, her backpack over one shoulder. I noticed she was holding a stack of papers in her arms. I recognized her face, but I didn't know her name.

She spoke slower, with her eyebrows raised. "Are you auditioning?" I had no idea what she was talking about. She pointed over my shoulder after I still hadn't said a word.

My head whipped around. "Oh," I said. Finally, everything made sense. There was a sign posted on the auditorium door that read: FOOTLOOSE AUDITIONS, 3:00 P.M. I looked back at her. "No, I won't be auditioning. That's not really what I do."

She tilted her head. "Not what you do, huh? What do you do, then?"

"I play football... I guess that's what I do," I said, shrugging my shoulders.

She rolled her eyes at me; my guess was she didn't like football players. "Well, reconsider, auditioning, I mean. We could use more guys like you."

"Guys like me?"

"Yeah," she said. "You know, Kevin Bacon types."

"Who's that? Does he go to school here?"

She laughed but I didn't understand why. "I love all those guys in there, but none of them are really perfect for Ren."

Everything she was saying sounded like a different language.

She noticed something through the auditorium window, then grabbed my hand and pulled me toward the door.

"Wait, what are you doing?"

"You're coming to the audition," she said without looking back at me, tugging me closer to the door.

"I can't," I scoffed, stopping her in her tracks. "I'm waiting for someone."

She turned to look at me. "Oh, do you have a girlfriend?"

That was direct.

"No," I said, but she was quick to pull me again before I could explain who I was waiting for.

"Good," she said with a smile. I didn't stop her that time. Her messy bun bounced up and down as she guided me through the auditorium doors. Steven had been there, holding it open for us. She didn't let go of my hand until we made it down the ramp. She parked me in front of the stage. Steven was trailing behind us.

"Lauren! I'm so excited!" Steven hugged the girl that forced me through the doors. She hugged him back with giggles. I looked around at the mostly empty seats. The front row housed most of the auditioners. I counted the number of girls versus guys. Only six guys had shown up and twenty girls.

"What's he doing here?" Steven's high timbre interrupted my mental investigation.

"He's gonna audition," Lauren said with a beaming grin. Steven glared at me.

"Landon," Steven said with a monotone voice.

"Steven," I said, matching his tone and giving a nod.

Lauren fluttered over to the hard plastic table that stood against the front row of seats and dropped her stack of papers, which I then realized were scenes from a script. I just stood there with my hands in my pockets while Lauren hugged everyone else in the room. I glanced toward the auditorium doors, wondering if Dan was on the other side waiting for me. I wondered why I was still standing there.

I'm not really going to audition.

Lauren finished her rounds and was back on me like white on rice. She sat me down in the front row and plopped in the seat to my right. Steven sat to my left. I heard coughing from behind us. I turned to discover an older man walking down the ramp toward the stage. He was dressed in a sweater; a button-up shirt and tie were peeking out of the top. A pair of khakis occupied his bottom half. His coughing continued the whole way down the ramp; he was covering his mouth with a handkerchief. The coughs sounded strong and phlegm-soaked. I assumed he was a chain smoker and turned forward in my seat, adjusting my posture. The cream orange upholstered seats weren't exactly luxurious.

"Welcome students," the old man said after his coughing subsided. "I have a list of your names here. I'll call all of you up to the stage in pairs to read the scenes. Break legs, everyone!"

I had no idea who this man was; I assumed he was the director of the school shows, but I wasn't sure if he was an actual teacher there. I also didn't understand why he told us to break our legs.

Lauren jumped from her seat, skipped to the table where the old man was sitting, and started writing on his piece of paper. She was adding my name to the list, meaning she locked me into it and I wasn't excited. Yes, I could've gotten up and left, but I was too nervous about what Lauren and the drama kids would do to me.

The older man looked over at me after reading my printed name. With his squinted eyes, I assumed he was trying to figure out who I was and if he had seen me before. I slouched in my seat, not wanting him to see my face. "Lauren will pass out the scenes and we'll start with a Ren and Ariel scene first," the old man said.

Lauren placed the scene down on my lap. At the top of the photocopy, someone had written FOOTLOOSE: THE MUSICAL in black sharpie. I leaned over to Steven. Without looking at him I whispered, "What's a Footloose?" My words caused him to stop reading and dramatically slap his lap with the papers.

He whipped his head at me and scrunched his eyebrows. "Are you serious?" I suddenly felt small. His words came at me like shards of ice.

I hesitated. "... yes." I imagined him turning into a cobra, and I was his prey. If I said one more word, he would swallow me whole.

"Wow, okay, you really don't know," he said with a sigh. I think he noticed my face turning red, so he eased up a little. "It's like one of the most iconic 80's movies of all time. The sound-track alone makes up the entire musical."

"What's a musical?"

"You're kidding..."

"Yes, that one was a joke," I said. The additional information made me even more reluctant. I am not a singer in the slightest. I'd describe my singing voice as a cat trapped in a burlap sack being set on fire. Lauren finished passing out the scenes and returned to her seat next to me. I leaned close to her, trying not to be heard by the others. "I can't sing, are they gonna make me sing?"

"No," she told me with a smile. "That part is tomorrow for the callbacks; maybe you'll make it through!" She looked at the pages and mumbled the lines to herself.

"God, I hope not," I said under my breath, leaning back into my seat. I stared down at the pages in my lap, reading over the scene. Ren and Ariel were the two leads of the show. The scene in question was very flirtatious. I kept telling myself to get up and leave. I couldn't go up on stage, not in front of everyone. My leg was bouncing. I could feel myself shaking the entire row of seats.

I stood, but as soon as I stepped toward the aisle, the old man shouted, "Landon and Lauren, you two can go first." I looked down at Lauren in shock. Her face beamed up at me as if she had planned it. I looked out to the small crowd of my peers; they were all staring at me, awaiting my performance. I swear my nervous gulp echoed throughout the auditorium. Before I could think about running out of the building, Lauren was pulling me onto the stage.

Standing in the middle of the stage, I was taken aback by how bright and hot the lights were and immediately started sweating. My eyes shot to my feet; all I focused on was the shiny wooden floor of the stage, feeling like I could pass out at any moment.

"Psst." Lauren caught my attention. "It's your line first."

"Oh," I said, clearing my throat a dozen times. I brought the pages close to my face; my eyes were struggling to focus on the words and my mouth went dry. I took the deepest breath I could. "You are something!" I shouted at her. My body had projected the words out of me as if they were a rocket launching into space. I looked to Lauren, who was standing about six feet from me. She didn't let my roar affect her at all; she was a real professional.

"What do you mean?" Lauren asked, without even looking at the paper. She already had her lines memorized. I stood there, watching her twirl her hair before I realized I had to say something back. I pulled the paper close again.

"I mean, the whole p-p-package," I stuttered. I licked my lips, trying to compose myself. "Minister's daughter, Ch-ch-chuck Cranston's girlfriend."

Lauren chuckled. "Guilty," she said, throwing up her hands.

"Just a cha-cha-church goin' gal with some b-b-badass red cowboy boots." I couldn't fathom what was happening. I wiped the sweat from my forehead and took a glance into the audience as Lauren said her next line.

"My father hates me wearing these things."

My quick look to the audience became a long, hard stare. I could hardly see anyone except for the old man sitting at his fold-out table. His hand was rubbing his forehead; everything I was doing appalled him. I imagined huge, white feathery wings sprouting from my shoulder blades, flying me straight through the roof of the stage. I could feel my breath getting sharper and I must have blacked out.

I remember things coming back into focus because Lauren said, "do you wanna kiss me?" I shook my head to find Lauren much closer to my face.

"Um... what?"

"That's not the line," she whispered.

"Oh... um." I pulled the paper back into my line of sight and realized I had spaced on most of the scene, but somehow made it to the end. "Someday."

"Someday?" Lauren took a step back. "What do you mean someday?"

"Ok, thank you, you two!" The old man barked at us. He had put me out of my misery and I'd never felt more grateful in my life. I stumbled off the stage and made a beeline for the doors. I dropped my papers on the table as I passed. I couldn't get out of there fast enough as I pushed through the doors, vowing to never step foot on a stage again.

A voice called out from behind me. "You were right," Lauren had followed me into the hallway. "This really isn't your thing."

"I told you," I said, wiping the last beads of sweat from my face. She just smiled and stared at me. I grinned back. "What?"

"You go do your thing, I'll do mine," she said, pointing a thumb behind her at the auditorium. "But, think we can do something together sometime?"

"Oh." I was a little shocked; she put me through the wringer because she was flirting with me? "Uh, yeah okay sure, that'd be cool."

"Cool, give me your phone," she said, holding out her hand. I gave in to her request and she typed in her number. "Text me?"

"Yeah," I said, still feeling jarred by my debut stage appearance. Lauren smiled at me, turned around, and disappeared back into the auditorium. Just as fast as Lauren vanished, Dan popped up behind me, shoving me down the hall.

"Dude! We have to get to practice, we're late!"

I shoved him. "Where have you been? I've been waiting for you." I chose to leave out the last twenty minutes of my stage adventures.

"I had shit to do. Don't worry about it, fireball."

It seemed a little odd, the way Dan had shrugged off my question, but at the time I let it slide.

A week later Lauren and I were hanging out, walking around the mall, and going to the movies. Everything seemed to happen so fast. Before I knew it, we were official. Lauren had become my very first girlfriend. I never would've thought to ask her out. She was the one to ask me. At the time, I wasn't sure I should say yes because I wasn't sure I liked her as much as she liked me. But I felt the pressure. Saying yes felt like something I had to do rather than something I wanted to do. Over time we got closer and I started to enjoy her company more. She became a person I liked being around and I loved her for that. But I never felt the way I was supposed to feel toward her or how I thought people would assume I should feel toward her. The first time we kissed was so awkward and sloppy, she actually stopped me and had to give me a lesson on how to do it well. I hadn't realized until later that throughout our entire relationship she was always the one to initiate a kiss.

———

SIX

"Goddammit," I whispered to myself. All I could feel was frustration. I'd been obsessing over Mystery Boy for days, and yet I had no details about who he was. I felt like I was so close to seeing him; my hopes were high, but instantly smashed. I thought maybe it was all a dream.

How could I go days without seeing this guy's face?

I ran my fingers through my hair, wondering what to do next. Standing in the courtyard, in the center of a human tornado, I watched my peers swerve around me. I didn't care that the sun was baking me.

"Landon..." Dan tried to grab my attention, but I walked away. I didn't want to lie about how I was feeling, so I started moving. I wanted to find him. I wanted to see him. He couldn't have gone that far; he had to be around somewhere. Dan and Chris didn't follow me. They just let me wander.

My eyes were scanning every person who walked by. The sun was causing me to squint and move my face away from the shining beams. I was afraid I'd miss a glimpse of him. I could already feel my skin burning and I'd only been outside for fewer than five minutes. I hadn't applied sunblock that day. I could picture the tube sitting in my backpack that had fallen off my shoulder when I crashed to the ground and left it there, in hopes of seeing Mystery Boy's face.

I pressed my hand to my forehead, creating a visor-like shape to shield the sun so I could look around without squinting. Taking giant steps, I walked to the front corner of the school. I was almost to the end of the street where an intersection started, about half a football field away from my house. Being that far from the school's entrance, kids still flooded the space. They moved like schools of fish. I heard bits and pieces of conversations as I passed by each mob. Discussions of homework, tv shows, who was having sex with whom, who broke up, and who got back together. Even conversations of hatred for a certain teacher. Some walked by me talking about volleyball, then another about tennis. The conversations would go in one ear and out the other, I was determined to hunt Mystery Boy down.

Face after face, I searched, and I scanned until I spotted a pair of tank-topped shoulders. In a sea of backpacks, he stood out like a great white shark. For a moment, I thought it was a mirage the sun made me see. But I had memorized the back of his body since the first time I saw it. I studied it in my mind every night before I fell asleep. I daydreamed about it in class, so I knew for sure it was him.

I stood there for a bit, waiting to see which way he would go. He was about to step onto the crosswalk through the intersection. I had the idea to cross to the other side of the street and follow him. There was no doubt in my mind that I wouldn't be able to see his face. My heart was pounding again; it was finally going to happen.

I dodged a few goth kids and was about to walk onto the crosswalk, until Lauren appeared, stepping in front of me. "Landon," she said. "Where are you going? People were saying you like, freaked out in the hall."

I couldn't believe I'd failed again. My frustration grew to sudden anger; if this were a cartoon, my ears would've shot steam, my face would've turned bright red, and my head would've skyrocketed off my body.

"Is this a dream?" My eyes widened. Steven was standing with her, looking as perplexed as Lauren. My eyes shot to my left, trying to see if Mystery Boy had already crossed the street. Once again, he disappeared. It was as if he had the power to evaporate into thin air. "This has to be a fucking dream, right?"

Lauren crossed her arms. "Landon, what are you talking about?"

Steven stepped toward me. "Are you all right?"

I couldn't answer their questions. I felt like the world was coming down on my head and I couldn't take it anymore. "I gotta go," I said as I pushed between them, crossing the street. I hadn't noticed the traffic was moving as a car came to a screeching stop before almost taking me out. My heart jumped into my throat as the person behind the wheel blasted down on the car's horn. I flipped them the middle finger and picked up my pace.

I reached the front door of my house and pushed through, hoping no one had followed. The cold air of the AC impaled me. It felt so refreshing, my temper cooled. My movements became slower as I ascended the stairs.

People were talking, Lauren said it herself. I needed to come up with an excuse in case anyone asked me about my freak out the next day at school. Maybe I could play it off as trying to catch my lab partner for a science project who'd been ignoring my texts. I could only imagine what people might've been thinking or saying.

The rollercoaster ride was over and my body was drained. Once in my room, I removed my shirt. I'd sweat through it. As I opened a drawer in search of a fresh one, my Dad knocked on my door frame.

"You didn't say hello when you walked in," Dad said.

"Sorry, I didn't know you were home." I hadn't noticed his car in the driveway. I grabbed a plain black shirt and slipped it over my head. The static sent a weird sensation through my hair.

My Dad was holding my backpack. "Lauren just dropped this off," he said.

I shambled over and took it off his hands. I wondered if Lauren had spilled the beans about my mini-meltdown. "Did she say anything?"

"No, but she seemed a little off. Are you two okay?"

"Yeah Dad, we're okay." I sat on my bed, letting the backpack fall to my feet. My Dad tilted his head as if to say he didn't believe me. The body language was there, but the words never came out of his mouth.

"Well," he said. "My campaign manager got sick, so they postponed our meeting. I figured I'd try cooking something tonight. Want to come to the store with me?"

"Yes!" I said as I shot to my feet. I don't think he expected that sort of reaction. I needed to do something that wasn't sulking in my room, obsessing over Mystery Boy.

As we pulled out of the driveway a song by The Chicks came on the radio and it reminded me how much I used to enjoy car rides with my mom. When I was little I'd always be singing in the backseat. As soon as we would get in the car, I would beg her to play whatever song I was obsessed with. Sometimes it was *The Lion King* soundtrack, other times it would be *Alvin and the Chipmunks*. I was even partial to "Achy Breaky Heart" by Billy Ray Cyrus.

My mom enjoyed her country music. The Chicks were one of her favorite bands. She and I would sing their songs at the top of our lungs, even if we didn't sound the best, we didn't care.

There's a special bond that develops between a mother and her only son; that's the only word I can fathom to describe it, special.

My Dad pulled into the parking lot of our local grocery store, Shop 'n' Go. Parking as close as he could to the entrance.

"I was thinking pork chops," my Dad said as he grabbed a basket before entering the automatic doors.

I smiled. "Whoa, that sounds risky. Think you can handle it?"

Dad chuckled. "I used to be a grill master back in my day."

"Oh yeah, sure."

The AC washed over us in a wave. I wondered what it would be like to live somewhere with different seasons, where it got cold. Maybe New York like Tasha had mentioned. I daydreamed about what it would feel like to throw a snowball or make a snow angel.

I followed my Dad, waiting for him to hand me the basket when he got tired of holding it. He started bopping along to a Stevie Wonder song playing over the loudspeakers. I grinned, watching him pick through heads of broccoli; I hadn't realized he was a Stevie fan. It was what I needed to mellow out.

"Hey," Dad said, handing me the basket. "Is that Steven Mori?" I took a glance behind me. It was Steven; he was shopping with his mom. His pink hair caused him to stick out from the cardboard cutouts of Shop 'n' Go customers.

"Yeah, that's him," I said, turning back to the produce, grabbing a hand full of green beans to shove into a plastic bag. I think my Dad sensed my discomfort.

"I haven't seen him much outside the school. Do you two still talk?"

"No," I said. "Not really." I tried to keep my back to Steven so he wouldn't see me.

"That's a shame." He looked over at me as I rearranged the green peppers. "You guys used to be so close."

"Well, people change," I said, staring down at the sea of veggies. "They grow apart."

———

FIVE YEARS AGO

Steven had come into our school district at the beginning of our eighth-grade year. He had lived a few towns over, but his Dad got a new job that forced them to move. I noticed him right away on the first day of school because he walked differently than the other boys. He wasn't obnoxious like Dan and the rest of our friends, but he didn't seem confident in his own shoes. He kept to himself the first couple of weeks, not saying much to anyone. But I kept my eye on him.

The first time we spoke was in gym class, about a month into the school year. I was in the locker room changing into my gym clothes. I'd gotten there a little early because I'd been to the nurse with a headache. She gave me some Tylenol and sent me on my way. I headed to the locker room instead of going back to class, knowing I had gym next. To my surprise, Steven walked in while I was changing.

"You're here early," I said to him, pulling on my shorts. He didn't make eye contact with me. I just watched him sway to his locker.

"My teacher lets me leave class if we aren't doing anything important," Steven said, looking in every direction but mine.

"Why?" I pulled off my shirt and caught him glancing at me out of the corner of his eye.

Steven hesitated. "I, um, I don't really like changing in front of people."

"Oh, okay," I said with a shrug, sensing he was uncomfortable with me there. I assumed he was just as surprised to see me as I was to see him. As someone involved in sports for most of my life, the thought of being uncomfortable changing in front of other boys was foreign to me.

I picked up my day clothes and shoved them into my locker, closing it and spinning the number dial. When I looked at Steven, he was already in a different outfit. He'd changed so quickly. I sat on the bench in the middle of the aisle, surveying his outfit. He was wearing black sweatpants and a long sleeve shirt.

"You're gonna die outside wearing those," I said, grinning in his direction. I thought his outfit choice was a joke. "You should wear shorts, you're gonna sweat big time."

"I can't," Steven said, looking down at the floor.

"You can't sweat?"

"No," he said, rolling his eyes. "I can't wear shorts."

I tilted my head like a confused dog. "Why?" Steven shrugged and sat on the wooden bench five feet from me. "Dude, you can tell me, no one's around," I said, holding out my arms. A moment passed in silence. I stared at Steven, trying to penetrate his mind to see what he was holding back. He sighed and lifted his pant leg. My eyes dropped, discovering what he had been keeping a secret. His leg was very hairy.

"My Dad says I'm an early bloomer," he admitted, letting his pant leg fall. "I'm like the sasquatch of the locker room. That's why I wear sweat pants because I don't want any of the other guys seeing my hairy legs and making fun of me."

I looked down at my legs, they were bare and pale with a few hairs here and there. Steven's Dad was right, he was an early bloomer. If there were a contest for the hairiest eighth-grader, he would've won. Puberty had hit him like a brick wall. Meanwhile, puberty had hit me like a soft feather to the cheek. I had two little hairs growing in my armpits.

"Hey, it's gonna happen to all of us," I whispered, trying to ease his embarrassment.

Steven pressed the toe of his shoe into the linoleum floor. "I know, but why did it have to happen to me first?"

"Hey," I said. "How do you think I feel? All my hair is gonna be orange!" Steven busted into a giant, squeaky laugh; it was the first time I'd seen him smile. His laugh was contagious, as I followed suit.

"Yeah, you're right," Steven said through his smile. "That is pretty bad." The bell rang and caught us both off guard; we jumped at the sound of it and started laughing again.

I slid down the bench closer to him and nudged him with my elbow. "Your secret's safe with me," I whispered. He smiled at me again. I could tell he was about to thank me when a group of loud boys clamored into the locker room. They surrounded me; Dan was among them. Steven stood and walked away. The guys had scared him off like a timid baby deer.

The next week I spotted Steven sitting alone at lunch. Dan and I were walking to our usual table when I stopped him. "We should sit with him," I said to Dan.

Dan looked at me as if I had two heads. "What? No, he's weird."

"He isn't that weird," I said, slapping Dan's arm with the back of my hand. "I talked to him last week in gym class, he's pretty cool." Dan wasn't convinced, so I looked him in the eyes. "I think I recall you sitting alone at lunch when you were the new kid. Who knows where you'd be now if I hadn't sat with you." I winked at him. Dan took a breath and weighed his options. He looked over at our usual table with our usual friends, and then back at Steven, and then back at our table, then back at me.

"Fine," Dan said with a huff. I took the lead, setting my tray down across from Steven.

"Hey man," I said. "This is Dan. Dan, this is..." My voice

trailed off and my smile faded. I realized I didn't know Steven's name yet.

"Steven, my name's Steven."

As I swung my legs under the table, I remembered he didn't know my name yet either. "I'm Landon," I said with a smile. Dan looked at me. I could feel his eyes digging into the side of my face. That first lunch was sort of awkward, but as time went on, it got easier. I had to convince Dan to sit with Steven a couple more times before he enjoyed it. The three of us got along well. Our duo that Dan and I had established was opening up to a trio.

Dan and I decided that we would let him into our bubble when we invited Steven to hang out with us on the weekends. We spent most of our time at my house. Being an only child, my house didn't have the burden of younger siblings. I also had violent video games that Steven and Dan weren't allowed to have. Over time, I noticed Steven liked our indoor activities much more than our outdoor ones. Anytime Dan and I wanted to throw a football around, Steven would either sit on the sidelines and watch or exclude himself altogether.

The three of us spent almost every weekend together for the entire school year. It was getting close to summer, and we were camping out in my basement. Each of us had a sleeping bag set up parallel to one another. I was in the middle, Dan on my right, Steven on my left. We stayed up into the early morning talking about what we would do over the break, like ride our bikes through the trails at Howard Hill. Or go to a trampoline park that just opened. Play basketball at Dan's house, or have as many *Mortal Kombat* tournaments as possible.

Things simmered down, but Steven had one last thing on his mind. "Guys, I have to tell you something," Steven said, breaking the silence of the room. The three of us were in our respective sleeping bags, staring up into the darkness.

"Okay," I said with a chuckle, not knowing where the conversation would go.

"I think," Steven started, chewing on those words for a moment. "I think I might be gay."

He'd sucked the air out of the room. It was silent as if we were floating in space with no tether to hold us. My young brain had no idea how to respond. Dan and I didn't speak, and Steven didn't say another word either. I could hear his breathing getting heavier. I expected him to laugh, admitting that it was just a joke, but he stayed silent. None of us knew how to react. Until that point, we had never heard the word gay used seriously. We always used it as an insult to our friends as a joke. Dan and I both knew what it actually meant.

The only real experience I'd had at that point with anything gay-related was watching reruns of *Will & Grace* with my mom. My Dad had a fit when he came home to us watching it. 'Landon shouldn't be watching this', he said. 'He's too young, I won't allow it. He doesn't need to be seeing that shit.' We never watched it after that. Anytime I would come across an episode being played on TV, I'd hurry to change the channel as if I'd committed a crime for even seeing a glimpse of it.

Dan finally broke the quiet. "I need to sleep, guys."

The sleeping bag made swishing noises, and he turned to his side, facing away from us. Then Steven's sleeping bag made the same noise as he turned away from me as well. I held my position, staring up at the ceiling until my eyelids got heavy enough to take me into a deep slumber.

The next morning I opened my eyes to a beam of light shining through the basement window. I propped myself up on my elbows and looked around. Both Dan and Steven were gone, their sleeping bags all askew. I walked upstairs, expecting them to be sitting in the kitchen as my mom served them breakfast, but the table was empty. I checked my room, no luck.

I called Dan's house to clear up the confusion.

Dan's mom answered the phone. "Hello?"

"Hi, Is Dan there?"

"Oh hi, Landon. He just walked in, let me get him." I heard a clunk as she placed the phone down.

I heard some mumbles before Dan spoke. "Hello?"

"Dan? Where'd you go? I woke up and you and Steven were gone. I thought we were gonna play Call of Duty today?"

"Sorry," Dan said. "I just felt weird."

"What are you talking about?"

"What Steven said." I had honestly forgotten the conversation. "Steven told us he was gay last night," Dan whispered into the receiver.

I let out a nervous laugh. "I'm sure he was joking. He always jokes."

"I don't want to hang out with him anymore."

"Seriously?"

"Yeah. I don't think we should, and if you're really my friend, you won't hang out with him either."

I tried to protest, but Dan had already decided. He gave me an ultimatum: Steven or him. He made me choose and of course; I picked Dan. I had no other choice; we'd been friends for much longer.

That Monday at school, Dan and I got off the bus together. Steven was waiting for us by the entrance like he normally did. Dan leaned over to me and reminded me not to acknowledge him.

"Hey, guys!" Steven said, waving at us. Dan never looked in his direction; he just kept walking. I wanted to stop, but I was too afraid of what Dan would do. I glanced at Steven, then my eyes shot to the ground. I walked past him without saying a word. Steven didn't follow us. He just let us go; I think he knew something in the air was different. I looked back at him and saw his face turn upside down. My heart dropped into my stomach; I felt so guilty.

The next day Steven tried to sit with Dan and me at lunch. Dan got up and walked away without a word. Steven sat across from me, his eyebrows furrowed, and he shook his head, not understanding what was happening. "I'm sorry," I whispered, before standing and following Dan to another table. I left Steven sitting alone like we had found him earlier that school year.

The summer came and went. Both Dan and I didn't speak to Steven at all. We didn't even see him around the neighborhood. We continued doing our own thing, and Steven became a distant memory. Three months of summer vacation could make a kid forget about anything.

That fall, we entered High School. It was great not having to take the bus. Now all I had to do was cross the street. Strolling down the halls, everyone had changed a little, including Dan and me. We were a little taller and had a little more fuzz on our upper lip. Dan greeted me with a fist bump as we gathered around some lockers with our other friends, updating each other on our lives.

"No fucking way," Dan said. His jaw went loose and his eyes were laser-focused on something behind me. I turned around, curious about his reaction. That's when I saw Steven walking toward us down the hall; he'd changed more than anyone. He'd grown out his hair and dyed it yellow, and he was wearing very tight jeans and black combat boots with rainbow laces keeping them in place. His bellowing T-shirt had the words 'Kiss Me' printed in a sparkly font. The guys in my cluster, including Dan, watched as he strode by us and greeted a group of girls gathered near a water fountain. "Look at this fucking queer," Dan said. This was the first time he'd said anything about Steven in months. "Guys, let's go fuck with him."

I rolled my eyes. "Why?"

Dan ignored me, walking toward Steven, motioning for the other guys to follow. I trailed behind the horde, watching. Dan was on Steven without warning and grabbed him by the neck of his shirt, slamming him against the wall. I heard the smack of Steven's head against the brick. I had never seen Dan that aggressive off the football field. The simple sight of Steven set something off in him.

"It's been a while, faggot," Dan sneered in Steven's face. I could see the spit from the F syllable fly onto Steven's shirt. "Do you realize where you are, fairy boy? What's gotten into you? Suddenly you decide to wear your mom's clothes to school?"

"You honestly pushed me to have more confidence in myself, Dan," Steven said with a devilish smile, feeling the pressure of Dan's strength. "You should be proud." Steven winked, setting Dan off even more. I remember thinking Steven's words sounded deliberate. Dan threw Steven to the ground and kicked him hard in the stomach as if he were kicking a football to a goal. I'll never forget the sound of air escaping Steven's body. He clenched his torso, gasping for a breath. Dan's aggression sent the surrounding girls screaming as they ran away.

The rest of the guys started in on Steven; like a pack of hungry wolves, they followed Dan's lead. The kicking was relentless. Stephen was crying out for help, as I stood there stuck. My eyes locked with Steven's. The desperation in his face crippled me. With just one look, he was begging me to make it stop, but I couldn't. I was a coward, frozen in fear, too scared to face repercussions from the alpha and his pack.

One of Dan's kicks met Steven's face, knocking him out cold. A teacher then rushed to Steven's aid, breaking up the pack. I looked down at Steven's helpless skinny body, holding back my tears. Blood was trickling off his face and onto the floor. That was the first time I had experienced actual violence, I felt so powerless.

Dan was suspended for the first week of school, while Steven spent time in the hospital. Steven's parents fought to have Dan expelled, but the principal wasn't convinced that the sole purpose of Dan's attack was because Steven was gay. When Steven eventually returned, I continued to ignore him, like nothing happened. I wouldn't have known what to say to him if he approached me.

———

"Mom used to do applesauce with her chops, remember that? Can you go grab some?"

"Sure," I said. I crossed the store, glancing at each sign as I passed an aisle, looking for the canned fruit section. I took a hard left down aisle six and reached the abundance of applesauce selection. I grabbed the cheapest jar and turned back the way I came, just to bump into a tuft of pink hair. "Shit, sorry," I said, composing myself.

Steven chuckled. "It's okay." He realized it was me and huffed. I walked away, but he stopped me, asking, "Why?"

I turned on my heels. "What?"

"Why did you talk to me the other day in the bathroom? You haven't really said a word to me in almost four years." Steven crossed his arms. "So why now?"

I stared at him, unsure of what to say. It took a moment for the words to form in my mind. "Like I said, research."

Steven scoffed, grabbing a can of mixed fruit off the shelf. "Research, right. And what about your scene at school today? What was that about?"

I scratched my head and straightened my shirt a little, nervous by his questioning. He was referencing my chase of Mystery Boy earlier that day. I must've looked like a freak. "I'm just kind of going through some stuff right now."

"Anything I can help with?" He was being uncharacteristically genuine for the sarcastic high school version of Steven I'd discovered over the years.

"No, no..." my words trailed off in an awkward chuckle. Then a light bulb popped on in my brain. "Well, maybe?" I took a deep breath. "If you wanted to find someone to like, find out what they looked like, how would you do it?"

"Easy," Steven said with a hand flick. "Do you know their name?"

"Um," I said. Why the hell hadn't I thought of that already? Finding out someone's name was the simplest thing in the world, I could've asked my Dad for it. "No."

"Well, it would be easy to look them up on Facebook if you knew their name. If that doesn't work, I usually use Grindr."

"What's Grindr?"

"Oh," Steven laughed. "Obviously you've never heard of it. It's like this hookup app for gay guys."

"Gotcha," I said. The thought of Steven hooking up with someone was weird. "Well, thanks, man. I appreciate it."

"No problem!" Steven said with a curtsy before walking away.

"Steven," I called out.

He stopped and turned to me with an eyebrow raised.

"I'm sorry... " I said, swallowing the lump in my throat. "...For not stopping Dan when I could have. I'm... I'm just really sorry."

Steven tilted his head, giving me a half-smile. "Wow. You know, never in a million years did I think those words would come out of your mouth after everything. I've had a long time to think about if I could ever forgive you, and I just might be able to, but I'll never forget." he said.

"Right," I said with a nod. Steven had every right not to forgive me, what happened to him was fucked up and I had a part in it. I turned to walk away but his words caught me.

"I never had the chance to say anything, but I was sorry to hear about... ya know..." Steven's voice got softer as he fiddled with the can of fruit. I knew what he was trying to say. "She was always nice to me. I never felt judgment from her."

My jaw clenched. It sent a chill through my body. "She was never the type," I said. He smiled before walking off. My shoulders relaxed around Steven for the first time in years. Anytime I'd been around him before that, I replayed the events in my head, causing me to keep my distance.

At that moment, I broke off from the pack to become an alpha of my own. My first order of business was to rush back to my Dad and ask for Mystery Boy's name.

SEVEN

M y eyes popped open, then closed again out of pain. I had opened them to a bright fluorescent light in the ceiling. I brought my hands to my face, rubbing my eyes. I turned my head and lifted my lids again.

What the hell? My eyes darted around.

I was in a hospital room, lying on a gurney. I looked down at myself; I was wearing a thin, white gown with nothing underneath. I moved my arms to prop myself up, but a sting from my left arm stopped me. I discovered an I.V. attached to the bend in my elbow. I ripped off the clear tape, pinched the needle, and held my breath as I dragged it from my skin. It felt like I was pulling out a shard of glass. I threw the needle to the ground and heard it clink against the floor. I swung my legs off the bed and connected my bare feet to the cold tile. I felt a breeze up my backside and realized my hospital gown was open, so I pulled at the strings and tied them while I looked for my clothes.

The room was bare, except for the bed and a single green cushioned chair; it stood out like a sore thumb against the stark whiteness of the area. I stepped over to the window and drew the curtains.

It was dark outside and foggy. I could tell I was a few stories up, but I didn't see the ground; all I saw was gray mist. I turned to study the space again. My body felt so cold. It confused me why I was there.

My eyes came upon a brown wooden door and I scrambled to it, turning the handle. It was the bathroom, just as barren. I glimpsed myself in the mirror. My breathing became heavier. I trudged closer, admiring my face. I reached up and touched my nose. It was bandaged and bloody. Both my eyes were shades of black and blue. I let out an exasperated sigh. I had no memory of how I got there or what caused my wounds.

A sound came from behind me. I twirled around with force, having to catch myself on the sink. "Hello?" I called out, but no one answered. I crept back into the room, walking on my tiptoes. The space was dead silent. My eyes caught another brown door, and I rushed for it. I slowly opened it, peeking my head out first. The corridor of the hospital was empty. I looked right and left, but all I saw were flickering lights. No one was around. The silence was haunting. I stepped into the hallway. "Hello?" I said again, hearing my voice echo. I walked down the white hall, feeling my left arm, discovering a skinny trail of blood moving down my skin from where I'd pulled the needle. Then I heard something in the distance. It was faint, but I could hear it. I moved toward the small sound, turning a corner before the sound became clear; it was a dial tone.

The lights flickered from above, which startled me to a stop. My heart raced. I continued to follow the sound; it was getting a little louder. There was a nurse station at the end of the hallway; that's where the dial tone was coming from. I picked up my pace and the dial tone got louder and louder as I approached. When I reached the nurse's counter, the dial tone became ear piercingly loud. Then I heard a splat as I felt a small splash hit my leg. I was standing in a pool of dark red blood. I screamed, stepping away, slipping on its slick layer, and falling against the wall. That's when I saw the body.

My hand covered my mouth, I couldn't believe what I was seeing. The blood was coming from a woman wearing white scrubs. She was face down in her own mess. Someone had stabbed her multiple times around the upper half of her body. I then realized that the dial tone had stopped and everything was silent again. That's when I heard the footsteps.

The steps were heavy; the person was wearing boots. The lights went out before I looked in the sound's direction, but I still heard the footsteps. They weren't fast, but a steady pace. I could tell they were getting closer. I pushed myself to my feet again, but my fear cemented me in my place. The lights turned on again, and I saw a dark shadowed man walking toward me at the same pace as the footsteps I'd heard. The light reflected off the long hunter's knife he held in his right hand; the blade was stained red. My eyes widened, and my heart dropped into my stomach. I tried to run but slipped and fell to the ground as my feet were still slick from the blood.

I felt a firm hand grab my ankle. I screamed and clawed at the floor, trying to get any sort of traction. My heart was beating out of my chest, I was terrified to look back at the person controlling my fate.

"Landon..." I heard a voice say, then again a little louder.

I jumped awake, struggling to catch a breath, I was in my Dad's car. I had fallen asleep on the ride home from the grocery store. My Dad had given me a good shake to wake me up. I was panting, and rubbed my face, and tried to calm my breathing.

"Didn't mean to scare you," Dad said.

I looked at him still sitting in the driver's seat. "It's okay. Just a weird dream."

I stood from the car in a daze, still shaken from my nightmare as I sauntered to the trunk to help with the groceries. I was used to having strange, vivid dreams but never that dark. My mind had been in a weird place. I assumed I was in a car accident in the dream which would make sense, being in a car when I fell asleep. But something dark was stalking me, something mysterious.

As I stepped through the side door, I remembered I was going to talk to my Dad about Mystery Boy. He was already paying for the groceries after my talk with Steven in the canned fruit aisle, so I waited until we got home to ask. I placed the grocery bags on the kitchen counter and emptied them. My Dad sat at the kitchen island and started watching a video on his phone. I walked to him, curious about what was keeping his attention. He was playing clips of football games from another high school team.

"Look at this," he said, feeling my presence behind him. "This team is slaughtering North Valley High."

I watched the screen, but I didn't respond to his comment. Whatever team this was, they were throwing some impressive plays on the field, but I couldn't care less at that moment about football.

"Dad," I said, but paused. I wasn't sure how to segue into my question. I determined there was no perfect strategy, I didn't have time to work it out like the perfect plays my Dad was watching on his screen; I had to come out and ask. My Dad strained his neck looking up at me, wondering what I wanted, but then focused on his screen again. "That guy working at the school, what's his name?" The words sounded glued together.

My Dad didn't take his eyes off his phone. "What guy? There are a lot of guys working at the school."

I moved around from behind his chair and sat to his left. "The guy doing community service or whatever."

My Dad paused the video. He looked at me, moving his upper body in my direction. "Why do you care?"

"I don't," I lied. "I just heard some people at school talking about him and I was wondering what his name was."

So I can look him up on Facebook.

"Oh, I don't know," he huffed, looking back at his screen.

"Come on, Dad."

"He doesn't report to me," he said, sounding annoyed.

I slouched in my chair. "You've gotta know something."

My Dad stared at me with curious eyes, I stared back at him and his mustache moved. "It's something with a C, I think." His eyes looked around the room, searching his brain for a name. "Charlie, maybe? No, Cole?" I perked up from my slouch, itching to get any piece of information about Mystery Boy. My Dad stopped talking to think. "It wasn't Chase, was it?" I could've started sweating from the anticipation. "I don't remember Landon, I'm sorry." Breath escaped my lungs like someone had let go of a full balloon. I was instantly deflated; he'd killed my high.

"All right," I said, standing from the table. "Thanks, I guess." I saw him un-pause the video and heard smacking football helmets start up again from behind me as I ascended the stairs. I tried to look at the positives, I at least knew the first letter of Mystery Boy's name was a C if my Dad's information was correct.

I closed my bedroom door and found my phone on my bed. I had hoped to be scouring Facebook for Mystery Boy, but of course, I wasn't so lucky. I looked at my screen and noticed I had a missed call from Lauren and three unread texts.

LAUREN

What happened today, are you okay?

You sort of snapped at me, so I'm kinda confused.

You're freaking me out.

She must've sent the texts as my Dad and I left for the grocery store.

ME

Hey, sorry I didn't respond, I fell asleep after school. Thanks for dropping off my bag.

She was already typing back.

LAUREN

You've been acting so weird this week, what's been going on?

ME

I just have a lot on my mind, it's senior year, things are crazy right now.

LAUREN

I understand that, but you've just seemed a little distant, I don't know. I feel like I've barely talked to you this week.

My fingers didn't move, I stared at the screen searching for the right words. I didn't want to lie, but I had no other choice.

ME

I'm sorry, but really I'm okay.

LAUREN

All right :/

Are we still on for Saturday?

ME

Yeah :)

I flung myself onto the bed and perched my pillow against the headboard for support and leaned back on it. I thought about what Steven said at the grocery store, that if he couldn't find someone on Facebook he used...

What was the name of that app?

I felt like my Dad. I played the memory of our conversation like a video in my mind, rewinding and fast-forwarding, scanning the way Steven's mouth formed his words, trying to figure out the answer.

Then it popped into my head.

Grindr!

My thumb moved around the screen of my phone. I searched the app store and found it within seconds. I hovered over the download button for a bit, fearing the unknown. I had no clue what type of door I was about to open. I wasn't sure how it worked or what my chances of finding Mystery Boy were. I didn't even know if he liked guys.

If someone sees this on my phone I'm screwed. If my Dad knew about this app he'd disown me. I'll just delete it when I'm done, it'll be quick.

I pushed the thoughts aside and clicked download. Suddenly I was in, but I needed to create a username first. It couldn't be my actual name, obviously. I pondered for a moment, then typed 'SportyGuy' and clicked next, but the app informed me the name had already been taken. So I added my jersey number to the end, and it let me continue.

Next, I had to fill in my stats, age, height, weight, and tribe. *Tribe? What the hell is a tribe?*

I clicked the drop-down menu to survey my options. There were about ten different tribes which included bear, twink, fem, sub, dom, jock, etc.

Overwhelmed and also not understanding what any of it meant, I clicked jock and moved on. Next, I had to add a picture. That part stressed me out, I knew I couldn't use my face. I thought about adding a picture of a celebrity, but that would make it seem like I was trolling people. I went with a picture of a Dallas Cowboys jersey. I skipped the part where I had to fill in my bio because at that point I just wanted to search.

The main dashboard of the app was just a bunch of square pictures. I had to click on one square if I wanted to talk to the person and read their stats. I realized that I wouldn't have any luck on Grindr either, because I had no idea what Mystery Boy's face looked like. If a picture of his face *was* on the app, I'd scroll right by it, not knowing it was him. I hoped that I'd see a picture of a guy's back and recognize it to be Mystery Boy. Then my phone vibrated, I had a message. I clicked over to a thread with a little blue text bubble on a gray background.

GUYLOOKING, 45

Hey handsome ;)

I had no idea how to respond. It surprised me; I wasn't expecting anyone to message me. And how did he know if I was handsome?

GUYLOOKING, 45

I'm looking to meet up with someone tonight to fool around.

"Wow," I said to myself, staring at my screen. "That was forward." It was making me nervous.

SPORTYGUY83, 18

No.

GUYLOOKING, 45

:(

GuyLooking sent a picture of his face. He had salt and pepper hair and looked like he could be my uncle. It made me feel weird. I clicked out of the chat and continued my search for Mystery Boy on the main dashboard. Scrolling through, I imagined Mystery Boy to have dark eyes to match his brown hair. I imagined him to have a dimpled chin with a little patch of hair growing under it.

Most of the pictures were bare chests, or underwear shots, or guys that looked like professional models. I suppose one guy could be him, but I'd never know. My phone vibrated again, I clicked over to the messages. HornyDaddy, 38, had sent me a photo. I held my breath and clicked the message to open it.

My eyes met a picture of HornyDaddy's erection.

"Jesus Christ!"

"What happened?" My Dad yelled from downstairs. "Are you all right?"

I clutched the phone to my chest, acting as if he were standing behind me trying to peek at what I'd seen.

"Yes!" I called back. "Nothing happened. I'm fine!"

I looked at the phone again. My jaw popped open. I didn't think anyone's dick could get that big. I was suddenly feeling very inadequate. I clicked away from the message and doubted what I felt for Mystery Boy because looking through all the faces on Grindr; I wasn't attracted to any of them. Another vibration.

THEATRENERD245, 18

Hey there, I don't think I've seen you on here before.

Finally, a normal thing to say to someone.

SPORTYGUY83, 18

Yeah, I'm kind of new.

THEATRENERD245, 18

That's cool, welcome! :) What're you looking for?

SPORTYGUY83, 18

Not really sure. Just looking around, I guess.

THEATRENERD245, 18

Cool. Wanna trade pics?

SPORTYGUY83, 18

What kind of pics?

I started to sweat a little.

THEATRENERD245, 18

Just face pics, for now.

Another vibration, GuyLooking was back.

GUYLOOKING, 45

Maybe you can send some nudes then?

SPORTYGUY83, 18

No thanks.

GUYLOOKING, 45

:(

THEATRENERD245, 18

I can send one first.

SPORTYGUY83, 18

Okay, sure.

HORNYDADDY, 38

You like my cook?

Cock*

GUYLOOKING, 45

Am I not hot enough for you?

HORNYDADDY, 38

Are you a top or a bottom?

GUYLOOKING, 45

You're probably some stuck up twink.

You don't deserve me, asshole!

HORNYDADDY, 38

I want to fuck you so badly.

Message after message kept coming, even though I wasn't responding to any of them. The app was scaring me, I didn't blame guys for being so confident and forward behind a screen but did those messages ever really work for them?. Another vibration, Theatrenerd245 had sent a photo. I opened it with caution and choked on my spit. Theatrenerd245 was Steven, in all his pink-haired glory, posing for a selfie in his room! I quickly closed the app and threw my phone face down on my bed as if Steven could see me through my front-facing camera. I ran my fingers through my hair, wiping the sweat from my head. I wasn't going to find Mystery Boy on Grindr, that much was clear.

EIGHT

The next morning I walked into school to find the *Monthly* had been printed and people were already reading it. My mind was still racing from the night before, horrified over my first Grindr experience. My eyes flickered from face to face as I shuffled through the mass of bodies, hoping I wouldn't see Steven. It was an irrational thought, but as soon as he sent me his picture I automatically assumed he knew Sportyguy83 was me. There was no way he knew that. But it's something I felt in my stomach.

"It's a hit so far!" Tasha said, popping up in front of me, taking me by surprise. "I'm so glad I added you to the team. Your stories are always the part people like the most, besides Corey's comic strip." Tasha smiled at me but noticed my face was stuck in a distant gaze.

"Of course," I said.

"Are you okay? You've been acting strange all week."

"I keep hearing that from people."

"Well, a lot of people saw your little freak-out yesterday. So I want to make sure you're okay."

"Yes, I'm fine," I said, dodging eye contact. "And it wasn't a freak-out. I guess I'm just tired of people saying I'm acting weird."

"Well," Tasha's expression became warm as she touched my arm. "If you need to talk about anything, don't hesitate. We can do coffee or whatever."

"Thanks, Tasha," I said, giving her a grin. I shrugged her off; my mind wasn't in the most conscious state. I headed toward the cafeteria; my stomach growled during my brief conversation with Tasha. I tried to look into each classroom as I passed by, hoping to notice Mystery Boy mopping the floor or removing pieces of gum from desks, but I didn't see him. I wondered if he came in every day, or every other day, or once a week. That was a question I should've asked my Dad; he might've at least known Mystery Boy's schedule.

As soon as I stepped into the cafeteria, Lauren flagged me down from a table ten feet away. Again my eyes darted from table to table as I walked over to Lauren's spot, searching for the pink-headed mop of hair.

Lauren spoke as I slipped into the bench seat across from her. "Are you feeling any better today?" She reached out and touched my hand. My eyes locked onto her for the first real-time in days. She smirked at me.

"Yeah. I think so." I lied. I was on edge, I was already so anxious to get a glimpse of Mystery Boy, and then I was even more anxious about seeing Steven, fearing he knew my secret.

"Ok, good," she said. She may have been unconvinced. "So, what did you mean yesterday when you asked me if this was a dream?"

I'd forgotten I blurted that out in frustration. She was calling me out about my freak out and I had no genuine answer for her.

I've been dying to see this guy's face and every time I get close, something gets in the way. Yesterday that thing was you.

That would've been too rude and more honest than I was

ready to be. That was the first time Lauren had seen me truly frustrated.

"I said that?" I was playing dumb.

"Yeah," Lauren said. "You seemed pretty annoyed."

"The sun, I was out in the sun too long." I lied again. It wouldn't be the last time I lied to her face. "You know it fries my brain sometimes." I gave a weak smile. "I have this group project due in chemistry and I was trying to find my partner, but he ran out before I could talk to him, so I was pretty annoyed. I'm sorry I took it out on you." I wondered how far I could go with the lie before it wore me down. I squeezed her hand a little, hoping she had believed my fairytale.

"Okay," she said with a genuine smile that told me she wasn't holding any grudges. "Oh!" Lauren perked up. "I made this new playlist last night! Can I download it to your phone?"

"Yeah, sure," I said without thinking. In one swift motion, I pulled my phone out of my pocket and placed it on the table in front of her.

"I need to grab something to eat," I said, glancing at the line at the food bar, it was long. I wasn't sure I had the patience, so I made a mental decision to wait longer until it died down.

"It's sort of this blend of 90s R&B and early 2000s pop," Lauren said, while she flicked through my phone. "Um," suddenly her face turned upside down. "Why do you have Grindr on your phone?"

My heart jumped into my throat. *Shit, shit, shit I forgot to delete it!*

After I'd seen Steven's selfie, my Dad called me downstairs to help him with dinner. By the time I'd gotten back to my phone after eating and doing homework, I'd forgotten the app was there.

I practically leaped over the table to grab my phone back

from her. My face felt flushed as I tried to think of an excuse. I cleared my throat.

"Dan must've downloaded it as a joke or something." I struggled to play it as smoothly as I could. "I'm deleting it now," I said, which was another lie. Suddenly, waiting in line at the food bar didn't seem so tiresome. "I'm gonna grab some food real quick. I'll be right back" I said as I stood, leaving Lauren there alone and confused by how quickly everything had happened.

While in line, I tried not to look back at the table, afraid Lauren would be staring me down. I hoped she believed what I said. I didn't think it would be beyond Dan's intellectual capacity to download a gay app onto someone's phone as a prank. Right? I pulled my phone out, deleting Grindr faster than I could say...

"Do you want to try the new breakfast burrito?" A woman in a hairnet asked from behind the bar. It took me a second to realize the line had moved, and I was standing there with a blank look on my face. I could smell the fresh eggs and bacon circling the air.

"Sure," I blurted, grabbing the foil-wrapped cylinder. As I moved toward the cashier, I looked over to Lauren's table. Dan, Chris, and a few others had joined her. I took a relaxed breath, hoping she'd become distracted enough to forget about finding Grindr. Hopefully, she wouldn't bother asking Dan about it. My stomach growled. I was getting excited to scarf down the burrito.

"Sup, Cheeto," Dan said as I reached my spot back at the table. I gave him a quick head nod and unwrapped my breakfast. The cafeteria had gotten louder with random chatter all around us as kids started piling in before the first bell. I started taking large bites, worrying I wouldn't have enough time to finish. To my very satisfying surprise, the burrito housed eggs with cheddar cheese, sausage, and bacon. It was everything you could want in the morning when your stomach yelled at you. I glanced at Lauren between a massive bite and noticed she was texting, seemingly unfazed by her recent discovery on my phone.

Dan was babbling about some girl he hooked up with the previous night, which I tried to tune out. But then he said something that caught my ear. "Have you guys heard the latest about this new janitor?" My eyes focused on Dan's face, ready to receive any additional information about Mystery Boy. My mouth was chewing, but everything else was still. I focused on his lips just in case I couldn't hear what he said over the roar of the growing breakfast crowd.

Everyone at the table was listening. It made me suspect that Mystery Boy's popularity was increasing. The gossip was spreading about who he was and what he did to get community service. "Someone told me they saw some sort of, like, anarchy tattoo on his hand. It's like an A marking," Dan said. My mind took the information and moved it to a little box labeled Mystery Boy with a small lock on the front.

A tattoo, interesting.

I whipped out my phone to google what an anarchy symbol looked like, wondering if it really meant what Dan said it did. The questions continued to build.

"The guy burns down his old school, AND has an anarchy tattoo? He's probably part of some cult," Dan said.

My thoughts traveled to a ridiculous vision of a man walking into the cafeteria. I couldn't see his face because a large hood attached to a Jedi-like robe covered it. He meandered toward a trash can and turned his back to me, removing his hood and dropping the robe. The familiar back was Mystery Boy. Then he pulled a large hunting knife from the waistband of his pants and raised it in the air, triumphantly displaying his tattoo. He was about to commit a sacrifice, but Chris's words brought me back to reality.

"Do you think this will all end in a murder spree?" Chris smirked.

"If anyone gets killed, he's definitely gonna be suspect number one," Dan said, causing the other meatheads to chuckle along with him. By that point, my burrito was gone and I could feel the grease coating my stomach lining. Then it made a sound that didn't mean I was hungry, it was bubbling up. I felt it rejecting everything I had just guzzled down.

I sat up straight, asking, "have any of you actually seen him?"

"How could you not?" Lauren said, looking up from her phone. "He's always doing something around here."

A pang of jealousy shot through me like a bolt of lightning. How had she seen him, but I hadn't? I felt like I was searching for him every hour of every school day. I wondered if I should interrogate her for more details, but it might be too soon after she found Grindr on my phone. The first bell rang and everyone stood from their seats, putting an end to my personal debate.

The day flew by faster than usual. It was a half-day because of parent-teacher conferences happening later that evening. My stomach got progressively worse throughout the day, bubbling up like a pot of liquid left on the stove for too long. I headed toward the locker room to change before football practice. As I passed the cafeteria, I got a strong whiff of pizza that made me want to vomit.

Stepping into the boy's locker room made my stomach turn again. The whole place smelled like decaying feet, mixed with Axe body spray. I threw my bag on the bench and walked over to a sink. I turned on the cold water and cupped my hands, using the puddle to soak my face. I leaned on the porcelain, which felt cold under my palms, staring at my reflection. The fluorescent light made my ginger buzz cut look even brighter than it was. I strolled back to my bag and grabbed my jersey. Pulling it over my head, it met me with a pleasant scent of floral breeze. It was my mom's favorite laundry detergent that my Dad continued to use. It didn't last long as I pulled my head back into the stench of the room. My stomach gurgled again, forcing me to the bench, feeling a bit light-headed. Other guys trickled in to change, and the smelly room filled with energy.

Our football field was behind the school. To get to it, you had to walk through the gym, out the backside of the school, and across a large parking lot. I was holding my helmet by the face-mask, letting it swing back and forth as I weaved through parked cars, still scanning for Mystery Boy at every opportunity. I hadn't seen him at all that day, so I assumed that he didn't work every day.

Then my eyes fixed on Dan. He was standing behind his car with the trunk popped open, already in his practice gear. His helmet was resting on the roof. I continued to walk toward the field, but my eyes stayed on him, confused by what he was doing. As I made my way through the cars, another person came into my line of sight standing next to Dan. He was a tall skinny guy with a goatee and stringy long hair. His clothes looked two sizes too big, and he stood with slumped shoulders.

The strange man pulled out some crumpled cash from his pocket and gave it to Dan. Dan gave a quick look in each direction before reaching for something in his trunk. He didn't realize I was watching him. Whatever Dan grabbed for, he kept it concealed in his fist before passing it off to the skinny man. The exchange had happened so fast, if I blinked I would've missed it. The man hurried away, and Dan closed his trunk, grabbing his helmet. I looked forward again and almost walked into a parked car. If I watched them any longer, I'd for sure have a bruised knee.

Who the hell was that?

My mind raced with questions. Surely I'd know if my best friend was selling drugs. Dan wouldn't be stupid enough to do it on school grounds. Then I thought it was probably something school-related, like a USB or something.

I stepped through the four-foot-high chain-link fence that surrounded the field area. My shoes first met the brown racing track that wrapped around the football field. I always liked the way it felt under my feet, it had a slight bounce to it that made it fun to walk on. I heard a whistle blow and saw kids were already running down the track. There was a group of guys huddled on the grass ten feet in front of me. I heard the grass crunch under my feet; it had just been cut and the smell of it made my stomach flip again. I closed my eyes and took a slow breath out of my mouth, letting my cheeks blow up like balloons. The nauseous feeling didn't go away, and I knew any strenuous activity would only make it worse. I wasn't sure which end the greasy breakfast burrito was going to come out, but I could feel it gearing up for its exit. It was just a matter of when.

"Looking a little sweaty, Griffin," Chris said, bringing all the attention to me. "We haven't even done anything yet."

"Never eat the breakfast burrito from the cafeteria," I said, dropping my helmet, and rubbing my stomach. "I'm learning that lesson the hard way." The other guys laughed it off, and it seemed to make my stomach angrier. It was pushing its way out, but I held it back. I wanted to get through practice.

I saw my Dad walk onto the field with Coach, which wasn't uncommon. They were good friends, and my Dad had to be on school grounds that night for the teacher meetings.

Coach's voice roared. "Take a knee, boys." We all turned around, doing as he commanded. Dan ran up from behind him and joined us. "We've got a lot of work to do," Coach said. His whistle hung around his neck and he held a clipboard in his right hand. His daily tie was loosened, and he undid the top button of his shirt. "We could've done better when we faced Glendale last Wednesday. What I saw on that field was not what

I expected from you guys." He stroked his goatee, while his eyes passed over us one by one. "I expect focus and hard work. That's not what I saw on this field. As you know, we have a game against Skowhegan in a few weeks. Those guys are serious business. I saw them kill the North Valley team last night." Coach must've been the one who sent my Dad that video. "I'd be scared if I were you because, with the shape we're in right now, they're going to use us to wipe their asses. Y'all need to show me what it takes to win. The work starts now," he said, pointing to the ground. "Fifty crunches, fifty push-ups, let's go."

"Yes, coach!" we all screamed.

Dan positioned himself next to me, giving me a greeting head nod. Lying on my back in the grass, I wanted to stay there forever. It made my stomach feel a little better. Everyone else had started, but I didn't. My Dad was quick to notice.

"Landon, pick it up!" he hollered in my direction.

I pushed up toward my knees and winced; I could feel the bile in my gut sloshing around. Dan was counting out loud, already ten crunches ahead of me.

"Who..." I said to Dan, speaking my words between each wince of a sit-up. "... was... that guy you were talking to?"

Dan's head turned. I could see the concerned look on his face out of the corner of my eye. "Don't worry about it," Dan said.

"He just seemed really odd. I haven't seen him around here before."

"Drop it, Landon. Like I said, you don't need to worry about it." He was being standoffish, more than usual. I winced again. "What the hell is wrong with you?"

"Fuck," I whispered, grabbing my stomach as I laid flat against the grass. "That burrito I ate this morning hasn't been sitting well with me all day." I felt a cramp building up in my bowels, I knew I needed to find a bathroom. I stood on my feet too quickly, getting a sudden head rush. "Coach," I called out, raising my hand.

He looked at me with scrunched eyebrows. "Why are you on your feet, Griffin?"

"I have to go."

"What do you mean? We haven't even started yet."

Then my dad walked over to us, looking annoyed.

"I need to find a bathroom," I said, holding my stomach.

"Landon, you can hold it, now get back down with the rest," Dad said, motioning me back toward the group.

"No, I'm gonna be sick. I think I have, like, food poisoning or something." My stomach flipped again, causing me to clench my jaw.

"Food poisoning?" Dad asked as if he had never heard of it. "From what?"

"Dad," I said, frustrated. "If you don't let me go now, I'm gonna shit all over this field." That statement alone turned my Dad's confused expression into a disgusted one.

"Go then, go!" He waved me off.

I power walked through the gate and into the parking lot, afraid that if I ran too fast, the bile in my stomach would push its way through. I was wearing tight, white padded pants, I didn't need that happening in front of everyone. I swayed around people getting into their vehicles to go home for the day. My eyes were laser-focused on the door to the gym, not caring to scan for Mystery Boy.

"Hey, Landon!" I heard a voice call out from my right. My power walk continued as I inched closer to the building. "Wait up!" The voice called closer than before. I stopped just outside the metal door and turned toward the voice. It was Steven, he was running to me.

"Goddammit," I mumbled under my breath. I avoided him all day, thinking I was scot-free. I clenched my jaw again, trying to keep everything in. I watched Steven jog to me in his red short shorts and a white T-shirt. The shirt's sleeves were short and hugged his shoulders at an angle, leading me to believe it was a woman's shirt.

"Hey," he said, catching his breath. "Sorry. I know you're busy, I just wanted to ask you something."

My heartbeat got a little faster, and my hands felt clammy.

He's gonna ask me about Grindr. Please don't ask me about Grindr. How does he even know Sportyguy83 is me?

Beads of sweat ran down the back of my neck.

"Are you okay?" Steven tilted his head. "You don't look so good."

I swear to god if someone asks me if I'm okay one more time.

"I don't feel well," I mumbled, reaching an arm out to support myself against the brick wall of the building.

"Oh, well, I'll be quick."

Please be quick.

"The story you wrote for the *Monthly*," Steven said. "It was great, by the way. But I was wondering..." His words trailed off as he hesitated over what he was about to say. "Was it about me?"

My breath caught in my throat. It was not the question I expected. The day that Dan and I ignored him flashed through my mind and I felt guilty all over again. "Uh," I couldn't form words fast enough. "No, it wasn't. Why would you think that?"

"Oh, I was just curious," Steven said. "It just seemed very familiar. A story about two young friends drifting apart? It felt like, too real, ya know?"

"Yeah," I said. "I get what you mean." I clenched my jaw again as another cramp hit me, reminding me of what was soon to come. "It wasn't specifically about us, no. But I mean people always say 'write what you know,' right? So maybe it just came out subconsciously."

"Right." Steven nodded his head, but he didn't seem to understand what I was talking about.

My stomach bubbled again. "Steven, I really gotta go, I'm sorry," I said as I ran into the building, not letting him ask any further questions. I took long leaps across the gymnasium, hoping that nothing would come out before I reached the locker room. My heavy steps echoed loudly in the empty changing area. I darted toward the stalls and pushed my way through the door and fumbled with the lock before pulling down my pants and sitting on the porcelain throne. My body knew it was time to open the floodgates as my stomach pushed out everything it had. I'd never felt so much relief, but with it came a smell that could only be described as ungodly.

When it was over, I felt like I could breathe again. I closed my eyes and rubbed my forehead, taking long unstrained breaths. I reached for toilet paper with my other hand, but my fingers clinked against an empty plastic rod where it should have been.

Are you kidding me?

I heard footsteps. Sneakers squealed across the tiled floor as they got closer to my stall. I watched the open space under the door as the feet passed by. The person was wheeling a yellow mop bucket behind them. I cleared my throat to announce my existence so they wouldn't attempt to open the door. But the smell of what I had just done probably gave me away first.

"Oh, sorry," a man's voice said. "I didn't know anyone was in here." The voice had a slight rasp to it but still sounded young. At first, I said nothing, I didn't want to further out myself as being the person who stunk up the bathroom. But then I looked at the empty roll and knew the guy was my only hope.

"Could you, um, possibly hand me some toilet paper? I'm all out in here."

"Sure, one sec," he said, sounding happy to do so.

"Thanks," I said. "You're a lifesaver, you have no idea."

"Here you go," the guy said, popping his hand under the stall door. I looked down, reaching for it. That's when I saw the tattooed A on his hand and stopped breathing altogether.

Holy shit. Holy shitty fucking shit.

It was Mystery Boy! A lump caught in my throat and my outstretched arm froze. I locked my eyes on the A. The placement of the tattoo was on the back of his right hand between his thumb and pointer finger. It was a simple letter A in a circle. But it wasn't the anarchy symbol where the lines of the letter came outside the ring. The letter fit perfectly in the middle of it.

"Are you gonna take it?" His voice brought me back to reality. I wondered how long I'd made him wait.

"Thank you!" I shouted, grabbing the toilet paper from him.

"No problem," he said, rolling his mop bucket out of the bathroom.

I pressed my face into the fresh roll of toilet paper and desperately wanted to scream. All that separated him and me was a thin door. His face was on the other side of it. It embarrassed me that our very first interaction, something I've literally dreamed about, was through a bathroom stall. I couldn't believe that he'd know it was me that stunk up the entire bathroom.

Wait, he doesn't know it was me. He doesn't even know who I am.

I used what he gave me and pulled my pants up, ready to storm out the door and find him in the locker room. He couldn't have gotten far. Then I stopped before unlocking the door.

If I go out now, he'll know who I am and he'll know that I created this horrid smell; that's even worse than him not knowing I exist.

I placed my palms and forehead against the door. "Why?" I whispered. "Why is this happening?"

NINE

I'd waited almost ten minutes to leave the stall after I was done in the bathroom. My body wanted to burst out to get my first look at Mystery Boy, but the fear of embarrassment held me in the small rectangular space. I waited there until it was silent in the locker room. Despite that, I tiptoed my way out of the stall just in case he was still lingering. Once I was out of the locker room, my searching eyes kicked back into gear. I felt like I was released from prison after a fifteen-year stint, free to explore the world for Mystery Boy once again.

I pushed my way through the rest of practice, doing the minimal amount of movement to exert my body, which felt like it had nothing left in it. I tried to chug as much water as I could between the running, the catching, and the tackling. I couldn't wait to get home just to lie in bed and let myself recover from the food poisoning.

On the field, my eyes would drift to the parking lot, searching. But again, no luck. I'd lost my chance. It really seemed he had the power of teleportation. Every time I saw him, he would disappear as fast as he came into my line of sight. After two hours of non-stop running and sweating, the practice was finally over.

"Y'all are off tomorrow," Coach said to us, huddled by the water cooler. "But I'll see you here again in two days. Rest up, we go hard again at practice on Sunday."

The guys started shedding their gear and walking toward the school; that's when I spotted Steven sitting in the bleachers with a couple of girls. They were chatting and laughing.

"I bet he gets off on watching us," Dan said, popping up next to me chugging a cup of water. He was watching Steven and his friends, just like I was. "Faggots shouldn't be allowed to just sit there and watch us; it gives me the creeps."

I thought back to the question Steven asked me in the parking lot before I got sick. "Do you ever feel bad for what we did?" I realize now it was a stupid question to ask someone like Dan.

"Hell no," Dan said. "Do you wanna be associated with queers? I sure as fuck don't."

"I feel bad sometimes; he was our friend."

"Don't tell me you're going soft, Griffin," Dan pushed my shoulder. "He stopped being our friend the second he told us he was gay. Besides, you weren't even part of the worst of it."

His words confused me. "What does that mean? What are you talking about?" My first thought was he meant the attack on Steven, but Dan's words made it feel like he was talking about something else.

"Don't worry about it."

"You know," I said. "You've been saying that a lot to me lately. What the hell is going on with you?"

Chris had caught on to our conversation and stopped before exiting the track to watch us.

"What's been going on with me? You're the one who's been acting weird. We've barely seen you out of school."

Chris jogged over to us before I could say anything. "Guys, chill. If Coach sees you arguing, he'll make you stay here all night doing drills."

Chris was right. The coach's way of making teammates work out their issues was to drill them on the field until he heard a sincere apology or their feet bled. I didn't have an excuse to prove Dan wrong. He was right. I had been distant from my friends that past week.

"I'm sorry," I said, picking up my gear and shoving it all into a duffle bag. "You guys should come over tomorrow. We can hang out and play video games or something. We haven't chilled in a while."

"Finally," Dan said, crumpling up his water cup and spiking it to the grass. "About time you started making sense. See you tomorrow, then." Dan ran off to the school with the other guys. Chris walked over, picking up the cup before we exited the field together. I wondered if he noticed the guy Dan was hanging out with in the parking lot earlier.

"Have you seen Dan hanging out with anyone weird lately?"

"Nah." Chris shook his head. He tossed the crumpled cup into a trash bin, just before stepping onto the asphalt of the parking lot. "Why?"

"I saw him with someone earlier, like someone who doesn't go to school here."

"Was it that weird janitor?" Chris let out a small laugh.

"No," I said with a chuckle. "It definitely wasn't him."

I wished it were Mystery Boy, then I'd finally know what he looked like. The thought of him never left my mind while walking home.

Where did he go? Where does he go when he leaves school?

Later that night, I was washing dishes after dinner when Lauren called me. She wanted to talk about our date the following night.

"We should go to La Villa!"

La Villa was a local Italian restaurant, and I suddenly craved chicken parm just hearing the name.

"Sure," I said. "I'll ask my Dad for some money. Though I don't think he'll wanna pay for both of us."

"That's fine. I can ask my mom for some money, too."

As I climbed the stairs toward my room. I felt a cool breeze come through my open window. My Dad turned off the central air and opened all the windows. I could hear the next-door neighbor's dog barking at a couple of kids skateboarding down the street. It was a German Shepard named Sparky; its owners made it sleep outside at night. My mom used to think it was cruel and unnecessary.

"We should see a movie after, maybe?"

"Dang," I said, laughing. "You're an expensive date."

"I thought you knew what you were signing up for."

"Apparently not."

"I'll swing by your place tomorrow then and we'll go, sound good?"

"Works for me,"

"Okay, babe, I'll text you."

"Sweet."

"Love you," Lauren said. She was saying it more, while I hesitated.

"You too." I had yet to say the actual words to her. It just didn't feel right. I hung up and sat on my bed, feeling the pull of social media, seeing as I hadn't checked it in hours. I scrolled through my phone intending to click on Instagram, but my thoughts gravitated toward Grindr, wondering if Steven had sent anything after his picture. I bit my lip a little, feeling the curiosity strike me again. I hopped up and closed my door before springing myself back onto my bed. Laying on my stomach, I re-downloaded the app, hoping my messages with Steven hadn't been deleted.

Once I opened the app, I was met with several vibrations. I'd received more messages while I was offline. The first one I opened was from a person with the username Anthonyorgy, 30. He didn't even say hi. All he sent me were naked pictures of himself standing in a mirror at several angles. I groaned and deleted the message thread. Then I noticed that Steven had messaged me again.

THEATRENERD245, 18

Gonna send me any pics of you?

SPORTYGUY83, 18

Sorry. But I don't think I'm ready to show my face.

I assumed he wasn't online at the moment, so I clicked away and scrolled through Instagram until a notification popped up, telling me Steven had written back.

THEATRENERD245, 18

It's okay, I get it. This app can be pretty intimidating sometimes.

SPORTYGUY83, 18

More like terrifying haha. Why do so many guys send random nudes without even saying anything first?

THEATRENERD245, 18

> LOL yeah you kind of get used to that. Some guys are into it, but it's mostly creepy. I like to get to know a guy before showing him the goods, ya know? ;)

Is Steven trying to flirt with me?

THEATRENERD245, 18

> So what're looking for on here then?

SPORTYGUY83, 18

> To be honest, I was looking for someone in particular. It's dumb because I don't even know what he looks like or what his name is.

THEATRENERD245, 18

> Hmm, well there are a lot of faceless guys on here, maybe he's already messaged you.

SPORTYGUY83, 18:

> Haha, I doubt it. I don't think he's on here. I call him Mystery boy, how lame is that?

THEATRENERD245, 18

> I think that's kinda cute. So you've never even met this guy?

SPORTYGUY83, 18

> Nope. Which sounds ridiculous. I've only seen him from afar, but he's completely taken over my thoughts. I've become infatuated with him to where I'm dreaming about what he might look like.

THEATRENERD245, 18

> Oh, so you're like a stalker?

. . .

I didn't know what to say. I felt like a total freak.

THEATRENERD245, 18

I'm kidding lol I've been in that situation before, crushing on someone from a distance. It happens to me a lot.

SPORTYGUY83, 18

Really?

THEATRENERD245, 18

Oh yes, Hunny. I've been at this a long time, lol. When did you come out, if you don't mind me asking?

I paused, thinking over the question. It felt great to talk about what I was feeling, but coming out had yet to pass through my mind. My feelings for another guy had hit me all at once. It was the first time they'd stuck. For me, attractions usually came and went faster than I could run a football to the end-zone. Seeing all the hate Steven got over the years, I didn't think all that pain was worth coming out and telling anyone about my feelings in real life.

SPORTYGUY83, 18

I'm not out, actually. No one knows about me, except you.

THEATRENERD245, 18

> *gay gasp* well clutch my pearls! I'm so honored! I'll just consider myself your fairy gay mother. You can come to me for anything.

Our conversation continued throughout the night. Steven gave me a crash course on all things gay. Which gay movies to watch, his favorite gay books I should read, even his favorite porn website if I was ever feeling extra gay. I felt confident in my anonymity. I felt like I wasn't being judged or laughed at. I still felt like me, but a different me. An honest me. I was actually enjoying my conversation with Steven. I wondered what he would do if he found out SportyGuy83 was me. I wondered if he would shout it to the entire school or if he'd keep it to himself. And I wondered if we would've enjoyed the same conversations if we had remained friends.

For the first time in a while, I felt I could relate to someone. The past week, it felt like I'd been screaming underwater while my friends watched from the shoreline, waiting to see if I would drown or make it back to the sand.

———

"Dude, wake up!" Dan's voice pulled me out of a deep sleep the next morning, howling through my open window. The sun shined so brightly in my room that it was hard to even open my eyes. I blindly reached for my phone to check the time. It was almost noon. I opened it, realizing I had to close out Grindr because I'd fallen asleep talking to Steven.

My body felt sticky. I propped myself up, noticing I'd sweat through my sheets. My Dad had forgotten to turn the AC back on, the heat was pouring in through the windows all morning. I walked to my window in nothing but my underwear and poked my head out.

Dan and Chris were standing on my front lawn, looking much more awake than I was. "Let's throw the ball around!" Dan said.

"I'll be down in a sec!" I stumbled over to my closet and slipped on a tank top and a pair of basketball shorts. I pulled my desk drawer open and grabbed a tube of sunblock, slathering on as much and as quickly as I could. I hurried down the stairs and grabbed a power bar before heading out the front door. "What's up, guys?" I said, unwrapping the bar. It only lasted three bites before it was gone. "Throw me the ball." I ran out to the middle of the street and caught the first toss. Chris and Dan followed. We formed a large triangle and tossed to each other casually.

"Get it in with Lauren yet?" Dan caught the ball that Chris threw at him.

I rolled my eyes. "No, I haven't," I said, stepping back to increase the distance between us. "Sorry to disappoint."

"You guys have been dating for what? Almost a year now?" Dan threw the ball to me, I jumped to catch it with both hands. Dan tended to throw a little high.

"Yeah, that's kinda sad, man," Chris said.

I brought the ball to the side of my face, prepping for a throw. The wind whipped against me and I could smell the leather before I chucked it toward Chris with a perfect spiral.

"I don't know," I said. "It just hasn't happened yet. It hasn't really been an issue." I could hear some kids laughing behind me and the sound of their scooter wheels racing toward us.

Chris and Dan both had sex before I had. A few months before I started dating Lauren, I went to my cousin's wedding in Houston. When I came back, I told the guys I hooked up with a random girl who was there as her friend's plus one. The guys believed me, even though none of it was true. I felt a lot of pressure from them since Dan lost his virginity sophomore year. Chris lost his a couple of months before the start of his junior year.

"You can't go into college a virgin," Chris said, running back to catch the ball. He jumped, catching it with one hand. "That's just weak."

We let the kids pass through our triangle on their scooters before resuming our game of catch.

"Landon, go long!" Dan shouted.

I turned and ran, sporadically looking over my shoulder at him. Dan threw the ball with power like the talented quarterback he was, but I undershot it. I tried to jump to reach it, but I was too short. The ball zipped through the air and into the front courtyard of the school.

"Weak!" Dan shouted, making Chris laugh.

I hopped the stone wall, landing on the grass. The ball was in my sights, but so was the sun. I approached it, squinting, not letting the rays burn my eyes. I was about to reach for the ball, but another set of hands grabbed it first. I was taken aback as I hadn't noticed anyone standing around in the courtyard. I stood up straight and locked onto the person whom the hands attached to. My entire body immediately turned to ice. It was Mystery Boy.

"Here you go," he said with ease, holding out the ball. I wondered if the sun was playing tricks on me. Had I been baking for that long I was seeing things I only saw in my dreams? I squinted harder. The sun was glowing from behind his silhouette like he was a muse sent to me from the Greek gods. Words couldn't form properly. I imagined my brain was a mess of nonsensical numbers, like binary code I didn't understand. I tried to speak, but nothing came out. My eyes were the only part of my body I could move. Again he was shirtless and sparkling. The front of his body was even more pleasing than his back. Mystery Boy's skin was a bronze color and looked smooth to the touch. His chest looked as if someone sculpted it from marble and his torso was long with toned abs. I couldn't see each individual square, but his stomach was flat.

I wanted nothing more than to see his face since the first time I saw him. The thought of it kept me from paying attention in class that whole week. And finally, I was staring into his big hazel-colored eyes. They were like quicksand and I was sinking fast. His eyebrows were thick and his hair was long enough to cover most of his forehead. But then his smile hit me like a brick wall. His teeth were almost as bright and blinding as the sun. But it was the dimples that formed at his cheeks that practically made my knees buckle.

He looked at me with one eye squinted. "You okay?"

I hadn't moved or said anything in what felt like hours. My mouth was so dry my tongue was stuck to the roof of it.

Speak! My brain was shouting. *Say anything!*

"Uh yeah," I said, reaching out to grab the ball. "Sorry. The sun, it um, gets hot."

What the hell did I just say?

I had no idea what was wrong with me. It's like I turned into a limp noodle. Feeling completely incompetent, I panicked, swiped the ball from him, and turned to walk away, feeling idiotic.

This may be your only chance, I thought as I flipped to face him again. "Landon," I spat out. "I'm...my name's Landon."

"Caleb," he said, extending a hand. I grasped it and I could feel the calluses on his palms, formed from hours of manual labor.

"You wanna join us?" I pointed a thumb behind me to the street. It was worth a try.

"Oh, no thanks," Caleb said with a smirk. "I still got a lot of work to do." He sauntered backward. "It was nice to meet you, Landon," he said before turning away from me.

"You too!" I said, causing him to look over his shoulder at me one more time with a smile. Then I stood there watching him walk away.

Caleb, holy shit, his name is Caleb.

The ice had melted away, and I could move again. I smiled to myself before jogging back to the street.

"So," Dan said as I came back into earshot. "What's his deal? Is he a psycho?" Chris moved in closer to us.

"Nope," I said with a grin. "Seems pretty normal to me."

"I'm not convinced," Chris said, stealing the football from my hands. "Someone told me he got expelled because he tried to bomb the place. Said he literally brought a homemade bomb into his school."

"You know that's all gossip, right?" I said, looking at Chris with a goofy smirk. "No one knows for sure."

"Got that right," Dan said. "Guy's a total mystery."

Not anymore. He's Caleb now.

Throughout the rest of that afternoon, I'd look over at the school, hoping to see him again, hoping Chris and Dan wouldn't notice.

———

Later that night I was in my room getting dressed, waiting for Lauren to pick me up for our date when I heard music play from outside. I glanced out my window and saw Caleb standing under a streetlight; he'd found a shirt since I last saw him.

Is he just finishing up now?

The music was coming from his phone; I think he started playing it before plugging his headphones in. He was failing to untangle his earbuds as the music continued to play. I checked my phone for the time. Lauren wouldn't arrive for another twenty minutes. I took a breath and decided to go talk to him. I felt like I had to prove I knew how to speak a proper sentence.

I barely touched a single step as I leaped down the stairs, worried that he'd be gone before I got outside. By the time I stepped out the front door, Caleb was halfway down the street. It was dark, and the air felt cool. I jogged and called out his name, but he had untangled his wires and had the earbuds in.

"Caleb!" I said a little louder. That time he heard me and looked back with his eyebrows raised. He pulled an earbud out of his right ear and smirked.

"Oh, hey," Caleb said, stopping in the middle of the street. "What's up?"

I caught up to him. "Figured I'd say hi. Are you just finishing...at the school I mean, it's kinda late."

"Yeah, the asshole guys that run the school thought it'd be best If I stayed until I finished their laundry list," Caleb said with a scrunched face. I walked with him. "They all need to take the stick out of their asses."

"Yeah." I looked at the pavement. "One of em's my Dad."

"Oh shit! The principal is your Dad?"

"No, no, he's the superintendent."

"Damn, that must suck. I'm sorry, I didn't mean to sound like a dick."

"You're fine. And you're right, he does have a stick up his ass. It's pretty annoying." We chuckled a bit then fell silent. We walked a few steps, looking forward until I spoke again. "Headed home?"

"Yeah. I live a town over."

"In Skowhegan?" I glanced at him. "That's like a two-mile walk from here."

"It's cool, I just cut through the baseball field. Makes it a little shorter," Caleb spoke with ease like he'd been doing it every night for years. I wondered why he didn't have a car.

Somehow we got lost in simple conversation and I ended up walking with him to the baseball field. His laugh was so damn charming, I could've listened to it on repeat. His voice had a rasp that could soothe anyone who listened. I'd once heard a 1940s radio host who told bedtime stories during one of my Dad's History Channel shows, making me picture Caleb's voice booming from an old radio.

The baseball field was creepy at night. It was dark, except for a light over one dugout. I wasn't going any further, so I sat down on a metal bench looking at the chain-link fence surrounding the field.

"You cut through the woods?" I looked up at Caleb who was standing next to me. A dark forest surrounded the entire back of the baseball field.

"Yeah," he said, looking toward the line of trees. "There's a clear path. It's not too bad; I just use the light on my phone."

"Seems a little too creepy for me." I felt a chill up my spine just thinking about walking through the woods alone. I figured Caleb and I would say a quick goodbye and he'd be on his way, but to my surprise, he sat down next to me.

"It's not like *The Blair Witch Project* if that's what you're thinking," Caleb said with a chuckle.

"What's that?"

"What?" His mouth dropped open. "It's a horror movie. You've never seen it?"

"No." I smiled. "I haven't seen a lot of movies. I auditioned for the musical *Footloose* once. I heard that was a movie."

"Go home," Caleb said, looking at me with a deadpan expression. He wiped his face with his hand, "You've never seen *Footloose*? That's like one of the best 80s movies of all time!" He was genuinely shocked. "Blair Witch I can understand, sure, but *Footloose*? Wow."

"I didn't watch a lot of movies growing up."

Caleb turned his entire body toward me and I felt our pinkies touch as our hands rested on the bench. It sent a shock wave through my body.

"Okay, uh... " Caleb looked to the sky. "...what about *Jurassic Park*?"

"Nope," I said with a sour face.

"Oh, my god!" He jumped from his seat and shook his head. "I don't know if I should even talk to you right now," he said with a laugh. I would've stopped time to watch a thousand movies if it meant he would continue to talk to me for the rest of the night. "*Jurassic Park* is an all-time classic, one of the greatest! For being made in 1993, it still holds up to this day! The dinosaurs look so real compared to the CGI bullshit they use now." Watching him spaz out made me smile.

"What are you? Some kind of movie buff or something?" I was genuinely amused by his tidbits of information.

"Maybe a little." He sat next to me again. I was taken off guard by how cute his dimples were, they melted my insides. They were pulling me in like a tractor beam from an alien space-ship. Then he switched gears so fast, it nearly knocked me off the bench. "You remind me of someone special to me." He paused. "You both have red hair."

I sat there staring at him staring at my hair. I didn't know what he meant by it, or how to take it. I could've stared at him until the sun came up.

He looked away before standing again. "Thanks for walking me this far." Caleb shoved his hand out for a shake.

"No problem." I stood and returned his gesture, noticing the A tattoo on his hand. "What's this stand for?"

"It's a long story," he said with a flat tone before brushing by me, heading toward the woods. "Catch ya later."

"Maybe tomorrow? Gonna be around?" I was feeling desperate, wondering when I'd see him again.

He turned on his heels to face me, walking backward. "Probably not. Got a date tomorrow." Caleb turned to the woods again. His words burst my bubble. I crashed hard from the high he had given me like a little kid after he'd downed five Pixie Stix. I wondered who the lucky girl could be. Was she the special one with red hair who I reminded him of? I tried to hide my disappointment.

"Careful of the Blair Witch!" I said, cupping my hands around the sides of my mouth to make sure he'd hear me.

"Watch the movie, kid!"

I smiled and watched him disappear past the dark tree line.

My phone vibrated as I walked back to the street. I pulled it out and the screen lit up my face, causing my smile to fade when I saw I had three missed calls from Lauren.

Fuck.

TEN

I jogged most of the way home, sweating through my date-night clothes. Though it was a bit cooler, it was still a warm Texas night. I was an idiot for letting myself get swept up with Caleb, forgetting all about my date with Lauren.

How did I not feel my phone vibrate? Three missed calls?

Lauren was going to have questions. I needed to make up an excuse fast.

On my jog home, though, I couldn't stop thinking about Caleb. I scratched out the label on the small box in my mind. Now instead of saying Mystery Boy, it read Caleb. A few more tidbits of information about him were downloaded and stored. He was a movie buff, and he lived in Skowhegan. I imagined the files being dropped into the box, like when you drag a file into a folder on your computer.

Skowhegan was one town over from Madison, but they couldn't be more different. My town was very suburban with lots of cul-de-sacs. Skowhegan was a bit more rundown. A lot of condemned buildings, a few trailer parks, and even a cornfield. I pictured Caleb living in a house that kids thought was haunted because it looked decrepit on the outside. I pictured him having to chase them away as they attempted to throw rocks through the windows.

As I approached my house, I thought about what Caleb said, that he had a date. Jealousy shot through me again. Though I was about to have dinner with my girlfriend, I desperately wanted to be on a date with Caleb.

A car horn had lifted me from my thoughts. I made it back to my house, about to step through the front door when Lauren honked her horn at me. I was so distracted by my dreamed-up scenario; I hadn't noticed she parked on the street in front of my house. I stood there on my front steps and watched as she got out of her car and stomped up the lawn.

"Where've you been?" she asked aggressively. "I've been calling you."

"I know, I'm really sorry."

Lauren crossed her arms. "Landon, we had plans. I thought you were ditching me. We missed our reservation."

"I'm sorry, I didn't feel my phone go off, I don't know how."

"You're all sweaty. What've you been doing?"

I searched my brain for an excuse. I knew I had to lie to her again, and it killed me. "I went for a walk," I spat out. "To think about some stuff. I lost track of time. When I finally realized, I ran back hoping you wouldn't be here yet."

"To think about stuff?" She uncrossed her arms. "Like what, Landon? What the hell is so important that you blew me off?"

I felt like I was on a witness stand. I was a pot of boiling water with a lid that was about to burst. "Wanna come inside?"

"Are you going to tell me what's going on with you?"

"Yes." The pot I'd become cooled as a lightbulb went off instead. I knew something I could tell her that wasn't necessarily a lie, but it wasn't my biggest secret either. I took her by the hand, leading her through the door.

"Where's your Dad?"

"Probably with his campaign team," I said, glancing over my shoulder at her. I led her up to my room and sat her on my unmade bed. She tossed a sock to the floor that was hanging out by my pillow.

"I haven't been up here in a while," Lauren said.

My Dad was pretty traditional with having my girlfriend over. He didn't like us hanging out in my bedroom, knowing what might happen if he left us alone behind a closed door. 'I was a teenager once,' he loved to say.

"Yeah, sorry it's such a mess," I said, stumbling over my football shoulder pads, trying to scrounge up anything I could from my floor to throw in my closet. I unbuttoned my sweaty shirt and threw it into the hamper as I looked for a new one.

"Landon, come sit."

I did what I was told before I could find a shirt. I sat next to her on my bed and apologized again. I felt terrible for blowing her off. Lauren popped up onto the bed and crossed her legs. Her jeans were skin tight. She grabbed my hand, interlocking her fingers with mine. "So, what's going on?"

"All this college stuff," I said, glancing at the floor. I couldn't bring myself to lie while looking her in the eyes. "It's really stressing me out. My Dad is putting all this pressure on me about football scholarships. But I don't think I even want to play football anymore."

"What do you want to do, then?"

"I think I want to major in creative writing, but if I tell my Dad, he's gonna go berserk. I feel like unless I make it to the NFL, nothing is gonna be good enough for him."

Lauren pulled my face up, forcing me to look at her. "You're gonna have to tell him eventually, babe, and soon. Application deadlines are coming up fast."

"I know. I think I'm gonna go see my counselor on Monday. "

"Have you thought about where you want to apply?"

"Not sure. Tasha recommended NYU, maybe."

"Oh my god." Lauren perked up. "How amazing would it be to be in New York City together?!" Lauren was trying to get into Marymount Manhattan's musical theater program,

I just smiled and nodded, wondering how many high school couples made it through college. "When is your audition, again?"

"Not this weekend, but the next, so like, two weeks?"

"What are you gonna sing? Are you nervous?

"Oh god yes," Lauren said, moving her hair from one shoulder to the other. "I'm singing 'Astonishing' from Little Women. It's a white girl song, but I feel like I'd just be a cliché, if I sang something from In the Heights or West Side Story, ya know?"

I nodded. "Yeah." I had no idea what she was talking about, the only words that made sense were Little Women, I loved that book. I stood and continued my hunt for a shirt.

"We can still make the movie if you wanna go," Lauren said as she stood. She walked to me, wrapping her arms around my neck.

I needed to redeem myself and get my mind off of Caleb. My thoughts turned into a hailstorm.

Maybe I'm bi. I could easily be bisexual. I just need to make a move.

My hands grabbed Lauren's hips. I wanted to prove that Caleb didn't have control over me. I wanted to prove that I could tell Dan I'd had sex with my girlfriend.

I leaned, pressing my lips against hers, kissing her passionately. The small buttons of her shirt were scratching against my bare stomach, tickling me. She kissed me back. Our breathing got more intense as my tongue found hers.

"I'm still mad at you," Lauren said between breaths

I smiled against her lips as she furiously unbuttoned my

pants, but before she could reach inside, I walked her backward, laying her on my bed. I came down easy on top of her, our lips never detached. Her hands continued their mission. My fly was down next and she pushed my pants and underwear down at the same time. It was the most naked I'd ever been in front of her or anyone for that matter. It was the first time another person had touched me where I'd only touched myself. Things had gone much further than they ever had between us

My heart raced. I wasn't sure what to do next. My hands stayed flat on the bed, holding myself over her. She reached down to discover I was still flaccid, while the image of my pinky touching Caleb's on the bench flashed through my mind, sending a shudder down my spine. It felt like an earthquake in my bones, causing me to stop kissing Lauren. I clenched my eyes shut and shook my head a few times.

"Are you okay?"

"Yeah.... sorry," I said, moving to continue kissing her. One of her hands slithered up to mine and guided it under her shirt to her chest. I tried my best to touch her in a way that I thought she would enjoy, but still, nothing triggered me. I assumed I'd feel a tingle in my stomach. I assumed I'd want her the way she wanted me. I assumed I was supposed to be erect, but I wasn't, I couldn't. Caleb's face flashed in the darkness behind my eyelids. Again, it felt like my bones shook, forcing me to leap off of her. I just stood there naked at the foot of my bed, rubbing my eyes.

"Landon, what's wrong? You're not even hard."

Thank you for reminding me.

I sighed, pulling my pants up from around my ankles. "I'm sorry... I..." I turned around, desperately searching for a shirt. Embarrassed, I felt the need to be clothed, not wanting her eyes to spend any more time on me.

"What's wrong?" Lauren asked again.

I opened a drawer and grabbed the first T-shirt I saw.

Lauren continued her questions. "Is it me? Are you, like, not attracted to me?"

That feeling of boiling water erupted in my stomach again. I didn't have an answer for her, and that scared me. I placed both my hands on my dresser, facing away, feeling like I could pass out at any moment from the pressure building inside me.

"Landon?"

"I think you should go," I whispered, still staring at the stained paint of my dresser drawer.

"What?" She stood from the bed, taking a step toward me.

"I want you to leave. I'm sorry."

"Landon, please tell me what's going on." She placed a hand on my arm. I wanted to look at her, but my body wouldn't let me. Lauren sighed and turned to go without saying goodbye. When I heard the front door slam, I felt I could breathe again.

I spun around and sat at the edge of my bed. My hands rubbed back and forth against my thighs as I took a few deep breaths. My face warmed and my eyes filled with tears. Caleb was corrupting my thoughts, corrupting my body. He *did* have control of me. But how was that possible? I'd only interacted with him twice. I was so confused about what I was feeling and why.

I could still feel the boiling pot inside me, and when it was too much to bear, I let out a visceral scream that filled my room until I had no breath left in my lungs. The tears made their way down my cheeks, but I wiped them away. My nose was running, I felt like a complete mess. I pulled the bottom of my T-shirt up, wiped my nose with it, and took a few more deep breaths. I laid back on my bed, staring at the ceiling. If Caleb saw me at that moment, he'd think I was psychotic. He had a date; he confirmed it. Some girl is taking up the attention that I dreamed he would give me. She's got him, and I've got...tears.

I guessed it was all but confirmed that Lauren thought I

must be insane. I was afraid to check my phone, afraid to see the inevitable texts from her. I thought it was something I wanted. Sex is what's supposed to happen with a guy and his girlfriend in high school. It's what's supposed to happen after you've been dating for a year. I'd imagined it so many times, Lauren and me hooking up. Talked about wanting it. And I thought I could do it when the time came. I'd imagined it would be this fantastic thing I could brag to Dan and Chris about, but I was wrong. When Lauren was touching me, I felt nothing. I seriously wanted to feel something. I tried to connect the dots in my body to make my dick work, but my body already knew something my brain didn't. My body didn't want Lauren. I laid back on my bed and closed my eyes, feeling depleted. I was so emotionally exhausted that it only took a minute for sleep to take over.

I saw myself sitting at a white cloth-covered table at La Villa, dressed in a button-up shirt and khakis. I was waiting for Caleb to arrive. I had told him to meet me there at eight. The server had asked me if I'd like to sample some wine while I waited, and I accepted. I checked my phone; it was eight-twenty. When I looked up, Caleb had arrived and sat across from me looking confused.

"What are you doing here?"

I tilted my head at him. "What do you mean?"

"I'm meeting a date here," Caleb said.

I stared at him blankly. "I am your…" I couldn't get the words out fast enough; there was a hand touching my shoulder. I looked to see a beautiful red-headed woman wearing a short black dress.

She looked at Caleb. "Who's this?"

"This is Landon. He and I met during my community service. Not sure how he ended up at our table."

I quickly realized she was his date for the night, not me. Caleb was about to introduce her…

My eyes popped open. I sat up and checked my phone. I'd only been asleep for ten minutes. I pulled my shit together and took a shower, washing away the embarrassment. I didn't bother sending Lauren any texts. I needed to get my head straight before I could talk to her.

After my shower, I walked back to my room in just a towel and sat at my desk in front of my laptop. I had left my phone charging with the USB plugged into my computer. I opened Grindr and swiped through my chat with Steven, looking for the recommendations he had given me for good porn sites. I wasn't that horny, especially not after what happened with Lauren but I couldn't get aroused by her. I needed to know if my body responded to gay porn instead.

I opened my computer and clicked the incognito window of my browser.

I should lock the door.

I hobbled over to the door and twisted the lock before plopping back down at my laptop. I typed in the first site Steven gave me. He listed three different ones, so I started with the first. The site popped up looking like YouTube, but with naked bodies in the thumbnails. There was a tab called 'categories' that I clicked on first. I wasn't sure what kind of porn I was into, or what kind of guy I might like. There were so many options. I knew I was attracted to Caleb, who wasn't super skinny but wasn't too muscular either; he was a sort of in-between. The image of shirtless Caleb popped into my mind from meeting him earlier that day. I licked my lips subconsciously. Thinking of Caleb shirtless stirred something inside me. I surveyed the options on my screen. They labeled one category, 'Gingers.' I chuckled to myself, not realizing that we deserved our own category. People had made fun of my red hair most of my life, leading me to think few people found us attractive.

I clicked on a category called 'College Guys,' and scrolled

through the countless thumbnails until I came across the title 'freshman learns a lesson'.

"Here we go," I whispered, as self-encouragement before watching gay porn for the first time. The video started with a guy in a white polo attempting to unlock a door. 'Hey, Michael,' another guy said out of frame. The guy wearing the white polo, who I gathered was Michael, spun around toward the voice. 'Yeah?' A taller guy stepped into frame, wearing a blue polo. I then wondered if I needed to stock up on polos before entering college. Both men had tanned skin and dark hair. Michael was also wearing a white puka shell necklace. It was hard to pinpoint the year they could have filmed it. Blue polo guy continued: 'heard you was talkin' shit'. Michael was then backed against the door, looking nervous. 'What?' Michael asked. I rolled my eyes; the acting was pretty cringe-worthy. 'Let's go to your room,' the taller guy said. 'I need to show you what we do with loud-mouth freshmen.'

I wondered if all gay porn started that way, with lines written for people who didn't have any acting experience, not that I was an expert on acting ability. Once they walked into the room, they started making out on the bed. Michael was enjoying it, which to me was a major plot hole. Two seconds ago he looked scared like he was going to get beaten up. But now they were smiling and taking each other's clothes off. I decided to fast forward the video a bit, hoping to get to the action. As soon as I hit play again, loud moaning played from my speakers and I quickly hit the mute button. My Dad had gotten home while I was in the shower. I listened attentively to my surroundings, making sure my Dad wasn't walking outside my door. Then I focused back on the video. I was subconsciously biting my lip, and my breathing became heavier. The towel around my waist had tented. I liked what I was seeing, and my body was responding.

I heard my doorknob jiggle.

Fuck!

My eyes widened and my heart stopped as I pushed myself out of my chair and stood. My Dad came barreling into my room, and I faced him in nothing but my towel, crossing my arms in front of me, trying to hide my erection.

"Jesus, Dad!" I shouted.

My Dad didn't even try to shield his eyes or look away; he was used to seeing guys in towels in the locker room. To him, it was nothing out of the ordinary...so far. "Sorry, I should've knocked," my Dad said with a dry tone.

"Uh, yeah! That's twice this week you've done that!" I needed to check if the lock actually worked.

I could feel the beads of sweat dripping down my forehead out of pure fear that he'd seen my computer screen. I realized my body was covering the video that continued to play. My half-naked, pale figure was the only thing separating my Dad's eyes from two men having sex. It terrified me. Thank God I'd muted the video. I needed to think of something to get him out of my room, and fast. Or, I at least needed to get his line of sight away from my computer.

"I think there's a leak," I spat out; it was the first thing that came to mind.

My Dad's face scrunched. "What?"

"I think there might be a leak... up there." I pointed up toward the corner of the ceiling behind him. It caused my Dad to turn his back to me, looking up to study it.

"I don't see anything,"

"It's there, just look a little closer." My voice cracked. I cleared my throat and walked past him. I could move now that all the blood from my crotch had rushed to my face. I stood in front of him so that his back was facing my computer and stared at him as he squinted at the ceiling, tilting his head back and forth. Out of the corner of my eye, just over my Dad's shoulder, I could see my computer screen; they were going at it like a pair of rabbits.

Jesus Christ, why didn't I close the screen?!

I wiped the sweat from my forehead with the back of my hand.

"Landon, I really don't see anything. I mean, I know my eyesight isn't getting any better these days, but maybe you should get yours checked." Then my Dad turned around. I panicked again; if I didn't stop him, he was going to see my screen.

"Wait!" I grabbed his shoulder. He looked at me with a furrowed brow. "My door, um, it's been, like, creaking lately? Can you just check that real quick?"

My Dad huffed. "I guess."

He turned and walked into the hallway to check the door. I took two enormous steps toward my desk. If it were the savanna, I'd have been a gazelle. I closed my laptop before sitting at the edge of my bed, finally able to breathe.

"Landon... " Dad was down on one knee, bent at the waist with his ear close to the bottom hinge. He was hanging on the doorknob, swinging the door back and forth. "I don't hear anything." He made a grunt, trying to pull himself back up. "Are you okay? You're seeing and hearing things that aren't there." He stood in front of me with his arms out to his sides.

I answered his question with a question of my own. "What did you want, anyway?"

"My computer is dead. I was hoping I could use yours for a second." Before he even finished his sentence, he was already reaching for my computer and opening the screen. I shot off my bed, almost losing my towel.

"WAIT!" I screamed, scaring him out of his skin. I felt like I was leaping into the air to catch a pass. I shoved his hands away and slammed the computer screen shut. Luckily, it didn't have enough time to turn on.

"What in the hell is wrong with you, boy?"

"You can't use it," I said, leaning against the desk, trying to be as casual as possible.

"Why the hell not?"

"It's broken."

"What?"

"Yep. It just died and never came back to life. I'm throwing it out, actually."

"What happened to it? I feel like you just got the damn thing."

"I don't know, just stopped working." I shrugged. "Technology man, I don't get it."

My Dad scoffed. "Yeah, me neither." He gave me an awkward stare and a nod and started for the hallway. "I guess I'll just wait for mine to charge."

"What did you need it for?"

My Dad stopped before stepping out of my room. "Facebook. My campaign manager set up a page for me that people could follow, I wanted to check it out before it goes live."

I rolled my eyes and crossed my arms; I was almost outed because my dad wanted to use Facebook.

"You know you can do that on your phone, right?"

"My damn phone screen is too small, I wanted to see it bigger." He waved me off before walking out. "Put some clothes on, will ya?"

I quickly shut the door and locked it before slouching back into my computer chair, opening my laptop, and there it was. The video continued to play where it left off. I closed out the tab. It proved its point in telling me I liked it, but I didn't need to go any further. I'd had enough gay stress for one night.

ELEVEN

The following Monday I stopped by the guidance office. I needed to talk to my counselor about college options before it was too late. To be honest, I'd already waited too long. Most students figure out where they want to go to college during their junior year, but I procrastinated. I'd already applied to a few state schools where my Dad was sure I could get a football scholarship, like the University of Texas in Austin, Texas A&M, University of Houston, and Rice University. I hadn't looked into any of them much. My Dad just handed me the applications and told me to fill them out. Now that I knew the major I wanted, it was best to visit my counselor.

I stepped to the counter in the main office to find eighty-six-year-old Mrs. Darcy about to announce something over the loudspeakers. It was a running joke at Madison High if Mrs. Darcy would still be there on the first day when everyone got back from summer vacation. Some people had running bets based on whether she would retire or die first. I watched her crypt keeper-like hands switch on the microphone. Then I heard her warble voice over the speakers.

"Reminder to students and staff," she said. "There will be a mandatory assembly held in the auditorium after the last lunch period." Mrs. Darcy clicked off the microphone, noticing me out of the corner of her eye. She reminded me of a sloth as she made her way over. "Can I help you, sweetie?"

"Yeah," I said. "I was wondering if Mr. Reily was available."

"Let me check." She wobbled over to her desk and picked up the receiver of her phone, dialing a number. She tapped her nails against the desk, waiting for him to answer. "Yes, hello, I have a young man here asking to see you. Great, thank you." She hung up the phone. "You can go on back, hun."

"Thanks," I said as I scooted around the counter, walking through a glass door to the back office. I knew where Mr. Reily's room was, as I'd visited several times over the years. I knocked on a wooden door, staring at Mr. Reily's nameplate. I heard a muffled 'come in' before opening the door.

"Hey Landon, what can I help you with?" Mr. Reily was an overweight African-American man with a bald head and goatee, who wore a lot of argyle sweater vests. He started typing something into his computer. I assumed he was pulling up my file.

"Hey, Mr. Reily," I said as I sat in a cushioned chair on the opposite side of his desk. "I was wondering about a few other schools. I wanted to apply to some that have a good creative writing program. It's sort of late to apply but I just wanted to get some options... if there are any."

"Hmm, it is pretty late in the game, but let me see." He started typing again. He mumbled to himself now and then as his eyes scanned back and forth. "I see you've already applied to a few state schools, which is good, you should be hearing from them soon. But let me see." My legs bounced as I became anxious. Mr. Reily finally looked away from his computer and said, "All right, plenty of schools have great creative writing programs, but I'm only seeing three here that take late applications. Those three are uh..." He looked back to his computer screen. "The University of Southern California, Emerson College in Boston, and New York University."

"Okay." I nodded my head.

"Looks like you have to turn in some work based on the prompt they provide and a letter of recommendation, of course."

The bell rang as a five-minute warning for the first period of the day.

"Thanks, Mr. Reily. I really appreciate it."

He smiled. "Of course. You can fill out the applications online but I'll print the list of schools for you, just grab it from the printer on your way out."

I gave a nod and headed out the door, whizzing by Mrs. Darcy, who was reading a book. I snatched the paper from the printer, shoving it into a folder in my backpack, I could look it over later.

I was hoping to find Lauren. She and I hadn't spoken for the rest of the weekend after she left my house Saturday night. I needed to apologize for acting cold toward her. I turned a corner and saw she had just closed her locker. There were only a few people left scattered around the hall. She didn't notice me before walking away. I jogged up to her, calling out her name.

"Hi," Lauren said flatly.

"Can I talk to you?"

"We don't have a lot of time." Again her words felt cold, which I deserved.

"I know." I leaned against the wall of gray lockers with one backpack strap around my shoulder. "I just wanted to apologize."

"I just don't get it," she said.

"I don't either, I sort of panicked. I thought I was ready, but I guess I wasn't?"

"You could've been nicer about it. You made me feel like I molested you or something."

"I'm sorry," I said. "I didn't mean for it to be that way."

"I just need to know if it's me."

I took a deep breath and held it, not on purpose but because I was becoming a pressure cooker again.

God, give me something so I don't have to talk about this anymore.

I pictured a tornado ripping through the school and taking out most of the hallway behind Lauren. It would scare her enough to forget about her question. Then I pictured the hallway filling with water and we needed to find a way out, again avoiding her curiosity. No natural disasters were going to save me, though. Then the bell rang.

Thank you, God.

"I should go. I'm late for first period." I grabbed her hand. "Can we sit together at the assembly later?"

"Yeah, sure." She walked backward and let our connected hands bring our arms in the air. Then she let go and walked away. I stood there, watching her, feeling like she was getting suspicious. I wasn't sure how long I could pretend everything was fine. I rubbed my hand over the top of my head and sighed. I wasn't ready to break her heart because I still wasn't ready to accept everything I was feeling.

I stepped away from the lockers and whipped around, crashing chest first into someone. My eyes scrunched closed on impact. It all happened lightning-fast; I didn't even hear anyone walking behind me. I felt my shirt become damp with splotches. I opened my eyes. It was Caleb. My bad luck continued. He was carrying a large bucket of gray-colored water. I realized when I slammed into him; it had splashed the water from the mop bucket all over his face. He was wearing a black T-shirt, so it was difficult to see where the water landed. But it was very clear I soaked his face. I wiped the drops of water from my face with the back of my hands as Caleb put down the bucket.

"Shit," I blurted out. "I am so, so sorry. I had no idea you were behind me."

At first, he said nothing; just stood there looking like a grumpy dog dripping wet after a bath he didn't want to take. Then he cracked a grin. "It's all right, Mad Max," Caleb said with ease. "Maybe pump the brakes a little quicker next time."

Mad Max?

I wondered if he had forgotten my name. Caleb lifted the bottom of his shirt, using it to wipe his face. My eyes took in his toned, smooth stomach. It was as if he was taunting me. Tempting me to reach out and touch it. My eyes became a camera; every time I blinked, it was like taking a picture and saving it in the Caleb box in my brain.

Seconds later his stomach was covered again, and I felt I could focus. "What were you doing?"

"There was a leak in the utility closet. They've been using this to catch all the water instead of fixing it."

Great, I covered him in dirty pipe water.

I looked at the bucket. "Why are you carrying it down the hall? I thought every utility closet had a sink."

"Oddly enough, this one doesn't. And someone's gotta dump it, that someone is me. The closet by the cafeteria has a slop sink, so I'm just gonna dump it there." Caleb scooped the bucket into his arms again.

I'd never been jealous of a bucket until that moment. Ugh, to feel what that bucket was feeling in Caleb's arms. The tightness he held it with made my jeans feel tight. I needed to think of another question before I exposed myself. I thought of asking about his date from the weekend. But what if he said it was great? I wasn't prepared to hear about the beautiful red-headed woman and how many kids they might have together in the future.

"Do you go to school?" The words came out of my mouth like a dragon spraying it's fire breath.

Caleb raised his eyebrows, probably feeling like the question came out of nowhere. He stared at me for a second. I could picture the gears in his brain, working hard to decide what to tell me.

"Maybe, maybe not," Caleb smirked, teasing me with one dimple as he strutted by. Was he playing with me? Was he being mysterious on purpose? Did he know he was killing me? As he passed by, I got a whiff of his mix of sweat and cologne that would haunt me in my dreams later that night. I watched him walk away as I had with Lauren moments before.

"Are you coming to the assembly later?" I called out to him. He didn't look back at me when he spoke; he let his voice echo the halls as he had at the baseball field, walking into the sea of trees.

"That's gonna be a hard no from me, kid."

I found it interesting that he called me a kid again. He wasn't much older than me. We were about the same height too, so I wondered where the nickname came from, and if he used it with everyone. He disappeared around the corner, and I already wondered when I'd see him again.

Mid-afternoon rolled around, and they instructed everyone to go to the auditorium. They already had the assembly for the underclassman. It was time for the juniors and seniors to congregate in the auditorium as there weren't enough seats to fit the entire student body. I shuffled along with the rest of the hoard. I pulled out a slip of folded paper from my pocket and stared at it. It was a detention slip that Ms. Pepper had given me for being late to calculus because of my distraction with Caleb earlier in the day. The detention was for the next day, after school.

I scanned the awful colored seats of the theater space,

searching for Lauren. I spotted her toward the front, sitting next to Dan and Chris. She had her backpack resting in the seat to her left, saving it for me.

"Hey!" Chris waved at me. He was sitting at the end, with Dan in the middle and Lauren to Dan's left. I moved Lauren's backpack and sat. The projector screen was pulled down on the stage, ready to show us whatever slideshow my Dad had come up with.

"Dude," Dan said, looking over at me. "I want to have a huge party for my birthday! I'm thinking a costume party."

"A costume party? Halloween was months ago."

"I know," Dan said with a smile. "It's not a Halloween thing, it's a costume thing."

"... okay," I said. "When?"

"Two weeks from now, on the weekend."

"It's gonna be sick," Chris said. "Our parents are visiting our uncle in San Antonio, so it'll be perfect."

"I'll be in New York for my audition," Lauren said with a pouty look. "So I won't be able to go."

"Damn, I'm sorry," I said, placing my hand on her thigh. She didn't respond to my touch. I felt she still wasn't over everything that happened. Then Tasha turned around; I hadn't noticed she was sitting in front of us.

"Did you say party?" Tasha said with a smile.

"Yeah," Dan and Chris said at the same time.

"You wanna come?" Dan asked.

"Duh," Tasha said. "Can I make a Facebook event for it? How many people are you thinking?"

"I want this party to be lit."

"Done," Tasha said before whipping back around in her seat. I peeked over her shoulder; she was already on her phone creating the event.

"Oh!" Dan said, tapping Tasha on the shoulder. "Make sure

you add that everyone has to be wearing a costume or they aren't getting in." Tasha nodded, and Dan sat back, looking proud as if he was the first person to come up with the idea of a costume party.

My Dad's voice boomed through the auditorium. He was on stage, speaking into a microphone, telling everyone to get to a seat. The roar of the chatter died down as my Dad continued to speak.

"As you all know, tomorrow is our second annual intruder drill," Dad said. "Today's assembly will be a reminder of how it works, and what to expect."

I'd completely forgotten the drill was happening. Last year the school brought in a non-profit organization that works with local police departments to run school shooting drills. They formed the program to give students and staff the best ways to stay safe in a school shooting scenario and plan out evacuation techniques and strategies. The company started about five years prior and was met with a lot of controversies. They strived to make the drills as realistic as possible. They even recruit the local police department as "shooters". The school goes into lockdown while the police officers walk around with paintball guns that look like real automatic rifles and they simulate actual gunfire sounds through speakers. Parents thought it could be too triggering, but the company insists that they had done countless studies on the program that proved the more realistic, the higher the success rate was of keeping students safe.

My junior year was the first year we did the drill; they instructed us on how to stay safe specifically inside the classroom. The school spent a bunch of money installing a specific type of lock on every door. During that first drill, I was in Mrs. Donahue's English class. The school went into lockdown, so all the students huddled together on the floor in the farthest corner of the room, away from the door. Dan was also in that class and kept mocking the drill and how stupid he thought it was. He said the obvious move would be to just attack the shooter if they ever came into the room.

Once we were all huddled in the corner, it was Mrs. Donahue's job to lock the door. But since the school had installed the new lock, she had trouble with how it worked. She couldn't figure out how to lock it shut. She eventually gave up and huddled with us. Four or five minutes later we saw a figure dressed in black pass by the small square window of the door. Then we saw the handle jiggle. Everyone stopped breathing. The man in black pushed through the door and pointed his gun at us, announcing we'd all been shot and killed. Dan got pretty angry afterward, blaming Mrs. Donahue for causing all of our deaths. She studied how the locks worked after that. She even told me it sometimes kept her up at night, knowing if it had been a real scenario, she couldn't have saved us.

In my senior year, things were a little different, things had gotten even more realistic. In the second year, we were told that we had the choice, leave the classroom, and evacuate using one of the practiced evacuation paths or stay put. Leaving meant you risked being caught by a shooter. If they saw you, the police could shoot paintballs at your legs, which meant they'd killed you.

It was an odd feeling, coming out of the assembly that day. The tension was high; you could tell people felt nervous about the drill the next day. Others were treating it as a game.

"I can't believe they can actually shoot us," Lauren said as we walked down the hall back to our respective classes.

"Yeah, but they're just paintballs," Dan said. "So it'll hurt, but only for like three seconds."

"Plus," Chris said. "They're only allowed to shoot our legs, believe me, it hurts a lot more getting shot with a paintball in the chest."

"Or the neck!" Dan said, grabbing hold of his neck and acting as if they had shot him.

"Shit, the neck is the worst!" Chris shouted.

"I'm staying in the classroom," Lauren said. She walked close to me and wrapped an arm around my waist. I threw my arm over her shoulder and pulled her close. "I do not want to get shot at, no thanks."

"I'm choosing to get the fuck out," Dan said. "Especially after what happened last year. I'm not getting killed this year; I'm in control of my own life. I'm not letting a teacher fuck us over again."

"Ease up," I said. "Mrs. Donahue made a mistake."

"Mistakes get people killed," Dan said.

Chris looked at me. "What're you gonna do?"

"I'm not sure," I said.

I continued to think about it for the rest of the day. At first, I had nerves about the whole situation but kept reminding myself it wasn't real. That nothing would actually harm me. The whole thing seemed like a scare tactic, which I sort of understood. They wanted us to be feeling the fear we would feel during a real-life lockdown. I wondered what I would do during a real school shooting. Stay put or run. Of course, there were pros and cons to both decisions. But what was stopping a gunman from shooting through the door or even the glass window of the door? Maybe it would be better to evacuate rather than sit around like a fish in a barrel. But then of course if you leave the classroom, you have a chance of running into the shooter, which might lead to your death, with no locked doors standing in between you and the gun.

I thought about who a shooter could be. I thought about plenty of people in my grade who had the motivation to bring a gun to school. My first thought was Steven. How many times can one person tolerate getting beaten up over four years for being gay? At what point would Steven snap and eliminate the entire football team?

There was also Susan Townsend, who had suffered from bipolar and schizophrenia most of her life. During our sophomore year, they hospitalized her for hearing violent voices in her head. Of course, when she returned to school kids were calling her Schizo Sue. Her depression got worse after that, which led to a suicide attempt in our junior year. She survived, but she didn't come back to school after that. What's stopping her from coming back and taking revenge on everyone who made fun of her?

Then there was Ms. Henderson, who worked with the special needs kids. She spent her days following the mentally challenged around the school and helping them in their classes. I'd seen her get cussed out and even bitten, pinched, and punched by these kids who don't know any better. Every time I saw her, it seemed like the circles under her eyes got darker. She was an exhausted and worn-down woman, which was justified; she had one of the most demanding jobs. One that got very little praise. How far could she go before they pushed her to end it all?

And of course, the last person I thought of was Caleb. I did a mental recap of the facts. He lived in Skowhegan, a run-down town, and he had a criminal record. He had a mysterious tattoo, and he was obsessed with movies. That was it. People already thought he was weird. Dan already said that Caleb would be suspect number one if someone turned up dead. What if he got his community service on purpose? What if he was hoping to get assigned to a school so he could scope it out? What if his love for violent movies inspired him to try his hand at some violence of his own? People say video games attribute to real-life violence, so why couldn't movies inspire the same?

I combated my thoughts, thinking there was no way that Caleb could do anything like that, but the thought of him pulling his shirt up to dry his face blinded me. He seemed normal, based on the few times I'd spoken to him face-to-face, but I had to be honest with myself, I had no idea who he was. I wanted to change that so badly.

The next day at school, everyone was on edge. No one knew when the lockdown would start. Any sort of loud noise would make people jump. First period went by, then second, and third, still, nothing happened. We were told to go on about our day as if everything was normal. I even had a lunch period with Lauren and Chris that day.

It was final period. I was in my chemistry class with Dan. He and I sat toward the back because we were the only seniors in a room full of juniors. We had both failed our biology class freshman year, which caused us to take an extra science credit during senior year. Mr. Butler was our teacher. Most kids called him the penguin. He was severely overweight, causing him to waddle when he walked. He had a pointy nose and wore thin-framed glasses. He had hair but only on the sides of his head; the only thing that connected one side to the other was a few long strands that he combed over the bald space.

Mr. Butler was explaining the chemical reactions of soap when we heard three industrial alarms over the loudspeakers and the emergency lights turned on.

"All right everyone, this is it," Mr. Butler said. "Everyone, please move to the back of the room."

We obeyed, shuffling to the back of the class while Mr. Butler waddled over to the door to lock it. Dan and I were sitting toward the front of the huddle, watching Mr. Butler struggle to join us on the floor. Then we heard the gunshots, which caused some girls in the class to scream.

Dan jumped to his feet. "All right, I'm not sitting here anymore!"

"Mr. Wilson, sit back down now!" Mr. Butler whispered.

"No, they said we could go or we could stay. I'm choosing to go. Who's coming with me?"

Everyone stayed quiet. I looked behind me at all the nervous faces before standing.

"I'll go," I said.

"Damn right you will!" Dan said as he slapped me on the back. Mr. Butler didn't bother to stop us. We started for the door, but when Dan tried the handle, he remembered Mr. Butler locked it. Dan looked over to the huddle. "How do you unlock this?"

"You need this key and the passcode. But if you leave, I can't let you back in," Mr. Butler said. Dan stomped over to our teacher and took the key from him. He jogged back to the door and inserted it. "Now keep the key turned," Mr. Butler said. "And type in three, six, eight, six, and four." I couldn't see what Dan was doing since I was standing behind him, but I could hear the beep of the number pad every time he pushed a button. The door then unlatched and Dan threw the key back to Mr. Butler.

"Let's go," Dan said to me over his shoulder.

We slithered out the door and closed it behind us, keeping our backs against the wall.

"Do you remember the evacuation route?"

"No," Dan whispered. "I wasn't paying attention to that shit."

"Dammit, me either. We're gonna have to wing it."

Again we heard gunshots, which made us flinch; they were louder in the hallway than in the classroom. The halls were deserted, it didn't seem like anyone else chose the option to leave their room.

My phone vibrated. It was a text from Lauren.

LAUREN
Landon I'm scared.

ME
It'll be fine, it's not real.

LAUREN
The gunshots sound real.

ME
I know, but they aren't. It's all fake.

"Who is texting you right now?"

"It's Lauren," I said, looking up from my phone. "She's scared."

"Tell her we'll come get her."

ME
Dan and I left the classroom.

LAUREN
OMG!

ME
He said we can come to get you.

LAUREN
You're insane.

ME
Where are you?

LAUREN
Second floor, room 204.

ME
Okay, we'll try to get there.

Be careful.

"She's on the second floor," I whispered.

"Okay, we need to get to the stairs then." Dan led the way. We moved quickly, trying to stay as light on our feet as possible. We were about to turn a corner, but Dan suddenly backed into me. He put his finger to his lips. I could hear footsteps, so we backed ourselves against the wall again. Dan peeked around the corner, then turned to me. "There's a guy holding a gun; he's walking to each door and checking the handles." Then we heard a whole classroom worth of screams. The man with the gun must have found a door that was unlocked. Dan turned me around, and we went running in the opposite direction.

"Stop!" someone shouted from behind. I saw a red paintball splat against the ground in front of us right before we slid around the corner. We ran as fast as we could until we came to the cafeteria. There were a bunch of lunch tables folded up and stacked close to a wall. Dan and I stayed low and hid behind the tables. The cafeteria had a wall of windows facing a small courtyard before leading into the staff parking lot. Within that wall of windows was an exit door.

"We have to go for it," Dan whispered to me.

"I don't know," I said. "There could be a shooter anywhere in this cafeteria."

We couldn't see past the stack of folded tables without exposing ourselves.

"This may be our only chance." Dan attempted to make a run toward the door, but I grabbed his shirt.

"Dan, this could be a mistake, don't."

"I have to take that risk."

"Mistakes get people killed, those are your words."

Dan stared at me with a furrowed brow and clenched jaw before he shoved me, running toward the door. I didn't follow him but I heard his clunky footsteps and then a single shot.

"Goddammit!" Dan shouted.

I peeked one eye in his direction and saw the red splat on his pant leg. A man dressed in black then escorted him through the exit door. I pressed my back against the tables, looking in the direction we came from. I needed to get to the second floor. Each corner I approached, I peeked my head out to make sure no one was around.

I made a left turn and saw the stairs in front of me at the other end of the hallway. I was about to run to them, but a man stepped out from underneath the staircase, pointing his gun. I panicked, jumping around the nearest corner behind me when I felt a hand wrap around my mouth and pull me backward.

"It's me, it's me," the voice said. I was turned around and face to face with Caleb. "What the fuck is going on?" He was wearing a white tank top and a janitor's jumpsuit, but it was unzipped halfway and the sleeves were wrapped and tied around his waist.

"What do you mean?"

"There are a bunch of guys walking around with guns," Caleb whispered. "Have you not seen them?"

"It's a drill."

Caleb's face twisted. "What?"

"A drill," I said again. "A school shooting drill. The guns are just paintball guns."

"Jesus Christ, it would've been nice if the principal told me about this."

"Hey, you're the one that skipped the assembly yesterday." I had a dumb smile on my face. "If the guys see us, they'll shoot us."

Caleb tisked. "They don't see me as part of the staff. I'm just a guy completing his sentence, they couldn't give two shits about me. Come on," Caleb said before grabbing me by the hand and pulling me down the hall. The top of Caleb's hand felt smooth. I would've let him pull me off a cliff. At that point, I didn't care, as long as he didn't let go. I didn't even look up to see where we were going. I just stared at our hands clasped together. Before I knew it, Caleb swept me into a closet and closed the door. It was pitch black and both of us were panting. He cracked the door, peeked out, and closed it again. "Someone was following us." My eyes widened. I couldn't see Caleb, but I could feel his breath when he spoke. "This is kinda fucked up."

"I agree, but it's intended to feel real."

"They sure fooled me," Caleb said.

Our hips were brushing together, and my heart raced. The closet was so small my chin was resting on his shoulder.

"I came in to clean the bathrooms today, and then I heard the alarm. When I came out, I saw these guys walking around with guns and I thought something serious was going on," Caleb said.

Beads of sweat made their way down my face; it was getting hot.

Caleb cracked the door open again. "We should head for the front exit."

I was about to mention Lauren on the second floor, but the door closed and Caleb pushed his hand against my stomach.

"Shh, someone's coming." Caleb's hand rested there, and a fire erupted inside me. I closed my eyes tight, trying to push down the flames.

Don't get hard, don't get hard.

I clenched my jaw, hoping it would help, but my body wasn't listening to my brain. Thank god it was dark. I heard heavy boots step past the thin wooden door.

"Think it's safe?" I whispered.

Caleb waited for another thirty or forty seconds before opening the door. The rush of cool air pushed against us. The heat of our heavy breathing turned the closet into a mini-sauna. Caleb grabbed my hand again and led me down the hall and around two corners before we reached the front foyer.

"It's clear, as far as I can see," Caleb said.

"Should we make a run for it?" I could see the front entrance, as well as half my house across the street.

"Go!" Caleb yelled, and we dashed down the hall. I ran as if I were on the football field, whizzing past the auditorium. Caleb was keeping up with me. I saw him out of the corner of my eye, smiling. We jumped down the front steps and through the court-yard. He slowed down, but I kept running until I reached my front yard. I collapsed on the grass and stared at the sky, breathing heavily. Then Caleb was standing over me, looking down with a smile. "So, did I just like, rescue you? I felt like I was in *Die Hard* or something."

I laughed, propping myself to a sitting position. "I have no idea what that is."

Caleb sat next to me. "You have so much to learn."

"And you didn't save me," I said, looking at the grass, ripping out chunks of blades. "I was already trying to escape. I was with my friend Dan, but he got shot."

"Jesus, this school is intense." Caleb leaned back on his hands. "So, what happened to him?"

"I'm not sure, I saw a guy escort him out after he shot him."

"How is this okay? I don't get it," Caleb said. I shrugged. "How come you were out in the halls? I assume they locked everyone else in the classrooms."

"This year, we had a choice, we could stay in the classrooms and wait or we could choose to leave the building ourselves."

"And you left, huh?" Caleb bumped his shoulder into mine. "How James Bond of you."

"Hey, I actually know who that is," I said, choosing to look at him for the first time since we took off running, getting trapped in his eyes.

Caleb laughed. "Thank God."

I was suddenly thrust into thinking about Caleb and his red-headed goddess. I imagined myself sitting in the audience at their wedding, watching them exchange their vows. They both looked beautiful. Caleb looked so happy holding her hands. I looked around, but I was the only one sitting in the space, surrounded by empty white chairs.

"How was your date?" I blurted out.

Caleb stared at me. "What?"

"Your date this past weekend?"

"How'd you know about that?"

I hesitated. "Uh, you told me about it."

"Oh," he said, looking toward the school. "Right."

"Did it go well? Was she everything you hoped?"

"Meh." Caleb shrugged. "It was all right, I guess."

"Think she'll want to see you again?" I was torturing myself, getting in too deep with the truth I didn't want or need to know.

"I hope so," Caleb said. We both went quiet and stared at the school. "But," Caleb said as he stood, wiping the dirt from his pants. "I never said my date was a she."

Holy shit.

TWELVE

My mind was reeling. I had to stop my jaw from hitting the ground. The street was so quiet; it was easy to hear the school bell ring and an announcement that the shooting drill was over.

"See ya, Lan," Caleb said as he strutted off across the street.

My brain was so rattled I couldn't even say goodbye, I just watched as Caleb walked away. I suspected he knew how much he was torturing me with every word he spoke and that he enjoyed it. Was he being honest telling me his date wasn't with a girl or was he just busting my balls?

My mind switched gears. He gave me a nickname. No one had ever called me Lan before, not even my parents. Thinking about it made me feel warm. Was it strange to think he cared about me enough to give me a nickname, or was I being childish? What made me so special?

My phone buzzed. I pulled it out, seeing texts from Lauren coming in.

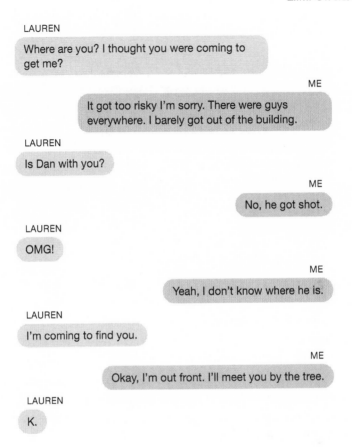

LAUREN
Where are you? I thought you were coming to get me?

ME
It got too risky I'm sorry. There were guys everywhere. I barely got out of the building.

LAUREN
Is Dan with you?

ME
No, he got shot.

LAUREN
OMG!

ME
Yeah, I don't know where he is.

LAUREN
I'm coming to find you.

ME
Okay, I'm out front. I'll meet you by the tree.

LAUREN
K.

I stood, patting the grass and dust off my butt. Kids were exiting the school as I crossed the street. I wondered where Caleb was off to. I assume he had things left to do since the men with paintball guns interrupted him.

There was a beautiful, large oak tree in the front courtyard of the school. It was the usual meeting place for Lauren and me most mornings. I leaned against it, noticing I didn't have my backpack with me. I'd left it in Mr. Butler's classroom, not even thinking to grab it amongst the chaos of the drill.

Could use some sunblock right now.

The tree's leaves were in full bloom, so I found a shaded area to stand under, shielding myself from the sun.

"Hey," Lauren said as she approached me.

I held out my arms so she could embrace me. She hesitated, but then gave in.

"That was so scary."

"I know," I said into her neck as I held her. I could smell the fruity-ness of the shampoo she used. My mind flickered to the scent of sweat and cologne I'd gotten from Caleb, wishing I could be as close to him as I was to Lauren.

"I hope we never have to go through that," Lauren said, pulling away from me.

"Same, but at least this is giving us some sort of prep if it does." Lauren held my hand as I spoke, I could sense her attitude toward me had eased.

"I'm sorry," she said, looking me in the eye. "I went too fast the other night."

"You have nothing to apologize for, I'm the one who started it. I could've been a little nicer about it. I just got nervous, I guess." I looked at her, feeling a wave of guilt. How could I say that getting physical with her may never happen at all? The last thing I wanted was to hurt her feelings, especially after all the time we'd spent together. I noticed more and more kids file out of the building and I let go of Lauren's hand. "Shit, what time is it?" I checked my phone, confirming I was late for my detention. "I gotta go," I said.

"What? Where?"

"I almost forgot that I have detention."

"For what?"

Getting detention wasn't a usual thing for me. I'm sure she found the words odd coming out of my mouth.

"Yesterday," I said. "Ms. Pepper gave me one for being late after I talked to you in the hall."

Lauren cocked her head. "Her class was right around the corner. How were you late?"

She caught me. "Caleb." I blurted. My words could no longer keep themselves in as if they had a mind of their own.

"Who's Caleb?"

There it was; I had to tell her, but I was so nervous. I was nervous my feelings for him would show in the words I used to describe him. I was nervous somehow she would know I was with him the other night and that I lied about it.

"He's that new janitor guy," I said, after searching the entire English language for words that wouldn't give me away.

"Okay..." Lauren's hands moved in a way that told me she wanted more information. "What does he have to do with you being late?"

My pulse rose, I felt like I was being interrogated.

Just tell her what happened, it wasn't a big deal!

I felt like Jekyll and Hyde going back and forth, deciding what pieces of information to give her.

"I bumped into him and made him spill mop water everywhere," I said.

"And now you guys are suddenly friends?"

I searched my brain as if it were Google, but all I kept seeing was the box labeled 'Caleb' and all the information files started shooting out of it like a magician throwing cards around a stage.

"Cool," Lauren said before I could even answer her question. "So is he weird? Is he scary?"

"Uh," I said. I was shocked by the outcome of the conversation. "No?" It was all I could muster to answer both of her questions. Then panic set in again. "I need to go, Ms. Pepper is gonna give me another detention for being late to this one."

Lauren nodded and gave me a quick kiss. "Okay, go. We can talk later."

"See ya," I said before jogging into the building.

"Late again?" Ms. Pepper said, looking over the frame of her glasses. I plopped myself at a desk in the second row. The woman had an awful fashion sense. She was wearing a long-sleeve, brown turtleneck and a long denim dress that looked like overalls.

"I'm so sorry," I said as I tried to catch my breath. I wiped some sweat from my forehead with my arm. "I had to run to Mr. Butler's room to grab my backpack first." Glancing around the classroom, I was the only one in the seats.

"I'll let this one slide," Ms. Pepper said. "Because of the hectic events today."

"Thank you."

"Ah, Mr. Montes," Ms. Pepper said as I was searching through my backpack for my water bottle. My ears perked up as I took a sip. Ms. Pepper stood from the desk, walking to the door. The clunk of her wedged two-inch heels echoed through the empty room. I almost spit the water as I saw Caleb walk in. Ms. Pepper and Caleb were standing side by side, looking at me. "This is Mr. Montes, he's going to be watching you during your detention." I saw Caleb smirk. His face looked devilish and handsome. Ms. Pepper continued, "I have a teacher's meeting about today's drill or else it would be me. Mr. Montes was the only one available to take over for me."

"Okay," I said with a hard gulp. My palms felt clammy, so I rubbed them against my jeans. I felt embarrassed.

"He's not allowed on his cellphone," Ms. Pepper said to Caleb. "That's about it. Sit at my desk and I'll be back in an hour to release Mr. Griffin."

It was official; we knew each other's last names. I pictured another file going into my Caleb box. The other scattered files from earlier whisked themselves up, placing themselves neatly back in the box.

"He's in good hands," Caleb said with a nod. I remembered the way his hand felt against mine. I wanted to feel his skin again. Caleb started for the desk as Ms. Pepper left the room. He sat and kicked his feet up, crossing his ankles with a smug look on his face. He was wearing tan work boots, dirt stuck in the grooves of the rubber soles. Caleb leaned back in the chair, interlocking his fingers behind his head, and asked, "Are you stalking me?"

"Ha! You wish," I said.

Caleb chuckled. "What're you in for?"

"You tell me first."

Caleb raised one eyebrow as if to say 'touché'. "It's complicated."

"Try me," I said as I sat up straight.

"I know people around here have been talking about me, spreading rumors."

"Are any of them true?" I was desperate for any sort of word that came from his lips.

"Like I said, It's complicated."

I sensed he didn't want to talk about it, so I made a joke. "They have you doing everything around here, huh?"

"What can I say? I'm a jack of all trades."

"Is this conflicting with school or anything?" I wanted to become an encyclopedia on Caleb and Caleb only.

"Nope, It's just easier not to be in school right now."

"Because of what?" I couldn't stop myself. I was a freight train bursting through the walls of Caleb's boundaries.

He was quick to change the topic. "You're lookin' a little red, kid."

"I just had to run from..." I stopped myself, I needed answers. "Wait, why do you call me that?"

Caleb sighed and took his feet off the desk, leaning on it with his forearms instead. "Sorry, It's a habit," Caleb said. The rasp in his voice was endearing. "You're younger than me, so it just comes out."

I laughed. "Oh, come on, how old are you?"

"Just turned twenty-one."

I threw my hands out toward him, smiling like a clown. "You're barely three years older than me!"

"You're right." Caleb smiled, flashing his perfect dimples. "I won't call you kid anymore."

I would've asked for an entire week of detention if it meant I got to spend time with him for an hour every day after school.

"I'm not saying it's a bad thing, I was just curious." I noticed Caleb get rosy in the cheeks, and I wondered if he could sense my playfulness. Then he split the air again.

"You can use your phone. I won't narc on you." Caleb whipped out his phone. It was two generations old.

"Thanks," I said through my smile.

I cupped my phone in my lap as I stared at the screen, keeping a low profile in case Ms. Pepper popped her head through the door. I texted Dan asking what happened after I saw him get led out of the cafeteria, but he didn't answer. Then, in a weird coincidence, I got a text from Chris.

CHRIS

Hey, do you know where Dan is?

ME

That's so weird, I just texted him asking the same thing.

CHRIS

lol.

I'll check around. I wonder if he left during the drill.

ME

I was in class with him.

I looked up and surveyed my surroundings, making sure no teacher was in sight. Out of the corner of my eye, I could see Caleb texting, and he'd returned his feet to the top of the desk.

ME

We left the classroom together during the drill.

I looked over at Caleb again, wondering if it would be weird to ask for his phone number.

CHRIS

I just found him and saw the red paint on his pants lol.

ME

He was an idiot and got himself shot haha.

CHRIS

Sounds about right.

When I found him by his car he was talking to a weird smelly guy.

ME

The guy I told you about at practice last week?

CHRIS

Yeah, I think so.

Dude, I think he's selling drugs or something because this guy was sketch.

ME

Are you serious?

It suddenly made sense why Dan got defensive when I asked him who that guy was. I wondered what Dan had gotten himself mixed up in, and if he needed help. Who was he selling drugs for, and why? Even though he'd been a major dick of late, I still didn't want him getting in trouble.

I sniffed the air, recalling a memory.

"What is it?"

Caleb caught me.

"Huh?"

"It looked like you were smelling something," Caleb said.

Was he watching me when I wasn't looking?

"I had a math class here during my sophomore year. Every time I'm in here, I smell the vomit."

"Why? What happened?" Caleb put his phone away before smirking at me.

"One day during class, a kid named Jared raised his hand saying he needed to go to the nurse, which the teacher allowed, but before he could leave the room, he threw up all over the floor in front of the desk you're sitting at."

"Gross," Caleb said with a chuckle.

"Oh, it gets worse." I grinned. "Everyone screamed. Jared curled over and vomited again, splashing some chunks onto the pant legs of other kids. I remember seeing the puddle of orange goo all over the floor. Then the smell dusted the room like a sandstorm. The smell was so rancid that it caused a girl named Alexis to vomit all over her desk, which then caused a boy named Dustin to vomit in his hands. Jared had single-handedly created a chain reaction so disgusting that people started running from the room in fear as if the vomit was poisonous. I remember laughing so hard, thinking it was something you'd only see in cartoons."

Caleb laughed. "Oh my god, I feel like I can smell it now!"

I remembered the smell lingered for weeks after the incident. I looked down at my phone in my lap as I thought about Dan's drug dealing again. The thought evaporated into thin air as the sudden screech of Caleb's chair startled me.

"I gotta go," Caleb said as he pushed the chair into the desk. "Tell Ms. Pepper I'm sorry."

"Wait!" I hollered, trying to stop him. "Where are you going?"

"A date!" Caleb shot through the door and took a hard left.

Another one?

The rest of the hour passed and Ms. Pepper returned to release me, shocked to see Caleb had ducked out. She commended me on staying the whole time before letting me go. As I walked back home, I wondered if Caleb was dating multiple people. I pictured him at a dinner table, sitting across from a man and a woman holding both their hands. I was depressing myself. Why was Caleb so hard to figure out? I tried to think of something else to occupy my mind, then remembered I hadn't looked over the college applications that Mr. Reily gave me.

When I stepped through the door, I smelled a Hot Pocket my

Dad had microwaved. He sat at the kitchen counter with his laptop open in front of him.

"Hey, son," he said without looking up.

I gave a nod as I walked to the fridge, before heading to my room. I had set the latest edition of the *Madison Monthly* on the counter next to the fridge as I liked to keep each one. I had the idea to frame them and hang them up in my room someday, but it wasn't there anymore.

"Dad," I said as I twirled around. "I put the *Monthly* here. Did you move it?"

He looked at me. "I might've accidentally scooped it up with my stuff. Check the office on my desk." His eyes went back to the computer screen while my heart abruptly sank to my stomach.

"Can you go get it?" I asked with a lump in my throat. "Please?"

"Landon, I have to finish this email. And I need the office for a Zoom meeting in ten minutes, so be quick."

What my Dad didn't know was I hadn't stepped foot in his office for months. I'd been too scared to even touch the door-knob, afraid I'd get a whiff of her perfume, or see a pair of her shoes in the corner and break into pieces. But I knew my Dad wouldn't budge. It was time I faced my fear.

THIRTEEN

There was a short hallway off the living room, with only two rooms, a bathroom, and my Dad's office. I hadn't stepped down that hallway in six months. Even a glance in its direction sent a chill down my spine. It was a dark place, a place of pain, anger, and sorrow. I avoided it at all costs. Anytime I needed to use the bathroom, I'd go upstairs.

I reached for the knob of the office and took a deep breath as if I were about to go underwater. I opened the door a crack just to peek in.

It's just a room.

It made a creaking sound as I pushed it open and stepped in. The hallway was carpeted, but the office had dark hardwood flooring. In front of me was a large bay window looking into the backyard behind my Dad's oak desk that he'd built himself when I was nine. I made a chip in the wood of one leg with a screwdriver, saying that I was helping with the build. It was the only imperfection on the desk. The walls to the left and right were floor-to-ceiling white shelves that made the room feel brighter. These shelves held everything from books to trophies, to miniature flags, to things my Dad collected from his military days. The ceiling was the only one in the house with exposed beams. There were a few potted plants that had seen better days.

I took in the room as I had many times before, but it was different that time. I could almost hear her voice, telling my Dad to come to bed after a long night, or her saying 'knock knock' before she entered the room to tell my Dad dinner was ready. My chest felt heavy. I closed my eyes for a second to regroup. When I opened them, I noticed a stack of papers on the desk.

I walked behind the large oak fixture and pulled out the leather chair. The sun was setting and reflected light off of a picture frame on the desk that caught my eye. That picture was the only one in my Dad's office. I picked it up as I sat in the chair. The chrome frame held a picture of my mom and me sitting on a haystack. I assumed we were at the annual fall county fair. I was only about a year old in the picture. We were wearing matching overalls. I was sitting between my mom's legs and she was looking down at me with the biggest smile. She had long wavy red hair.

God, she looks so young.

It was before she lost her hair, long before the pain, and before the depression hit. She looked so carefree. The longer I stared at it, the easier it was for me to hear her laugh. It was loud and contagious. I missed it so much.

"I wish you were here," I whispered. My chest felt heavy again as my eyes watered. I wiped them, sniffling a bit, setting the picture back down. I rubbed my forehead, wondering what she might say about my feelings for Caleb.

You probably already knew.

She told me when I was in second grade, I would come home every day gushing about a boy named Aaron. 'Aaron said this today,' I would tell her. 'Aaron wore this today.' 'Aaron and I played catch today! You're never gonna believe what Aaron had for lunch today!' All the signs must've been there, but they weren't important to her. As long as I was happy, she was happy.

I shuffled through the papers until I found the *Monthly* and stood, taking one last look at her before I started for the door. The air in that office felt cold, even without the AC running. It was a different cold, an empty cold. When I closed the door behind me, I felt like I could breathe again.

I walked into my room, slapping the paper on my desk, plopping into the little wheely chair that always hurt my tailbone the longer I sat in it. I pulled the list of colleges out of my bag, picturing myself walking around each campus while googling them. The prompt of each application was simple: write an original short story no longer than 50 pages and no shorter than 20.

Easy.

I could have it done and send them out the next day. I opened my laptop and clicked into a new word document ready to type anything that came to mind, but I sat there. I stared at the blank screen for five minutes, watching that little cursor line on the page blip in and out. Nothing was coming to me. I wiggled my fingers over the keyboard as if to conjure up any sort of inspiration. I had several stories saved on my desktop, but most of them were shit and underdeveloped. I wanted something new.

"Landon!" My Dad called out from downstairs. I sighed and cupped my hands around my face in frustration that my thinking process had been interrupted.

"Yeah?" I yelled back.

"I need you for something!" The neighbors could probably hear us from down the street. I hopped down the stairs, eager to see what he wanted so I could get back to thinking.

"What is it?"

He collected his computer off of the table starting toward his office. "I need you to deposit that check for me," he said as he pointed his free hand at the kitchen island. "The card is there too, it's a donation so I need it done today."

"Dad, you know you can deposit it from your phone right?"

"I don't trust that." He headed down the short hallway. "Just do it, please. I have to get to this meeting." The last words were muffled as he'd already closed himself in his office.

I sauntered over to the counter and picked up the check. The donation was $2,000 from a woman named Ruth Steinberg. I checked the back for my Dad's signature before folding it in half, slipping it in my pocket. I grabbed the ATM card that had COLOSSAL BANK in bold letters across the front. Colossal was a local bank unique to Madison County. It was a good ten-minute drive away.

Colossal Bank was in a plaza with a few other businesses. I parked just in front of the ATM attached to the outside wall of the bank. As I stepped out of the car, I heard a small high-pitched laugh. I looked over, seeing a little boy exiting Sal's ice cream shop. The window to the shop had a large cartoon cow painted on it, wearing sunglasses.

I walked up to the ATM, inserting my Dad's card. Every time I hit a button, an obnoxious beeping sound would occur. I slid the check into a slot on the machine and it sucked the paper in. I imagined a round, furry monster inside the machine who fed on paper and threw up dollar bills. I chuckled to myself, thinking what the monster might sound like until a familiar voice caught my ear. The voice was youthful but a little raspy. I knew right away it was Caleb.

I turned my head to follow his voice and there he was: sitting at a picnic table outside Sal's ice cream shop, across from the boy I had seen seconds before. They were both laughing. I felt so confused. Hours ago, Caleb ran out of my detention flustered, saying he had a date.

BEEP! BEEP! BEEP! The machine startled me, yelling at me to take my Dad's card. Caleb had noticed too.

"Landon?" Caleb yelled over.

I pulled the card from the machine and slipped it into my pocket. I turned around, trying to act surprised that I was hearing my name. Looking everywhere but the ice cream shop, I tried to play it cool as if I wasn't just watching him and the boy. Then I focused on Caleb.

I waved "Oh, hey!" To my surprise, Caleb motioned me to join them. I nodded and took a deep breath, trying not to freak out. As I made my way over, my mind raced with so many thoughts.

Holy shit. That's his son.

My eyes tried to survey the ice cream shop through the window, searching for a woman that would be Caleb's girlfriend. My hands were in my pockets as I squeezed them into fists, I wasn't ready to know that Caleb had a kid or a woman in his life. As I got closer, I saw that there weren't any customers inside. Caleb and his son were the only ones there. I shuffled to the front of the picnic table, I could smell the sweetness of sugar in the air.

"Wanna sit?" Caleb looked up at me, squinting his eyes from the setting sun.

"Uh, yeah, sure." My body felt so stiff as I sat next to Caleb, still unsure of what was going on.

"Hi!" the little voice said from across the table.

"Hey," I said. I looked over to Caleb again, I think he could tell I was confused.

"This is Parker," Caleb said. "My little brother."

I felt the weight of confusion and worry lift off my shoulders after Caleb spoke. Then I felt like such an idiot.

"Oh," I said with a dopey smile before looking over at Parker. "I'm Landon."

"Hi, Landon," Parker said. His words came between each lick to his soft-serve cone with rainbow sprinkles. "I'm nine, how old are you?"

"Sorry," Caleb said. "He's very inquisitive."

I smiled. Parker and I had that in common.

"I'm eighteen."

Caleb's ice cream of choice was a banana split. Then he caught me looking.

"You want a bite?"

"Um," I said, lingering on the word. "Sure." I reached for the utensil, but Caleb was already moving to feed me a clump of vanilla and chocolate stuck together. I accepted his offer as I closed my teeth over the cold spoon, making a small clink sound that sent a chill down my spine. I just nodded my head as I moved the ice cream around the roof of my mouth to melt it.

Caleb returned his spoon to the frozen dessert. "Good, right?"

"Yeah," I said, raising both my eyebrows. I let the ice cream melt before I spoke again. "What happened to your date?"

Caleb flashed his dimples. "He is my date." He took a big spoonful. He was the type of person who chewed his ice cream. My teeth ached just watching him do it. "Once a week, we see a movie, and then we have ice cream," Caleb said.

Everything about him was a surprise. I never knew what he was going to say next. I felt like a sponge, letting every one of his words seep into my pores. I imagined the small box labeled 'Caleb' in my mind overflowing with files.

"Yeah," Parker said before another lick of his cone. "We like movies."

"Listen to this," Caleb said to Parker, pointing a thumb at me, "he's never seen Jurassic Park."

"What?!" Parker said. He had gone into a complete sugar

rage, standing out of his seat. "That's impossible! It's like the best movie ever made!"

"That's what I said!" Caleb pointed his spoon at Parker, matching the younger boy's excitement. They laughed together, making me laugh too.

"I'll see it soon, I promise," I said as I covered my face in shame.

"Caleb has the Blu-ray," Parker said proudly. "Come to our house, you can watch it!"

The words made Caleb go silent. He just sat there looking down at his ice cream as he cleared his throat.

"Finish your ice cream kid," Caleb said, breaking the silence. There was a weird amount of awkwardness in the air.

"So," I said to Caleb. "Your date from this past weekend you told me about..."

Caleb nodded. "I was with Parker."

Wow, now I really feel dumb.

All the women I had conjured up in my head, all the restaurants I pictured Caleb sitting in, it was all for nothing. I was so naïve. Nothing about Caleb so far was stereotypical, I had to stop thinking about him that way.

"Our home life isn't the best," Caleb said, looking at me. "So we try to get away every once in a while."

"Yeah, Luke is a real asshole," Parker spouted.

Caleb shot a look at Parker, "Language, kid. I told you, you can't say that till you're ten." Caleb looked at me again. "Luke's a real asshole."

I saw Parker smile out of the corner of my eye.

"Who's Luke?"

"Our mom's boyfriend," Caleb said.

"Oh, okay," I said, unsure how to respond appropriately. "Cool." My eyes widened. "I mean, not cool as in like, cool that your home life isn't the best." I felt a warmness in my cheeks.

"No," Caleb said, chuckling. "I get it."

I thought it was cute that he took his little brother to the movies. My eyes traveled to Parker again, inspecting him. He was a unique-looking kid. He had a similar face shape as Caleb and even had the same bronze skin, but he had red hair and freckles all over his face. Caleb's words played back in my mind from that night at the baseball field as if they were on a tape recorder being rewound and played over and over.

You remind me of someone special to me. You both have red hair.

The realization crashed over me like a tidal wave. Caleb was talking about Parker. Just thinking about it made me smile again as I noticed something else unique about the boy. His left eye caught a bit of reflective light, helping me realize his pupil was cloudy.

"I have to pee," Parker said. "I'll be right back."

"I'll be here," Caleb said before Parker stood and glided back into the shop. Parker was already crunching through his cone at that point.

"I didn't know you had a brother," I said as I watched Caleb take another bite. He was close to finishing himself.

"You don't know a lot of things about me," Caleb said with a mouth full of ice cream and a smirk.

"Okay," I said, slapping my hand against the wood of the picnic table. "Do you like, get off on being mysterious or something? I don't get it."

Caleb laughed before wiping his mouth with a napkin. "No. I just don't need everyone knowing my business."

"How does anyone ever get to know you then?"

"Fine." Caleb placed his napkin on the empty bowl and swung his leg around to straddle the bench and face me. "Today's your lucky day. What do you wanna know?"

My eyes widened. The lights and circuits in my brain were going off at a rapid pace.

Anything?!

It was an impossible decision. I imagined an arrow hitting the bullseye of a target, as I found my question. "What's going on at home?"

"Wow." Caleb chuckled. "I was expecting, like, 'what's your favorite color?' Or, 'what's your favorite movie?' But you're starting deep."

"I'm sorry." I waved my hands in front of me. "You don't have to answer that, that's way too personal."

"No, no," Caleb said. "You took the leap, you're in deep now, Lan."

Hearing him call me Lan again made me warm in the chest. "All right, all right," I said, resting my hands in my lap.

"We don't have much." Caleb glanced into the ice cream shop. I looked behind me and noticed Parker had sat at a table inside, flipping through a magazine. "We don't have the nicest clothes or even a car. We walk everywhere. And we don't have the nicest house. We live with our mom and her shitty boyfriend. The house is his. Our mom is only with him because he keeps her doped up. The roof over our head is just a bonus." Caleb spoke directly and to the point, not adding any unnecessary detail. "They fight all the time. We all do. He hits her, so I hit him, he hits me back." Caleb rubbed the top of his right hand without realizing it. I glanced and noticed minor bruises on his knuckles that were in the last stages of healing. Caleb looked toward Parker again. "He knows I'd kill him if he ever touched Parker."

"Has he tried?"

"Not yet," Caleb said, looking at me. "I hate that Parker has to be around all that."

"So, you and Parker have the same Dad?" I felt like I was prying, but he answered me quickly.

"Yeah." Caleb leaned his arm against the table. "He left when I was eleven. I used to think it was my fault," Caleb laughed.

"Wow," I said with a lump in my throat. "I'm sorry." I was so stunned by Caleb's honesty. He wasn't this beast of a criminal that everyone at school thought he was. He was a person with real trauma and feelings.

"Soon after my Dad left, my mom found out she was pregnant with Parker. We moved around a lot until she found the only guy who didn't mind a woman with two kids. And we've been with him ever since."

A bell rang from behind me as the door of the shop swung open. Parker walked out and up to Caleb, putting his small hands on Caleb's broad shoulders. "Can we go home now?"

"Sure, kid," Caleb said with a smile.

"Let me give you a ride," I blurted.

"Oh, no," Caleb said. "You don't have to."

"It's no problem. I swear."

"You probably have other things you could -"

"Please, Caleb?" Parker said, smushing his face into the side of Caleb's. "I don't feel like walking back."

Caleb hesitated, staring at his brother. "Okay, fine," he said, wrapping his arms around Parker's little body and squeezing him. I could tell Parker held Caleb in the palm of his hand. Watching them together really warmed my heart.

FOURTEEN

"I like this car," Parker said after he'd been sitting in the back seat for all of ten minutes.

Caleb twisted toward Parker. "Why this car of all cars?"

"I don't know."

I glanced in the rearview mirror just in time to see Parker's exaggerated shoulder shrug. We laughed as Caleb uncoiled back into his seat.

"Seems legit," I said, taking a glance at a smiling Caleb, I swear his teeth could reflect the sun.

"Oh," Caleb said. "Take this right coming up."

He pointed to a large wooden sign. Written in an old western font, the sign read: 'Skowhegan Trailer Park Housing.'

I turned through the gate onto the dirt road. It was a straight and narrow path that looked forgotten about, and it continued as far as my eyes could see. On each side were trailer houses, all similar in build but different colors.

"It's the sixth one in, on the right," Caleb said.

He wasn't looking at me, he just stared out the window, scratching at his jeans. I pulled up in front of a gray trailer. It was one of the longer ones. The porch was unpainted wood as if it had just been built. Two beach chairs were resting to the right side, with a small white plastic table in between them.

I had barely come to a stop before Parker unbuckled himself and rushed out the door.

"Parker!" Caleb shouted through his open window. Parker stopped in his tracks before ascending the three small steps of the porch. "What do you say to Landon?"

Parker rushed to the passenger side window with as much of the excitement as he used to exit the car. He popped his head into the car and looked me in the eye, "thank you," he said, making two words into a one-syllable sound. And just like that, Parker was off in a flash, returning to his original route.

"Anytime!" I shouted just before he slipped through the screen door. I glanced at Caleb, who was smiling as he watched Parker run into the house. "His eyes are-"

"I know," Caleb said as he looked at me. "It's one of the first things people notice."

"I've never seen anything like that before. Do you mind if I ask why it's like that?"

"My mom caused that one," Caleb said as he scratched the back of his head. "Cocaine is her favorite, but meth has always been cheaper." I turned the car off as Caleb spoke. "She started using after my Dad left. Even though she knew she was pregnant, she didn't stop. The doctors noticed something was wrong while giving him an exam a week after he was born. They figured out that his left eye wasn't responding to light at all. The meth my mom was smoking had destroyed Parker's retina, making him lose sight in that eye." Caleb glanced out the windshield as a woman walked toward us with her small dog on a leash trailing behind her. "There wasn't anything the doctors could do. As time went on, his eye just started getting cloudy."

"Damn. That must be tough for him."

"Naw, he's never known anything different, so I don't think it bothers him much."

"Everyone has their imperfections, I guess." I shrugged, feeling like that was something my Dad would say.

"What're yours?" Caleb chuckled. "Red hair and pale skin?"

"Oh, okay!" I said, acting offended. I pantomimed, opening the driver-side door to storm out. Caleb laughed. "We can't all have perfect tanned skin!"

"I get it from my Dad's side of the family," Caleb said with a smile. Every time I saw the dimples in his cheeks, it sent me soaring through the air. "He's Puerto Rican. Luckily, Parker got most of my Dad's traits. He's kind and curious... for now."

"And your mom?"

"She's white. You're all Irish, I assume?"

"Oh, completely! My mom is..." I paused and then tried to speed up my next set of words as if I had lost no time in between. "... She was a redhead too." I watched Caleb as he just smirked and nodded. I hoped he couldn't tell I was thrown off. As much as I loved Caleb opening up to me, I just wasn't ready.

"Parker gets his red hair from our mom too."

The conversation came to a lull and the awkward air returned. We stared as the woman with her dog passed the car.

Caleb waved at her. "Hey, Mrs. Watson."

The woman gave a weak wave back to Caleb as she walked by.

"Do you ever talk to Parker about your Dad?" It surprised me I hadn't scared him off yet.

"We've shown him a few pictures," Caleb said, unfazed by my constant flow of questions. "I tell him things I remember. I tell him how gentle he used to be. He was the polar opposite of the guy that my mom's with now. I try to remind Parker that not every guy is a bully." Caleb's eyes met mine, and I glanced down at my lap after feeling a bolt of lightning shoot through my stomach.

"My Dad used to be more of a hard ass," I said. "He's cooled down a lot over the past couple of months. But he used to talk to me like a drill sergeant."

"At least he had the balls to stick around," Caleb said with a tone I hadn't heard from him. It was colder. It seemed his Dad leaving had a powerful impact on him.

"So," I said, unsure if I should continue with my question. *He's still in the car, I haven't scared him off yet.*

"Earlier you said you felt like it was your fault, why is that?"

Caleb let out a small huff. He didn't answer right away.

I panicked and said, "You totally don't have to answer that. My questions are way too much, I'm sorry."

"You're good," Caleb said as stared out his window. "It was almost ten years ago, but it still feels fresh in my mind. The Christmas before he left, he was excited to give me a specific present. I remember him handing me the gift and I noticed how messy the wrapping job was." I stared at him. His eyes followed a flock of birds that flew by. "I ripped through the paper and stared at what was inside. It was a baseball cap." Caleb looked at me and laughed, "I swear it was the ugliest hat I'd ever seen."

"Oh, no," I said through gritted teeth.

"It was like this weird combination of blues and browns like someone had stitched two separate ugly hats together into one. I kind of made a face and tossed it aside with a quick thank you. 'Well, try it on.' my Dad said. I reluctantly grabbed it off the floor and put it on. I wasn't a kid that was into wearing hats." Caleb was reenacting the scene with his hands, pretending to put on the hat and unwrap a gift. "I pulled it off just as quickly as I put it on. My Dad was disappointed, but I was too excited for more gifts to notice. I remember just tossing it under my bed that night and forgetting about it." Caleb's hands calmed. "Two days after Christmas, I woke up and could hear my mom crying in her bedroom. I checked on her and the room was a mess. She was sitting alone on the bed, just sobbing. I was so confused. Then I noticed the top of their dresser was empty. All of my Dad's deodorants and colognes were gone. The closet door was open and most of his clothes were missing, and hangers were scattered on the floor."

A small pit formed in my stomach as I listened to Caleb tell the story. I knew what it felt like to find a parent crying alone.

Caleb continued as he fiddled with the strings hanging from his thin hoodie, "I asked her where Dad was and all I could hear between her sobs was that he left. I didn't believe her because I remember searching every room, hoping he'd be there, but he wasn't. Then I thought about that ugly hat." The sun was set and the street lights popped on around us. Both of our eyes caught the porch light turn on from Caleb's trailer. "Every time I left the house, I'd put on the hat he got me. I wore it everywhere, I guess just hoping that somehow he would see me wearing it and want to come back home with us. But we never saw him again."

I pictured a smaller version of Caleb with the same face but shaggier hair, walking around the mall, with his ugly hat on, holding his mom's hand with hope in his eyes, hope that would never be fulfilled.

"As I got older," Caleb said, "It was probably my mom that drove him away with her budding drug habits. Of course, we've never talked about it. Her relationship with drugs got stronger. I was always the one taking care of Parker. Made me feel like an adult real quick."

"I'm sorry. That's a lot to go through as a kid."

"You'd be surprised."

Suddenly the screen door was thrown open and a tall, bald man stepped onto the porch.

"Speak of the devil," Caleb mumbled as he looked through

the window at the man wearing a dark blue jumpsuit with grease stains all over it. His beer belly seemed to be pushing the buttons to their limits. He stood there barefoot, staring at us.

"Yer ma needs ya fer somethin'," The bald man said toward us with a southern twang.

"Coming," Caleb said before turning back to me. "So, think you've got enough information for the book I assume you're writing about me?" He smiled.

"Damn, I forgot to take notes, can you say all that again?"

It felt good to make Caleb laugh.

"Thanks again for the ride," Caleb said as he opened the car door. "I'll see you around."

"Yeah," I said as I watched him walk up the steps, his work boots clunking against the wood. He pushed past the tall man without a word of acknowledgment. My eyes were locked on the porch, I didn't want Caleb to leave. The tall man stood there, giving my car the once over before disappearing inside. I turned the key in the ignition and rolled up Celebs open window before doing a U-turn and driving back toward the main road.

The car was so quiet after they left. I couldn't stop thinking about Caleb and the story he told me, still surprised that he opened up to me. I wondered if he had that kind of relationship with anyone else or if I was a fluke. Maybe my questions were enough to nag him into submission, maybe he told me just to get me to stop asking questions. I couldn't stop thinking about how he acted with Parker either. For a guy so mysterious and brooding, he was so warm and patient with Parker. Seeing the two of them eating ice cream, I would never imagine them having a tough time at home. I could imagine Caleb having loud arguments with the bald man, who I assumed was his mom's boyfriend. I pictured Caleb playing with army men in Parker's bedroom to distract him from the voices growing louder as their mom and the bald man got drunker. I wondered if Parker knew that Caleb was forced to do community service. After seeing them together today, I couldn't imagine Caleb breaking the law. But as he said, there's a lot I don't know about him.

I remembered my college applications as soon as I walked back into my house. Inspiration had hit, and I was ready to write my short story.

"You were gone a while," my Dad said from the couch, scaring me half to death. The entire living room was dark besides the small lamp that was lit next to the recliner he was sitting in. He was reading the newspaper from that day.

"Yeah, sorry, I ran into a friend that needed a ride," I said, moving toward the stairs.

"Hang on, son," he said before I could touch the first carpeted step. I was eager to get to my computer before the inspiration faded. I stopped and turned toward him with a sigh, waiting for him to speak. "This article says I'm a few points ahead in the race."

"That's great, Dad," I pretended to care and started for the steps again before his voice stopped me.

"Landon, can you wait just a second?"

"I'm sorry, but I have this assignment."

"Well, the team recommended I speak at a church tomorrow, and they think it would look good if my son was there with me."

"Dad, I have school tomorrow, it's a Wednesday."

"It's after school."

"I have practice, I can't," I said, thankful that I could use it as an excuse. I didn't want to go to church.

"Coach told me he pushed practice to Thursday. He's gonna announce it tomorrow morning." He folded the newspaper as my excuse burned up. I rolled my eyes. Of all the days to reschedule practice.

"Who goes to church on a Wednesday?"

"A lot of people." My Dad stood and walked toward the

kitchen counter. "And we'll be two of them tomorrow, so come home right after school and put on something nice. You don't have a say in this one."

"Fine," I said as I started up the stairs, leaping over every other step. I sat at my desk and revived my sleeping laptop. The familiar blank page popped up on my screen and my fingers started their usual dance across the keyboard. For the next two hours, I was transported into my little world, where characters came to life and all I could hear was the clicking of the keys.

FIFTEEN

"I can't believe you got yourself shot," I said to Dan as we stepped out of the school and into the front courtyard.

Dan puffed his chest. "I told you that if it came down to it, I was gonna control my fate."

"You're such an idiot." I laughed, shoving him. "Did it hurt?"

"Have you ever been shot with a paintball, Griffin?"

"No, I can't say I have."

"Well, it hurts like a bitch."

"You got shot in the leg, princess," I said with an eyebrow raised. "I'm sure you'll survive."

Dan returned the shove. "Fuck off."

I tried to catch my footing, but I backed into someone. I turned around, apologizing. It was Steven. He turned to face me, I'd caused him to spill his green juice all over himself. Steven's white shirt was splattered with what looked like an infant's vomit. Dan started laughing.

"Steven, I'm so sorry. Dan pushed--"

Dan cut me off with a shout, "Did we ruin your blouse, faggot?" Dan then acted as a crying baby, bringing his fists up to his eyes to wipe the fake tears.

"You're such an asshole!" Steven said as he stormed off toward the school's entrance. His words were an instant trigger for Dan, sending him into rage mode.

"What did you call me?!" I had to put my body in front of Dan to stop him from going after Steven. "Come say that to my face, pussy!"

"Dan, stop!" I tried to get him to focus on me. His eyes remained on Steven, but his body language calmed. "Why does he set you off so easily?" My hand dropped off his chest.

"Because he's a fuckin' freak, bro. Every time I see his fairy face, I just want to slap the shit out of him." Dan bent down, picking up his backpack that fell off of his shoulder. "His parents should send him to one of those conversion camps or some shit and set him straight."

"You don't seriously think that works, do you?" Tasha asked as she and Lauren approached us on the sidewalk. Dan was speaking loud enough for everyone to hear.

"I remember my pastor talking about it when we would go to church," Dan said. His breathing had gone back to normal. "One time he brought this guy up to the altar as an example. He said the guy went through this program that turned him straight after being gay his whole life."

"That's impossible," Lauren said. "You can't just switch it off."

"Yeah, it sounds like a bunch of bullshit to me. Not all Christians and Catholics support conversation therapy. " Tasha said, giving Dan a suspicious look.

"The guy had a wife and kids!" Dan gestured out with his hands. "They were sitting right there in the front row! It fuckin' works, trust me."

I pictured older versions of Lauren and me. We were living in my parent's house. Everything was the same except for the baby playpen in the living room. And there was no carpet going up the steps, everything was glistening hardwood. I had a few gray hairs poking through on the sides of my head, and I could hear Lauren in the upstairs bathroom laughing. I also heard a smaller laugh echoing down the stairway, accompanied by water splashing about. Could this be my future? I saw myself standing at the kitchen counter watching the side door as the knob turned and Caleb walked through. I was startled back into reality as soon as I saw his face in the vision.

"You can't argue science!" Lauren said with a scoff as she reached for my arm.

"Someone needs to check that guy's browser history," Tasha said with a chuckle. "Then we'd know for sure." We all started laughing.

I wondered if my Dad would send me away if he found out I had feelings for Caleb. He might see conversion camp as a sort of boot camp. From the way my Dad reacted to *Will & Grace*, it wouldn't surprise me if he knew about conversion therapy. I pictured myself running away from pastors trying to force me onto a bus.

Dan's voice broke my thought when he said, "Me and Chris have our costumes for the party. You guys are still in, right?"

"Duh!" Tasha said. "That reminds me, I need to update the Facebook event. I should do that tonight."

It reminded me I had to pull a costume together for the ridiculous party.

Lauren sighed. "I'm gonna have serious FOMO you guys! Why'd you have to have a party when I'm in New York?"

"My birthday gets rescheduled for no one!" Dan said dramatically. "I gotta go, since practice got moved to tomorrow, I'm gonna go see this chick." Dan put his fist out and I gave him a bump back.

"Wear protection!" I shouted at him as he walked away. Dan turned on his heels and walked backward, flashing us a peace sign that he then flicked his tongue between.

"He's disgusting," Tasha said. "All right girlie, I got shit to do. I'll text you later!" Tasha hugged Lauren goodbye, and I got a wave. "Bye Landon."

"See ya," I said.

Tasha walked away before Lauren placed herself in front of me. Things still felt awkward between us since the night she tried to hook up with me.

Lauren's hair was pushed to the left by a small breeze that smelled like gas from all the cars leaving the parking lot. She wasn't wearing her fake glasses that day. "What're you gonna wear to the party?" She moved her windy hair to the back of her ear, staring up at me.

"I haven't thought about it yet," I said. "I just want something simple, ya know?"

"I can get you some tights from the costume closet, maybe you can be Peter Pan."

"You think Dan would ever let me live that one down?"

"Absolutely not." Things got quiet, I wondered if she told Tasha or Steven about how I couldn't get hard that night. I could feel the embarrassment wash over me before Lauren broke the silence. "Let's go to Lucky's."

"I can't today, I'm sorry," I said with a frown, even though I had been craving a chocolate milkshake.

"How come?"

"My Dad is making me go to church with him." I could see the confusion set in as she scrunched her face. "His team wants him to speak there, hoping to draw in some more voters or something. He's making me go with him. Said it would be good if people saw him with his family. Lucky me..." I raised my fists in jest of celebration, "... I'm the only one left." Lauren slapped my arm. She didn't like my dark humor.

"That sounds nice. Maybe we can go on Sunday, that's the next day I'm free."

I shrugged. "Yeah, that works for me." Lauren grabbed me by the hands, pulling me closer to her.

"I feel like we need to have some us time and like, reconnect."

"I agree," I said as I tried to push away the thoughts of the night I rejected her.

"It's a date then!" Lauren smiled widely. I nodded, and she stood on her tiptoes to kiss me. It surprised me when she slipped her tongue between my lips, giving me a deeper kiss. My hands let go of hers, but I continued to kiss her back.

"Landon!" My Dad shouted from across the street. I unlocked from Lauren, quickly turning my attention to my Dad, who was standing next to his car. "We have to go! Get upstairs and change."

"Coming!" I looked back at Lauren. "I'll text you later?"

"Okay," she said as she grabbed my hands again. "Have fun."

"Yeah, I'll try." I tried to pull away from her, but I could feel she wanted another kiss, so I planted a quick one on her lips before running across the street.

"Love you!"

"You too!" I yelled without looking back.

I opened my closet door and spotted a black blazer I hadn't worn since my junior year homecoming dance. I grabbed it off the hanger and threw it on my bed. My jeans that day were dark and a tighter fit, so I left them on. I glided to the bottom drawer of my dresser, popping it open. My mom always said I should keep my dressier clothes in the bottom drawer because I'd probably wear them the least. I pulled out a red button-up I had gotten from my grandma for Christmas two years ago. I pulled my T-shirt over my head and slipped on the red one. As I buttoned it up, it kept getting tighter and tighter around my shoulders. It was almost impossible to button the top button without choking myself, so I left it undone. I stared at myself in the mirror and winced; I could see every rib and muscle I had. "I can't wear this to a church," I said to myself as I turned to see what it looked like from the back.

I heard my Dad's car horn blare. He was becoming impatient. I quickly undid the buttons and let the shirt fall to the floor. I jogged back over to my bottom drawer, pulling out a blue button-up shirt instead. It fit a lot looser.

"Things seem to be going well with Lauren," Dad said as he turned the steering wheel, pulling off our street.

"Yeah." I shrugged, embarrassed that he'd seen us making out. I was standoffish, I had a lot on my mind and the last thing I wanted was to sit in a stuffy church.

"How'd the assignment turn out last night?"

"Fine, actually," I said, staring out the window. "I got it submitted."

The car in front of us didn't move when the light turned green, so my Dad knocked on his horn, "c'mon man."

I hadn't told my Dad about the college applications, about them being out of state, or that I was submitting for writing programs.

"You should hear from the state schools any day now," my Dad said as if he could read my mind. "I know you'll get a scholarship. I can feel it."

A pit formed in my stomach again. I wanted to make him happy, and to make him proud, but how do I tell him I didn't want to pursue football? Thinking about seeing his face shrink into disappointment filled me with dread. I looked out the window, everything was so cookie-cutter in Madison. Every house looked the same. Every other front yard had kids playing in it. People were walking their perfect little dogs. I thought about the vision I had, hearing Lauren laughing with a baby in the upstairs bathroom. Could I feel fulfilled in that kind of life? I'd never even visited a big city. Who knows if I would even like it? I'd be a fish out of water, and everyone would be able to tell how phony I was.

As we pulled into the parking lot of the church, I read their marquee sign that was facing the street. It was red at the top, with white bold letters, letting everyone know it was 'Madison Catholic Bible Church.' Underneath the header, there was a digital screen where they could display the events being held that day. It read 'Guest Speaker: Republican Mayoral Candidate Curtis Griffin.'

We stepped out of the car after parking in a spot reserved for someone named Pastor Williams.

I looked at my Dad. "Where should I go?"

"You can go through the front," a voice said from behind me. I could hear the clunk of her heels against the pavement. I turned around to see my Dad's campaign manager, Grace. She was around my Dad's age and had her hair up in a tight bun. She was wearing a burgundy blazer and skirt. She held a clipboard in one hand as if she were about to take roll call. She honestly looked very put together and professional to me. "I'm gonna take your Dad around back with me."

"Okay," I said.

"You look very handsome, Landon," she said as she flanked my Dad.

"Oh." I smoothed out my blazer. "Thanks." Compliments made me feel awkward. "Good luck, Dad."

"I'll see you in there, buddy," he said, walking away with Grace. I lingered on them for a moment to catch her pass him some note cards. I shoved my hands in my pockets and walked toward the entrance.

I followed the crowd of mostly older white people into the church. There were a few empty pews in the back where I sat, hoping no one would join me. Most of the men were dressed in suits. Each seemed to have a woman attached to his arm, wearing a nice dress, some form of pastel color that reminded me of a carton of Easter eggs.

The pews were filling up, I never expected so many people wanting to listen to my Dad speak, I always thought his speeches were a snooze. The air smelled like old wood and upholstered fabric as if they hadn't changed the seating in a hundred years. The acoustics were strong. The echoes of everyone's voice floated up through the high ceilings, bounced off the rafters, and returned to my ears as one collective sound of chatter. A white-haired man approached the podium at the altar. I wondered if he was Pastor Williams.

"Welcome everyone!" The Pastor said into the microphone, shutting down all forms of conversation from the crowd. "We are so blessed to have Mr. Griffin here to speak to our congregation today, thank you all so much for being here." The pastor pulled out a notecard from his pocket and placed it on the podium. "Before we bring out our guest, I just wanted to remind you of all the upcoming fundraising events." That's when I tuned out.

My family was never the church-going type. My mom would ask us to go to Sunday mass at Easter and Christmas, but we were never in church every week. I assumed it was a ploy by my Dad's campaign team to string in the votes of the conservative church folk. I squirmed in my seat a little. Religion always felt cult-like to me. I never quite understood the draw to it. I was a co-captain of a football team, so I could understand camaraderie and a sense of community, but fearing God while telling other religious people that their beliefs weren't valid just seemed very off to me. But those were the people my Dad hoped to represent. He had been lucky enough to stay clear of hot-button political issues so far, like abortion or gun control. He got by on being a blue-collar, military family man. That was enough for most people in Madison.

"Good afternoon, everyone!" My Dad said enthusiastically from the podium. He had been superintendent of Madison High School for three years by then, so he had no trouble speaking to an audience, he was quite good at it. "It's an honor to speak in front of you today..."

My Dad was just going into his plan to boost the jobs and wages for working families in Madison when I felt my phone vibrate. I inched it out of my pocket as if my Dad had eagle eyes, afraid that he would catch me not paying attention and call me out in front of all the people. I had a Grindr notification. Every night before bed I would see the app on my screen and think about deleting it, but my fun conversations with Steven always pulled me away from doing it. I ignored every other message I got. I opened the app, seeing a message from Steven.

THEATRENERD245, 18

Hey!

SPORTYGUY83, 18

Hey, how are you?

THEATRENERD245, 18

I'm okay. Kind of having a shitty afternoon.

SPORTYGUY83, 18

Oh, I'm sorry. You wanna talk about it?

By that point, Steven and I had had some lengthy conversations on Grindr. I was getting to know him and he was getting to know the real me, not the fake me I portrayed when I was at school. I was weightless and free when I messaged him. I was able to talk about Caleb, without using his name of course. It felt great to talk about Caleb's dimples and how sexy they were, and how I could stare into his eyes for days. Now and then Steven would try to slip in questions to figure out who I was, but I always caught on and changed the subject.

THEATRENERD245, 18

There's just this guy at school who continuously makes my life hell.

SPORTYGUY83, 18

Oh?

THEATRENERD245, 18

He seems like he goes out of his way to embarrass me in front of people or threaten me.

SPORTYGUY83, 18

I'm sorry, man.

THEATRENERD245, 18

I've been dealing with this for four years, I'm so tired of it you know? I can't wait to get out of this white bread town and finally start living.

That sounded nice to me, too.

THEATRENERD245, 18

We used to be friends. The things I know about him could ruin his life. But I'm a nice person!

Steven piqued my curiosity. What did he know about Dan that I didn't?

SPORTYGUY83, 18

What do you mean? Like what?

THEATRENERD245, 18

Ugh, it doesn't matter. I need to get out of this negative headspace! >_< What're you up to?

SPORTYGUY83, 18:

Believe it or not, I'm in a church right now, haha.

THEATRENERD245, 18

OMG no way! How are you not burned to a crisp by now? Lol, I never pictured you as a closeted bible boy!

SPORTYGUY83, 18

Yeah, I'm not exactly.

THEATRENERD245, 18

Well, you better get out of there before they make you straight! Lol

Nothing sounds worse right now than being straight lol

I heard my name come from my Dad's booming voice, and quickly put my phone away. He was gesturing to me, introducing me as his son. Everyone sitting in the pews turned around and smiled at me. I slid down in my seat a bit, seeing all of their smiling faces gave me the creeps. Luckily, my Dad moved on quickly and brought the attention back to him. I sighed, laying my head against the back of the pew. It seemed like the speech would last for eternity.

SIXTEEN

I opened my eyes to see the high rafters of the church. A beam of light was shining through a stained glass window that led to a huge wooden cross at the altar. I sprung up in the pew, realizing the crowd whittled down to a select few. I saw my Dad helping arrange folding chairs into a circle in front of the altar stage. The people who were left congregated around the circle.

"Landon," my Dad said. "Come join us, please."

I stood and brushed my hands down my blazer, confused about where everyone had gone and without me noticing.

I walked down the aisle as the others took their seats in the circle. "What's going on?"

"Take a seat," Dad said, motioning to an empty chair.

"Um... okay." I glanced at the others who were seated. There were no women, only men of varying ages. Across from me was a man with a thick beard and bandaged wrists. Next to him was a skinny teenager, no older than fourteen. The more I looked at everyone's faces, the more I realized how miserable they looked. Then I noticed something even more strange. Everyone was wearing white slacks and a white shirt; some long sleeves, some short but all the same shade. My Dad was standing behind me, I looked up at him over my shoulder. "Dad, what is this?"

"They're here to help, son."

"Help with what?" His eyes fixated on something. Following his gaze, I saw the white-haired pastor step into the chair circle, taking the last empty seat. "Dad..." I said, wondering why he hadn't answered me.

"Don't be nervous, Landon," the pastor said. "My name is Pastor Williams. We are all here today for you."

"What do you mean for me?" I glanced to my right to see a man with a freshly shaved head. He was looking at his lap and fiddling his thumbs, not making eye contact with anyone.

"Your father came to me with concerns," Pastor Williams said. "I recommended that you join our program here at the church so we could help set you on the right path."

I tilted my head, still in the dark about what was happening. "What? What path?" I looked up at my Dad again. "Dad, what is he talking about?"

My Dad shushed me and placed his hands on my shoulders.

"These men," Pastor Williams said. "Have all been set free under my guidance." He pointed at the man sitting to my right, "long feminine hair afflicted Kyle. People would often mistake him for a woman. We started him on his path by shaving it off." My eyebrows furrowed as I looked at Kyle. He remained silent with his eyes in his lap. "And Carson." I looked at the white-haired pastor in time to see him point at the bearded man. "He was so distraught over his addiction to pornography that he tried to take his own life." Carson then pulled down his sleeves to hide his bandages. "And this poor boy, Ryan," Pastor Williams said as he kneeled, placing his hand on the teenage boy's thigh. Ryan moved his leg away, not wanting to be touched. "They caught him fornicating with the son of the family next door, so his parents sent him to me."

"This has nothing to do with me," I said as I stood from my chair, but my Dad pushed me back down from my shoulders and held them.

"Oh, but it does, Landon," the pastor said as he walked behind Ryan. He stroked Ryan's hair like he was petting a puppy. Just watching it sent a chill down my spine. "Every man in this circle is plagued by homosexual perversion."

"I'm not!" I squirmed in my seat, trying to get my Dad to ease his grip. "Dad, tell him!"

"We know, Landon," Pastor Williams said as he penetrated the circle again, sauntering toward me. "We know about the videos you've watched." He inched closer. "We know about the app on your phone. We know..." He kneeled in front of me. "... about the feelings, you have for Caleb." My eyes widened. I wanted to refute the claims but suddenly couldn't speak. Pastor Williams placed both hands on my thighs and crawled them toward my crotch. "Do you admit to these sins?" His face moved closer to mine as his hands inched up my legs. I wanted to scream, but my voice was trapped in my throat. "Can you repent for your sins?!" The pastor screamed in my face. Flicks of saliva hit my cheeks. My jaw was clenched and I could feel my teeth grinding together. The pastor let go of my thighs and stood. "We must start you on your path to righteousness," the pastor said as he walked around the circle again, his hands clasped behind his back.

My Dad pulled me up by my shoulders and guided me onto the altar stage. I felt my voice break free. "Dad, stop!" I shouted. "What're you doing?!" I glimpsed his face. His eyes were glazed over. He was a shell of the man I knew. He was a bodyguard of God, hauling me toward my fate. He pushed me face-first against the wooden cross that stood behind the podium where he'd given his speech. My right cheek burned from the hard slap against the mahogany, and it smelled like a campfire. "Dad, please!"

Two men dressed in white tied my hands around the other side of the thick cross. I could feel the rope getting tighter around my wrists, digging into my skin. It was all happening so fast that it was difficult for my brain to catch up and understand. I could hear the slicing of fabric as Pastor Williams slid a pair of scissors up the middle of my blazer and then again to my blue button-up shirt. The frayed fabric tickled my sides as I felt them fall, revealing my bare skin. My knees shook.

"What the fuck!" I could hear my voice echo through the church. "Dad, make them stop!"

"This is for the best, son," Dad whispered.

I felt the searing sting against my back. I scrunched my eyes closed and let out a yelp.

"This is where we all must begin on our path!" Pastor Williams' voice boomed through my ears. I opened my eyes and looked behind me, struggling to break free from my restraints. Every man dressed in white lined themselves in a single file, ready to take the whip from the person in front. The second man stepped toward me. It was Carson with glazed eyes. He raised his arm and shot down the whip against my back with no remorse. The pain splintered into my skull and I let out a loud cry.

It was the fourth lash that sent me crumbling to my knees. The teenage boy held the whip, he raised it with no hesitation and connected it to my body with an overwhelming force. My skin had ripped open, sending spits of blood into the air. I went numb after the sixth time they hit me. All I could feel was the blood trickling down my back and tears running down my cheeks. I pressed my forehead against the wood, opening my eyes to a stream of blood pooling around my knees.

"Dad, please make them stop," I said through my shortened breath. I was sobbing and squeezed my eyes shut as another strike of the whip hit. The tears pushed from my eyes. "I don't want to be gay, I promise!" I screamed, not able to withstand the torture anymore. I hoped my words would make them subside, but I heard another crack of the whip before feeling the burn.

"Tell God what you're thankful for!" The pastor yelled. "If you continue to deny this disease that put you here, you will never become clean!"

I felt like I was dying. I had no more blood left to lose and no more tears left to cry. I opened my eyes to look to my father for forgiveness, but he was no longer there. Instead, I saw my mother standing where the shell of my Dad was moments before.

"Landon," she said. I missed hearing her voice. It was gentle and warm. I gave her a weak smile, finally feeling at peace.

"Landon!" I was shaken awake by my Dad. I sat up straight in the pew, rubbing a hand down my face. I looked around the church, people were filing out. "Were you asleep for my entire speech?"

"No," I said with a crack in my voice. "Of course not." I wiped some drool from the corner of my mouth.

"Go to the car," Dad said. I don't think he believed me. "We're going home."

I did what I was told. Walking into the parking lot, I felt bad I was asleep for most of the speech, I couldn't even remember when I dozed off. I sat in the passenger seat of my Dad's car, still thinking about the terrifying nightmare. I had no desire to step foot in a church again. I knew my dream was extreme but I'm sure that's how a conversion camp could feel to some people. It wouldn't have even been in my head if Dan didn't bring it up. I made a mental note to be more aware of my surroundings while on Grindr. My Dad could've easily seen my phone if it was open while I was asleep.

I looked out the window as people passed by getting back to their cars, noticing my Dad and Grace having a conversation, standing three parking spaces away. My eyes zeroed in on their lips, trying to read them. I saw Grace reach to fix my Dad's tie. The way she was smiling and looking up at him made my stomach turn. Her hands swiftly moved from his tie to his chest, placing her hands flat against him. I felt a fire in my chest as my eyes squinted.

I opened the car door so my Dad could hear me shout. "Dad, let's go!" He stared at me with a furrowed brow. He may have been taken aback by my tone. His attention went back to Grace, and they said their goodbyes.

"Bye, Landon," Grace called out to me, but I just slammed the car door.

"You were incredibly rude," Dad said as we walked into the house. I'd been silent the whole ride home. I was about to ascend the stairs, but my Dad stopped me with his voice. "What the hell has gotten into you?"

I whipped around and glared at him, taking off my blazer. "It's been six months!" I shouted. "Mom has been gone for six months, and Grace is all over you as if mom died six YEARS ago!" I threw my blazer on the stools resting at the kitchen's island.

"Oh, come on, Landon. You don't know what you're talking about."

"Come on, what?! I saw it. She couldn't keep her hands off you!" I could feel my face getting warm. "Are you guys like... a thing?"

"No, son," my Dad said, sounding deflated. "It's professional, I promise."

"Is that why you have so many late nights? Are you spending them with her?"

My Dad pointed at me. "You watch your mouth when you talk to me."

I stood my ground as he sat on one of the island stools. "Do you even think about Mom anymore?"

"Landon, do not go there with me," he said as he raised his hand to stop my questioning.

"Well, do you?!"

"Goddammit!" Dad smacked his fist on the counter. "Of course I do! I can't *stop* thinking about her! I see her everywhere in this house!" He stood from the stool, taking a step toward me, I could see the redness around his eyes. "I thank God every damn day that you aren't the one who found her. You're lucky you don't have to live with that. You think it's easy for me to step foot in that office every day?!" He pointed his gorilla-sized arm toward the small hallway that housed his office. "It kills me, but I do it because I HAVE to, Landon, to give us a fuckin' life worth living!"

I felt a shooting pain down my stomach and my eyes well up. "Dad, I'm s--"

"Go to your room," he said, cutting me off before I could finish my apology. "I'm done with your attitude today."

He sank back onto the stool, rubbing his forehead with one hand. I sighed as I grabbed my blazer and climbed up the stairs.

I felt awful for what I said, not realizing what my Dad must've been going through. I got so heated when I saw Grace touching him; it wasn't like she didn't know about my mom. I'm sure my Dad liked the attention, or maybe he was oblivious to it all. I knew he eventually had to move on and find someone new, but not that soon. Everything was still fresh and sore. I thought it tortured me, but my Dad was right, I'm lucky I wasn't the one who found her in the office. I can't imagine the nightmares I would've had.

I pulled out my phone. My conversation with Steven was still open. I swiped the app closed and opened my photo album. I wasn't the type to take a lot of pictures, that was Lauren's thing. She would take selfies of us all the time and text them to me.

I scrolled past the pictures of me and Lauren, and covers of books I had seen at Barnes & Noble. I finally reached the pictures I wanted of me and my mom. I took them when she was in the chemo phase of her treatment. She encouraged me to take them in case things got worse, and I'm glad I did.

I clicked on a picture to make it full-screen, staring at it. My mom was sitting in a recliner under the fluorescent lights of the room, tubes running from her arm. I was sitting in a folding chair next to her. She was wearing a pink and purple silk scarf around her bald head that had flower patterns on it. A gossip magazine rested on the lap of her hospital gown; it splayed large yellow letters across its cover that said 'WILL BRAD AND JEN GET BACK TOGETHER?' My mom loved reading those things, especially when she was in the hospital. She said reading about the lavish life of celebrities made her forget about her situation.

Our faces were pressed together, looking into the camera lens with big smiles. I cherished that picture so much. Weeks after she died, I would look at it every night before going to sleep. Sometimes I'd cry, other times I'd laugh, thinking about the stupid celebrity gossip she would relay to me. But I always kept my phone open on that picture next to my pillow, just to feel like she was still there. As I stared, thinking she was just as beautiful bald as she was with hair, I realized it wasn't fair that I'd accused my Dad of not thinking about her. I wondered if he looked through pictures at night too when he was alone. I can't imagine the pain that came with losing your spouse.

I wiped the tears forming in my eyes and placed my phone

on my desk, with the picture still on the screen. I opened my laptop to check my email, hoping I'd have something from the schools I'd submitted to.

It's only been a day, idiot.

It was too soon. All I had from the schools were confirmation emails that I'd submitted my applications, with NYU's at the top of the list. I closed my laptop with a sigh and thought about Caleb, wondering what he might be doing. Maybe watching a movie with Parker. I pictured them sitting in front of a big TV with a gigantic bowl of popcorn. Then I imagined Caleb tossing a piece at Parker, which caused an all-out popcorn war. That made me smile.

SEVENTEEN

I hadn't seen Caleb in two days until I noticed him raking leaves around the perimeter of the football field during our rescheduled practice. Dan and I were discussing a play with the guys when Caleb caught my eye. He was wearing a pair of khaki shorts and running shoes. I felt like he knew he was teasing me with the number of tank tops he wore, and on that Thursday afternoon, it was a black one. I could see the definition of his triceps every time he pulled the rake.

"Do you think it'll work?" Dan said to me, but I was a million miles away. He looked up and caught me staring. "Landon," he said, waving a hand in front of my face.

I woke up from my trance and nodded, not truly understanding what he was talking about. Not that I needed to. We had done the plays on the field a hundred times.

"All right, break!" Dan yelled.

Everyone got into formation. I dazedly walked to my spot on the twenty-yard line.

Coach split the team up into sub-teams, one side wearing yellow mesh over their jerseys, the other side wearing blue mesh. Dan and I were on the yellow team. Waiting for everyone to get to their places, I heard a tick of rain hit my helmet as it started to sprinkle.

"Red thirty-three!" Dan shouted as he stood behind the guy playing center.

Dan had the ball snapped into his palms and everyone started running. I needed to get out half a yard before Dan could throw the ball my way. I was watching for anyone around me in case I needed to weave through them, but I caught another glimpse of Caleb through the slit of my helmet. He was wiping the rain off the back of his neck. I'd never been jealous of the rain until I saw the way it slid down his shoulders. I wanted to touch him like the water had, with no hesitation or doubt.

SMACK! Someone had laid me out against the soft grass of the field. The crack of our helmets sent an echo through the empty bleachers. I groaned for a second as I laid there, the rain trickling through my helmet, onto my face. He pushed his weight off of me, it was Chris.

"Sorry, not sorry," he said, looking down at me with an evil grin. He reached out his arm to help me up, but I waved him off.

"I think I'm just gonna lay here for a sec," I said through a quick breath.

"Take a five-minute break, guys!" Coach shouted, causing Chris to run toward the bench for water. I sat up, trying to find my bearings after the tackle. Looking ahead of me, Caleb was leaning his forearms on the chain-link fence that separated the football field from the rest of the open greenery. He gave me a small wave and a smile. I glanced behind me, thinking it might be one of those situations where he was waving at someone else, but no one was there. He was waving at me. I swallowed with a gulp, pushing myself off the ground. I jogged over to Caleb, noticing my chest was a little sore from the impact as I stepped onto the soft asphalt of the track that surrounded the field. I could hear my cleats clicking against the ground as I approached the fence.

"You okay? Looked like you got hit pretty hard."

"Yeah." I took off my helmet. "I'm all right. Chris forgets this is practice, not an actual game," I said with a groan, rolling my shoulder.

"It sounded like a car crash."

"Yeah, it's even louder when you're the one getting hit."

"I'm actually glad I saw you," Caleb said with a smirk.

"Really?" I tried to keep the excitement from bursting through my stomach.

"Yeah, I wanted to thank you again for the ride the other night."

"It was no problem." I noticed I was grabbing the facemask of my helmet so hard that my fingers stung.

"Parker won't stop talking about you, believe it or not." Caleb was completely wet from the rain at that point, and his tank top was vacuum-formed to his chest. I tried my hardest not to stare. "He's been asking if we're gonna see you again."

"I'd like to see him again, he's a cool kid."

"I'm taking him to see a special screening of Jurassic Park at the old theater in Millbrook tomorrow for the movie's anniversary."

"Oh, awesome."

"Since you've never seen it, I was hoping you'd come with us?"

"Oh." I tried to play it cool, but on the inside I was jumping and squealing in an imaginary room, bouncing off the walls like a Looney Toons character. "I don't want to interfere with your sibling time."

Caleb laughed, gripping the top of the chain-link fence. "Parker insists."

"Well, how could I say no to Parker?" I said with a smile. Caleb chuckled.

"What time are you done tomorrow?"

"2:30ish, since I won't have practice."

"Perfect, the movie starts at three-thirty."

I wanted to stay at the fence until my legs gave out, but Coach was blowing his whistle. I looked behind me to see the guys running onto the field. "Sorry, I gotta get back."

"Yeah, me too."

"You're doing great!" I said as I slipped my helmet back on. I ran backward, still staring at him as he walked back to pick up the rake. "Hey! I'll pick you guys up!"

"Perfect!" Caleb gave me a salute. "Later!"

I turned around and jogged back, hanging on Caleb's last word, 'later'. Not a 'see you later' but just a simple 'later'. I liked that. I pushed through some guys and noticed Chris waving me over, still standing by the benches.

"I think Dan is high on something," Chris whispered.

"What? What makes you say that?"

"His eyes are like, out of control. His pupils are huge."

I looked over to the crowd of players. Dan was doing leaps. "I thought he was selling them, not taking them."

"Guys, c'mon, let's go!" Coach shouted to us.

"Let's keep an eye on him," I said as we started back to the huddle. Chris gave me a nod.

As practice continued, we noticed Dan getting more angry and aggressive. If he threw the ball and someone didn't catch it, he followed it with immediate harassment. I kept reminding him it was only practice and he would tell me to go fuck myself and move on to the next play. We eventually switched up the sub-teams. The rain had gotten harder, making the turf extra slippery. We were starting the next play as I looked to see if

Caleb was still around, but he was gone. He wasn't dressed for the eventual downpour, so I assumed he retreated inside.

"Blue sixteen! Hike!" And just like that, we were off to the races.

Chris was on Dan's yellow mesh team that round. Chris ran off in a different direction than the other players, oblivious to the play that Dan called out. Chris accidentally ran into another yellow mesh player who was supposed to catch Dan's throw. They both smacked the wet grass, causing a splash from a puddle that hit some other guys.

"Dammit, Chris!" Dan screamed as he charged in his direction. Chris was getting off the ground before Dan ran over and pushed him back down. Chris jumped up and shoved Dan back. Some other guys got between them before they started throwing punches. "I said blue sixTEEN!" Dan was being held back by his arms as Coach ran over.

"I thought you said sixty," Chris said. "I'm sorry."

"You're a fucking idiot!" Dan screamed at his brother.

"Wilson!" Coach stepped in front of Dan. "Off the field, you need a break."

"Are you kidding me?" Dan broke free of the restraining grip. "It's not my fault that everyone on this fucking team is too stupid to catch a ball!"

"Go now," Coach said, pointing to the school. "Before I bench you for next week's game."

"Fuck you, this team needs me! Bench me and we'll lose!" Dan said as he pulled off his helmet, spiking it to the ground. We all watched as he walked back toward the school, ripping off his jersey and shoulder pads, dropping them one by one as if he were leaving a trail of breadcrumbs to find his way back. I was disappointed seeing Dan like that on the field. I've seen him be a major douche in school, but he was never like that when we were in our jerseys.

Coach's jaw tightened. The disrespect Dan showed would've gotten any other player benched for a month but he knew Dan was right, we needed his arm.

"Griffin," Coach said, turning his attention to me. "You're calling the shots now."

I was still flying high from Caleb asking me to the movie that they could've asked me to give the okay on a nuke strike as president and I wouldn't have hesitated.

By the time practice was over, the rain had passed, but my uniform was still soaked. As we filed back into the locker room, we were expecting to see Dan, but I should've assumed he wouldn't wait around. I opened my locker and took off my shoes. My socks were sticking to my feet. I reached into my backpack, grabbing my phone to check the time when I saw the text from Lauren.

LAUREN:
Hey, babe, meet me in the parking lot.

ME:
Sorry, practice just ended. You still there?

I peeled off my jersey and pulled the shoulder pads over my head and hung them in the locker to dry.

LAUREN:
Yeah!

ME:
Okay, be there in a sec.

"Dan's been getting worse, it feels like," Chris whispered as he approached me. "He has to be on something, right?"

I was pulling on a pair of jeans and dry socks. "Yeah, something seems off."

"I'll try to talk to him about it tonight."

"Good luck." I scoffed, grateful the duty wasn't on my shoulders.

He held out a fist, and I gave it a light bump with my own. "Thanks, I'll see ya." I had seen Dan and Chris argue a few times over the many years I'd known them, but what happened on the field felt different; I'd never seen Dan show that much aggression toward his brother.

I stepped into the parking lot, hiking my duffle bag over my shoulder when I saw Lauren standing outside her beat-up car. She held her arms up when she saw me, in hopes to wrap them around my neck in a hug.

"I'm really sweaty," I warned her with a smile.

"I don't care," she said, mocking my tone with her voice. I walked into her as she wrapped her arms around me and we stumbled against the car. "Okay, you smell," she said as she gave me a light shove.

"I told you!"

Lauren wiped my sweat off her cheek with the sleeve of her sweater. "What're you doing tonight?"

"Homework, unfortunately, I have a pile of it," I said.

"Same, I'm going to Tasha's now so we can finish our history project."

"Whoa, so fun!" I raised my fists in a fake celebration, which was met with a slap on the chest.

"We're still on for Sunday right?"

"I wouldn't miss it. I can taste the chocolate milkshake already!"

Lauren laughed, pushing herself up on her toes to kiss me. "Good," she said as her lips left mine. "I'll text you."

Lauren turned on her toes, opening her car door as I said goodbye.

. . .

I was walking into my bedroom when my phone rang. I flung my duffle bag on my bed and reached into my pocket and clicked the green button.

"Hey, Dad," I said. "What's up?"

"Wanted to give you a heads up that we're pulling a late one tonight," he said. I could hear a lot of chatter in the background.

"All right,"

"I left you some money on the counter for when you get hungry."

My stomach growled on cue. "Got it, thanks."

"Gotta go,"

"Oh wait, can I use the car tomorrow after school? I'm gonna see a movie with a friend."

"Uh." my Dad lingered on the word for a while. "Yeah, sure, I think we're doing tomorrow night's meeting at the house, anyway."

"Awesome, thanks."

"All right stay out of trouble," my Dad said before I heard him start to talk to someone else, then hang up, all before I could say goodbye.

Friday rolled around and I couldn't sit still in any of my classes. My excitement for seeing Caleb kept me fueled better than six shots of espresso. I watched the clock in every class, counting each excruciating minute. I had never felt a day go by so slowly. When the last bell finally rang, I sprinted home, not even bothering to say goodbye to anyone. I burst through my bedroom door and I could smell my rotting football gear. The smell filled the room, forcing me to open a window. I was trying to move fast so I wouldn't make us late to the movie, but the clothes needed to be thrown in the wash.

I tripped down the stairs, almost face planting onto the kitchen floor. I grabbed the wooden railing attached to the wall to save myself, causing my clothes to spill down the stairs. I regained my footing and collected them before rounding the corner to the basement when I heard my Dad shout, "Where's the fire?"

"I don't want to be late!" I said into the air, hoping my voice would find my Dad's ears. I shoved the clothes into the washer and poured some liquid soap over the top of them. With a push of a few buttons, I was back leaping up the stairs. I had already wasted ten minutes.

I ripped open a dresser drawer and pushed through my clothes before landing on a black v neck T-shirt. I pulled it over my head, doused myself in cologne, leaped down the stairs and out the door. I pictured the wind from my speed blowing my Dad over as I ran by as If I was the roadrunner.

My excitement manifested itself into a lead foot. I remembered the route to Caleb's house perfectly. I had passed their trailer community a hundred times, but I'd never been inside until I dropped them off that night after ice cream.

The sixth one in, on the right, I thought, but it was Caleb's voice saying it in my head.

I pulled the car in front of their trailer and honked the horn. I could smell the dust creeping in through my open window that had been rustled up by the car's tires.

Parker came running out first, bursting through the screen door. He was wearing a Jurassic Park T-shirt and a pair of khaki shorts. He rushed to the passenger side door and opened it. His small freckled face beamed a smile at me. "Hi, Landon!"

"Hey man," I said, trying to match his enthusiasm.

"Hey!" Caleb's raspy voice rang out as he descended the porch steps. "Backseat, kid."

"Dang," Parker said to himself. He moved to open the back door, revealing Caleb behind him. I swear I felt like I had to catch my breath every time I saw him. Caleb had on a gray tank top with a matching *Jurassic Park* logo on the front, but he wore an open white button-up over it.

"I don't think I got the memo for the matching shirts," I said with a smile as Caleb sat next to me.

"It was Parker's idea."

"Landon," Parker said from the backseat. I put the car in drive and started the U-turn. "I can't believe you've never seen this movie! It's gonna blow your mind!"

"Seatbelt," Caleb said, looking over his shoulder. I smiled into the rearview mirror to see Parker fumble with the belt before clicking it in. "It smells like a Macy's in here," Caleb said with a laugh. I apologized before rolling the windows down from the control panel. I hadn't realized just how much cologne I sprayed. "No, it's fine, I kinda like it." I glanced at him with a smile, catching the dimple in his left cheek.

Millbrook was a twenty-minute drive from Caleb's house. I pulled into the theater's parking lot with ten minutes to spare before the movie started. The theater was a small building with a big neon sign that read OASIS. I hadn't been there since I was a kid. My mom took me to see my first movie ever at OASIS. They were having a special screening of Snow White. I was only four years old and I remember my mom telling me I fell asleep to the tune of 'Heigh-Ho'. The OASIS Theater looked ancient. It only housed four screens. They were known for playing two new movies and two old movies. That day they had been showing *Jurassic Park*, *Dirty Dancing*, and two new movies called *Hashtag Love*, and *Millennium Now*. The building had four spots on the front wall outside where they displayed the posters of the movies they were showing.

"Aw, I wanna see that!" Parker said, pointing to the poster for

Millennium Now. I had no idea what the film could be about. My only clue came from the spaceship on the poster.

As we walked through the swinging front door, we were hit with the overwhelming smell of popcorn. There was a wide gray desk straight in front of us, with one woman standing behind it selling tickets. To the right was a large concession booth surrounded by different colored neon lights. Three people were standing in line waiting for popcorn. The entire floor was a dark blue carpet, with different neon shapes sprawling in different directions. The entire place was stuck in the 80s, but that was part of its charm.

"God, I love this place," Caleb said as he leaned into me to get my attention. He looked around the space with a big smile. Parker was next to him, holding his hand, eyeing the concessions booth.

"I haven't been here since I was like four years old," I said. "I almost forgot about it."

"Welcome back," Caleb said, looking at me. His smile was like an infectious disease taking over my body, inflicting me with a smile that I couldn't get rid of. The three of us stepped up to the counter, and Caleb pulled out his wallet. "Three for Jurassic Park, please." The woman tapped a few things on her computer screen before I heard the printer shooting out the tickets.

"Caleb," I said, "You don't have to--"

"I got it. The old movies are only five bucks each, it's fine." He handed a twenty-dollar bill to the woman, who took it with haste. "You can get the next one." Caleb said nonchalantly, which sent me into a frenzy thinking about the possibility of a "next one." Did that mean he already planned on seeing me again, that he already wanted to? I tried not to hyperventilate over the thought and followed the boys toward screen number three.

"Welcome to Jurassic Park!" Parker said in the deepest voice he could muster.

"Hold onto your butts!" Caleb said as we stepped into the theater. They laughed at each other's imitations, while I had no idea what they were talking about.

EIGHTEEN

"I can't believe how real they looked!" I said as we busted through the doors of the OASIS.

"I told you!" Parker said. "And what about that part when the T-Rex was like, ROOAARRRR!" Parker jumped out in front of us with his arms tucked into his sides. He continued to stomp around as if he were forty feet tall and roaring as loud as he could. Caleb and I watched with smiles on our faces.

"The scene with the raptors in the kitchen is iconic," Caleb said.

"You guys were right, I can't believe it took me until now to see that movie, it was so good!"

"Now you gotta see the second one!" Parker said as he rushed over to me, grabbing my hand.

"Wait, there's more?" I was genuinely curious.

"A lot more," Caleb said. "None of them as good as the original, but yes, there are a few more."

Parker let go of my hand as we approached the car and rushed to Caleb's side. "Can we go to the playground?!" Parker jumped up and down.

"I don't know, kid," Caleb said. "It's gonna be dark soon and Landon has to drive us back, we can't take up more of his time."

Parker's excitement turned to disappointment in the snap of a finger, and I felt bad.

"What playground?"

"I'm sorry," Caleb said, looking at me. "It's tradition when we come here, we go to the playground across the street after. But-"

"Why break tradition?" I said, cutting him off. "We should go."

"Really!?" Parker's high voice jumped over the car.

"Yeah, why not?" I said with a shrug as I smirked at Caleb.

"YES!" Parker shouted.

"Get in, we can drive over." I caught Caleb's smile as we all jumped into our seats.

The playground was across the main road; we cut through two lanes of traffic to the next parking lot. The area was a kind of desolate, with few cars parked in the area. The playground was off the parking lot, with an open field behind it before hitting a line of fenced-in backyards. Caleb and I were a little slower to get out than Parker, who raced like a greyhound toward the metal structure. The play structure was painted green, complete with three slides, a firefighter's pole, even a small rock-climbing wall to get to the top tower. There was also a pair of swings that hung just to the right of everything. Wood chips surrounded the entire area.

Caleb and I sat on a wooden bench facing the playground to monitor Parker. A lot of Texas never saw the change of seasons, but that day it smelled like fall, even though spring was upon us; maybe it was all the woodchips. We watched as Parker played with the only two other kids that were there. I wondered if they lived in the houses that occupied the edge of the field because there weren't any parents around. Parker was laughing as he jumped onto the slide at the top of the tallest tower and slid down with ease. The other two weren't far behind. His laugh was one of the most innocent things I'd ever heard. It reminded me of a chipmunk mixed with Woody Woodpecker.

"Wanna hear something ridiculous?"

"Always," Caleb said.

I looked at Caleb, hesitating, thinking how stupid I was going to sound. "When I saw you guys at Sal's, eating your ice cream, I thought Parker was your son."

Caleb started laughing, throwing his head back.

"I told you it was ridiculous," I said.

"No, it's not ridiculous. You're not the only one who's thought that. We get mistaken for father and son all the time." I scoffed and gave him a light shove for laughing at me. Caleb went with it, pretending to fall off the bench. "It's funny, 'cause when Parker was little he would call me Dad sometimes. And I'd say 'no, kid. I'm your brother.' He'd get confused a lot 'cause I was the only one taking care of him most of the time." Caleb's gaze followed Parker, who was playing tag with the other kids. "He would see Dads on TV or at school, and just assumed that I was his, I guess. Do I look old enough to have a nine-year-old?"

"I don't know," I said with a shrug. "I'd say you're old enough."

"What?!" Caleb spat out. "That means I would've been a very sexually active twelve-year-old."

"Stranger things have happened."

"Naw, I was a late bloomer," Caleb said with a scoff. "I wasn't getting anyone pregnant at twelve."

My jaw tightened. My pinky finger touched Caleb's. Both of our hands were resting on the seat of the bench. I tried my hardest not to bring attention to it, even though it felt like a magnet was pulling my hand closer to his. He was oblivious while I couldn't stop thinking about it.

"I even looked around for your wife," I said, just to get my mind off our small connection.

Caleb pulled his hand away, severing the spell over me. "Seriously? I had no idea I gave off this married Dad vibe."

"It's all Parker's fault," I said, smiling.

"I gotta get rid of the little twerp."

Caleb's phone rang. He swiftly pulled it from his pocket and checked the screen.

"Sorry," Caleb said. "It's my probation officer, I'll be right back."

"Yeah, of course."

I headed to the swings to see what Parker was up to, but he'd already run off for more tag. I sat on the chained seat, swaying back and forth. I hadn't been on a swing in years; I'd forgotten how fun it was. I pumped my legs to get some air flowing, getting higher and higher, swinging back and forth, and remembering how it made my stomach flutter.

Caleb appeared out of thin air. "Having fun?" I put my feet down to stop myself, knocking wood chips into the air.

"That was a quick call," I said, feeling embarrassed that he'd caught me swinging as high as I could.

"Yeah." Caleb sat in the swing next to me. He spun in a circle, twisting up the chain. "He was just reminding me I have to check in with him tomorrow at the courthouse. It's annoying." He stopped twisting and pulled his legs up, allowing the chain to unwind itself, sending Caleb into a spinning frenzy. I used to do that a lot, as a kid. I'd imagine I was the Tasmanian Devil from those cartoons. I pictured turning into a little tornado of dust and woodchips, spinning across the playground, knocking people over.

"Sounds like it sucks, I'm sorry," I said as I watched him bring his legs down to stop his spin. Everything was untwisted, and we both faced the parking lot, staring straight ahead.

"Yeah, he really has a way of snapping me back into reality,"

"How long do you have left?"

"The rest of the year." He stared at his lap. I noticed Caleb did that a lot when the conversation got serious. "I'm sure rumors are running wild around your school about what I did."

"A few, but I haven't--"

"Like what?"

"Uh. They're all really dumb."

"I wanna know."

"Okay. Um, I heard one about how you like, burned down a school or something."

Caleb scoffed. "Yeah. It wasn't a school."

"Oh," I said. "Caleb..." I tried to get him to look at me, but he only glanced at me before looking back at his lap. "I'm not gonna judge you."

"It happened while Parker was at school," Caleb said with a sigh as he swayed back and forth in his swing. "Luke was beating on my mom pretty badly, over something as dumb, like forgetting to buy him cigarettes. I was in my room when I heard it happening so I came running out and I threw a punch at him. Then all hell broke loose, and we started pushing each other all over the house, connecting punches anywhere we could. I remember hearing my mom screaming for us to stop." Caleb got an eye on Parker, who was drawing in the woodchips with a stick. "I finally pushed him off me. I was so done with his bullshit that I just wanted out, so when I saw his car keys hanging by the door, I swiped 'em and ran. I didn't even care about leaving my mom. I swear I've begged her for years to leave him but he keeps her so doped up that she wouldn't have the energy to move out even if she wanted to."

I listened, imagining what it would feel like to have parents that never cared about me. It felt awful thinking about everything Caleb had been through over the years, and what Parker might've witnessed.

"I had no idea where I was driving to," Caleb said. "I just wanted to get as far away as I could. I found a bottle of whiskey in the glove box and downed it. You know that stretch of road by the train tracks over in Oxford County?"

"Yeah."

"That's where I was when I thought about Parker. I turned the car around so fast that I lost control. Next thing I knew I was waking up, realizing I'd wrapped the car around a telephone pole."

"Holy shit," I said, thinking that he was lucky to be alive.

Caleb was nodding as if he could hear my thoughts. "I pulled myself out through the window before the engine caught fire. By the time the cops found me, most of the car had burned up and I was sitting nearby with nothing but a nosebleed."

"And they arrested you?"

"Charged me with a DUI and Grand Theft Auto, and took away my license." Caleb paused. I feel like he was waiting for me to give him a reaction but I stayed listening. "The judge took pity on me since I'd never been in trouble before. I was looking at jail time for at least three years." Caleb looked at me. "But I got a year of probation and three hundred hours of community service. I got so fuckin' lucky. I could barely look Parker in the eye after everything was settled. I was selfish."

"You were fed up, it's understandable."

"I hate thinking about Parker having to live with them while I could've been in prison. I would've gone crazy."

"You're an amazing brother."

Caleb stopped himself from swaying and stared at me as if no one had ever said those words to him before. That was the first time Caleb looked at me and made me feel like he wasn't just passively seeing me but studying me, taking me in.

"Sometimes I feel like he's all I have," Caleb said.

I fought back the urge to hug him. I wanted to jump off my swing and wrap him in my arms.

"God damn!" Caleb jumped from his swing. He pointed at me as he chuckled. "Is that your superpower or somethin'? Because I open up to you without even realizing it, so spill it!"

"You caught me," I said as I stood, raising my hands in defeat. "You figured out my superpower."

Caleb smiled. "Your secret's safe with me."

If only he knew my real secret. I wondered how he would react if I told him how beautiful I thought he was. Everyone at school thought he was an anarchist who burned schools to the ground, but he was the complete opposite. He was funny, kind, and he was a big nerd that could talk about movies for hours.

Being wrapped up in the world of Caleb, I hadn't noticed how dark it got until he called out to Parker saying that it was time to go.

Caleb pointed as I pulled the car into the trailer park.

"Sixth one in, on the right," I said. "I remember."

"I'm impressed."

I parked in front of their gray trailer and turned off the engine. I looked in the rearview to see Parker slumped over in the backseat.

"He's passed out," I whispered.

"I'll grab him," Caleb said as he opened the passenger door. He then leaned down with his forearms resting on the open window. "I should get your number, you know, just in case we ever need a ride anywhere." I could tell he was joking by the size of his smile. How could I say no when his dimples were staring me in the face?

"Oh, but of course, sir," I said in a terrible British accent, tipping my invisible hat. Caleb pulled out his phone and typed in the numbers as I said them. He gently opened the back door. I watched as he unbuckled Parker and scooped him up in his arms, pulling him out of the car like a firefighter carries a person from a burning building. He bumped the door closed with his hip and stopped at the open window again.

"Later," Caleb said as he crouched to see me one more time. "Thanks for today. We had fun."

"Me too." I felt like it was the first time I'd genuinely smiled in weeks.

NINETEEN

I woke Saturday morning to the sound of my phone vibrating. They were three quick vibrations that meant I was getting multiple texts. I had been checking my phone all night, hoping Caleb would text me, but it never came. I sat up, feeling groggy, and wiped the crust from my eyes. Sunlight filled my room and I could smell clean laundry. I peered over to my desk and saw a small wicker basket with my washed football clothes hanging over the edge. My Dad must've dropped the basket in my room while I was asleep.

I reached for my phone, realizing it could be Caleb texting me. I unplugged it from the charger. To my dismay, none of the texts were from Caleb.

LAUREN

Heading to my grandma's house soon. I'm not looking forward to the two-hour drive. I can't wait to see your face tomorrow!

CHRIS

I tried talking to Dan.

He got pretty defensive.

TASHA

Mr. Reily told me you were applying to NYU. Are you actually going through with it?

I responded to Chris first.

ME

What did he say?

CHRIS

He said to stay out of his business. Typical Dan.

ME

Did you tell him what you saw, though?

Then I jumped to the text with Lauren.

ME

Same! Have fun with grandma, tell her I said hi! Haha

Last was Tasha.

ME

That seems like a serious breach of counselor/student trust.

TASHA

Boy, you know I have the magic skills to get info out of anyone.

ME

haha yeah sure.

TASHA

Is it true?

ME

Yes, I applied. But I haven't told anyone, so don't spread it.

TASHA

OMG, yes! I'm so excited for you. It is pretty late in the game, though.

ME

I know, I only applied because Mr. Reily said they take late applications. I feel like I'm constantly refreshing my email.

TASHA

Be patient! They'd be foolish not to take you! What did your Dad say?

ME

I haven't told anyone, remember? My Dad included. I'm terrified. I don't think I'll tell him unless I get in. I still haven't heard from any state schools.

TASHA

Me either, but I know a few people have so they're coming! Slowly but surely!

LAUREN

I will! She always asks about you, she loves you. Lol.

What're you doing today?

. . .

Waiting for Caleb to text me, is what I wanted to say. It tore me apart knowing that I was going to hurt Lauren. My feelings were becoming too strong for Caleb to ignore. The more I saw him, the longer I wanted to be around him. I didn't even know If Caleb was gay or bi or straight. It felt like I was living in purgatory. Either I'd be let down when Caleb told me he was straight or happy when he told me he wasn't. Regardless, I'd still be breaking Lauren's heart.

ME

Not sure what I'm doing yet.

Chris texted me back.

CHRIS

Yeah, but he told me I was wrong. That I didn't see him do anything.

ME

Damn, I guess we need more evidence because he's not going to admit it.

CHRIS

What's the point in lying? He knows he can tell us anything.

I wished that were true. I could relate. If I told Dan my biggest secret, he'd probably beat the shit out of me no matter who was watching. I felt my phone vibrate. A notification popped up from an unknown number. My heart skipped a beat as I shot upright off of my bed.

UNKNOWN
Hey, it's Caleb.

Holy shit, holy shit. I saved the contact in my phone before sending a text back. *Don't look desperate.*

ME
Hey. What's up?

CALEB
Was wondering if you had any plans tonight?

ME
Tonight? No, I don't think so. Why?

CALEB
I was thinking about meeting up with some friends at this club. Since it's 18+ night, I was gonna ask if you wanted to come?

Holy fuck, holy FUCK!

ME

Sounds awesome.

CALEB

Great. Mind if I meet you at your place at like 9?

9 P.M.?! That seemed so late to only be starting the night, but I'd never been to a club, so what did I know?

ME

Yeah, sure.

CALEB

Perfect! See you tonight.

ME

Can't wait!

I stared at my phone, hoping to see those three little dots pop up. I couldn't believe I had sent the words 'can't wait'. I hoped he wouldn't think I sounded too needy.

My stomach made a loud growling noise, I needed to eat something; I pulled on some basketball shorts but stayed shirtless. I ran pretty warm most of the time, so I took any opportunity not to wear a shirt.

"Hey, Dad," I said cheerfully as I came down the stairs. He was sitting at the counter with a cup of coffee, staring at the screen of his laptop. He was fully dressed, he just needed to tighten his tie, throw on a jacket and he'd be ready to give another speech. He looked at me as I was pouring some cornflakes into a bowl.

Dad removed his glasses. "What's wrong with you?"

"What?" I closed the door to the fridge, milk in hand. "Nothing. Why?"

"That goofy grin on your face, for starters."

He closed his laptop and placed it into his satchel. I hadn't even realized I was smiling to myself.

"I don't know what you're talking about," I said, shoving a spoonful of cereal in my mouth before sitting at the counter.

My eyes widened when I remembered I told Caleb he could come here. I then had a flashback to my Dad telling me not to involve myself with a delinquent like Caleb.

"It's gonna be another late one tonight," my Dad said, almost on cue. I let out a sigh of relief.

"Oh," I said, spitting out milk. "Can I use the car again tonight?"

"For what?"

"Just hanging out with a friend again."

"Who is this friend, do I know them?" He wrapped his satchel around his shoulder.

"Just a guy from my school."

Technically, I wasn't lying. My Dad stared at me through squinted eyes for a moment, wondering if he should trust my word.

"Sure," he said tentatively. "I'll leave you the keys. Grace is picking me up today, anyway." I nodded my head and started for the kitchen sink as I had already scarfed down my cereal. The clink of the bowl forced my Dad to turn around before walking out the door. "Wash that bowl," he said as he caught me trying to walk away. I turned on my bare heels and reached for the soap.

I watched my Dad get into Grace's car from the window above the sink. I still felt unsure about Grace and her motives, but I had a lot more to worry about.

I spent the entire day cleaning the house, something I'd never done. I vacuumed the living room rug, I wiped down every surface in the kitchen, I even made my bed! My mom would've fainted in shock if she'd seen it. I didn't even expect Caleb to come inside the house, but I couldn't take the risk of him thinking I was a slob.

It felt like I was thinking about Caleb every second of that day. I wondered what he would wear; I wondered what he would smell like; I wondered if he would do anything different with his hair.

My phone vibrated, I pulled it out and read the text.

DAN

Dude, come over tonight! We're gonna get drunk and jump off the roof into the pool. It's gonna be sick.

ME:

Exhilarating as that sounds, I can't. I have plans tonight.

DAN

With who? We're your only friends!

He wasn't wrong.

ME

I'm just busy, man. Sorry.

DAN

gaaaaayyyyy

. . .

Rolling my eyes, I placed the phone on my desk. I was trying to decide what to wear. Unsure if I should go in shorts or jeans. I slipped on a pair of khaki shorts and a white T-shirt and stared at myself in the mirror. I was about to take the shirt off when I heard the doorbell ring. My stomach sank and then filled with butterflies. I ran down the stairs, around to the front door, pulling it open a little too forcefully.

"Hey," Caleb said with a head nod. My mouth got dry as I took him in. He looked so good. I couldn't believe he was standing on my front steps. He was wearing black skinny jeans with rips in the knees, a pair of black boots that made him look taller, and a red flannel over a black T-shirt. His hair was pushed back under a black, flat-brimmed hat he wore backward. Silver studs poked out from each earlobe. I hadn't realized his ears were pierced until that moment.

"Hi," I said, trying not to smile as hard as I wanted to.

Caleb looked me up and down. "Is that what you're wearing?"

"Uh..." His forwardness took me by surprise. "I don't know, I was just trying stuff on."

"Mind if I help?"

"Oh, yeah, sure," I said, pointing a thumb behind me. "My room is upstairs."

Caleb walked in while I closed the door behind him. I turned around to find him looking at our framed pictures on the wall.

"Is that your mom?" Caleb was pointing to a picture with a golden frame.

"Yeah," I said with a hoarse tone. The saliva was coming back.

"She's really pretty."

I just smiled and headed up the stairs, Caleb stayed close behind. My room was spotless for the first time in my life. I would've felt comfortable eating off of the floor that night.

"This is where the magic happens," I said as I presented my room, instantly regretting the words.

"Cool." Caleb looked around with his hands in his pockets. The first thing he studied was the collection of sports trophies on the top of my dresser. I hadn't touched them in years, he could probably see all the dust they collected. Of course, that was the one thing I didn't clean. He turned around, giving me another once over. "We're going to a club, Lan. You gotta wear some jeans." Caleb pulled off his flannel and tossed it on my bed.

"Jeans." I pointed at him with a finger gun. "Got it." I stepped to my dresser and pulled out a pair of blue jeans. He seemed satisfied with my choice.

"Put 'em on, I'll find you a shirt."

I nodded and did what he asked as he approached my closet and opened the door. He moved through the shirts on hangers as if he were swiping through Tinder, making little noises to disregard each one. Then something caught his eye on the floor of the closet.

"Is this one clean?" he asked as he reached down, picking up the red button-up shirt. I'd forgotten to hang it back up after I tried it on before going to my Dad's speech at the church.

"Yeah, but it's too tight."

"Perfect," Caleb said with a Cheshire-like grin. "Put it on let's see."

Caleb tossed me the shirt, which hit me in the neck before I caught it. I placed it on the back of my desk chair while I pulled off the white T-shirt I had on. I was standing there with my bare chest exposed, wondering if Caleb liked what he saw, or if I was just another shirtless guy you paid no mind to in the locker room. My face warmed as embarrassment crept in on me. I was confident that my body was in better shape than most, maybe a bit on the skinnier side, but my thoughts raced to wonder what Caleb thought of it. I tried to watch him for any clue that leaned in my favor, but as usual, he was stoic. I slipped into the red shirt. The silky fabric felt cool against my warm skin. I buttoned it up to my neck and walked over to my closet, closing the door to reveal the full-length mirror to check myself out.

"See, it's way too tight," I said.

"It's actually perfect for where we're going," Caleb said as he flanked me, looking at me in the mirror. "One more thing." He stepped close to me, his chest against my back as he wrapped his arms around my shoulders, reaching for the top button of my shirt. The warm breath from his nostrils flowed against the back of my neck, giving me chills. He unbuttoned the top two buttons of my shirt to expose my chest. I stared at him through the mirror as he stood behind me, yearning to feel his touch again. I closed my eyes, enjoying his arms around me.

The last time someone was in my room, it didn't go so well. I couldn't help but wonder what Caleb would do If I pushed him over to my bed like I had with Lauren. I wondered how differently my body would respond. The way his breath teased my neck sent a fire through me. I wanted to feel his breath move down my torso. I imagined myself leaning over him, in the same position I had Lauren in.

Breaking my fantasy, he stepped away from me to observe his work, saying, "There, now you're ready."

———

"Take a left at Perkins," Caleb said as he pointed. I was more than happy to go wherever he asked me to. I imagined us as

Lewis and Clark. "So what do you do when you're not driving me around?" He glanced at me with a smirk.

"I write a lot," I said as I turned the wheel, pulling onto Perkins Street. "Read books. When I have time I mean, homework and football keep me pretty busy."

"I never would have pegged you as a writer. What do you write, poetry?"

"Fiction, I've never actually tried writing poetry," I said with a nervous chuckle, hoping he wasn't a poetry buff too.

"Cool. Is that what you want to do, like write books and stuff?"

"Yeah, that's the dream." We came to a red light. "I have, like, this weirdly active imagination. I'm constantly picturing myself in absurd situations or coming up with stories in my head. My dreams can get pretty wild too."

"Okay," Caleb said as he turned himself toward me in his seat. "What's in your head right now? Come up with something."

"All right," I said as confidently as I could while feeling pressure to impress him. "I look at these traffic lights and I see a love story." I pointed up to the one we were in front of. "This one is in love with that traffic light across the street." Then I pointed to the light opposite of us. "They used to be on the same wire, for years and years. Until one of their lights went out. Someone removed the traffic light from the wire altogether to get it fixed. For weeks this one here was left on the wire alone, never thinking it would see its soulmate again. Until the day that the traffic light came back, except they reinstalled it across the street on that wire." Caleb followed along as I pointed, nodding his head. "They used to change lights in sync when they were on the same wire, but now the only way they can communicate is by displaying the opposite lights to keep the traffic moving." I paused for a second as the light turned green. I pulled off the brake. "It's a work in progress," I shrugged, uncertain that the story was good enough to impress him.

"I like it." Caleb chuckled. "It's cheesy, but I liked it."

"It wasn't good," I said, shaking my head in shame. We both busted out laughing.

"No, it wasn't good," Caleb said between fits of laughter.

"I'm better than this, I swear!"

Caleb dried his eyes. "I hope I can read your stuff sometime."

"Me too," I said as my laugh was calming down. "I write short stories for my school newspaper every month, maybe I'll let you read one of those."

"All right." Caleb rolled down his window. The fast wind felt amazing against my flushed cheeks. I got a whiff of hot dogs as we passed a vendor standing at his cart on the sidewalk. "What's your favorite book?" Caleb blurted out. "Oh, take a left up here."

"That's a hard question." I took a wide turn on the street that Caleb pointed out. I had so many favorite books that it was hard to pick just one, I'd imagine Caleb felt the same about movies. "I feel like it changes every week."

"All right then, what's your favorite you've read recently?"

"Um..." It had been weeks since I read a book. I was racking my brain trying to remember, then it hit me. "Oh! Ready Player One by Ernest Cline. It was so good! It's about this guy who lives in a dystopian future where everyone thrives in a virtual world, like a video game. But you can do anything you want pretty much." Caleb nodded along. "It's really entertaining, and there are all these references to movies and pop culture, which I didn't always understand, but I bet you would love it!" The nerd in me had jumped out, but it made Caleb smile.

"Sounds good," Caleb said.

I glanced at him, taking my eyes off the road for a second. He was looking at me with his beautiful hazel eyes. I could've crashed the car if I didn't look away.

"I'm not much of a reader, but I'd love to check it out," he said. Caleb turned his attention back to the road. His leg was bouncing. Was he getting nervous?

"It's up here on the right," he said.

Caleb pointed at a tall sign with bold white letters painted on it that read 'PARADISE'. There was a neon palm tree that lit up coming off the top right corner. I pulled into the lot, noticing how packed it was with cars, but I found an empty spot that was facing the small brick building.

An eccentric array of people were walking around. A tall person wearing a skin-tight dress that stopped at their thighs, and high-heeled boots turned the corner. They wore a big afro wig that was pulled into two poofy buns. Then two men walked by our car. Both of them were buff with hairy chests. Instead of shirts, they wore leather harnesses around their bulging shoulders. I would've thought they were twins if I hadn't seen them holding hands. A gaggle of girls rushed past the car, all greeting a skinny, younger-looking boy with a hug. Each person walked around the side of the building, assuming that's where the entrance was.

"I should've given you the heads up," Caleb said as he unbuckled his seatbelt. I think he could tell I was putting the pieces together.

"So, this is a gay club?"

I was barely treading water with my sexuality and being in that parking lot felt like jumping into the deep end, head first.

"Yeah," Caleb said as he twisted his leg up into his seat. "If that makes you uncomfortable, we can leave. We can go somewhere else."

"No, no. I'm fine." I lied. I could feel the sweat form at my hairline, wiping it away before Caleb could notice.

"She isn't much," Caleb said, looking at the brick building. "But she's felt like home for the last few years."

"I didn't know there was one so close."

"Closest in two counties."

He smiled at a group of four people standing by a red jeep that was missing its doors and roof.

"I didn't realize you were..." I couldn't even say the word, I was such a coward.

Caleb looked at me, "I didn't realize I had to tell you I was."

He was right. He didn't owe me anything. We hadn't known each other long. I flashed back to the day we met outside the school when I was playing catch with Dan and Chris. I imagined him shaking my hand, saying, 'Hi, I'm Caleb. I'm gay.' I looked at him with nothing to say, but I felt relief finally knowing his sexual orientation. Maybe I'd have a chance if I gained the balls to tell him how I felt.

"Those are my friends," Caleb said before looking at the folks standing next to the Jeep. "Are you sure you're all right with this?"

"Yeah," I said, fighting against the pit forming in my stomach.

If anyone sees me here, I'm fucked. Maybe I should say I don't feel good and I can go home.

My hand was on the door handle but I wasn't ready to open it. Caleb had already gotten out of the car. I closed my eyes and took a few deep breaths. When I opened my eyes I caught a bus driving by with my Dad's face on the side of it. He was smiling right at me with his campaign slogan etched above his head.

"Jesus Christ, he's watching me," I whispered to myself.

This is a sign, leave now. Go!

Caleb knocked on the window, startling me. "You comin'?"

Goddammit.

"Yeah," I said with a fake smile as I opened the door.

TWENTY

"Oh, my, who is this fresh meat you've brought us, Mr. Montes?!" One of Caleb's friends shouted as we approached the group. The short man stepped out from the huddle and tiptoed toward Caleb with his arms stretched out. He was wearing a mesh tank top that exposed all of his dark skin. He buzzed his hair short like mine and had a thin goatee. One long earring was hanging from his right earlobe.

"Don't scare the boy off, Miguel!" A husky person in small heels said between puffs of a cigarette. I looked them up and down. They were wearing a feminine pants suit as if they had just come from a law office. They wore a long black shawl-like scarf that wrapped around their neck and shoulders, and held a cigarette dramatically with two fingers, taking puffs as if it were a prop. Even though their clothes were feminine, the thick beard told a different story. And yet their hair was long and straight, just passing over the shoulders. It was a complete blend of masculinity and femininity.

Caleb let go of the embrace and looked at me behind him. "This is Miguel, pronouns are he/him," Caleb said as he gestured to the short man wearing the mesh tank top. Miguel then tiptoed toward me with a big embrace. My hands stayed in my pockets, unsure of what to do. My chin rested on Miguel's shoulder as he squeezed me. I was taken aback by how touchy-feely he was with someone he didn't know.

"It's so nice to meet you!" Miguel said excitedly as he eased his hold on me. "What are your preferred pronouns, honey?"

"Um..." I hesitated as I'd never been asked that question before, thinking it was obvious. "He/Him."

"Girl, let him breathe," another shouted at Miguel. The guy was tall, with the build of a professional football player and pale skin. His head was shaved bald except for a short strip of mohawk down the middle. He also had a beard, but he kept it trimmed shorter than the cigarette-smoking person. He looked like a guy you saw in a biker gang. "Sorry, Miguel can't resist a fresh twink," he said as Miguel guided me toward the group. I had no idea what a twink was, but I assumed he was referring to me.

"Oh, bitch," Miguel said, pointing a painted fingernail. "Do not try me tonight." He started spitting out something in Spanish. It made all of them laugh, but I had missed the joke.

"This is Dennis," Caleb said as he gestured to the person wearing the black shawl. "Pronouns are they/them."

Before Caleb could finish his words, Dennis was already holding out their hand daintily, waiting for me to shake it. I reached out and felt I was shaking hands with the Queen. It took a second for my brain to wrap itself around calling someone by the pronouns they/them, I knew it was going to be tricky as I'd never met anyone who used those pronouns.

"This is Patrick," Caleb said as the biker reached out his hand. "Pronouns are he/him."

"Hey," I said softly as I returned the handshake. Patrick's grip was strong.

"And finally," Caleb said as he gestured to the only person

who had yet to speak. "The woman of the hour, Mallory!" Caleb hugged her, and she wrapped her arms around his neck with a smile. Mallory was wearing a purple cocktail dress that cut off at the knees and white pumps on her feet. Her long, curly hair was a strawberry blonde color that reminded me of a sunset. She was wearing purple, glittery eye shadow that matched her dress. Caleb came out of the hug with one arm still wrapped around her shoulders. "We are celebrating her approval for her gender confirmation surgery!" The others clapped as I smiled awkwardly.

"What does that mean?"

They all laughed at me. I shrunk into myself feeling like an idiot.

I shouldn't be here. I clearly don't fit in. but if I leave his friends will talk shit about me. I want Caleb to like me, leaving might put me on his shit list.

"OH, he's serious," Mallory said.

"What kind of backwater swamp did you find this one in, Caleb?" Dennis asked. Miguel slapped them on the shoulder.

"It means I'm becoming the woman on the outside that I've always been on the inside, sweetie," Mallory said with a smile.

Oh my God!

The realization hit me like a Mack truck. I was shocked. I would've never suspected that she was assigned male at birth. It made me think about all the people I've passed by in my life, anyone could be transgender and I'd never know. I was naive. Steven was the only person in my day-to-day life that was outside the norm. If I had opened my eyes a little sooner I might've been able to see all of the colors of the rainbow instead of the black and white I was used to.

"Oh, cool. Congrats," I said to Mallory.

"Now that he's educated," Caleb said. "This is Landon."

"So how'd you two meet?" Mallory asked with a thick Puerto Rican accent.

"Caleb rarely brings guys around unless it's serious," Dennis said before taking another drag off their cigarette. I hated the smell of cigarettes and of course the wind blew the smoke in my direction.

"Oh, I'm not..." I stuttered as I put a hand up in defense. "I have a-"

"We're just friends," Caleb said, cutting me off as he stepped to my side, looking at the others.

"And you wanted to bring him to this dump?" Miguel asked.

"He...needed a change of scenery," Caleb said as he glanced at me with a smirk. "Get out of his bubble, ya know?"

"We can all relate," Patrick said as he leaned back against the red Jeep. I wondered how Caleb knew them, as they all looked older than him. But Caleb was right, I needed something new. Just standing in the parking lot, I felt very out of my element. It was both exciting and scary. I'd never seen so many queer people in one place or even knew they existed

"How do you all know Caleb?" I asked the group. Miguel threw his hands up first.

"Oooo child, he was just a sweet lil' gayby when he walked into Paradise for the first time," Miguel said. "You and Andy, remember?"

"Yes," Caleb said, shaking his head in embarrassment.

"They looked like two lost puppies," Patrick said with a chuckle.

"And we kind of just took them under our wings," Mallory said.

"I think that's the night Miguel went home with that foot fetish guy," Dennis said, causing a burst of laughter from everyone.

"Bitch, why you gotta do that?" Miguel said to Dennis as he

puffed out his chest and stepped in front of them. "You always gotta air my dirty laundry, in front of somebody new."

It was funny to see Miguel standing in front of Dennis acting tough when there was such a big height difference between them. I was concerned that his anger was real but his demeanor flipped on a dime.

"Best damn foot massage I ever had in my life though, I'll tell you that." Miguel spat out as Dennis nudged him away. Everyone laughed again. The whole dynamic of the group shook the foundation of my small world.

"So if it wasn't Grindr," Mallory said. "Then how'd you guys start hangin' out?" She looked to Caleb for the answer. I thought about how I stalked him until he noticed me.

"We met at his school," Caleb said, shoving his hands in his pockets. "I'm doing my community service at Madison High School. He's a senior there."

My cheeks got warm. I suddenly didn't feel old enough or cool enough to be there.

"How's that going, by the way?" Patrick asked.

"It's not too bad. Though my probation officer is a dick most of the time."

"Fuckin' cops," Mallory said under her breath.

"He has this power complex going on," Caleb said. "He treats me like I'm lower than him."

I felt sorry for Caleb, he didn't deserve to get treated that way.

"There have been so many times where I'd love to just put him in his place, but I can't risk getting in more trouble. I gotta think about Parker."

"Oh, how is that little nugget?" Dennis asked with a baby voice.

"He's good! He's saying more outrageous things every day."

Miguel eagerly interjected. "This one time, I was at the

grocery store, right? And this little boy pointed at me and asked his mother if I was pregnant." This sent all of them into a laughing fit. "I swear I was ready to go to jail that day, I said lord you betta stop me from slappin' the shit outta this boy. Best believe I was on the treadmill that night!"

"I don't think it's working," Patrick said through his big smile, trying to catch his breath from laughing. Miguel screamed and started laughing along with everyone else. It felt like they had known each other for decades. It was so easy for them to bounce words off one another in a lighthearted way. It felt like I was watching a sitcom, it eased my anxiety. I finally cracked a smile and it felt amazing.

I could hear bursts of loud music spill into the parking lot every time someone stepped through the entrance. I noticed Mallory perk up when she caught a sample of the current song playing.

"Oh shit, that's my jam!" She cheered. "Let's go, henny!" She turned around, rushing toward the entrance. Her calf muscles looked strong. I assumed she gained them from wearing such high heels. We all followed suit and formed a line in front of the entrance as the bouncer checked everyone's I.D.

The closer I got to the door the higher my anxiety filled my stomach. It reminded me of when I was little and my parents would take me to a haunted house during October. The antici-pation and screams from inside killed me.

I stepped to the closed door and handed my license to the large man dressed in black. His T-shirt had the word 'SECU-RITY' written across the chest in bold white letters. He shined a small flashlight on my license and asked me to hold out my hand. I followed his command and he drew a big X with a black marker. He opened the door, and I followed Caleb inside.

A wave of booming music slammed us. The sound of the bass knocking on my chest. The building wasn't very spacious.

We were plunged into a crowd waiting to get to the bar. There was a strong smell of alcohol and dry ice, seemingly from the machines built into the ceilings that were shooting out mists of fog. I could see bodies pressed together all over the dance floor. Strobe lights of reds and purples plastered everyone, then it would switch to blues and greens. Mallory had left us all behind and I caught her squeezing herself between two shirtless men on the dance floor. Seeing everyone dancing made me self-conscious. I never considered myself a good dancer. I was always too afraid I'd look like a fool so I never fully let loose. I wondered what Caleb was expecting of me. The thought of getting sweaty next to him though was one I liked.

"What's this for?" I yelled to Caleb, grabbing onto his shoulder to get his attention. I held my hand up to show him the black X.

"It means you're under twenty-one," Caleb yelled back. "So the bartenders know not to serve you alcohol."

"Oh, gotcha."

"Don't worry, I won't be drinking tonight either," Caleb yelled as he turned to face me. "Not allowed to." It was so dark, I had trouble seeing his face. I'd get a glimpse of him every time a spinning light flashed by us. Caleb looked around for his friends, noticing that they were ordering drinks at the bar. He walked toward them when he was pushed from behind and he fell into me, grabbing me by the arms to steady himself.

"My bad!" We heard someone yell back to us as they headed to the dance floor.

"Sorry," Caleb said, his face three inches from mine. "It's so crowded on Saturday nights."

The spinning light came around like the beacon of a lighthouse, and I saw Caleb's dimples on full display. I fought the urge to kiss him as he held onto me. No one would've batted an eye. I could be free to kiss a beautiful man and no one would judge me. Then I recognized a familiar head of pink hair bouncing toward us and my heart sank to my toes.

"Fuck!" I shouted, turning my back to Caleb.

"What's wrong?" Caleb strained his voice over the music, trying to turn me back around.

I peeked over my shoulder, Steven was weaving between people, looking to reassure himself that he'd spotted me. My gaze shot to the front door and I bolted. I threw the door open and was struck by the silence of the parking lot. A small ringing sound hung in my ears. I walked back around the side of the building to my car.

"Landon!" Caleb shouted from the entrance, but I kept walking. The ringing in my ears faded as I heard Caleb's footsteps galloping behind me.

"I have to go," I said. "I can't be here."

Caleb caught up before I got to the car and stepped in front of me.

"Why? What's going on?" Caleb's eyebrows were raised. He looked concerned.

"I saw this guy Steven from my school."

"Okay, so," Caleb said, not realizing the gravity of the situation.

"Everyone at school knows he's..." again I couldn't even say the word. "I just don't need him telling people that he saw me here, then everyone is gonna say that I'm..." I stopped speaking as I pulled my keys from my pocket, feeling disoriented.

"Gay?" Caleb said flatly. The word stopped me as if it had all the power in the world.

"Yes."

"Is that so bad?" The look on Caleb's face broke my heart.

"It is when you have a Dad like mine," I said, moving toward the driver's side door. "It is when you go to a school like mine. You don't know what it's like."

"You're right. I'm sorry," Caleb said as he followed behind.

"It's not your fault." I jingled my keys into the lock and opened the door. "I wasn't thinking. If my dad found out I was here, it could ruin his entire campaign."

"His campaign? What're you talking about? I thought your Dad was the superintendent of your school."

"He is," I said as I stood in the open door. "He's also running for Mayor of Madison. His picture is all over town."

Caleb looked as if he was sifting through his memories.

"I think Miguel has the hots for your dad," Caleb said.

I was so flustered from seeing Steven that I couldn't even crack a smile.

"Look," I said. "I enjoy hanging out with you and it was fun, but I can't be here." I tried to get in the car, but Caleb reached out and stopped me.

"Let's go somewhere else then."

"No. You're here to celebrate your friend, you should be with them."

"They're very understanding people," Caleb said as he glided around the car. He opened the door and sat inside in one swift movement. "I have the perfect place, get in!"

I hopped into the car, feeling like an idiot for not thinking I would see someone I knew. Steven was the only person at my school that was out of the closet, of course he would be at a gay club on 18+ night. I shook my head at the thought as I turned the key in the ignition and shifted the car into reverse.

I pulled onto the main road. "Where are we going?"

"You'll see," Caleb said slyly.

TWENTY-ONE

We parked in front of a chain-link fence and the headlights lit up a big sign that said 'NO TRESPASS-ING.' The fence was covered in overgrown vines and foliage. The trees on the other side of the fence had grown over the top, making it difficult to tell how far up it went. I wondered what was beyond the gate, and if it was Caleb's plan all along, to take me to an abandoned factory to murder me. I turned off the car, and the headlights faded, leaving us in total darkness.

"You sure this is the place?"

"Yup," Caleb said, stepping out of the car. I followed suit and opened my door, feeling the gravel under my feet.

"It looks like it might've closed down since the last time you were here," I whispered. The area was so silent, aside from a few crickets chirping. Caleb led us off the beaten path as there were no other cars or people in sight. He pulled out his phone, switching on the flashlight.

"This place was closed long before I got here," Caleb said as he touched the fence. I shined my phone's flashlight. My beam followed Caleb as I watched him run his hands against the chain-link.

"What're you doing?"

"Trying to find the spot," he said with a huff. "I haven't been here in a while."

I continued to wonder what was happening as he crouched down and started pushing against the fence.

"Got it," Caleb said.

I stepped closer to him, shining my light on his hands as he pulled the chain-link apart. The metal fence had been cut into, allowing Caleb to bend a chunk out.

"Wait," I said as I grabbed his shoulder to get his attention. "We're going in there?"

"Yeah," Caleb said, looking up at me, still crouched and holding the fence open. "Andy and I used to come here a lot. It was our favorite spot." That was the second time that night I'd heard the name Andy. The thought threw me into a guessing game, but Caleb was unfazed. He pushed through the opening, getting his T-shirt caught against one of the cut links. I crouched down behind him and released him, still feeling uneasy about the whole situation.

"It says no trespassing. Aren't you supposed to be staying out of trouble?" I shined my light through the hole in the fence at Caleb. His eyes squinted at me.

"I promise you, no one is ever here," Caleb whispered as he tried to shield his eyes from my light. "C'mon, scaredy-cat."

I gave him a look of unrest before checking behind me to see if anyone was around, but all I saw was darkness. I pushed myself through the small hole and let the fence bounce back into place behind me. Caleb started walking, and I followed close behind. The overgrowth was thick, but there was a small path of broken branches and leaves. I flashed my light to the right of us, a few empty beer cans were scattered in the bushes. As we continued, the air got mustier. It smelled like we were close to a body of water.

Our path ended at a single white door of a small wooden structure that was covered in moss and vines. Caleb reached for the doorknob and twisted it.

This is it. This is where he kills me.

The door opened toward us and lead into a small booth. I felt a breeze push through. A half-wall was installed at the front of the structure.

"Whoa," I said as we walked through the threshold. The structure was one of those squirt gun game booths where people shot a stream of water at a target to make their stuffed animal race to the top. Everything looked decayed, a few stuffed animals were left on the ground torn apart by wildlife. The water guns were covered in rust.

Caleb jumped over the half wall of the booth and into the dark open area. I shined my light at him as he threw his arms out to the side.

"Welcome to Rocky Lake Amusement Park," Caleb said with a smile.

I hopped the half wall, landing my feet into the overgrown grass. I'd heard stories of the place, but I'd never seen it in real life. My parents used to tell me about going to Rocky Lake when they were teenagers. It was the spot to hang out. My Dad told me it was a famous date spot for him and my mom. Dad would try to win my mom's affection by collecting game-winning prizes for her.

The entire park took up the north side of Rocky Lake, a two-mile round body of water. The park was complete with a carousel, a swing ride that brought you up into the air. A bumper car terminal, a small rollercoaster where you rode on the back of a giant fish, and a huge Ferris wheel that allowed you to take in the entire surrounding landscape. There was an unbroken stretch of game booths and food huts that lined up with the one we walked through. I followed Caleb as he started walking and spotted a booth that read 'Ned's Burgers & Dogs.' Seeing it all in the dark, I couldn't imagine it lit up and functioning without the overflowing bushes and trees.

Rocky Lake Amusement Park closed down in September 1990 because of health and safety regulations. The rides were getting old, and the owner was too cheap to fix them. I remember reading about the swing ride breaking down while people were on it. The swings were flying high as usual until smoke started pouring out of the top, then it suddenly dropped everyone back toward the ground, causing over ten people's legs to snap on impact. Attendance faltered after the incident until the place went under and the owner filed for bankruptcy. Oddly enough, the state never removed any of the buildings or rides. The park had slowly turned into a place of legend as it sat there rotting.

Caleb pointed things out to look at. My amazement slipped into realizing just how creepy the place was. We walked past the bumper car terminal, seeing that most of it had been spray-painted with graffiti and every bumper car was left flipped over or taken apart.

"This place is awesome, isn't it?" Caleb's voice split the silence in the air.

"Yeah." I nodded, looking in every direction to spot something new. "It's crazy that it was just left here."

"I know, right? It feels frozen in time." Caleb was like a kid in a candy store, smiling ear to ear with every step. My flashlight was facing the ground as we walked, so I wouldn't trip over anything. We were approaching the enormous Ferris wheel. The entire structure was white, with white carriages that had blue-colored roofs. The wheel was so rusty that you could get tetanus just looking at it. "You can probably see the entire lake from the top," Caleb said.

"We're not going up there, are we?"

"Hell no," Caleb said with a laugh. "Do you see that thing? It looks like it's gonna shatter with the next gust of wind."

I laughed in agreement, feeling relieved that he wasn't bringing me to the top.

"So," I said, lingering on the word. "Where are we going then?"

"The best spot in the park," Caleb said. "Right behind the Ferris wheel, looking out onto the lake."

I nodded my head, keeping pace, and heard the rustle of a nearby bush that caught my attention. I snapped my head and saw a squirrel run out from the leaves.

I imagined a hoard of zombies pushing through the tree line. I saw their mangled faces glisten under the moonlight as they reached toward us, hungry for our brains. Then I imagined Caleb whipping out a pistol from his waistband, shooting each one in the head, causing them to drop like flies. Next, I imagined hearing more shuffling footsteps coming from behind us and we see zombies flooding out from the bumper car terminal. Caleb throws me a shotgun that appears out of thin air and I shoot. The place is becoming overrun, so we dash toward the lake where we find an old wooden rowboat, our only hope of escape. I pictured us jumping inside and I grab the single paddle, while Caleb is shooting at the wave of undead getting closer.

"Climb through," Caleb said, pulling me from my apocalyptic thoughts. We had reached the metal poles that surrounded the perimeter of the cement slab at the base of the Ferris wheel. I ducked under the fence and stepped onto the cement. It was all cracked with nature pushing its way through. I looked at the Ferris wheel and it seemed as tall as a New York City skyscraper. "This was our spot," Caleb said. I assumed he was talking about him and Andy again. "We thought we were so cool at seventeen," Caleb said as we walked past the big wheel and to the back fence that faced the water. "We had our fake IDs that got us into Paradise every weekend, then we'd come here and just look at the water and talk."

Caleb leaned against the horizontal pole. It wasn't much of a fence. He sat on the cement, there was enough room to hang his legs under the fence and over the edge. I did the same. I looked over and saw it dropped a few feet into the lake.

The area was the brightest spot in the park. The moon was reflecting off the surface of the water, spreading streams of light in each direction. We stared across the lake, taking in a few houses with their windows lit up on the other side. Caleb pointed at two turtles sleeping on a stump. The light was bright enough for me to notice the circled A tattoo on his hand.

"A for Andy?"

Caleb dropped his hand in his lap and rubbed the A with his other thumb.

I asked, "Who was he? If you don't mind me asking."

"He was... a lot," Caleb said. "It's a long story."

"Hey," I said, looking at him. "I got all the time in the world."

Caleb glanced at me with a weak smile. His eyes weren't on me long as they looked back at the water. A cool breeze brushed my skin, giving me goosebumps. The light wind caused a small splash of water to erupt on the shoreline under our dangling feet.

"We dated when we were in high school," Caleb said. "But it was always a secret. We were in the same film class and talking about movies led to hanging out after school to talk more about movies. Hanging out turned into other stuff and I fell pretty hard for him. We were each other's first everything." Caleb's voice trailed off, flipping through the memories in his head. "I was already out to a few friends at school, but coming out never seemed to interest Andy. His family was really conservative, so his parents just thought we were best friends; we were insepara-ble. Things got serious, and we came up with our own signal for when we couldn't say I love you out loud." Caleb reached for my wrist and turned my hand so my palm was facing up. "Like, if we were at dinner with his parents or something, he would reach for my hand under the table and draw a circle on my palm." Caleb traced a circle in my palm. His light touch sent a chill up to my shoulder. "And that meant that he was saying I love you to me without saying the words." Caleb let go of my wrist, I could tell from his eyes he was living in that memory. His smile was as bright as the moon.

"So what happened with you guys then?" I made a fist when he stopped touching me, still able to feel his circle.

"I didn't wanna be a secret anymore," Caleb said as he peered back to the water. "We got into this big fight over the phone one night. I was so frustrated, I wanted to love him outside the walls of Paradise, ya know? I wanted to hold his hand at school, kiss him in the parking lot, say I love you at the dinner table. But he was too scared, he didn't want any of it." Caleb took a big breath, then exhaled slowly. "After we hung up, I texted him to meet me here at the park. I was gonna tell him to his face that things had to change or else I was gonna break it off."

"And did you?" It felt like I was reading the last chapter of an excellent book.

"He never showed up," Caleb whispered. "I waited for a long time, so I hopped on my bike and rode home." Caleb continued to stare out at the water, but I could see it in his eyes: he was reliving every moment. "When I got to the main road, I saw the flashing lights of the cop cars. I sped up and saw Andy's mangled bike in the middle of the road. A cop stopped me as I tried to run to it, looking for him, but all I saw were drops of blood smeared across the cement. I just collapsed in the cop's arms as I screamed 'what happened?' The cop sat me down and asked if I knew the kid who owned the bike and I just remember nodding my head yes because I couldn't keep my eyes off the stained street. The cop told me a car had hit a teenager, they could tell it was a drunk driver by the tire marks on the road."

My heart sank as I listened to Caleb recount the events of that night. I could hear the pain in his voice. I wanted to reach out and hold him close and tell him it was going to be okay. Picturing him crumble into the cop's embrace crushed me.

"They'd already gotten him into an ambulance by the time I got there," Caleb said. "The cop was nice enough to drive me to the hospital. Andy's parents were already there. I came to them in a waiting room crying, and they told me Andy was gone. I swear it felt like I had just been stabbed by a thousand knives."

"My God, Caleb," I whispered. "I'm so sorry."

Caleb reached above him, grabbing the pole of the fence, and let his arms hang.

"The worst part was that his parents didn't let me go to the funeral," Caleb said. "They went through his phone and found our texts and figured out we were seeing each other. Then they blamed me for his death." Caleb let his arms drop, and he stared at his hands, rubbing the tattoo again. "For a long time, I actually agreed with them. If it wasn't for me, he wouldn't have been riding his bike so late."

"Caleb, you couldn't have known," I said as I shook my head. He seemed to accept the words.

"They never found who hit him. I came to this spot almost every night for a month, just to cry," Caleb said, scoffing at his own words. "It felt like I could feel his ghost when I was alone here. It was the only way I could feel some sort of resolution."

"My Dad likes to say grief is just love with nowhere to go," I said. "So, I understand feeling stuck. I've felt stuck for the last six months." I admitted, not realizing I was exposing my own pain. I leaned back on my hands, and a rock dug into my palm. I scooped it up and tossed it into the water below us.

"How come?" Caleb sounded genuinely concerned. He pulled his right leg up onto the ledge and sat facing me with his other leg still hanging.

"My mom she..." The words trapped themselves in my throat. My jaw tightened. I wanted to tell him everything but my body wouldn't let me, it knew If I started to talk about her I wouldn't be able to stop crying. "I'm sorry. I haven't really talked about this with anyone, so."

"It's okay," Caleb said.

"No, you weren't done talking. I shouldn't have brought it up." I looked out at the water again. Every ounce of my being was telling me to run, to get up, and walk back to the car.

"Landon," Caleb said with a gentle tone. "I'm a great listener if you give me the chance."

I looked him in the eyes, realizing he'd given me so much about his life and his trauma and I'd given him next to nothing in return. I cleared my throat, and my jaw loosened. He deserved to know.

"My mom...died a little over six months ago." My voice trembled.

"Shit," Caleb whispered. "I had no idea."

"It all happened so fast," I said. "She went to a dermatologist on a Sunday and was diagnosed with Melanoma by Friday. They said it was stage three by the time they started her on chemo. We spent weeks in the hospital but nothing seemed to work. The cancer was spreading too quickly to too many vital organs." The words came out fast like I had been rehearsing them in my head for months, knowing one day they'd have to come out. Reliving everything out loud for the first time felt awful. I could feel my chest fill with the same dread as the day we were told the treatment wasn't working. "She had gotten so depressed and so skinny because she refused to eat most days. It felt like my Dad was getting weaker every day too. The cancer was draining the life out of our entire family."

"I can only imagine."

"They let us bring her home one weekend," I said as I stared at the moonlit water. "We were told she only had a few weeks left. She looked so different by that point, she was so frail-looking, I hated seeing her that way." I took a deep breath, filling my lungs with the cool moist air, and held it for a second as I remembered her last day. "That Monday at school, the principal told me to go home. I walked into the house to find my Dad sitting at the kitchen counter with a piece of paper in front of him and his face in his hands." I could feel the tears collecting in my eyes as I hesitated to say the words. "He told me she was gone, that he found her hanging from the rafters in his office. I couldn't believe what he was saying until I read the letter she left on his desk." I felt the tears overflow and drip down my cheeks. I didn't want to cry in front of Caleb, but I was picking at a scab that had yet to heal. "She wrote about how she wanted to end her pain, and that she wasn't suffering anymore. She wrote how proud she was of me, and that she'd always be watching me." I felt a lump forming in my throat, trying to hold everything back. "She ended the note with 'I love you more than anything.'"

Caleb reached, gently placing his hand on the back of my neck. I looked at him with a wet face, trying not to sob. He raised his left hand and wiped the moisture from my cheek with his thumb.

"Sorry," I said with a sniffle, wiping my nose on my sleeve.

"You never have to apologize for showing emotion."

"I feel like I've cried myself to death," I said. "And yet my Dad hasn't shed a single tear, at least that I've seen. Even when we were at her funeral, he was like a statue."

"Do you resent him for that?"

"Kind of," I said as I wiped the remaining tears from my face.

"I feel like I'm suffering alone, ya know? It would be nice if he showed any type of emotion. It's not fair that he gets to feel numb. It's not fair."

"I'm sure he's suffering in his own way, Lan. You should talk to him about it."

"I don't know. You haven't met him. He isn't the easiest person to talk to." I looked out at the water and shook my head. I was feeling the embarrassment creep through now that the tears had passed. "I'm sorry, I didn't mean to make this about me after everything you told me."

Caleb's hand never lifted from the back of my neck. He held it there, stroking my hair with his thumb.

"Thank you for telling me," Caleb said. "It means a lot."

He stared at me with a soft smile, looking like an angel. I felt like a troll with snot running down my face.

"I have an Idea," Caleb said. He was full of them that night. He pulled out his phone.

I raised an eyebrow. "Yeah?"

"We never got the chance to dance tonight, so," Caleb said with a smile. "Come on, stand up."

"I don't know," I groaned. "I don't dance."

Caleb jumped to his feet. A song played with a single tap on his phone's screen. He slipped his phone back into his pocket halfway so that the speaker was facing out, making it easy for us to hear the song. I pulled myself up using the pole of the fence. I was already embarrassed enough and didn't want to push myself deeper into that hole by dancing.

The song echoed through the tall trees. It had a funky 80s beat with a strong synth presence.

"What is this? It's got a cool sound."

Caleb bopped his head.

"It's one of my favorite songs by this band Walk The Moon. It's called "Aquaman," Caleb said as he reached to turn up the volume. "It always puts me in a better mood. it's so easy to dance to." Caleb beamed his smile at me. I could feel the beat of the song as a guy sang.

Caleb swayed his body, and I thought about how nerdy he looked, but I'd never seen a cuter human.

"Come on," Caleb said as he pointed a dancing finger at me as the chorus hit.

I had no choice.

He's not gonna let up, I thought.

I followed his lead and swayed my body at his tempo.

"There we go!" Caleb said. I laughed and moved a little smoother. I could feel my body loosening up. Caleb wasn't afraid of look ridiculous, so why should I?

Caleb did a swift spin and raised his arms. I was being drawn into his self-confidence. I was becoming hypnotized by the way he moved his hips. He stepped closer to me as he swayed back and forth like a snake being charmed by its flute player.

I did an awkward spin as I stepped toward him and rocked back and forth. It was apparent that he had much more experience than I did. He noticed me trip over my foot a little and chuckled. He reached out and grabbed my hand and spun himself under my arm. We both laughed at each other, moving closer as the music boomed through us. Caleb reached for my other hand as we swayed smoothly back and forth. I couldn't take my eyes off of his perfect face. His smile was all the light I needed for the rest of my life. I held onto his hands with a slight grip. He inched closer to me with his dancing feet and my heart felt like it was beating out of my chest.

I took a small step toward him, not able to control what I was doing any longer. It felt like years of instinct were kicking in. The music was building. We continued to move our hips in unison and Caleb let go of my hands. I thought he would pull away, but his arms glided up and rested on my shoulders. I could feel his fingers running through my hair. I wrapped my hands around his lower back and pulled him in even closer. Our stomachs were flat against each other. I felt so free dancing this close to him under the night sky. My heart beat faster.

Caleb's hand slid out from the back of my neck and caressed my cheek, and we looked into each other's eyes as we swayed. The song continued to build and then the key change shot through us.

I closed my eyes and felt Caleb's lips press against mine.

Our bodies kept swaying with the music as we continued to kiss. It felt like a thousand fireworks were going off in my stomach. I was in a kind of euphoria I'd never felt. I reached, feeling his smooth face with my palms. Our tongues mimicked the dance of our bodies and I didn't want it to end. My heart was pounding a mile a minute, excited and nervous. Nothing had ever felt as right as kissing that boy in front of that decaying Ferris wheel.

The song faded and so did the kiss. Caleb pressed his forehead against mine, still holding onto my face. I opened my eyes and saw him looking at me with the biggest smile. Everything I'd felt for him since the first day I saw him came to fruition. I could've stayed in that moment, staring into his hazel eyes for all of eternity.

TWENTY-TWO

W e broke our hold of each other when we heard fits of laughter coming from the distance. It caused us both to scatter to the nearest Ferris wheel carriage and hide behind it. Caleb reached for his phone, turning off the music. We stared at each other as we crouched behind the carriage and smiled with heavy breaths. It felt like they had caught us committing a crime.

"I thought you said no one ever came here," I whispered.

"I didn't think anyone did. I've never seen anyone here."

As I listened to the distant chatter, I recognized one voice.

"I think that's Dan," I whispered.

"Who?"

"He's a friend, it's all right." I pulled Caleb up from his shirt. "C'mon."

I stepped away from the Ferris wheel and toward the small gate where previous patrons would have entered the ride. Caleb followed behind me. I saw Dan and a few others stepping out from the shadows and into the moonlight. They were laughing and pushing each other playfully. I reached for my phone to switch on my flashlight so they would notice us. My heart was still beating from our dance. I looked over my shoulder and saw Caleb standing there patiently with his hands in his pockets. I wondered if he was thinking the same thing I was: did any of them see us kissing?

"Griffin?" Dan called out, realizing I was standing there with my flashlight on. "What the hell are you doing here?"

"I could ask you the same thing," I said with a smirk. The four guys flanked Dan. I knew three from the football team, but the fourth guy was new to me. I gave a quick 'hey' to the others as they approached.

"Who's this?" Dan gestured to Caleb standing behind me. I noticed Dan was a little jittery and kept wiping his nose with his fingers. He seemed to sniffle between each word.

"That's Caleb. Caleb, this is my friend Dan, and some guys from the football team." Caleb stepped toward us with his hands still in his pockets, offering a nod to the group.

"Wait," Dan said, pointing a beer bottle at us. "You're that guy who's been working at the high school."

"That's me," Caleb said with a flat tone.

"Guys," Dan said over his shoulder to the others. "This is the guy I told you about. The psycho who burned down a school."

"Don't believe everything you hear," I said.

"Most of the rumors are true," Caleb said sarcastically. I knew Dan wouldn't understand Caleb's tone.

"I knew it," Dan slurred as he looked at Caleb. It was apparent he and the guys had been drinking for a while. "Kinda weird finding you two here."

I rolled my eyes. The last thing I wanted to deal with was an intoxicated Dan. I'd been having a good time with Caleb and he was ruining it.

"I come here to think," Caleb said. "It's one of my favorite spots."

"You must bring all the boys here," Dan sneered. The other guys laughed at his words.

"It's not like that," I said, the words sprung out of my mouth like a jack in the box, and I could feel the theoretical daggers that Caleb was giving me. Dan approached Caleb and met him at eye level. He sniffled as he looked Caleb up and down, analyzing him. "Dan cut the shit," I said as he walked around Caleb as if he were a predator hunting his prey. Caleb seemed unfazed by Dan's idiotic display of dominance.

"Only fags wear earrings like that," Dan said.

"You seem to know a lot about fags," Caleb said as he stood face to face with Dan. "Wonder why."

Dan's goons busted out laughing. Dan grabbed Caleb by his collar and squeezed the fabric in his fists.

"Dan!" I stepped to him. "What the fuck is wrong with you?" I grabbed his shoulder. Caleb was stone-faced. Dan eased his grip and let go, raising his hands in defense.

"I'm just fuckin' with him!" Dan said. His voice echoed through the trees. The other guys started laughing like hyenas again, pushing my patience even further. "You seem cool, you seem cool," Dan trailed off.

"What a compliment," Caleb said under his breath.

"What're you doing here, Dan? What happened to jumping off the roof?" I tried to sound as calm as possible as I feared any sort of raised tone would set him off like a firecracker.

"We got bored," Dan said, wiping at his nose again. "We wanted to tear some shit up. Gary said this was the perfect place."

I quickly figured out Gary was the odd one. I shined my flashlight to get a better look at the crew and realized Gary was the tired-looking guy I'd seen with Dan in the school's parking lot, giving him crumpled-up dollar bills. Gary's eyes were bloodshot, he looked like one of the zombies I'd imagined walking out from the tree line earlier.

"Have fun," I said. "We were just leaving."

"Oh, C'mon!" Dan yelled as he spiked the bottle he was holding to the ground. The glass shattered in a thousand different directions. "Stay with us, the nights just getting started!"

"Sorry," Caleb said. "I gotta get up early for work tomorrow."

I couldn't tell if Caleb was telling the truth or using an excuse to get out of the awkward situation.

"C'mon," Caleb whispered as he walked by me. I gave the guys a nod and followed close behind Caleb.

"Hey Caleb," Dan called out to us. We both stopped and turned around. "I'm having a birthday party next weekend, you should come." Caleb gave a quick salute to confirm. "Bring a costume." Dan pulled a skinny can of spray paint out of his back pocket and shook it before we continued on our way.

We jumped through the game booth and passed the white door into the woods. "I'm sorry about him, he was really drunk," I said as I pushed branches away from my face.

"He was a lot more than drunk," Caleb said, leading the way through the path.

"What do you mean?"

"I've seen a lot of people on drugs in my life."

"You think he was high?" I said, holding the fence open so Caleb could step through.

"Very." Caleb ducked through the gate with a grunt. "He was sniffling a lot and couldn't stop touching his nose. I've seen it enough to know."

I crouched down, pushing myself through the fence. I believed Caleb knew what he was talking about, I just couldn't believe Chris's suspicion was right.

I turned the car off the dirt path and onto a paved road, still thinking about our kiss. I'd never felt that same electricity when I kissed Lauren. Then the guilt flooded over me when I realized that I'd just cheated on her.

"You okay?"

"Yeah," I said after a pause and shot him a smile for insurance.

"What did Dan mean when he said to bring a costume?"

"Oh," I chuckled. "His birthday is also a costume party."

"Halloween was months ago..."

"That's what I said! You don't actually have to come. It's just gonna be a bunch of drunk high schoolers. That doesn't seem like your kinda thing."

"Hey," Caleb said, putting a hand on my thigh. "If you're gonna be there, it's my kinda thing."

Feeling his grip against my leg made me smile.

"Do you have a costume?" I felt the giddiness trying to escape my stomach.

"I have a decent Michael Myers mask," Caleb said as he watched the trees speed by out his window. "I can steal a jump-suit from my mom's boyfriend."

"Who's Michael Myers?" I winced, knowing Caleb would tease me.

"Oh, come on!" He threw his head against the seat. "The killer from the Halloween movies?"

"I haven't--"

"Seen them, I should've known." Caleb shook his head with a chuckle. "There's so much to show you."

"Teach me," I said in an exaggerated southern accent. "I'm just a poor sheltered boy!"

Caleb laughed. "You have to know the mask. Everyone knows the mask." Caleb looked at me for an answer, but all I gave was a shrug. "It's a white face with messy brown hair?"

"Oh yeah. I've seen that one before." I racked my brain,

trying to see it, but I was coming up empty. Caleb pulled out his phone and started typing.

"This one," he said as he shoved his phone into my field of vision.

"Yep, that's the one I was thinking of." It wasn't, but I said it anyway. Caleb pulled the phone away and stared at it as he scrolled through the pictures.

"Did you know the first movie was so low budget that they just used a William Shatner mask that they painted white?" Caleb's tone was cheerful. He was naïve to think I knew who William Shatner was, but I was so fascinated by his random nuggets of movie trivia.

I shifted the car into park in front of Caleb's trailer and he was sending a text before noticing we'd arrived. He put his phone in his lap before looking at me. "Thanks for tonight."

"I didn't do anything," I said with a shrug. I should've been the one thanking him for opening my eyes to something I didn't know I was missing.

"It's not easy opening up to someone," he said. "Especially about losing someone close to you." Caleb rested his hand on my thigh again, and I realized how badly I was craving his touch.

I placed my hand on his. "Thanks for listening."

"I should go, I need to check on Parker."

I just nodded my head, already wondering when I would see him again. He smiled at me and his dimples looked as if they were glowing. He touched my face before moving in for a kiss. I closed my eyes, gladly accepting his lips. Their softness made me feel like I could fly.

. . .

As I walked into my house, all I thought about was Caleb's lips. I could still feel the prickly sensation from his small amount of stubble. That was a big difference between kissing Lauren and kissing Caleb, I'd never kissed someone who shaved their face.

I tore up the stairs and heard my Dad rustling around his room. I tried to tiptoe, but the floor was too creaky. My Dad popped his head into the hallway.

"It's a little late, Landon."

"I know, I'm sorry," I said, placing my hand on the doorknob of my room.

"Text me next time you're gonna be out late, or else I won't be lending you the car again." His hair was wet, he'd probably just showered.

"I will."

I stepped through the threshold.

"That shirt's too tight, might be time to retire it, no?" My Dad called out as I shut my door. I rolled my eyes, surprised he didn't mention my dumb smile again because I felt like it became a permanent fixture on my face. I could feel myself gleaming like a cracked glow stick.

I unbuttoned my shirt and took it off, feeling like my skin could breathe again. I tossed it into the hamper. My eyes widened as I turned toward my bed. Caleb had left his flannel there. I sat down next to it and pulled it into my lap, feeling his softness between my fingers. I slowly lifted it to my face, closed my eyes, and took in his scent. I imagined it was how Caleb's bedroom smelled. I imagined it was how all of his clothes smelled. I knew it had recently been washed by the fresh linen smell, but there was also a hint of cologne. Not the fancy kind you get at a department store, but more like a spray from a can.

I laid down on my bed staring at the ceiling. I laid Caleb's flannel over my naked torso, pretending he was keeping me warm. I wanted to feel that explosive high again.

A rush of guilt hit me again as I remembered my date with Lauren was the next day. I needed to tell her how I was feeling before things got in deep with Caleb. Lauren didn't deserve to be strung along.

————

Lauren and I agreed to drive separately to Lucky's the next morning for our 'reconnection date', as she called it. I felt the anxiety building in my stomach the entire drive, feeling awful that I cheated on her. But I had to figure out how I would tell Lauren. I played out a few scenarios in my head. I pictured us sitting at the table eating pancakes and suddenly I blurt it out, jumbling the words together so frantically that she doesn't understand what I said so I'm forced to say it a second time, only slower. I pictured myself saying 'I kissed Caleb' in slow motion, followed by her throwing her coffee all over me. I then switched to another scenario where I say 'Caleb and I kissed last night,' and she says 'who's Caleb?' Then I imagined a scenario worse than the previous ones. A scenario where she shrugs it off and guilts me into staying with her for the rest of our lives.

She wouldn't do that, right? She has gay friends. She knows what it's like. She wouldn't hold me back from being happy, would she?

I saw Lauren's bug-like car as I pulled into the lot and parked next to her. I looked over through the passenger side window and gave her a wave. She smiled and reciprocated. We met behind our cars. She was wearing light blue jeans and a simple gray T-shirt. She pulled her hair into a ponytail and hugged me, before giving me a peck on the lips. My mind immediately flashed to kissing Caleb.

"You okay?"

My face must have gone blank for a second.

"Yeah, of course," I lied. "How was your grandma's?"

"Boring," she said with a huff as we walked toward the diner. "I was on my phone like, the whole time. But we did talk about my audition next weekend."

"How's your prep going?"

I opened the glass door and the sound of sleigh bells rang through the air.

"I feel ready. Confident."

Stephanie was behind the bar, tattoos on full display. She spotted us and said, "sit anywhere you'd like."

The diner was bustling every Sunday morning. Lauren and I surveyed the tables. Only two were empty. We ended up sitting at a booth next to a large glass window that faced the parking lot. The theme of the table was puppies and kittens.

I let Lauren choose which side she wanted and I sat next to her. I always thought it was dumb when I saw couples do that when they weren't sitting with anyone else. It was harder to eat or have a conversation. But I felt it might make Lauren feel like I cared. I wrapped my arm around her and smiled.

Tell her. Tell her now!

She was staring me in the eyes as if she were waiting for me to tell her. I knew if I told her what happened with Caleb the previous night that it would mean we'd have to break up, and I knew she would probably cry, so I decided I couldn't embarrass her in a public place. I needed to tell her somewhere private so she could feel everything she wanted to feel. She could even scream at me if she needed to.

I got so nervous that I just kissed her. I moved in quickly and I could tell it took her by surprise. I wanted to make it a passionate kiss so she wouldn't suspect anything was wrong. Mid kiss, I heard a familiar voice approach our table.

"Hey guys, welcome to Luck-" the voice cut out as I unlocked from Lauren's lips and turned my attention to the person standing there. It felt like I stopped breathing when I saw Caleb, wearing a Lucky's T-shirt, and a pad and pen in hand, ready to take our order. Our eyes locked onto each other and remained silent, held in place by shock. Then Caleb turned around and walked away. I watched him approach Stephanie behind the bar and say something to her. It was impossible to hear over the chaotic chatter of the other customers. Stephanie glanced at our table, then took his pen and pad.

"That was weird," Lauren said. "Wait, wasn't that the guy that works at our school?"

My throat felt so dry that I couldn't respond. I locked my eyes on Stephanie, who was walking toward us.

She's gonna ask us to leave.

My mind was firing in a hundred different directions. If Stephanie asked us to leave, then I would have to explain why. I could feel a bead of sweat form on my forehead as Stephanie arrived at our table.

"Sorry about that, I'll be taking you guys from Caleb," Stephanie said, "What can I get you?"

"Can I do the avocado toast, with poached eggs please?" Lauren said.

I felt like a block of ice stuck to my seat; it paralyzed me from the neck down.

"And for you, sweetie?"

I didn't acknowledge her question. My eyes had focused on the movement behind her. I glimpsed Caleb look at me, then he bolted to the restroom.

"Landon?" Lauren nudged me. The ice holding me in place shattered, and I looked up at Stephanie.

"Um, the French toast," I said with a groggy tone, as If I had just woken from hibernation. "I'll be right back." I pushed myself from the booth and started for the restroom. I thought about how to explain everything to Caleb. If I knew he worked at Lucky's I would have suggested we go somewhere else. I weaved through the tables, feeling like I was running a marathon because I could barely catch my breath.

The restrooms were at the back of the restaurant, close to the kitchen. All I could smell was bacon as I pushed the door open. The bathroom was small and stark white with fluorescent lighting, and the smell changed to an overwhelming scent of bleach and urinal cakes. Two stalls lived next to two urinals and two sinks on the opposite wall. Caleb was standing at the sinks, with his arms crossed against his chest.

"So you have a girlfriend?"

"Yes," I said. I stood three feet away from him, worried about how much he was hating me.

"You couldn't have told me that last night when I was kissing you?"

"I'm sorry."

"Sorry?" Caleb let his arms fall. "Are you even gay?"

"No," I blurted. "Yes," I said even quicker. "I don't know... It's complicated."

"After everything, I told you last night," Caleb said as he rubbed his forehead. "I've already done complicated. I can't go through that again."

Everything I was hearing Caleb say was valid. I was scratching at an old wound.

"I know, but nothing about this has been easy for me. Everything is so new! I've never felt like this."

Caleb frowned. "I can't be someone's secret again, Landon."

He walked past me, and I smelled his cologne in the breeze. It made my heart sink.

"I loved kissing you," I said before turning around. Caleb's hand was on the doorknob but hadn't pulled it open. He just stood there with his back to me. "I've never felt happier kissing anyone in my life. I don't know what it's supposed to feel like, but I know that when I'm with you, I finally feel free."

Caleb turned to me with his hand still on the doorknob. I'll never forget the disappointment on his face.

"Figure your shit out, Lan," Caleb whispered before walking out, leaving me alone under the white light.

I exhaled, leaning against the sink. "Goddammit," I said to myself as I stared into the drain. I pictured myself falling through the dark hole and never reaching the bottom, just being stuck falling for eternity.

I walked at a steady pace back to our table, afraid to see Caleb if I glanced around the diner. Lauren was swiping through her phone when I approached. I didn't sit back down. "I gotta go," I said.

"What? We haven't even gotten our food yet."

"I know, I'm sorry," I said as I pulled out my wallet. I placed a folded twenty-dollar bill on the table. "I don't feel good. I just have to go home." I couldn't look at Lauren. I could hear it in her voice, I confused her. Panicked, I fled from the diner and got into my car. I just wanted to be alone. My heart was racing, I had no idea how I was going to fix anything.

TWENTY-THREE

I was on autopilot the next four days, going through the motions of my day. School, practice, shower, homework, sleep and do it all again the next day. I'd texted Caleb I was sorry the night after the confrontation in the restroom, but never got a text back. I'd completely ruined any chance I had with him.

I felt drained anytime I would see Lauren, all I was doing was lying to her, lying to my Dad, lying to myself and it took a toll on my emotional well-being. I was good at faking it in front of my Dad; he had no idea what I was going through; I doubt he would have understood it. All he asked about was football practice and moved on with his business. I sat at my bedroom desk, going over a practice quiz for my calculus class. My mind wondered as I scribbled little circles around the page. Suddenly my phone buzzed. I'd never moved so quickly to grab it in my life. I saw a text from Lauren on the screen.

LAUREN

Mind if I stop by tomorrow before school to say goodbye.

ME

Goodbye?

LAUREN

We're leaving for New York tomorrow...

I had forgotten Lauren was leaving for her audition during my week of numbness.

ME

Right, I'm sorry.

I'll meet you out front.

I threw my phone onto my bed; I didn't want to continue to check it. I was losing hope that Caleb would text me. The phone buzzed again. Assuming it was Lauren responding, I let it be.

I was back at the amusement park, and everything was fully operational and new. Kids were running around with big puffs of cotton candy on a stick. I could smell fresh popcorn, and people were screaming as the roller coaster sped down the track. I was standing at the entrance of the Ferris wheel alone, watching crowds of people pass by. Then everyone stopped in their tracks, parting like the red sea, revealing Caleb. He walked over to me, looking dashing in a black tux, smiling widely. He reached for my hand and pulled me in close to kiss me. I felt the familiar prickle of his upper lip against mine and it felt like we were floating. I stopped kissing him and looked around as our feet left the gravel. I panicked, but Caleb tightened his arm around my waist, holding me close to his body. "Everything will be okay," he whispered. I looked him in the eyes, feeling safe in his embrace. We heard everyone clap as they watched us floating higher and higher. Caleb moved in for another kiss before my eyes popped open and I was back in my room, discovering I'd drooled all over my practice quiz.

The digital clock on my desk glowed with red numbers; it was close to midnight. I huffed and pushed myself from the desk, groaning as I felt my neck stiffen. I'd fallen asleep at a terrible angle, causing a knot to form. I rubbed it with a strong thumb as I approached my bed. I took off my shorts and pushed them to the side with my foot, pulled my shirt over my head, and plopped down. I shuffled through my blanket to find my phone so I could plug it into its charger. Grabbing it, I checked the screen and my stomach dropped. The buzzing earlier wasn't Lauren responding to my text, it was Caleb, and I'd left it unread for hours. I swiped, going directly to his message.

CALEB

Hey, sorry, I haven't texted you back. I just needed time to think about everything.

I frantically started typing, hoping he was still awake.

ME

Sorry I didn't see this earlier, I knocked out early.

I stared at my screen, waiting for the three little dots to pop up, showing me he was typing a response, but nothing came. I sighed, plugged my phone into the charger, and placed it on my bedside table before clicking off my lamp. I rested my head on the pillow but I didn't want to close my eyes, I just stared at the dark ceiling wondering what Caleb might say next. I guessed he would ask me to delete his number, not wanting anything to do with me anymore.

My phone vibrated loudly against the wood, sending my heart through my chest. I reached over so quickly that I knocked the phone off the table instead of grabbing it.

"Shit," I whispered, leaning my upper body over the edge to search in the dark. It had bounced under my bed. I pushed myself back up and clicked my phone open.

CALEB
Sorry if I woke you up.

ME
You didn't, it's okay.

How are you?

CALEB
I think I'm all right.

I just needed time to think about everything, so I'm sorry I didn't text you back.

ME
That's understandable.

CALEB
To be completely honest, it hurt me after I saw you with your girlfriend, sorry what's her name?

ME

Lauren.

CALEB

I assume she doesn't know that we kissed?

ME

No, she doesn't. I swear I wanted to tell her that day, but I just couldn't find the courage.

CALEB

Coming out is tough, and everyone's journey is different. I realized that I have to respect that. But damn it hurt seeing that because I really liked you.

ME

Are you saying you don't anymore?

CALEB

I go back and forth. I wasn't lying when I said I've already done complicated. What you did was really shady.

ME

I promise I'll tell her. I like you a lot. It's just not gonna be easy to break up with Lauren.

CALEB

Believe me, I know that. And I don't want you to do this just for me. If this is how you really feel, then it isn't fair to her.

ME

I know. That's why I feel awful.

CALEB

Once you come out, it never really stops for the rest of your life. But every time it gets a little easier, you chip away at the insecurity and gain confidence in its place.

ME:

That's good to know.

I'm sorry I hurt you, I want you to know that it wasn't my intention.

CALEB

I keep thinking about what you said, that when you're with me you feel free. I want to feel that way too. I don't want to be your secret.

ME

I know, I don't want you to be either.

Staring at the bright screen in the dark was making my eyes hurt. I lowered my brightness before I went blind.

CALEB

So what do we do?

I sat there frozen for a minute, thinking of how to respond to his question. I didn't want to call it off just yet. There was still so much I wanted to explore with him.

ME

I just know that I don't want this to end.

CALEB

Don't let it.

ME

I think you should come to my game tomorrow night.

CALEB

I don't know, won't Lauren be there?

ME

She's actually gonna be gone the whole weekend. She's gonna be in New York for a college audition.

CALEB

I don't know. Won't it be weird?

ME:

ot unless we make it weird.

CALEB

Okay. I'm fine with seeing you, but nothing beyond that until you're a single man, all right?

ME

Works for me.

CALEB

I don't know much about football...

Maybe I'll bring Parker. He might have fun.

ME

Yeah! :)

CALEB

Maybe I'll watch Friday Night Lights, or Varsity Blues to get in the zone.

ME

Haha, whatever you need to do. The game starts at 7:30. Don't be late!

CALEB

I'm never late ;)

> **ME**
> Good. :) I'll see you tomorrow night then!

> **CALEB**
> Sleep tight.

> **ME**
> Night!

I placed my phone on the bedside table and went back to staring at the dark ceiling, but I was smiling. Tomorrow I had a reason to play now that I knew Caleb would be watching. I closed my eyes, feeling like I was crawling out of my self-loathing.

———

Friday night games always had special electricity to them. Even when we were in the locker room, we could hear the chants of everyone in the stands explode. The marching band was playing, and the cheerleaders were gleefully screaming their cheers to get everyone pumped. We were playing against the Skowhegan Saints that night, a team known for playing aggressively. They intentionally tried to hurt guys with their tackles, knocking players out one by one to make it an easier win, or so the rumor went.

"We know how these guys play," the coach said to us as we sat on the benches.

A few guys were still tying their shoes up. I sat on the wooden bench in front of my locker with my arms resetting on my padded thighs. I wedged my helmet between my feet on the floor.

"I want you guys to keep a cool head out there and watch out for each other," Coach said.

Everyone was nodding their heads. There was a big fight night energy in the room. Everyone was amped up, ready to get into the game. My Dad stood at the exit door, leaning against the frame. He gave me a head nod before the Coach ended his speech the way he ended every pre-game speech,

"Let's go give 'em hell!"

All the guys bounced to their feet and hollered, myself included.

I picked up my helmet and turned to close my locker, reaching into my duffel bag first to check my phone. I had a text from Lauren and a text from Caleb.

LAUREN
Good luck tonight! I love you!

ME
Thanks! <3

I swiped over to the text from Caleb. He'd sent me a selfie of him and Parker sitting in the stands. Parker was holding a bag of popcorn and they both had enormous smiles on their faces. Parker even had two thick painted lines under his eyes, one black and one red; representing my school's colors.

CALEB:
Turns out you're playing my old high school team. Feel free to kick their asses! ;)

ME
I'll do my best!

. . .

I placed my phone back into my bag with a smile. Seeing Caleb and Parker, knowing they were in the stands was all the fuel I needed. I felt so strong like I could pick up a bus over my head. I turned on my heels after slamming my locker shut and squeezed on my helmet. I glimpsed Chris from across the room; he was looking at me with concern on his face. He gestured to Dan with his eyes before slipping on his helmet.

I searched the locker room for Dan until I caught his Jersey number, 14. He'd just turned away from his locker and wiped his nose with his fingers, then wiped his fingers on his pants. Whatever he was taking, he wasn't hiding it very well, and I was concerned. He pushed his head into his helmet and filed out with the other guys.

The crowd went wild as we ran onto the field. The cheerleaders were throwing girls into the air and the band had never sounded louder. I heard the announcer call out our team's name over the loudspeakers, and the stomps on the bleachers boomed across the field. I searched through the sea of people in the stands, trying to get a glimpse of Caleb and Parker. I had limited vision through my helmet, but I spotted them. They sat toward the bottom, closer to the running track that surrounded the grassy turf. Parker was frantically waving and jumping to get my attention. I smiled and waved back, then spotted Tasha and Steven sitting close by, sipping from Styrofoam cups.

I looked across the field and saw the other team staring us down. Their uniforms were blue and gold, and they had two medieval-looking S letters stretched across the sides of their helmets. It was our second time facing the Skowhegan Saints that season. They had beaten us in the first game, so we were looking forward to revenge. Dan popped up in front of me and grabbed the face mask of my helmet.

"Let's kill these motherfuckers!" He shouted before running onto the field.

I wanted to beat the team just as badly as he did, but I wasn't about to intentionally hurt anyone. We lined up in the middle of the field, and I looked across to the guy that would guard me and he flipped me off. A part of me wanted to tackle him right there, but that wasn't my job. My job was to get the ball from Dan and run it as far as I could.

"Blue sixteen!" Dan shouted out to us.

I slouched and pushed the ball of my foot into the grass; I was ready to run. Knowing Caleb was watching from the stands made me feel invincible.

"Hike!"

The ball was snapped to Dan, and I shot off running. The guy that flipped me off barreled toward me. I needed to fake him out. The both of us were on the same train track, rushing toward each other. He was a bull that only had eyes for me. As soon as he jumped for me, I twisted around him with a spin, causing him to hurtle to the ground.

I looked over my shoulder; I was open for the pass. Dan always threw a little high. I saw the ball spiraling toward me and caught it with a jump. As soon as my feet met the turf, I was struck from the side. We both crashed to the ground as I heard a whistle through the small holes in my helmet.

"Fuck you, pretty boy," the other guy said as he pushed himself off of me.

I stood, still feeling the pain in my ribs. I glanced over to Caleb who had his hands over his mouth; the tackle must've looked brutal. Parker had both fists raised in the air, mouthing my name. I shook off the pain and smiled as I jogged back to the scrimmage line. Caleb seeing me get tackled during the first play bruised my ego, but it only fueled my fire more.

I pushed my way into the huddle of guys as Dan pointed at me.

"Landon, watch your fucking nine and three. Don't fuck this up for us."

"Dan, chill out," I said. "We have a hundred plays left."

"We can't play like pussies. Not against these guys."

I rolled my eyes at him. "Just call the next play and let's go."

The other team got more aggressive during the second quarter. We were on defense with three minutes left until halftime. I stood on the back line. My job was to force the player with the ball to run out of bounds. Chris was in the line in front of me. His job was to not allow the player with the ball to get very far.

The Saints hiked the ball, and we were off. I followed close behind Chris as he pushed through two players, rushing for the ball. If Chris failed, it was on me to run the guy holding the ball off the field. A husky guy with the number 43 on his chest came barreling toward Chris like a Mack truck. Chris tried to evade him but 43 wrapped an arm around Chris's waist, bringing him down, but Chris wiggled free before another player, 30, grabbed Chris's face mask and brought him down to the grass. Luckily, a guy from our team took out the guy with the ball at the seventy-yard line.

The whistle blew, but the ref never called out player 30 for the face-mask.

I jogged closer to the old man dressed in black and white, shouting, "you need to flag 30 for the face-mask."

"I didn't see it," he said calmly.

"I'm telling you it happened," I said, pulling off my helmet.

Dan ran up to us, looking heated. "Don't tell me you're that fucking blind!"

"He said he didn't see it," I said to Dan.

"The fuck he didn't! Call the penalty!"

Chris jogged over, removing his helmet too.

"No," the ref said, shaking his head and walking off the field. The three of us stood there dumbfounded while the other team strutted by us. 30 pulled off his helmet and kissed the air in Dan's direction.

"Pull that shit again, asshole!" Dan shouted at 30. "Come try it on me!"

30 had no hesitation stepping to Dan. The two were in each other's faces screaming back and forth. Chris and I held Dan back, unfortunately to his detriment because 30 took a swing and connected with Dan's jaw. Dan overpowered us and broke free of our grip and tackled 30 to the ground and kept punching him until the refs and coaches rushed in to separate them. The animosity between our two teams cranked up to eleven after that.

The Saints were beating us by six points during the third quarter when they finally took out a member of our team. Dan had thrown the ball down the center of the field to me. Two Saints flanked me and I knew I had to get rid of the ball fast. Ray Bloom was running parallel to me and was the only guy close enough. Ray and I locked eyes, and I tossed him the ball. I was tackled but able to keep my sights on him. Ray ran the ball another two-and-a-half yards before two linebackers came out of nowhere from opposite sides. The linebackers lunged, one connected with Ray's torso and the other with Ray's legs, practically ripping him in half. The linebacker's weight landed on Ray's leg, twisting it backward. Ray let out a blood-curdling scream that was heard even over the rowdy crowd.

I rushed over to him as other team members did the same. The ref called the coaches over to inspect Ray's leg. All of us took a knee and watched in horror as Ray cried and screamed.

"Those fuckers did this on purpose!" Dan shouted.

I looked over my shoulder at the Saints standing on the sidelines laughing and making crying faces, mocking us. It made my blood boil. They had no respect whatsoever.

The crowd cheered as they wheeled Ray off the field on a stretcher, holding his fist in the air.

We were four points away from overturning the game, with fifteen seconds left in the last quarter. The energy on the field was electric. The crowd was booming. I glanced over at Caleb before walking into the huddle. He looked like he had gotten more into the game as time passed. Parker was on Caleb's back and they were both cheering.

We all locked arms and listened to Dan take the lead.

"It's now or never, y'all. We can pull this off, we just need to be perfect."

Everyone was drenched in sweat. The pressure was on and we knew it.

Dan continued, "I want to use Purple Twenty Three. Landon, do you think you can do it?"

"That's twenty yards," Chris said. "It's too risky."

"If Landon says he can do it, then we're doing it," Dan said. "We need risky if we're gonna win this."

All eyes were on me. I glanced at Caleb again; he was mouthing something to me. It was hard to see, but I think he mouthed "you can do this." But it could've easily been my imagination.

"I can do it," I said, snapping my eyes back to Dan.

"Let's fucking go!" Dan yelled at us. He put his fist out in the middle of the circle and we all slapped our hands on top of it before we broke.

I stepped to the scrimmage line with my heart pounding. My eyes were laser-focused on the end zone. I slowed my breath and the noise of the crowd faded away and all I heard was Dan's voice yelling, "Purple Twenty Three! Purple Twenty Three! Hike!"

I was shot from a cannon, with the kind of speed that could split molecules. I dodged three players before I even looked over my shoulder for the ball. I felt telepathically connected to Dan; he knew exactly when to throw the ball as I turned, running backward. It was the first time in a long time that he didn't throw high. The ball was a perfect spiral and my chest was its target.

I gripped the ball between my arms and turned toward the end zone, and my legs kicked into fourth gear. Five yards, then ten, I was soaring. I checked my left, there was one Saint's player trailing me. It was player 30. I shot my eyes forward again; the field was clear, but 30 was gaining on me.

I was speeding across the field like one of those lizards running on water. I glanced to my left again, 30 was even closer. He could've nabbed me if he lunged far enough. I could tell he was about to jump for me when I saw Chris charge at 30 like a bull seeing red. Chris lunged, wrapping his arms around 30's waist, slamming him down hard.

The end zone was mine and mine alone. I jumped for it and rolled onto my padded shoulder across the line, scoring the touchdown, pushing our score six points ahead and winning the game.

I ripped off my helmet and slammed it to the ground, letting out my best war cry. My head got colder as the wind swept the condensation away. The entire team came stampeding toward me until they smashed into me with open arms, cheering and hollering. It was hard to keep my balance as each body crashed into the pile. It was a huge win for us. The crowd's cheers were deafening even while "We are the Champions" blasted from the loudspeakers. I had never played better in my entire high school career. I felt like Sonic the Hedgehog on the field that night. No one could catch me.

———

I was chatting with Dan and Chris in the parking lot as Tasha and Steven walked up to us. Tasha hugged the three of us, gushing about how great the game was. Steven stood by with his hands in his pockets, staring me down; it looked like he wanted to say something, but was keeping his distance from Dan.

"Landon Griffin?" A voice asked from behind me. I turned around to see a broad-shouldered man with salt and pepper hair. He was holding some folded-up papers in his hand. The others focused their attention on him as well. None of us had ever seen him before. He looked upper class based on what he was wearing.

"Yeah, that's me," I said with raised eyebrows, still in my muddy gear.

"Hi, my name is Chester Redfield." He reached out to shake my hand. "I'm from The University of Texas." I felt like a soldier who went to attention and firmly took his handshake.

"Oh, nice to meet you, sir,"

"You played a fantastic game tonight," Chester said as he pushed the folded papers into the inside pocket of his jacket. "We've had our eye on you for a while now and we like what we see."

"Thank you, sir."

"We would love to offer you a full scholarship to come play for us in the fall," Chester said with a half-smile. I heard Tasha gasp from behind me. I was in complete shock, wondering if I misheard him. "I know this is very informal telling you in a parking lot full of people, but we like to approach our guys before going over the official stuff."

I felt Chris's hands grab onto my shoulder pads and shake me with excitement, which brought me out of my state of shock. "Wow, I don't know what to say," I said. My mind felt blank. "I'm honored, thank you. Thank you so much." A smile filled my face, and I wished my Dad had been there to hear the news with me.

"We'll be in touch," Chester said before reaching his hand out again.

"Thank you, sir. I look forward to it," I said as I returned the handshake. We all watched Chester walk away. I waited until he was out of earshot to turn around. "Holy shit!" I said through my teeth. Tasha screamed with excitement and jumped up and down, whereas Chris picked me up off my feet in a big bear hug. Even Steven was clapping along with Tasha and smiling. Everyone seemed happy for me except for Dan. Chris put me down and my eyes went to Dan who was leaning against a car, looking defeated.

"That should've been me," Dan mumbled.

Tasha shot daggers in Dan's direction. "What?"

"I said that fucking should've been me!"

Chris tilted his head. "Seriously, bro?"

Dan pointed at me but looked at Chris. "I played just as good as he did!"

"No one is saying you didn't," Steven said.

"No one fucking asked you, faggot! What the fuck do you know?" Dan yelled as he took a step toward Steven, but Chris stepped in front of him.

"Landon's your best friend," Chris said. "You can't be happy for him?"

"For what? Because he's some fucking hot shot now?" Dan said as he shoved Chris. "Fuck all of you." Dan grabbed his helmet off the car and walked back to the locker room, while I stood there feeling deflated.

"He's an asshole, guys," Chris said as he turned to us. "I'm sorry."

"You shouldn't be the one apologizing," I said as I glanced across the parking lot. Dan pulled open the door and stomped inside the school.

"I'm gonna make sure he cools down," Chris said as he crouched to pick up his helmet. "You guys are still coming to the party tomorrow night, right?"

"Of course!" Tasha said.

"I won't be coming for obvious reasons," Steven said as he crossed his arms.

"I know it's Dan's birthday, but I invite everyone no matter if Dan likes them or not," Chris said with a smirk. "It's my house too."

"Maybe I'll make an appearance then," Steven said as he tossed his invisible hair, making Tasha chuckle.

"Cool," Chris said as he jogged away. "See you guys tomorrow! Congrats again Landon!"

Tasha tackled me with a hug. I laughed and hugged her back. A line of cars had formed as everyone was leaving the lot.

"I'm so freaking proud of you!" Tasha squealed.

"Yeah, you should be really proud Landon," Steven said as he watched us.

"Thanks, guys. I should go tell my Dad."

"Yes, yes, go," Tasha said, slapping me on my shoulder pads. "We have face masks to get to." She trotted over to Steven and wrapped her arm around him.

"I'll see you guys at the party," I said with a head nod.

"Can't wait!" Tasha said with a smile. I'd almost forgotten about Caleb and Parker in all the excitement. I walked back toward the field with my Helmet edged between my body and my arm.

"Landon," Steven called out to me. I whipped around and

saw he had hung back while Tasha walked to her car. "Eighty-Three must be your lucky number." I looked down at my jersey, I could smell the sweat seeping through.

"Since day one."

Steven daintily spun and walked away.

Okay? I thought to myself, heading for the field again.

I spotted Caleb and Parker sitting alone in the front row of the stands. Everyone else had gotten to their car at that point. Caleb was throwing pieces of popcorn into the air as Parker tried to catch them in his mouth. Seeing that made me smile. I jogged over to them through the empty field. I could feel my legs begging me to stop, I was exhausted.

"Landon!" Parker shouted as he saw me. A piece of popcorn accidentally hit him in the face as he glimpsed me running over. I slowed down and approached them with heavy breaths. Parker threw himself at me with a big hug.

"Hey, bud," I said as I wrapped my arms around his head. "Did you enjoy the game?"

"It was so cool!" Parker said as he pulled away from me. He jumped up onto the first step of the bleachers with excitement. "When you made that last touchdown and you were like aaahh-hhhh!" Parker mimicked me throwing down my helmet and even added a strong-man flex for good measure. I laughed, watching him try to flex his scrawny arms.

"I think you have a new fan," Caleb said as he stood from his seat with a crooked smile.

"And what about you?" I said, taking a step toward Caleb.

"Oh, I'll be first in line for your autograph."

"Shut up," I said with a chuckle. I felt the butterflies wake up in my stomach and start fluttering their wings. "Something insane just happened though." Parker jumped off the step and settled next to his big brother. "I just got offered a scholarship to play at the University of Texas."

"Holy shit!" Caleb shouted, stepping to me with a hug. His force knocked me back a bit, causing me to drop my helmet. I wrapped my arms around him, thinking how lucky I was just to touch him again. "That's incredible, congrats!"

"Thanks," I said with a smile as we came away from the embrace.

"What's a scholarship?" Everything had gone over Parker's head.

"That means Landon gets to go to college for free and play football there."

"Sounds cool," Parker said as he looked up at Caleb. "But wait, people have to pay to go to college?"

Caleb and I nodded.

"That's dumb," Parker said.

"He's not wrong," Caleb said, looking at me before we laughed.

Caleb and Parker walked me back to the school, where we stopped in front of the big metal door that led into the gym. The parking lot was empty. Everyone was probably at Lucky's or Joe's Pizza Place by then.

I leaned against the door and looked around the parking lot, we were the only three people around. I reached for Caleb's hand and pulled him close, hoping I didn't smell too badly.

I wanted to kiss him more than anything and I think he could tell.

"Hey, remember what I said? Are you a single man yet?"

"You're right, I know, I know."

Caleb squeezed my hand and smiled before letting go. Not being able to touch him more killed me.

"You still wanna go to the party with me tomorrow?" I asked.

"Yeah, I think so. Just text me the address."

"Will do." I smiled as Caleb and Parker walked by me,

headed toward the street. "Hey," I called out, causing Caleb to look over his shoulder at me. "You looked really cute tonight."

Caleb smiled, looking a little flushed. "So did you, football boy."

Caleb winked at me and my chest got warm.

Parker grabbed Caleb's hand as they continued on their way. I kept my eyes on them.

Parker looked up at Caleb. "Are you and Landon boyfriends?"

"No," I heard Caleb say with a laugh.

"You must really like him then."

"Yeah," Caleb said, looking down at Parker. "I like him a lot."

Just hearing him say that sent me to the moon. I walked into the building, unable to hide my smile. It had been one of the best nights I'd had in a long time.

TWENTY-FOUR

I checked my phone as I walked home. The first text I saw was from Lauren. I crossed the street, looking both ways before clicking my phone open.

LAUREN:

TASHA JUST TOLD ME THE NEWS!
CONGRATS BABE!

ME:

Haha, thank you! I couldn't believe it.

I walked through the side door. To my surprise, my Dad was already there in the kitchen. He suddenly popped the cork from a bottle of champagne and it scared the hell out of me.

"Congratulations, son!" My Dad yelled as the bottle overflowed. "Oh, shit, shit." He held the bottle over the sink as the fizz poured out. I laughed and tossed my duffel bag on the floor.

"I've been saving this for when we got the news. I know you're not twenty-one but one glass won't hurt."

"Okay." I shrugged with a smile as I sat at the kitchen Island. "How'd you find out?"

"Mr. Redfield talked to me and coach after he approached you," Dad said as he filled two glasses with the bubbly liquid. "I'm proud of you son, I knew this would happen!" He extended his arm across the counter and handed me a glass.

"Thanks," I said as we clinked our glasses together. The bubbles of the champagne tickled my nose when I took a sip. It was my first time tasting the drink, I wasn't expecting it to be so sweet. I wondered if my Dad would've been that proud if I got into the writing program at NYU. "Dan seemed pretty upset."

He wiped his mustache with a paper towel. "About what?"

"I don't know, he just seemed like, jealous I got a scholarship and he didn't."

"That's ridiculous. There's still time. Another school could approach him."

"Yeah, you're right." I took another sip. The bubbles continued to crackle down my throat, and I thought about how much Dan had changed throughout high school. I looked up from my cup and saw my Dad smiling. "I wish we could tell mom," I whispered. Dad's smile faded as if he had forgotten she was gone until I spoke.

"She'd be just as proud, and she'd already be planning a party to celebrate," Dad said as he gulped down the rest of his cup.

"I miss her."

My Dad poured himself another cup, ignoring what I said.

"I'm gonna head to bed, I'm pretty beat," he said before ascending the stairs, gripping the bottle of champagne in one hand and his full cup in the other.

I sat in the kitchen alone and took my time sipping my cup. I hadn't thought about all the things my mom was missing. She wouldn't be there to take pictures of us before prom. She wouldn't be there to see me graduate. She wouldn't be dropping me off at college with tears welling up in her eyes. I thought of an entire lifetime of events where moms celebrate their sons, and how I'd never get that.

I downed the rest of my drink and placed my glass in the sink. I grabbed my duffel bag and climbed the stairs. Sitting, I felt the bounce of the mattress underneath me. I pictured myself playing college football, going to parties, skipping class to sleep in. Then I imagined how different it would look if I was in New York, not playing football, but writing on my laptop at the library.

I felt my phone vibrate and remembered Lauren had been texting me. I pulled it out, laying down on my bed.

LAUREN

If anyone deserves it, it's you!

ME

Dan didn't seem to think so.

LAUREN

Ugh, Tasha told me. :(I wish for once he would think of someone other than himself. I'm sorry, babe.

ME

It's whatever. How's NYC?

LAUREN

OMG it's amazing!

Our hotel is so nice! We're staying at this place on 50th street like right next to Times Square. It feels so alive here, everyone is always moving. I love it!

. . .

I wanted to visit New York so badly and get a taste of the fast-paced life. I wanted to feel the wind of a subway train as it rushed by, and walk through a crowded Times Square, bumping shoulders with tourists.

ME

I'm jealous, haha.

LAUREN

Well, if I get in, you'll have to come to visit me all the time!

I wondered what a long-distance relationship would be like if she moved to New York. Maybe she would know about Caleb by then and I wouldn't have to break up with her over the phone. My anxiety level rose just thinking about it.

ME

You're gonna get in, you're too good not to!

LAUREN

Awww, you're so sweet! <3

Oh!

My Dad just told me that my prom dress is ready! And he'll be picking up your tux this week.

ME

Holy crap, I can't believe prom is a little over a month away.

LAUREN

I know, right?! I'm so excited!

I have to sleep cutie, we're getting up early to head to the audition. I miss you so much!

ME

All right, break a leg! Sleep tight. :)

LAUREN

Goodnight! <3

I wondered if she was catching on to my non-reciprocation. I missed her being around of course, but the way I missed her and the way I missed Caleb were two very different things. My guilt got worse, and I could make it go away if I just had the balls. I plugged my phone into its charger and placed my head on my pillow. I wanted to text Caleb goodnight, but I couldn't keep my eyes open. Not even having the energy to get up to turn my light off or get undressed.

I spent most of the next afternoon figuring out my costume for Dan's party that night. I wanted something that showed a good amount of skin to make sure Caleb couldn't take his eyes off me. I wanted to look sexy for him. Browsing Pinterest boards I ended up with the idea of an ancient Greek person.

It was simple but hopefully effective. I knew everyone would go the simple route. I had to remind myself that it was a birthday party, not a Halloween costume contest. I wondered if Dan would still hold a grudge when I showed up, not wanting to deal with the awkwardness; I hoped to have a calm night and to play beer pong with Caleb. I'd probably have to do all the drinking since Caleb couldn't during his probation. Then I realized, maybe he shouldn't be around underage drinking. He'd get into more trouble if the cops showed up. I grabbed my phone and sent him a text, airing all of my anxious energy.

CALEB

lol, I'm not worried about it. Let's just have fun.

He was annoyingly easygoing about everything.

I pulled a vine off the drainpipe in our backyard and tied it together. Then I glued a bunch of green leaves to it that I picked off one of our bushes and made a very poor-looking crown that rested on top of my head. I pulled a white sheet from a shelf in the upstairs closet and brought it to my room. Opening my laptop, I'd already queued up a YouTube video on how to make a toga.

My phone vibrated on my desk. I hopped over to it.

LAUREN:

Okay, I think it went well.

ME

How do you feel?

LAUREN

I was so nervous, but I think I did the best I could.

ME

Don't worry then! I'm sure they loved you!

LAURE

I hope so! Getting ready for the party?

ME

Yeah, figuring out my costume now!

LAUREN

Aw yay! Send me pics when you're done. We're gonna find a place to eat. I'll text you later!

I placed my phone on the desk. I stripped down to my white boxer briefs and held the sheet in one hand, then pressed play on the video. A buff frat bro appeared on-screen, showing off the toga he was wearing. "Hey guys, welcome back to my channel," his deep voice said from my speakers. "No college experience is complete without a toga party. Today I'm gonna give you ten easy steps to turn your basic bed sheet into a kick-ass toga!"

I kept having to stop the video and rewind as he went through the steps pretty quickly. The guy was a pro. He seemed to be in the living room of a big house, I could see a coffee table made of beer cans behind him. It felt like it took hours to get the toga configuration correct. I wrapped it over my shoulder and tied a knot and then through my legs and tied another knot and then around my waist, tying another knot. I already knew that unwrapping it was going to feel like one of those brain puzzles where you have to unlink the two metal pieces.

After tying the last knot, I looked in the mirror. I placed the leaf crown on my head and smiled; the look was complete. I just needed a pair of flip-flops. The sheet was mostly wrapped around my waist and under my crotch. My hips looked wider than they were thanks to the fluffiness of the fabric. The sheet rose across my torso and wrapped around my right shoulder. It exposed the whole left side of my upper body. I could see my hip bones poking out from the sheet. I pulled the waistband of my underwear down just enough to make it look like I wasn't wearing anything underneath. I was proud of what I'd accomplished, and I hoped Caleb would find me irresistible.

I glanced at the digital clock on my desk, I was already late. "Shit!" I said as I opened the door and searched the floor of my closet. It was dark, so I had to find my one pair of flip-flops by feeling around aimlessly. I felt the rubber against my palm and grabbed them. I slipped them on one foot at a time as I stumbled over to my bed to close my laptop. I ran down the stairs and out the door, then around to the backyard to collect my bike. My Dad was using the car, but Dan's house was only ten blocks away. I had planned on taking my bike anyway in case I drank too much.

I pedaled and regretted wearing flip-flops, not realizing how much more difficult it would be. It was already dark, and I felt my exposed nipple get hard as I pushed through the breeze. The street lights popped on and I heard a whistle. I glanced to my right to see two women sitting on their porch drinking. They started hollering at me and I felt like a woman passing a group of horny construction workers on the street.

I was panting by the time I got to Dan's block. I jumped off my bike to walk the rest of the way; already sweating through the sheet. The butterflies jumped around my stomach as I thought about seeing Caleb. I couldn't wait to introduce him to everyone and prove he wasn't the criminal they thought he was. Instead, I could show them how charming he was.

I approached Dan's house and could already hear the music. His house was bigger than mine. It was a split-level style, four-bedroom home with red siding, and white shutters on every window. They had a big front porch where people congregated, sipping out of red solo cups. I ditched my bike in the front yard and started up the cement path that shot down the middle of the grass. I flip-flopped to the porch, noticing everyone's costumes. Katie Bear was dressed as a nun, which seemed appropriate. Zach Richards was dressed as a military person, wearing camouflage shorts and a camouflage T-shirt, completing the look with a set of dog tags around his neck. Kyle Dempsy was dressed as a cop, wearing a jacket with 'POLICE' across the back and a pair of aviator sunglasses.

I opened the front door and was hit with a sound wave of chatter and loud music. Someone had blown up a bunch of colored balloons and littered the entire first floor with them. I surveyed the space, there were more people there than I expected. Every room in the house looked shoulder to shoulder crowded. I could smell marijuana creeping down from upstairs. It overwhelmed me, as I hated showing up to social events by myself. It made me feel lost.

I looked around the crowded room. *I wonder if Caleb's here yet.*

"Landon! What's up!"

I followed the voice. It was Chris. He'd called out to me as he was leading a girl upstairs. I almost didn't recognize him. He was wearing a long wig, with a tie-dye bandana around his forehead and a tie-dye shirt and shorts. I assumed he was a hippie.

"Hey!" I shouted back, giving him a wave before he disappeared.

"Landon, here!" Tasha walked toward me holding out a plastic cup. "Catch up!"

"Oh," I said as I took the cup from her. I lifted it to my mouth and immediately breathed in the smell of hairspray. I took a big gulp, and the liquid burned my insides. I was never much of a drinker, but when Tasha tells you to do something, you do it. "Jesus." I winced. "What is this?"

"Dan's special!" Tasha yelled over the music as she bopped around. She acted as if she'd already downed a few cups of the special drink. I watched her dance. She was dressed as Catwoman, in fake leather pants and a whip that wrapped up around her torso. Cat ears connected to a black mask over her eyes. She looked amazing.

"Hey, girl!" Steven yelled as he approached us. Tasha screamed and hopped around with him as if they hadn't seen each other in years.

Steven was practically naked. He wore very, very short, white shorts and nothing else but angel wings and a sparkly halo that attached to a ring secured around the top of his head. His eyes were made up with gold eye shadow and his lips sparkled from the pink lip gloss he had on. His entire body was shimmering with glitter. He looked sexy as hell.

Am I attracted to Steven? No, it's just the outfit. Right?

"You look amazing, Landon," Steven said after he and Tasha finished bouncing.

"Thanks, so do you," I said, causing Steven to cheers me with his drink. "I'm kind of hungry. Is there any food around?"

"Yeah, I just saw some in the kitchen. C'mon." Steven gestured that Tasha and I follow him. We pushed through the crowds of dancing teens, and I spotted Betty Grass making out with Tommy Deckler, and people around them were cheering them on. It was strange because I don't think I'd ever seen them talk to each other during our four years at Madison High.

I took another gulp of my mystery drink and it sent fire ripping through my throat. We reached the kitchen, and the counters were filled with bowls of assorted snacks. Beer cans littered the space between them. I took a quick look in each bowl, before I reached for some pretzels and then some baked potato chips, swallowing them down with more liquid fire.

Jordan Palicki popped in to place a plate of brownies in front of us, knocking some beer cans to the floor, and walked away.

"Oh my god, those look so good," Tasha said. Steven and I both agreed, but only I reached for one and gobbled it down. The brownie was so fudgy, it kept sticking to my teeth. Chewing it made me crave a glass of milk but all I had was the kerosene in my little red cup so I downed it before taking another brownie. I noticed a weird aftertaste but hurried on to another handful of pretzels.

"I'm empty," I said, shaking my cup.

"On it." Tasha grabbed my cup and disappeared into the crowd, leaving Steven and me alone. I could feel the awkward tension as we both stood there bopping our heads to the music. Neither of us knew what to say to the other.

Steven broke the ice. "Can you believe Lauren's living it up in New York right now?"

"I know, I'm so jelly," I said with immediate regret. I'd never abbreviated the word jealous in my life.

"Samesies," Steven shot back without a blink of an eye. "She said she slayed the audition."

Steven must've gotten a different play-by-play than I had. Lauren seemed unsure when she texted me earlier. Maybe she was catching on to my dismissiveness. The anxiety poured into my stomach like the Dan special, quick and fiery. I wondered if Lauren had brought up anything to Steven about me.

"Yeah, she told me. I'm excited for her," I said over the music. I could already feel my voice getting scratchy from the strain.

Steven leaned an elbow on the kitchen counter. "So are you guys gonna do long distance if she moves to New York and you're here?"

Am I being interrogated? Will he report my answers back to Lauren?

"Uh, I mean, I guess?" I shoved more pretzels into my

mouth. "We haven't really talked about it yet." I wanted to get off the subject of Lauren. "You should try a brownie. They're so good!" I'd already felt the effects hitting from downing one cup of Dan's Special.

"I can't. I'm trying to stay away from sweet stuff lately," Steven said as he rubbed his stomach. His fingers caressed his smooth, rippled abdomen.

"Steven, I can literally see each ab of your six-pack. I don't think one brownie is gonna change that."

"Better safe than sorry," Steven said with a shrug.

Tasha came bounding into the kitchen as if she had just run through a tornado. She was holding my red cup, but she also had a half-empty bottle of vodka under her arm. She held three smaller shot-sized cups in her other hand. She handed me my drink first and I could smell the familiar hairspray aroma.

Steven took the bottle from under her arm and read the label. "Where did you get this?"

"Corey Bashoff," Tasha said with ease. "He just handed it to me before going to the backyard."

"Are you trying to kill me?" I asked. My drinking habits were very few and far between. Other than the cup of champagne I had with my Dad, I hadn't touched a drop of alcohol since the night of junior prom.

"Just one shot!" Tasha said with a smile.

"I don't know," I said.

"It's senior year!" Tasha said. "Who knows what'll happen when we all go off to our separate schools. This might be one of the last parties we have."

"Well, there's still prom, and graduation," I said.

"He's got a point," Steven said before Tasha gave him a light slap on the arm. She then gave me a look that said she would ruin my life if I didn't take a shot.

"Fine, I'll do it! But just one, this drink is already fucking me up," I said, raising my plastic cup.

Tasha yelped with excitement and poured the vodka to the rim of each shot cup. We each grabbed one and raised it. Some of mine had spilled across my hand before I threw it back. I clenched my jaw and squeezed my teeth together as the alcohol slid down my throat. Straight vodka was the worst. Tasha and Steven seemed to take the shot a lot easier than I had.

Steven glanced around the kitchen. "Do you think anyone here is gay?"

"Good luck with that," Tasha scoffed.

"Hey, a bitch can dream okay!" Steven laughed. I almost spat my drink out, laughing as well.

"Where's Dan?" I asked after another gulp.

"I saw Dan when I first showed up," Tasha said, reaching for a handful of chips from a blue bowl. "But that was like an hour ago."

Steven was bopping his head when he asked, "Can we go dance or something?"

"Yaaaassss!" Tasha yelled as she grabbed both of our hands and pulled us toward the living room.

We pushed through the sweaty bodies and found a spot in the middle of everyone. The music was even louder in the living room. Everyone was dancing to the sound of a techno beat.

"Does this feel familiar?" Tasha yelled.

My heart skipped, I thought she was asking me, but Steven responded quickly.

"Yes, except there usually aren't this many girls!" Steven shouted back. My mind flashed to seeing him at club Paradise when I was with Caleb. Anxiety popped its head into my thoughts.

Steven would've said something by now if he'd seen me, right?

"Dude!" I heard a guy yell as he approached Jordan Palicki, who was dancing next to us, dressed in all white. "Where did you put the pot brownies?"

"They're on the kitchen counter!" Jared yelled back.

My world stood still when I realized what I'd done.

"Oh my god," I yelled to the others. "Fuck!"

"What?" Tasha yelled before doing a body roll.

"I ate two brownies!"

"Yes, we watched you do it," Steven hollered. "So what?"

"I just heard someone ask where the pot brownies were!" I'd never smoked anything, let alone eaten a pot brownie. Tasha and Steven busted out laughing. I tried to put on a serious face. "Guys! This isn't funny. I've never been high before!"

"Boy, you are about to have a great night!" Tasha said between fits of laughter.

My tongue felt dry, so I took a mouthful of my drink. We continued to dance and laugh, and I tried to remember if I put on deodorant. I raised my arms into a dance move to give myself a whiff. No one seemed to notice or care. I felt reassured when I could smell the familiar scent of Old Spice.

I looked around the party as we danced, hunting for Caleb. I told him what time the party started, yet I didn't see anyone walking around looking like Michael Myers.

I finally spotted Dan through the sliding glass doors that led into the backyard. "Dan's outside, we should say hi," I said with a slight slur of my S syllables. Steven rolled his eyes but followed Tasha as she followed behind me. I slid the glass door to the right and stepped into the grass of the backyard. It was noticeably cooler outside, and separate music was playing a lot quieter. There was a large rectangular, in-ground pool in the middle of the yard that was lit up from under the water. A dozen balloons had found their way inside and floated on the surface.

The whole yard was lit up by lantern string lights that lined the wooden fence surrounding the yard.

"Dan!" I called out. He was huddled in a small group and looked up when he heard his name. He was dressed in khaki shorts and an oversized Hawaiian shirt. A flower lei hung around his neck and sunscreen covered his nose. A pair of sunglasses were tucked into the top of his shirt. He came staggering over to me and bumped my fist with his. "Happy Birthday," I said with a smile.

"Thanks, man!" he said as he sipped his beer. He looked at Tasha and Steven behind me and said, "Guys, we're about to play a game, but I wanna talk to Landon for a sec." Dan wrapped his arm around my neck and dragged me away from my two comrades. He brought me to the corner of his yard, where it was a little quieter. "Hey," he whispered to me. His sniffles started up again, and he wiped his nose with his fingers. "Are you drinking the Dan Special?"

"Yeah, what the hell is in it?"

"Uh," Dan said as he looked at his feet, racking his brain for the answer. "Tequila, Rum, Vodka, some orange juice," he paused. "And Sprite!"

"Jesus, it's awful," I said with a smile before downing the rest of it in my cup.

"You should try some of this," Dan said as he reached into his pocket. He looked around the yard before, he opened his hand, revealing a little plastic baggie filled with white powder.

"Dude, what the fuck," I said as I moved my body in front of his hand so no one would see.

Dan poked his finger through the top of the bag and scooped a bit onto the tip, brought it to his nose, and snorted it with ease.

"This'll give you energy for hours, bro," Dan said. "It makes me fuck like Superman."

"Dan, where did you get this?"

"I know a guy in Skowhegan. I can hook you up."

"I don't want the hookup. Where do you get the money for this?"

"I sell a little too."

"A little what?"

"Whatever he wants me to. Coke, meth, weed, rocks, whatever."

"Jesus, Dan! Do you know how badly this could fuck you up? If Coach finds out, you'd be kicked off the team! You could say goodbye to getting a scholarship."

Dan closed the bag and pushed it back into his pocket. His face was twisted, looking offended.

"Fuck, Landon, it's not that serious," Dan said with a deep sniff.

"Are you insane? Of course, it is!" I said through gritted teeth. "And if the cops caught you-"

"Guys!" Tasha yelled from across the yard. "Come on, let's play!"

We both looked over, sending a nod in her direction.

"Don't show anyone else," I whispered to Dan as we walked past the pool. Dan wiped his nose again as we approached, saying nothing.

Ten people surrounded a circular plastic table where someone had placed an empty beer bottle in the middle. My legs tingled as I stood next to Tasha.

"Okay," Jordan Palicki said. "We're gonna play Spin the Bottle Truth Or Dare."

Tasha leaned over to me and whispered, "What is this? Middle school?"

I covered my mouth, trying not to laugh as Jordan explained the rules.

"It starts with someone spinning the bottle. Whoever it lands on, the spinner gets to ask that person a Truth or Dare. If the person refuses that Truth or Dare, they have to kiss. No matter what you decide to do, you always gotta take a drink." Jordan finished by picking up a full bottle of vodka out of nowhere and everyone cheered.

I rubbed my left eye, feeling lightheaded. My fingers tingled too. The alcohol and weed brownies started hitting me all at the same time. I blinked and felt like my head was full of sand. Jessica Walters spun the bottle. My eyes locked on it as if I was being hypnotized. I felt my head wobble back and forth; the sand was getting heavier. The bottle slowed and landed on Max Gibbons, who was dressed as a magician. I wanted to see him do a magic trick so badly.

"Truth or dare?" Jessica said as she played with her teased hair. She was dressed as an 80s chick, obnoxiously chewing a piece of gum.

"Dare," Max said.

Please dare him to do a magic trick. I hope he pulls a bunny out of his hat.

"I dare you to take this gum from me," Jessica said with a wink.

Max had no hesitation, jumping over the table to get to her. He pushed his face against hers and I could see their tongues fighting to the death for the piece of gum. I felt like I had robot eyes, I swear I could zoom in close and see every string of spit coming off their mouths. I breathed heavier as my head filled with more sand about to overflow.

Focus, focus. You might miss the magic trick. Bunnies are so cute. I hope it's a white one.

My head was swaying back and forth, feeling heavier. I could no longer resist the weight. I let my head swing backward, looking at the night sky as the sand poured down my neck and my spine. It felt so good. The sand was rushing down my back as if it were a water slide. It pushed past my tailbone and under my crotch, out my groin, causing me to laugh uncontrollably. It tickled.

I hadn't noticed the bottle was being spun again, or that it stopped on me until Tasha nudged me.

I'm so fucked.

TWENTY-FIVE

"Landon, hello?" Tasha waved her hand in front of my face.

"Yeah, hi. What's up?" I said with squinted eyes, trying my best to focus.

"She asked you a question," Tasha fired back with a grin. I looked across the table, seeing Maddy Houser dressed as a construction worker, I'd never seen a pink hard hat before.

"How many tools can you fit in your tool belt?!" I blurted, pointing down at her waist.

"No," Tasha said, pushing my pointed arm down. "She's asking *you* a question."

Everyone laughed, it all felt so loud, like I was in the audience at a comedy show.

"Oh," I said as I stared at Maddy with a confused look. "What's the question then?"

"Truth or dare?" Maddy said flatly.

"Truth!" I shouted as I stood up straight like one of those Christmas nutcracker statues.

"Would you kiss a guy for a hundred dollars?"

All eyes were on me. I glanced at Steven. The way he was looking at me made me paranoid.

He knows. He knows I kissed a boy, and that I did it for free. Where would the hundred dollars even come from? Who just has a hundred dollars they would give away?

I sat on the question for way too long.

"No," I said. "Not enough money." Everyone laughed at me. Even Steven chuckled.

I want to kiss Caleb. Where is he?

I looked around the backyard, whipping my head back and forth, but I still couldn't spot him. The bottle of vodka had made its way to me and Dan was pushing it to my chest. I forgot I had to take a shot after answering the question. I leaned back and let the liquid fill my mouth, and tasted a hint of blueberry. I thought the pleasant taste might help with the burn on the way down, but I was very wrong. I passed the bottle to Tasha and she gestured to the table. It was my turn to spin.

My whole body felt covered in pixie dust like I could jump off the ground and start flying around the house. I gave the empty bottle a delicate spin as it terrified me I would break it somehow. Watching it spin, my head felt like it was spinning with it. I kneeled, putting my face inches from the bottle, studying it, eager to see where it would land. It stopped, and I looked up, following the neck of the bottle. It landed on Jordan Palicki.

"TRUTH?" I shouted, then whispered, "Or dare?" I closed my left eye and scrunched my face, trying to act like a pirate when I said the word 'dare'.

"Dare," Jordan said with a stoic tone.

"Wait," I said. "Who are you dressed as?"

"John Lennon," Jordan said with an offended tone as if I should've known.

"Okaaayyyyy. John," I spat back like a second-grader. "I dare you..." I stalled. I had no idea what I wanted him to do. I turned on my heels and looked around the backyard. People were coming outside more and more. I did a complete turn with my body and placed my groggy gaze back on Jordan. "I dare you to jump in the pool... naked." Everyone around us made some sort of snicker or gasp. Jordan thought about it for a second. He then casually walked to Tasha, took the vodka bottle from her, and chugged it for a few seconds. He took off his clothes with confidence as he strutted to the pool. Everyone cheered him on. Jordan was a lanky kid who looked older than eighteen. He stripped off his white shirt and white pants until he was standing at the edge of the pool in his tighty whities. People chanted his name. I joined in screaming "Jordan!" at the top of my lungs. Then, in the blink of an eye, he pulled down his underwear, exposing his flat ass that had never seen an ounce of sun. Some girls at the party shielded their eyes. Everyone else watched as he catapulted himself into a cannonball, headed for the water. Unfortunately for him, his balls got stuck hanging out between his legs as he pulled his knees to his chest, so his nut sack was the first thing to slap the water. All the guys watching groaned with a collective wince. I couldn't stop laughing.

Jordan seemed unfazed as he pulled himself up out of the water. I couldn't help but stare at his wet, naked body as it emerged. That was the first penis I'd seen in real life that wasn't my own. The alcohol rushing through me sent all the blood to my crotch, and I forced myself into a lawn chair to hide my erection. Jordan pulled his dry clothes over his wet body as fast as he could and strutted back to the circle, it was his turn to spin the bottle.

Jordan's spin landed on Steven, who was glistening.

"Truth," Steven replied to the age-old question.

"How many dicks have you had?" It was as if Jordan had the question queued up for years, waiting for it to release from his lips. I sat upright in the lawn chair. Steven's eyes shot right to Dan. I followed his gaze and saw Dan clenching his jaw. I assumed Steven looked to Dan because he was afraid of being ridiculed if he gave an honest answer.

"Okay, that's enough," Tasha said. We could all feel the tension.

"It's all right," Steven said. "I don't have to answer."

"If you don't answer, that means you guys have to kiss," Maddy said.

"Exactly," Steven said with an evil grin. I imagined devil horns popping through his forehead, knocking his halo to the ground. Everyone in the circle laughed, realizing it's what Steven wanted the whole time, everyone except Dan.

"Rules are rules," Jordan said with a shrug as he stepped through the circle. Steven placed his hands behind his back and puckered up. It reminded me of Betty Boop in those old cartoons my mom used to watch on Youtube. Jordan bent his body toward Steven and gave him a swift peck on his glossy lips.

"This is fucking disgusting," Dan said, turning away. "Fuck this game!" Dan stomped to the sliding door and stepped inside.

There was a smile on Steven's face as Jordan walked away. The circle of people playing dispersed in different directions after Dan stormed off. Honestly, I was jealous of the kiss. I didn't want to kiss Steven, and I sure as hell didn't want to kiss Jordan. I wanted to kiss my perfect boy. I wanted to feel his smooth face and touch his dimples while he smiled. I wanted to feel the stubble of his upper lip against mine. I wanted to smell the musk erupting from his pores after a long day of working outside. I wanted to run my finger through his thick hair. I wanted the confidence to kiss him when everyone was looking. I realized why I was jealous of Steven. It was because he got to be himself with no apologies while I was too afraid to twist the knob of the closet door.

"Snacks?" Tasha said, looking down at me in the lawn chair. She and Steven were holding hands.

"Oh my god, yes!" I said as they helped me up. We walked toward the house and I took one more glance around the yard for Caleb. "Holy shit, I smell pizza," I said after we stepped into the house. I imagined myself turning into a bloodhound, frantically sniffing at the floor until I found the pizza. Three boxes were laid out on the coffee table. Everyone sitting on the couch was feasting. I swooped in like a seagull in a Burger King parking lot and grabbed a piece that had pepperoni on it. I shoved the cheesy triangle into my mouth and realized how hot it was. I was chewing but blowing air out to cool it down. "This is soooo good," I said to Tasha and Steven. Tasha grabbed a piece, but Steven held off. "Who bought this?" I questioned as I did a merry dance. "I want to personally thank them right away." I had never been that wasted in my life, but I was loving every second. Someone accidentally knocked into me and I dropped what was left of my slice. I tried to catch it but ended up squishing it against myself, smearing the red sauce on my white costume and my bare chest.

"Jesus," Steven said as he grabbed some napkins from the table. "This is why we can't have nice things," He chuckled as he wiped the sauce from my chest. I felt grateful that I couldn't grow chest hair, it would've made for a much harder clean-up job. I shoved the last bit of crust in my mouth as I let Steven wipe me down. I looked him in the eyes for the first time since eighth grade and noticed how blue they were.

"Thanks, @TheatreNerd," I said sloppily with a mouth full of crust. My head was feeling heavy again. Steven shot a look at me and stopped wiping. He had gone completely white.

"What did you just say?" Steven's eyes were wide.

I glanced to the sliding door and saw Caleb wearing his full Michael Myers costume. He was standing in the backyard, leaning against the shed that sat in the back corner. Instead of acknowledging Steven, I turned away and started for the door with tunnel vision.

I wiped the pizza sauce from my mouth as I pushed through a circle of girls that were dressed like slutty farm animals and made my way past the pool. Jordan and a few others had jumped in after the game and were splashing at each other. A cold mist hit my bare legs. Caleb was holding a drink in his hand, talking to the girl dressed as a nun.

Why didn't he come to look for me?

He was wearing exactly what he said he would: a dark blue jumpsuit and a white mask with messy brown hair.

"Hey!" I said louder than expected. The nun looked over her shoulder and walked away as I approached. He gave me a head nod under his mask. "I've been looking everywhere for you," I said as I grabbed him by the wrist, pulling him to the small space between the back of the shed and the tall wooden fence. It was a tight fit, but I wanted to make sure we weren't visible to anyone. "I can't believe you're here. I mean, I'm so glad you are. I haven't been able to stop thinking about you." I reached out and touched his shoulder before sliding my finger to the top button of his jumpsuit. "I haven't stopped thinking about our kiss at the Ferris wheel and how perfect it was. I want to taste you on my lips again." It was complete word vomit, and it showed no signs of stopping. "You drive me crazy. Caleb. Since the first time I saw you, I was so enamor-, what's that word? En something. I know it starts with an E. Whatever, I already thought you were perfect, but then we started hanging out, and I saw how amazing you were with your brother and I fell even harder for you." I didn't let him say a word, I was spewing everything I had at him without taking a breath. I reached for his hand and pulled myself closer to him. "I know I have a girlfriend and I'm gonna deal with that I promise but being around you has made me feel so many things I've never felt, and I want more. I want to kiss you again." I placed his hand against my bare chest and continued to guide it down my stomach, making him caress my skin. His fingers felt like heaven. "I want to feel you against me," I whispered as I moved his hand lower, past my hip. I got his fingers to the waistband of my underwear when he flinched, jerking his hand away from me. I was so confused as I watched him back out of our small space. "I'm sorry," I said to him as I squeezed my way out, but he didn't hear me, he was already halfway across the yard. I wanted to chase after him, but my head was spinning hard. I blinked a few times, feeling like I was in the eye of a tornado, everything around me was twisting at breakneck speed.

What did I do wrong? I thought to myself as I stumbled into a lawn chair. I remember taking a deep breath and closing my eyes as everything faded to black.

———

I woke up face down in my bed. I could feel the warm rays of the morning sun against my bare back. I lifted my head an inch off my pillow before I felt the bass drum pounding against my temples. I laid back down with a groan, realizing my pillow was sticky with drool. I rolled over onto my back and shielded my eyes from the sun. I collected all the strength I had to prop my torso up with my forearms. That's when I saw a head of familiar curls sitting at my desk, staring at my open laptop.

"Hello?" I mumbled. "What's going on?"

"Oh," Tasha said as she whipped around in my desk chair. "You're up." She sounded surprised.

"Am I dead?" I mustered up the strength I had to prop myself against the headboard.

"You probably feel like it," Tasha said as she shut my laptop and sauntered over to my bed for a seat. I scratched my head and rubbed my eyes and realized I wasn't wearing any clothes. I was just sitting there in my underwear.

"Um," I said before touching my underwear. "Why am I damp? Please tell me I didn't piss myself."

Tasha rolled her eyes. "You thought it would be a good idea to jump off the roof into the pool. You were soaked when I finally got you into bed. I took your costume off, but there was no way in hell I was changing your underwear too."

"Holy shit. I jumped off the roof?"

"You don't remember that?"

"I don't remember much of last night, no."

"Here, I made you some coffee," she said, reaching for the steaming cup on my bedside table.

"Oh my god, my Dad," I whispered as I took the cup from her.

"It's fine. He was already asleep when I brought you home last night. He must be sleeping in because I didn't see him this morning either."

"Thank god," I said as I brought the cup to my lips, blowing on the liquid. "Were you on my computer?" I wondered if I dreamed of seeing her at my desk.

"Yeah, I was checking my email. Which reminds me." Tasha said as she sat back at my desk, clicking through my laptop. "I'm releasing a special edition of the *Monthly* and I noticed you had some stories already written on your laptop. Can I take one?"

"Let me guess," I said with a groan. "You already read them?"

Her jaw tightened and she squinted one eye. "...maybe."

"Sure, take whatever," I said, giving my coffee another light blow.

Tasha spun around and started typing herself an email.

I took my first sip of coffee. It was a warm welcome compared to the poison I drank the night before. The coffee tasted creamy and sweet.

"So," Tasha said as she stood from the desk. "Who's Caleb?"

My heart leaped from my chest and I choked on my drink. I placed the cup on my nightstand, looking at Tasha dumb-founded.

"What?"

"Boy, don't play stupid," Tasha said. "You couldn't stop talking about him during our walk home. You said he wouldn't kiss you at the party or something?"

"Fuck," I said through gritted teeth as I pressed my hands to my forehead. I felt so stupid, I remembered nothing after Caleb rejected me behind the shed. And my idiot drunken mouth went blabbing about it to Tasha. I panicked. "Did I tell anyone else?"

"No, I don't think so." Tasha calmly picked up clothes around my room and tossed them into the hamper. "It was just you and me when I brought you home."

I couldn't even look at her, I was so embarrassed.

"I was drunk, and saying stupid shit," I said, trying to backpedal my way out of it.

"Landon," Tasha said as she sat next to me. "What is going on? Who is Caleb? Was he someone at the party?"

"Just forget it," I pushed back before standing up too quickly. My vision went hazy for a second as I stepped to my dresser and pulled out a pair of basketball shorts and slipped them on. "You should go, I need to shower anyway, and..." I was panicking as I paced back and forth in front of my desk.

"Landon, relax, it's just me," Tasha stepped in my path and grabbed me by the shoulders. "Whatever happened, I won't judge you."

The drunk cat was out of the bag. I stared at her and felt my nostrils flare, I was breathing heavily.

I clenched my jaw.

If I tell her it's all over. There's nothing left, I'm fucked.

I think she could tell my gears were turning hard and fast, as I just stared at her.

"Landon...I want to make sure you're okay. You can tell me anything."

"Caleb is that guy who has been working at our school," I said with a sigh.

"Okay..." Tasha said.

"We've kind of been like seeing each other?" I spat out. I leaned an arm on my desk and stared out the window. "It's complicated."

"Oh, um, okay," Tasha said. She sounded shocked. I saw her sit on my bed out of the corner of my eye. "Are you gay?"

"I don't know."

"All right, that's okay," Tasha reassured me. "So what happened?"

"We started hanging out," I said before I took a deep breath and sighed. I still couldn't look at her. "One thing led to another and we ended up kissing."

"And you liked it?" I could feel her eyes on me.

"I loved it," I said. "And now he's all I think about. I can't get him out of my head."

"Been there," Tasha said with a smirk.

I swiveled my chair and looked at her. I couldn't believe I was saying all of it out loud to another person. I knew Tasha would ask about Lauren. They were friends. The guilt pushed its way up my chest and my face got warm. I dropped my face into my hands and let out a sigh.

"I fucked up, Tasha."

The pressure was building in my eyes.

Tasha kneeled in front of me and placed her hands on my knees. "I assume you haven't told Lauren?"

I looked at her with damp cheeks. "No. I've been too much of a fucking coward. I've never felt like this. I thought it would all just go away after a day. And now I'm scared because I know it's gonna shatter her."

"I'm not gonna lie to you," Tasha said. "It will. She's crazy for you, Landon. But it's not fair to her. If you're not happy with her, you need to tell her."

"I know. Please don't tell her. I want to be the one to do it."

"Your secret's safe with me, but I can't let it go unsaid that what you did was wrong and I don't support it. As Lauren's friend, I want to smack you upside the head. But as your friend I want you to know I'm here for you to help you figure this out. Was it just a kiss?"

"Yeah."

"Don't lie to me."

"I swear, it was just one kiss."

"Okay." Tasha stood and sat on my bed, before looking at me again. "Does he know about Lauren?"

"He saw me kissing her actually, at Lucky's. Where I didn't know he worked."

"Damn, this is some *Gossip Girl* shit."

"He actually said he wouldn't kiss me or anything again until I was single."

"That's somewhat redeemable." Tasha took a deep breath, taking everything in. "So, Caleb was at the party last night?"

"That's the last thing I remember." I moved to my dresser again and sifted through some T-shirts. "It was so strange, I was, like, trying to get him to touch me and he totally rejected me. Maybe he doesn't want me after all."

I heard my phone vibrate against my desk as I pulled a white T-shirt over my head. I'd left it there all night. I scooped it up and saw one text from Caleb on the home screen that said, 'hope you enjoyed the party! :) Text me when you're up.'

What?

I opened the text thread, I had other messages from him that were already marked as read. I scrolled to the last time I texted him and saw he texted me back over an hour after I left my house.

CALEB

Hey I'm really sorry!

Parker has been throwing up for the past hour.

I'm not gonna be able to make it to the party.

I can't trust my mom to take care of him all night. I can make it up to you. Sorry again. :(

The text I'd read from my home screen was the latest he'd sent:

CALEB

Hope you enjoyed the party! :) Text me when you're up.

I collapsed into my desk chair, staring at my phone with my jaw in my lap. I felt like I was going to throw up. I tried to steady my breathing. Tasha could tell something was wrong.

"Landon?"

She sounded a million miles away. I couldn't stop reading his texts.

"Shit," I whispered. "Fucking shit. No, no, no."

"What?"

"Caleb wasn't at the fucking party," I said with a panicked tone as I threw my phone on my desk.

"What're you talking about? You said he was behind the shed with you."

"It wasn't him!" I stood and paced, trying to remember everything from the night before. "Caleb told me he was gonna dress up like Michael Myers for the party. And I brought a guy behind the shed who was definitely wearing a Michael Myers costume, but it wasn't Caleb because he just sent me a text saying he was taking care of his sick brother all night. But I didn't get the texts because I forgot my phone here before I left."

"Oh my god."

My skin itched, I was burning up. "That means someone else knows about me."

TWENTY-SIX

"It's okay, we can figure this out," Tasha said, trying to calm me down.

My Dad popped his head into my room. "Figure what out?"

I was too freaked out that he might've heard our conversation, I couldn't come up with an excuse. Luckily Tasha was quick on her feet.

"This Physics project that's due next week," Tasha said with a smile.

My Dad looked satisfied enough by the lie. He sniffed the air. "Did someone make coffee?"

I rolled my eyes. "Yeah, it's downstairs."

My Dad nodded and continued on his way. We waited to hear the clink of the mugs from downstairs before we started talking again,

"I'm such an idiot," I said. "Why did I get so fucked up last night?"

I walked across the room, grabbing my cup from the nightstand. I sat on the bed next to Tasha. My hands trembled. "What if that person goes straight to Lauren, or Coach? Then Coach tells my Dad, I'd be so fucked. What if I lose my scholarship?"

"Whoa, Landon, relax," Tasha said, placing a hand on my forearm. "Being gay isn't the end of the world. This isn't nineteen forty. Gay people can play sports too."

I stared down into my cup, knowing she was right, but my mind couldn't stop racing.

"My Dad is a republican running for mayor. He'll never win if people find out about me."

"He loves you. He'll understand."

"You don't know him like I do."

"Let's just take this one step at a time. I have to get home, but I'll go through everyone's posted pictures from the party and see if I can hunt down Michael Myers for you. Maybe someone tagged him."

"Thank you," I said.

Tasha stood and collected her things. I noticed she wasn't in her Catwoman costume anymore. Instead, she was wearing yoga pants and a flannel. "Did you stay here last night?"

She scrunched her face. "Hell no. My mom would've killed me. I dropped you off and you gave me your keys so I could check on you this morning."

"You're the best."

"Never forget it!" she called back over her shoulder as she left my bedroom. But she popped her head back in and said, "oh, and I suggest you tell Lauren sooner than later."

"I know. I will."

I laid back onto my bed with my coffee mug clutched between my hands resting on my chest. I took a deep breath to relieve my anxiety, but it wasn't working. Then I remembered I left Caleb on read. Pushing myself up with a groan, I placed my mug down. My head was still aching. I grabbed my phone off the desk to call Caleb. A new text from Lauren popped up as I clicked the green button to start the call.

. . .

LAUREN

Just got on the plane, can't wait to see you!

"Hello?" Caleb's voice sang in my ear. It felt good to hear his raspy tone.

"Hey," I said. "How are you?"

"I'm really sorry about last night."

"It's totally fine," I said as I laid on my bed. "I actually forgot my phone at home so I didn't even see the texts till this morning."

"I was wondering why you never responded, I thought you were mad at me."

I could hear a TV on in the background.

"Of course not. How's the little guy feelin'?"

"He seems a lot better now. We're watching cartoons on the couch."

"Good, that's good." My voice trailed off.

"Are you okay?"

"Something kind of happened last night."

"Hold on, let me go outside," Caleb said. I heard Parker mumble, and the phone sounded like Caleb slipped it into his pocket. Then I heard the screen door squeak and slam shut. "What happened?"

"I got super drunk, and I ate two pot brownies by accident and it just really fucked me up."

Caleb started laughing. "That's hysterical. You had me worried for a second."

"Oh, there's more."

"Okay... "

"Someone was there dressed as Michael Myers, and I thought it was you. I was so messed up that I pulled him behind a shed and started touching him, and he freaked out and stormed off."

"Oh, shit," Caleb said.

"And now I'm going crazy because someone knows about me."

I rolled onto my side, holding the phone between the pillow and my face.

"I don't think it's the end of the world, Lan."

"Yeah, I keep hearing that. It's easy for you to say. You're out, you're proud, I get it. But I'm not. Your reputation isn't on the line here!"

"You're right," Caleb whispered. "I'm sorry."

"All of this screwing with my head. On top of everything I have to tell Lauren, just thinking about it makes my skin itch. And now I have some mystery person walking around that could blab about it. And while I was drunk last night, I told my friend Tasha about you."

"Oh?" Caleb's voice perked up. "How'd she take it?"

"She was cool about it."

I felt my stomach gurgle, I wasn't sure if it was hunger or the stale alcohol wanting out.

"That's great then! If anyone is really your friend, they won't care," Caleb said.

It all sounded too cliché for me. In Texas, at my school, with my Dad, it wasn't as simple as Caleb made it sound.

"Any advice on how I should tell Lauren?"

"Coming out is a really personal thing. It's never the same for anyone," Caleb said. "You like books, so maybe there's a book about it?"

"About coming out?"

"Yeah, maybe you should look into it." Caleb's voice cracked as if he was just hitting puberty, which caused us both to laugh. The more we talked, the calmer I became. His voice soothed my anxiety. His advice was perfect. I turned to books for almost everything else, so why not try?

That Monday at school felt like hell like everyone knew what was going on in my head. With every stare I got in the hallway, it felt like they were reading my dirty thoughts about Caleb. I wore my hood all day, just trying to blend into the crowd. I barely said anything at lunch, just listened to Lauren tell the others about her audition and how amazing New York was. She went on about shopping in SoHo, eating in Chinatown, and seeing a Broadway show.

Dan spoke next, bragging about how awesome the party was and how he hooked up with a college girl visiting a friend. I noticed he wasn't touching his nose as much, and I wondered if he had gotten rid of the cocaine like I suggested. I poked through the pasta pesto I'd gotten from the cafeteria. It tasted fine, but I didn't have much of an appetite, as the anxiety flooded my stomach.

I pictured someone dressed in a Michael Myers costume standing up on one of the lunch tables in the middle of the lunchroom. I imagined him taking off the mask and shouting, 'Landon Griffin is a faggot!' I pictured everyone booing and throwing food at me.

The bell rang, signaling the end of lunch, and I picked up my food and headed to my class without saying bye to anyone.

The rest of my day was slow. When the last bell finally rang, I bolted. I'd planned on getting straight into my Dad's car and driving to Barnes & Noble to find a book about coming out. I had the car in my sights before I crossed the street, but Lauren found me before I could look both ways.

"Hey, you," she said with a smile.

I looked at her with a blank stare.

"Are you okay?"

"Yeah, I'm fine," I lied, wondering when she would stop believing me.

"Tasha told me you got pretty messed up at the party. I would've loved to see that."

"Did she say anything else?"

"Like what?" Lauren said, sounding taken aback by my sudden words.

"Never mind, I gotta go."

"Wait," Lauren called out as she followed behind me. "Where are you going?"

"I need to go to Barnes and Noble for something," I said, avoiding eye contact. I reached the car and opened the door to the backseat, tossing my backpack inside as Lauren approached.

"Want some company?"

"I'm sorry," I said. "I need time alone for a bit, okay?" I hated being standoffish to her. It wasn't fair, she had no idea what was going on in my head.

"Oh, all right." She frowned. "Text me after then?"

"Yeah," I said, before kissing her on the cheek.

I pulled out of my driveway, giving Lauren a weak wave. I needed to figure out how to tell her as soon as possible.

I scoured the fiction section of the big box bookstore, looking for any title that jumped out at me. I picked up a book, read the synopsis, then put it back down. I repeated this about ten times before I realized I was procrastinating on purpose. I knew the LGBT section was on the back wall of the store, but I was avoiding it like the plague.

I got a strong whiff of coffee being made from the small cafe that was nestled in the store. I walked by and saw a mom reading to her little boy as they both sipped their drinks at a metal table. I passed the kids' section where foam chairs were splayed across a dark blue carpet. Puzzles were left unfinished on the small tables, and *Diary of a Wimpy Kid* books were on heavy display.

My mom used to take me there when I was young. Once a month the store would hire someone to do a reading for kids. We used to sit cross-legged on that same dark blue carpet and listen to someone read chapters from *Harry Potter* or *The Chronicles of Narnia*. I loved it; it was something I would look forward to. I could picture everything so clearly in my head as it was being read aloud. It was as if I was creating the movie out of the words I was hearing.

I reached the LGBT section and gave it a once over. There wasn't much, as it was only four shelves out of the stack. I got closer, reading the titles of some fiction options. A title caught my eye and I reached for it. *Rainbow Boys* by Alex Sanchez, I did the same as I had with the others, picked it up, read the synopsis, put it back. It sounded interesting, but fiction wasn't what I needed at that moment. Then I spotted a book titled *It Gets Better* by Dan Savage and Terry Miller. I pulled it off the shelf and read the back cover. It was exactly what I needed. I suddenly heard footsteps and glanced over my left shoulder. To my surprise, I saw Steven walking toward me. "Fuck," I said under my breath as I threw the book back on the shelf and turned the corner to another aisle, hoping Steven hadn't spotted me.

I wanted out. I couldn't focus on finding a book when I knew he was in the store. I looked behind me as I walked as if I was being stalked by a monster. I almost bumped into an old woman who was scanning the cookbooks. I could see the front door and hear the parking lot calling my name. I darted around the new arrivals table and passed the checkout counter, pushing open the heavy glass door. It was the last stretch; I was home free until I heard my name being called. I tried to ignore him as I approached my car.

"Landon, stop!"

I was caught. I could feel it. My stomach sank as I leaned my arm against the roof of the car and rested my head on my wrist. I took a deep breath and spun around, thinking I could play it cool.

"Hey, Steven," I said with a fake smile.

"I knew I saw you at Paradise," Steven said as he stomped toward me.

"What?" I acted as if I'd never heard of the place.

"Don't play dumb, Landon," Steven shot back at me. He was standing at the back of my car with furrowed eyebrows. "That was you! But what really confirmed it for me was seeing the eighty-three on your jersey. I can't believe I didn't put it together sooner!"

I had never seen Steven that angry, not even with Dan.

He continued, "Then you called me TheatreNerd, and that's when I knew I wasn't crazy."

I had no memory of calling him by his Grindr alias. Drunk me really wanted to push sober me out of the closet.

"We've been talking for weeks on Grindr!" Steven said. "Why are you doing this? Is this some sort of elaborate plan you and Dan cooked up?"

"What? No," I said, unsure what he was accusing me of.

"Oh, fuck you!" Steven shouted. I could see people around the parking lot staring at us. "You made my life fucking hell for being gay. You stood by while I got the shit kicked out of me by *your* best friend, and yet you were just like me this whole time!"

I just stood there and let him yell at me because he was right.

"How could you make that Facebook page about me and continue to sleep well at night? You fucking outed me to everyone!"

"Wait, Steven, what're you talking about?" I was genuinely confused.

He shook his head, and his eyes welled up.

"Why do you think I didn't come back to school after Dan attacked me that first day, freshman year? You guys made the Facebook page, and I saw all the comments, and I thought fuck it, everyone wants me to kill myself so why not give it to them?"

"Oh my god," I whispered as I stepped toward him. "Steven, I swear, I don't know anything about a Facebook page."

I was telling the truth. My stomach was in knots and my heart broke for him.

"Yeah, right," Steven said before turning and walking back toward the store.

"Steven, hold up!" I ran ahead of him, forcing him to stop in his tracks. "Let's sit in my car and we can talk." I looked him in the eyes, hoping he knew I was being sincere. "Please."

Steven sighed and nodded. We walked back to my car, and I unlocked the doors so he could sit in the passenger seat. My mind raced, I was unsure what to say first.

"I had no idea," I said as I stared at my steering wheel. "I had no idea what you were going through." I looked at him. "We were friends. The only person who changed was Dan, and I'm sorry I took his side. I'm sorry I never stood up for you, I always wanted to, but I was too scared of what people would think of me. I was too scared of what Dan would do, but I should've stopped him every time he harassed you, I'm sorry I didn't."

"You really didn't know about the Facebook page?" I shook my head, and he leaned back in the seat with a sigh, trying to come to terms with everything. "I knew it was Dan. I just assumed you had something to do with it too because you guys were inseparable."

"What was it?"

I was unsure if Steven would want to dive back into the memories. He just stared out the windshield as cars drove by.

"When I got back home from the hospital, after he attacked me, I saw a Facebook notification on my computer. It was an invitation to a private group titled 'Steven Boyer is a Flaming Faggot.' It already had at least thirty people following it. I was an idiot and clicked confirm and went through the page."

"If you knew Dan made it, why would you join?"

"I just said I was an idiot. I'm a queer that lives for the drama, I couldn't help it. I had no idea it was gonna be as bad as it was," Steven said.

"I'm afraid to ask what you saw."

"People were reposting my profile picture and drawing things on top of it. Most of them were knives to my head or dicks. Everyone commented that if I killed myself, no one would feel bad. That Madison High would be better off."

"Jesus Christ," I whispered. "I'm so sorry, Steven."

"I felt numb, I just didn't want to deal with anything anymore. So, I went into the bathroom and swallowed every pill I could find in the medicine cabinet, and just sat on the floor waiting. I was done with the snarky comments as a defense mechanism. I was done feeling alone and unwanted. I thought it's not gonna get better, so why wait around while it gets worse?" Steven paused, wiping his right eye with his sleeve. I was crushed by listening to his words. "The dumbest part of it all was that I tried to justify it in my head while I was laying there."

"What do you mean?"

Steven sniffled. "When I was little my grandma moved to the states from Japan. She used to tell me stories about samurai that took their own lives as an act of bravery. So I kept thinking, well, maybe this is a good thing. This is what I was meant to do because those stories lived in my head my whole life."

"But think of how much she would've missed you," I said. "Your whole family would've been devastated."

"It just didn't feel like it at the time."

"Losing someone to suicide is one of the worst things a person can go through, believe me."

"Landon, I'm sorry I wasn't thinking. I didn't mean to..."

"No, it's okay," I said, cutting him off. "That's a kind of pain I'd never wish on anyone. So I'm glad your parents didn't have to go through it."

"Yeah, luckily my mom found me passed out on the bathroom floor and called an ambulance."

"If I would've known, I would've come to see you in the hospital."

"No, you wouldn't have," Steven said, glancing at me. "You said it yourself, you were too scared, and honestly I don't blame you. Being gay can be scary sometimes. Especially when you look like me."

"What do you mean?"

I leaned a shoulder against the steering wheel as I faced him.

"Look at you. We're very different, Landon," Steven said with a small chuckle. "You're a jock, you blend in with the crowd. I'm a fem boy who practically sweats glitter, it's obvious. No one suspects you because you have a deep voice and the clothes you wear are normal."

I'd never thought of it that way.

"It all feels like a facade most of the time," I said. "The person you were texting with, that's the real me. When I talked to you on Grindr, I felt like my authentic self, not the coward I am in real life."

"I liked that person. He's in there you just gotta let him out," Steven said with a half-smile.

"I don't know how. That's why I was looking for books on how to come out."

"You don't need a book, just say it."

"What?"

"Say the words," Steven said again. "It's just us in the car. No one else will know."

I scoffed, sitting back against my seat. "I can't. That feels dumb."

"Girl, how the hell are you ever gonna come out if you can't even say the words?"

"What do you want me to say?"

"You tell me," he said flatly.

I closed my eyes, sitting there thinking. All I could see behind my eyelids was Caleb's face. I felt a collection of butterflies fill my stomach and took a deep breath.

"I'm..." I hesitated. "...gay," I whispered.

"I'm sorry, what was that?"

"... I'm gay," I said a little louder with my eyes still closed.

"I couldn't hear you, speak up, please,"

"I'm gay," I said with a raised voice. I could feel the butterflies building as they pushed their way up to my chest.

"One more time for the people in the back!"

The butterflies forced their way to my throat, and I squeezed my eyes shut and let them escape. "I'M GAY!" I screamed toward the roof of the car, releasing the butterflies into the air with my words of affirmation. My chest felt like I lifted an anvil off of it.

Steven's hand clutched mine, and I opened my eyes to look at him. He smiled. "Welcome to the party."

TWENTY-SEVEN

Steven and I stayed in my car talking for hours. We laughed a lot. He told me stories of his nights at Paradise. He knew one of Caleb's friends, telling me he went home with Miguel the first night he stepped foot in the gay club on 18+ night. He went on about how Miguel worshipped Barbra Streisand; he filled his entire apartment with memorabilia from records to coffee mugs to framed posters, even a few blankets with her face on them. Steven said it felt like he was in a museum.

I told him how I'd figured out Mystery Boy's name and everything that had happened with him. I told him I accidentally came out to Tasha while I was blackout drunk, and about the Michael Myers mystery. We also talked about Lauren and how I should address the situation. There was no way around it; it would break her heart no matter how or when I told her.

"As much as I love your revelation, Lauren is my friend too," Steven said. "If this were any other situation I'd immediately tell her what's going on, but I'd never out someone."

"I appreciate it. I just really want her to hear it from me. But every time I'm around her all I can think about is how upset she'll be. And then I start thinking about all the fun we've had over the last year and it makes me feel even worse so I chicken out."

"Girl, the longer you wait, the harder it's gonna get," Steven said. "I wish I could help more, but this is something you gotta figure out for yourself."

"She's gonna hate me."

"She'll be hurt, but I don't think she'll hate you. Dan on the other hand..."

"That's another thing I'm dreading."

"Maybe he doesn't have to know."

"He wasn't always like this," I said. "We hit freshman year, and he was a different person. I don't know what happened."

"I might know," Steven whispered.

The parking lot was almost empty, and the sun had set. The tall light posts illuminated the last remaining employees heading home after their shifts.

I perked up in my seat. "What do you mean?"

"He made me swear that I wouldn't tell anyone, but it's been over four years. With all the shit he's put me through, there's no point in hiding it anymore."

"Wait, did you guys..." Steven looked at me and I could tell he was trying to hold in his laugh, but it didn't last long before he covered his face and laughed into his hands, nodding his head. "No fucking way!"

"I swear to Ariana Grande," Steven said as he held up his right hand as if he were under oath.

"I can't believe this," I said as I swiveled in my seat, leaning my back against the door. "What happened?"

"The summer before high school started, long after you guys stopped talking to me, Dan asked if he could come to my house," Steven said with an animated expression. "I was shocked but excited because I thought it meant he wanted to be friends again. When he came over, I could tell he was nervous. It just felt awkward, you know?"

"Okay," I said, giddy with anticipation.

"I can't believe I'm telling you this." Steven chuckled. "So we ended up sitting on my bed and we were talking, then he just kisses me out of nowhere."

My eyes widened. "You're lying!"

Steven laughed. "I swear!"

"Okay, so, then what?"

"I let it happen! I'd been fantasizing about kissing boys since I was eight years old, so of course, I didn't want to stop him."

When I was eight years old I had a poster of Tom Brady next to my bed that I would stare at every night before I fell asleep and it made me feel warm, but I never fantasized about kissing him.

"Then things went further," Steven said. "We were making out. And oh my god it was so sloppy, we had no idea what we were doing. Then our clothes were coming off."

All I could do was listen, with my hand under my chin to stop my jaw from hitting my lap.

He continued, "Hands were exploring uncharted territory if you know what I mean, and it was awkward but exhilarating. When we finished, I could tell he felt different about it than I did."

"How so?"

"It felt like he was ashamed? Like he'd just committed the worst crime in history," Steven frowned. "It felt like the room went cold and all he said was 'I'll kill you if you tell anyone.' Then he left, and it all felt like a dream. I think that's when everything changed. His internalized homophobia hated what we did so much that he's been taking it out on me ever since."

"It probably doesn't help that his parents are super religious too," I said.

Knowing Dan, everything Steven said sounded impossible.

"Also, he's slept with so many girls..." I said.

"I'm not saying he's gay. Maybe he's bi, I don't know. Only he knows for sure." Steven gave me some side-eye. "Did you guys ever..."

"Oh god no," I never thought about Dan in that way, and I never wanted to.

Steven laughed before giving me a look. "But you have, like, done it, right?"

I felt a little insecure. I could've lied but what was the point, I'd owned up to everything else that day so why not my virginity too? I squinted my eyes at him, shaking my head no.

"Oh honey," Steven said. "So, no one has ever touched your 'between me down there'? Not even Lauren?"

"I mean, she's tried. But nothing... happens."

"Ah, I gotcha."

"Yeah, that was one of the most embarrassing nights of my life. I figured she would've told you and Tasha about it."

"She's never complained about you, at least not to us."

My stomach filled with rocks. Lauren really was the perfect girlfriend. I didn't deserve her.

Our conversation didn't go on much longer. We got out of the car and said our goodbyes with our first hug. He squeezed me tight and smiled at me before walking back to his car. It felt great to reconnect with him, things felt normal again. It reminded me of all the weekends we spent at sleepovers, getting hyper off of Mountain Dew, and playing video games all night. It felt like completing a puzzle after years of avoiding it, letting it collect dust on the shelf.

The next few days flew by, but my anxiety never flatlined. It was still in the back of my mind that a mystery person knew about me and Caleb, but they hadn't told anyone yet. I was sure it would've spread through the school like wildfire if they had. It helped that I got to steal looks at Caleb when I passed him in the hallways or watch him from a classroom window as he mowed the grass in the front courtyard. It was easy to forget about everything when I was able to look at him.

———

It was the Wednesday after Steven and I had our conversation in the Barnes & Noble parking lot; I was standing in the lunch line holding my tray, ready to see what was being served. I noticed Jordan Palicki's tall presence standing two people ahead of me, causing a flash image of his naked body emerging from Dan's pool. I'd never been able to look at him the same. I knew from that point on that every time I saw him, I'd also see his dick swinging in the wind.

I tried to focus my attention on the food. The line moved quickly for once. I stepped up to the sneeze guard and surveyed my options. I grabbed a paper plate that sat in a stack next to the salad bowl and loaded up, accidentally dropping some lettuce on the floor. Moving farther down the counter, I saw a bunch of burgers wrapped in foil, each labeled with a red font. I grabbed one that said 'cheeseburger' and felt content.

I heard people gasp, and it forced me to turn around. I could see people moving out of their seats, avoiding the action, but there were a few that stepped toward it. I bobbed my head to see what was happening. A group of girls blocked my view until a couple of guys moved them out of the way, that's when I saw Steven's bright head of hair whiz by. Dan had pushed him to the ground. My heart raced as I watched Dan approach Steven. The quarterback was the apex predator and the gay boy was the innocent baby zebra.

"Say it again!" Dan yelled down at Steven. The whole cafeteria was watching, and no one was trying to stop him from pouncing. I gripped my lunch tray, wondering what might've gotten Dan so worked up. Could Dan have overheard Steven talking about a guy he had a crush on? Or maybe Steven made a snarky comment about something Dan was wearing? Even from across the cafeteria, I could see the rage in Dan's eyes.

After reconnecting with Steven, there was no way I could continue to let Dan harass him. I had to be the one to put Dan in his place if his attacks were going to stop. My heart pumped as I threw my tray onto a nearby table and pushed through the crowd. I was moving as fast as I could, seeing red.

I threw a folding chair to the side and heard it crash against a table. It was the last object standing between me and them. Steven was on the tiled floor, waiting for Dan's inevitable strike. I stepped in between them before Dan could rain down his hatred. I grabbed Dan's shirt, crumpling it in my left fist as I cocked my right arm. My fist felt like it was being shot from a cannon before connecting with Dan's nose. The power of the smack sent an echo through the observing crowd. I saw a short rope of blood shoot from Dan's face and it splattered against my shirt. I reared back again, sending another fist hurling against his left eye. The second punch sent Dan crumbling to the ground with an explosive thud. My heart pounded. I'd never punched anyone in my life. It felt like I was no longer in control of my body.

The entire cafeteria had gone silent.

"Touch him again and I'll fucking end you," I said, standing over Dan.

He was holding onto his nose as blood dripped off his chin. A few guys from the football team rushed to his side, helping him off the ground. Dan spit a wad of blood on the floor in front of me as he stared me down with fire in his eyes. We were both panting, and I knew that if the guys weren't holding him back, he would've lunged for me.

"You're gonna choose this faggot over me?" Dan wiped his blood on his pant leg. "Then fuck you, Griffin!" Dan yelled as the other guys pulled him back and escorted him from the cafeteria. Everyone watched as they led Dan out, swearing the whole walk down the empty hallway.

I turned, seeing Steven on the ground. I reached out my left hand and helped him to his feet.

"Thank you," Steven whispered. People were returning to their tables and the chatter started again.

"I should've done that a long time ago," I said. "I'm sorry it took so long."

Steven smiled at me with hope in his eyes.

"What the hell set him off?"

Steven rolled his eyes. "I called him a neanderthal."

I smirked, shaking my head.

He pointed at my bloodied fist. "You better go wash that off. That's pretty gross."

I went home for the rest of the day, noticing my Dad's car wasn't in the driveway as I crossed the street. I was thankful I didn't have to explain why I'd come home early. I opened the door and went straight for the kitchen sink. As soon as my knuckles hit the stream of warm water, I winced. So much adrenaline was pumping, I hadn't noticed how much my fist was throbbing in pain. I guided my hand back and forth slowly under the water and watched the red spiral down the drain. Patting my hand with a paper towel, my knuckles already started bruising. I knew nothing was broken as I could still move my fingers, but it still hurt like hell.

I sat on the couch, feeling like I could breathe at a normal rate. I reached for the TV remote. I couldn't remember the last time I sat on the couch and mindlessly watched TV alone.

My phone vibrated. It was a text from Lauren. I knew words would travel fast.

. . .

LAUREN

OMG Steven just told me what happened, are you okay?

ME

Yeah, I'm fine, just a little sore.

LAUREN

Where are you?

ME

I went home after everything. I didn't feel like getting stared at for the rest of the day.

LAUREN

I'm proud of you.

My phone buzzed, and I clicked over to the new message.

CALEB

I think something just went down in the cafeteria. I heard some people talking about it.

ME

Yeah, I don't think Dan and I are friends anymore.

CALEB

Wait, what? Why?

ME

Because I punched him in the face. Twice.

CALEB

Seriously?

ME

Yeah. For years Dan has harassed this gay kid Steven that we used to be friends with. I just kind of snapped. I couldn't stand by and watch it happen anymore.

CALEB

You're a fucking legend! A hero to gays everywhere!

ME

Yeah right haha

CALEB

It's kinda hot ;)

I smiled at Caleb's text, thinking about what to respond with as my eyes drooped. The drone of the TV and the way my body sunk into the couch made my eyelids feel heavy. After school naps were something my mom never allowed me to do. She would always wake me up if she noticed me falling asleep. It felt good to let it take me away from everything that had happened.

I found myself on a stage in front of hundreds of people sitting in the audience. A spotlight was on me. I looked down to discover I was shirtless and wearing tights and ballet shoes. Then the violins started.

It was so strange when my body started moving. I'd never taken a dance class and yet my moves were effortless. I leaped into the air with ease, I'd never felt so flexible. I let my body take over and I started to enjoy the ride. I reached out a hand and Lauren came running onstage and held me. She too was dressed as a ballet dancer. I lifted her and she slithered around my body like a snake.

We continued our perfectly choreographed dance together until we were interrupted and I was taken away by Caleb dressed in a leotard. The audience gasped as Caleb picked me up into a spin. As he and I danced intimately with leaps and spins and dips, Lauren danced around us looking distraught.

Caleb let go of me and started dancing with Lauren, but the choreography wasn't sweet and sensual, it was dark and menacing. They pulled me into it and it felt like we had been doing the same dance for years. They pulled me in all directions around the stage until everything went dark and the music halted.

A spotlight popped back on, showing me at center stage, alone, breathing heavily, and crying. The whole audience started to clap and one by one they all stood up, cheering.

The sound of my Dad rushing through the door jolted me awake. I grabbed my phone and saw it was almost 4:00 p.m.

My Dad walked into the living room with his hands on his hips and a stern look on his face. "Coach called me," he said. "He told me you and Dan got into a fight at school today?"

I adjusted myself and sat up straight, sliding to the edge of the couch. "It wasn't exactly a fight," I said as I rubbed my neck.

My Dad crossed his arms. "What does that mean?"

"Well, I punched him. He didn't punch me, so it wasn't a fight."

"Jesus, Landon. I want you to go to his house and apologize. Now."

I shot up from the couch. "What? No!"

"He's your best friend, Landon. I get that friends don't always see eye to eye, but we didn't raise you to work it out with your fists. You guys should talk it out."

"You're not even gonna ask me why I punched him? He was bullying Steven!"

"Oh."

"Oh? That's all you're gonna say? How about nice job, son, for sticking up for someone?"

"I'm not saying Dan didn't deserve it, but I won't let you ruin your friendship over it. We still need you guys working together on the field."

"Jesus Christ, Dad. Is that all you care about?" I pushed past him and headed for the side door that led to the driveway. "There's more to life than fucking football!"

The door slammed behind me, and I heard him yell my name from the other side, but he didn't follow me. I was so aggravated; I needed to take a walk before I said something I'd regret. I dreaded the thought of seeing Dan at the next football practice, sure he'd take his anger out on me on the field. My punch had changed everything.

TWENTY-EIGHT

I wanted to bike around the neighborhood to clear my head. I glanced around the driveway but my bike was nowhere to be found. I sighed, remembering I'd left it in Dan's front yard when I rode it to the party.

Dammit, now I don't have a choice.

I looked at the sky, noticing how damp the air felt. The setting sun was locked behind a sheet of gray, ominous clouds. I was already two blocks from my house and didn't feel like going back for an umbrella. The whole walk I debated if I should grab my bike and go or ring the doorbell to talk to Dan. I thought about what I would say. I didn't regret punching him. It was something that needed to happen. I was over all of his bullshit, his bullying, his homophobia. We didn't have to be friends, but I wanted to be civil, so it felt less awkward when we were forced to be around each other.

I shoved my hands in my pockets as the breeze gave me goosebumps. I thought about Chris, and if our friendship would change over what happened. He and I were never as close as Dan and I, but we had been in each other's lives for so long. Chris often followed Dan's lead, but I could tell Chris wanted to forge his own path, especially after Dan became more of a selfish bigot.

I reached Dan's house, nestled on the corner of Packard Street and Lancaster Drive. I surveyed the yard for my bike, deciding I was going to grab it and go. I walked into their front yard, remembering I'd left it in the grass close to the sidewalk, but it wasn't there. I huffed, realizing I'd have to ask someone in the house if they'd seen it. I walked up the cement path to the porch when I felt a drop of rain hit my forehead. I hoped I could get my bike and race back home before it started to downpour.

My shoes knocked against the wooden floorboards of the porch. I rang the bell as my mind raced, trying to find the words I could say to Dan. It took seconds before I heard the click of the doorknob. My shoulders tensed, but relaxed when I saw Chris standing in the open doorway.

I looked him in the eyes. "Hey."

Chris raised his eyebrows, surprised to see me. "Hey man. What're you doing here?"

"I left my bike here the other night." I looked over my shoulder at the empty yard. "I was hoping to grab it, but it's not where I left it."

"I think my Dad moved it," Chris said as he stepped through the doorway, closing it behind him. "C'mon, I'm pretty sure it's in the back."

I nodded and let him pass me, following him around the side of the house. Their fence had a gate that led into the backyard.

"Everyone's talking about what happened," Chris said.

"Is Dan around?"

We stepped into the backyard and I let the gate swing closed behind me with a loud smack.

Chris stopped at the circular table where we played spin the bottle during the party and faced me. He leaned against the edge of the tabletop. "No, he split. He seemed pretty angry over everything."

"I figured he would be," I said. Another drop of rain hit my head, and another on my shoulder.

"I'm worried about him. He's touching his nose all the time and his temper is getting worse."

"He was snorting coke at the party, and wasn't afraid to show it off," I whispered, unsure if Chris' parents were home.

Chris rubbed the side of his face and kept his gaze low. "I found a gun in his car."

Living in Texas, it was common to see people walking around with their holstered gun so I wasn't taken aback by the idea of Dan having a gun.

"Okay," I said, wanting to give Dan the benefit of the doubt. "Doesn't your Dad have a gun?"

"Most people from our church do. My Dad has one but it's locked up. And Dan knows how much our mom hates guns."

I stood there staring, unfazed by his words.

"This was different though. The serial number was scratched off."

I stepped toward Chris. "Jesus, are you serious?"

Chris nodded,

"He's fucked if he's found with drugs and an unlicensed gun."

"No shit." Chris glanced at the sliding glass door, I assumed he didn't want his parents to hear us chatting. "I feel like every day I see him hanging around a new guy I don't recognize. They always look sleazy as fuck."

I paced, reflecting on what Chris was saying. "Tell your parents, this is getting scary now."

"Dan will kill me, I can't. Plus, my parents are dealing with a lot of shit right now."

"Okay," I scoffed. "Then let's get rid of it."

"I was going to. But when I went back to his car to get it, it was gone."

"Fuck." I sauntered toward the pool, thinking about what I could do to help. The smell of chlorine penetrated my nostrils as I took a breath. "Maybe I'll text him when I get home, see if I can talk to him about everything."

Chris pushed himself off the table and paced toward me. "Don't mention the gun. He's gonna know it's me that told you."

"I won't, I won't."

What the fuck has he gotten himself into?

I watched Chris's face shift before he walked to the shed at the corner of the yard. My bike leaned against the barn-like door of the small structure. I followed but saw something that stopped me. Chris grabbed onto the handlebars and steered the bike toward me. I watched in shock as he calmly ran the tires over a Michael Myers mask that was laying in the grass. I rushed over, snatching it off the ground.

I looked at Chris. "What is this doing here?"

His eyebrows scrunched together as if I had three heads. "What do you mean?"

"Whose mask is this?"

"Mine, you psycho." Chris chuckled. "I probably left it out here when I was drunk."

A wave of panic washed over me. "Holy shit, it was you?"

"Yeah. Who else would it be?"

"No, no. I saw you going upstairs. You were dressed like a hippie."

"Yeah," Chris scoffed. "That was before that girl threw up all over me when we were making out in my room. It was nasty, bro."

I closed my eyes. My stomach dropped when I thought about my confession behind the shed.

"The Michael Myers costume was my backup anyway so I changed after cleaning up the mess," Chris said.

I tossed the mask on the table. "Do you not remember?" I had a flashback of pushing Chris's hand toward my underwear.

Chris tilted his head and laughed. "Remember what? I was so fucked up that night."

"Never mind. I gotta go."

I rushed toward him, grabbing my bike. The rain dropped faster.

"All right." Chris watched me lead my bike through the yard. "See ya."

I pushed the gate open and hopped on my bike so fast that I smashed my butt bone against the seat and grunted in a quick burst of discomfort. The rain got heavier. I could feel my back tire splashing the water from the slick pavement against the back of my legs. I pumped the pedals, pushing through the sharp droplets. The streets were quiet, no cars, no kids playing, no birds chirping, just the sound of the rain pounding the pavement. I could hear thunder in the distance, so I assumed everyone was sheltering themselves from the storm.

Am I that lucky?

I didn't think I could get away with Chris not remembering a single second of my drunken rant. It felt too good to be true. I needed to text Tasha and let her know. By the time I pedaled into my driveway, I was soaked. I set my bike against my house and rushed inside. I stumbled to take off my shoes. My socks felt slimy between my toes as I peeled them off my feet. Every inch of my shirt was sticking to my body.

I hurried up the stairs and into my room. I could smell the musty air realizing my windows were wide open, and the rain was cutting through. I slammed them shut as fast as I could, but the surrounding areas were already damp. I pulled off my pants and shirt as if I were shedding a layer of skin before grabbing a towel out of my hamper to sop up the water from the windowsills. I felt a slight chill down my entire body and used the dry side of the towel to pat my damp skin.

I looked around for my phone, remembering it was still in the pocket of my jeans. The screen had a little perspiration on it, but it still worked fine. I wiped the screen against the side of my underwear before opening it. I saw I had a text from Caleb.

CALEB

Doing anything tomorrow after school?

ME

I don't think so. Why?

I swiped the text thread away and clicked on Tasha's name.

ME

It was Chris.

I swiped back and saw Dan's name. I sat staring at it for a second before clicking it.

ME

Hey, can we talk?

My phone buzzed.

CALEB

It's just gonna be me and Parker at the house tomorrow. I was hoping maybe you could come over and keep us company?

ME

Too scared to be on your own? Haha.

CALEB

Lol, we need a strong football player to protect us.

ME

When you find one, let me know. ;p

CALEB

Maybe I can wine and dine you.

ME

In that case, I'm in!

My phone buzzed.

TASHA

Wait, what?!

ME

Chris was Michael Myers.

TASHA

How did you find out?

ME

I was at his house and saw the mask in his backyard. He said it was his.

TASHA

OMG! What did he say?

ME

I didn't tell him what happened. He told me he was blackout and doesn't remember much. He didn't say anything about what I did, so I just left.

TASHA

Do you think he's telling the truth?

ME

I hope so.

My phone buzzed.

DAN

Why? As far as I'm concerned, we aren't friends anymore.

ME

I'm sorry I hit you, but I'm just tired of seeing you torture Steven.

DAN

He deserves it!

ME

Why?

DAN

Because he makes me sick.

ME

Are you gonna be a bully in college too? You
need to grow up and stop choosing to hate
people who are different than you.

DAN

Fuck off, Landon.

ME

I'm worried about you. If you're going through
some shit, I'm here to help you figure it out.

DAN

I don't need your help. FUCK OFF!

I wanted to tell him I knew about the gun, to grab his attention,
but I didn't want to cause any trouble for Chris. I had so many
questions for Dan. I wondered who the new guys were that he
was hanging out with. I wondered if he was getting in over his
head with the people he was selling drugs for. I wondered if he
had the gun for protection or intimidation.

My phone buzzed.

CALEB

Want to come over around 7?

ME

Sure.

CALEB

Or whenever, doesn't matter.

ME

No, 7 is fine. Sorry I'm just dealing with Dan
stuff.

CALEB

> Is everything okay?

ME

> I don't know. Dan just seems like he's in over his head with some stuff and I tried to apologize for the fight but it didn't go well.

CALEB

> You can't help someone who doesn't want to be helped.

I saw Dan in the hallway the next day at school. He was sporting a shiner under his left eye and the bridge of his nose was a little purple. He stared me down as he walked by; I was on his shit list. With a clenched jaw, he puffed his chest as he walked by, showing his alpha status. I half expected him to jump me in the bathroom or trip me in the cafeteria, but he showed his disdain with silence and sharp looks.

Lauren met me by my locker after the last period. I was shoving my math book onto the top shelf when she walked up behind me and squeezed my ass, causing me to jump out of my skin.

Lauren laughed. "Jeez, what's got you all tense?"

"I just wasn't expecting it," I said with a smile. I grabbed my backpack off a hook and closed the door. "I tried texting Dan last night to apologize, but he wanted nothing to do with me."

Lauren slid her hand into mine as we walked toward the exit. "I'm sorry, babe. I'm sure he'll come around."

Two freshmen dressed in basketball gear whizzed by us, and I heard an announcement that they were holding an AV club meeting in the auditorium.

"That's the thing, I don't think I'd be upset if he didn't." I shrugged. "We've been growing apart, so maybe it's for the best." I squinted my eyes as we walked outside. There wasn't a cloud in the sky.

"I have to start this chemistry project with Dan tomorrow, I hope it's not awkward," Lauren said.

"I'm sure he won't even talk about me, he told me to fuck off last night."

We walked to the sidewalk, and I let go of Lauren's hand as Steven approached us.

"Hey guys," Steven said with a cheerful wave.

Lauren and I said hi at the same time.

"We're seeing a movie later, wanna come?" Steven asked.

"I can't," I said. "I'm meeting up with a friend tonight."

Lauren raised an eyebrow. "Oh, who?"

I hesitated. "We're doing this writing project for Mrs. Donahue's class. We really need to get it done."

I had avoided answering her question like a scared dog avoids a mean cat. I glanced at Steven, who tilted his head at me with wide eyes; he knew full well I was talking about Caleb. Every lie I told felt like a single brick of guilt being added to the wall I was building between Lauren and me. Soon enough, I wouldn't be able to see her on the other side.

"Okay," Lauren said as she looked between me and Steven. "I guess I'll text you later and let you know how the movie was."

"All right." I leaned over and pecked her on the cheek. "Have fun," I said before spinning around and crossing the street.

I felt a pit in my stomach, feeling bad that I couldn't stop thinking about Caleb that whole day, but what else was new? Thinking about getting to kiss him again made me giddy but I wouldn't be able to do that until I ended it with Lauren.

Walking up the driveway, I noticed my Dad's car wasn't there. I unlocked the side door before shooting him a text.

. . .

> **ME**
>
> Hey Dad, Are you gonna be home later? I kinda need the car to get to my friend's house.

I took a stride to the fridge to grab the package of sliced cheese. I put two pieces between some bread and popped it into the toaster oven.

I felt my phone buzz from my pocket.

> **STEVEN**
>
> That was so awkward. Do you realize what kind of position this puts me in?

> **ME**
>
> What do you mean?

> **STEVEN**
>
> I know you're going to see Caleb. Now you're making us both liars. How long are you going to drag this on before you tell her?

> **ME**
>
> I feel just as shitty, believe me.

> **STEVEN**
>
> Doesn't seem that way.

> **ME**
>
> I can tell her tomorrow then okay? Just give me the night to think about how I'm gonna do it.

> **STEVEN**
>
> Try not to do anything tonight that you'll regret, all right SportyGuy?

ME

Who are you, my Dad?

STEVEN

Only if you call me Daddy!

ME

Omg, shut up haha

DAD

Sorry bud, I need the car for the night. Won't be home till late.

Damn.

I would have to ride my bike to Caleb's place. I leaned against the counter and checked my email. Nothing had come yet from NYU. I opened Instagram and typed NYU into the search bar and scrolled through their photos. So many students wore purple hoodies or T-shirts with the purple NYU logo on them. I wanted to be one of them so badly. Their Instagram featured a lot of single pictures of students with purple backgrounds behind them. I clicked on one where a guy was standing next to a purple tree, with purple buildings behind him. They quoted him in the caption, saying "you belong here," and it filled me with hope. I pictured myself walking the streets, admiring the architecture of the surrounding buildings, and writing in their massive library that reminded me of a beehive. My thoughts of NYU made me so much happier than picturing myself at the University of Texas. I'm sure I could find a writing program at UT, but I'd have to play football for all four years. Thinking about it exhausted me. I wanted to focus on writing the next influential novel that everyone became obsessed with, not getting tackled by guys who were twice my size.

I heard the ding of the toaster oven and opened it. A puff of smoke escaped as some cheese had burned against the rack. I laid down a paper towel and used my fingers to grab the bread, burning myself for a moment. I wrapped the paper towel around the crunchy bread, licking my lips in anticipation. I brought the sandwich up to my room to do some homework before heading to Caleb's house.

Riding my bike took double the time it would've taken to get to Caleb's with the car. I left early so I could get there around 7:00 as he'd suggested. I was dripping in sweat by the time I turned into the trailer park. My handlebars vibrated under my grip as I cycled over the rocks and potholes. My lower back is where I would sweat the most, I could feel my shirt sticking to it. I panicked, wondering if I smelled bad.

I squeezed the brakes as I approached the trailer and hopped off my bike. I looked down at my shirt and regretted choosing a gray one. I pinched the fabric and pulled it back and forth away from my body, trying to fan my damp skin. I did not feel cute.

I had tied Caleb's flannel around my waist during the ride but slung it over my shoulder as I made my way up the narrow wooden steps and knocked on the door. I swallowed the dryness in my mouth; I hadn't brought any water. I must have looked like an ogre who ran a marathon. I lifted my arm to take a sniff, and that's when Caleb opened the door, catching me in the act.

TWENTY-NINE

I swung my arm down as fast as I could, hoping Caleb didn't notice, but I could tell by his smile he had.

"Hey." Caleb leaned in to hug me.

"Sorry, I'm really sweaty," I said as I hugged him back. My arms fit perfectly around his broad shoulders. I smelled garlic whip past me in the air.

Caleb pulled away, but his hand lingered on the side of my ribs. "What happened?"

"My Dad had the car, so I had to bike here." I wiped my forehead with the back of my hand, feeling embarrassed.

"Damn, I'm sorry."

I handed Caleb his flannel shirt. "You left this in my room, I kept forgetting to give it to you at school." The truth was, I didn't want to give it up.

"Thanks," he said, taking it back with a smile.

Caleb stepped back and gestured for me to come inside. I stepped in, and a chilly breeze hit me. I glanced at an old AC unit in the living room window. It was loud as if it had been on for ten years straight, working its hardest to stay alive. The inside was wider than I thought it would be. The floor was worn down wood, and a long fluffy brown couch sat in front of a beat-up TV stand. A matching coffee table nestled in between. A forty-two-inch TV rested atop the stand, being held up by two skinny legs, looking like they could give out at any second. To the left of the TV was a wide, five-foot shelf filled top to bottom with DVDs.

I pointed to the shelf. "I assume those are all yours?"

"Yup," Caleb said, looking proud with his chest puffed and his hands at his hips. "My pride and joy."

I laughed. "How many are there?"

"Close to four hundred?"

"Holy shit! I've never even watched a hundred movies in my life."

"Well, hopefully, that'll change," Caleb said. He winked at me when I looked at him, which made my knees feel weak. There was a small dining table that took up the rest of the living room. Caleb pointed a thumb behind him and said, "we're in the kitchen."

"Mind if I used your bathroom first?"

"Sure."

Caleb stepped the few feet it took to arrive at the tiled floor of the kitchen. It was narrow with a fridge and stove on the left side and a sink on the right with some counter space. The bathroom was just before the kitchen. I closed the door behind me. The space made me feel a little claustrophobic. There was a small sink, toilet, and one of those rectangle standing showers that reminded me of a casket stood up on its side. Through the foggy glass door, I could see the hint of a little square window. I stepped to the mirror and raised my arms, revealing wet stains on my armpits. "Shit," I whispered, frantically reaching for a wad of toilet paper. I crumpled up the thin stack and reached under my shirt to dab the moisture. I tossed the paper into a small trash bin that rested under the sink.

If I don't raise my arms, he won't see the sweat stains.

I slowly opened the mirror, trying not to make a sound that would alert Caleb's attention. Inside were four toothbrushes in a cup, mouthwash, toothpaste, a few pill bottles, and a stick of deodorant. I reached for it, hoping it was Caleb's before pressing it into my sweaty pits and returning it to the shelf. I washed my hands, splashing some water on my face, hoping to get rid of any redness in my cheeks.

"Landon!"

Parker rushed me as I walked out of the bathroom, wrapping his arms around my waist.

"Hey!"

Parker grabbed me by the hand. "You *have* to see our room!" I didn't have a choice in the matter as he pulled me through the kitchen. I glanced at the stove, seeing a pot of boiling water and a pan of red sauce simmering. The smell of fresh herbs made my stomach growl. We pushed past Caleb, and I gave him a quick smile. Parker pulled me to the end of the trailer with two doors across from one another. He pushed open the door on the right and pulled me inside. The rooms' walls were painted baby blue, reminding me of a clear sky. The square room was big enough for two twin-sized beds and a nightstand between them. A single lamp and a digital clock rested on top.

Parker hopped on the left-side bed and sat cross-legged, saying, "this is my bed." He pointed to the other bed with gray sheets and a single pillow without a case. "And that's Caleb's bed."

It was clear which side of the room was Caleb's as he'd covered it in movie posters. At the head of the bed, there was a poster of *E.T.* with the image of the little boy on his bike and his little alien friend in the front basket. The other posters lining his wall were more films I hadn't seen. One called *The Departed*, another titled *Pulp Fiction*, both of which I'd never even heard of.

The last poster was a silhouette of four boys walking on train tracks, titled *Stand By Me*.

Caleb poked his head in as I noticed a book resting in front of his pillow. I sat on his mattress and picked it up to reveal the title; surprised to see it was *Ready Player One*.

I smiled, looking at Caleb who was leaning against the door frame. "You're reading it?"

"Yeah, it's great so far."

I placed the book on the nightstand. "Which part are you on?"

Caleb looked around the room, searching his brain, "Um, they just blew up his house."

"Crazy, right? It gets even better."

"Caleb," Parker said. "I'm starving."

Parker slumped over on his bed as if he'd passed out.

Caleb chuckled, "All right, the pasta is almost ready. Go set the table."

"Okay!" Parker rose from the dead and shuffled into the hallway. I stood to follow Parker out, but Caleb didn't let me pass. His shoulders almost filled the skinny door frame. He pinched my shirt and pulled me close to him, forcing our stomachs to touch. He looked me in my eyes and smiled.

"I'm glad you're reading the book," I said. "No one ever takes my recommendations."

"How could I not?" Caleb cupped my hand in his. My face scrunched as he grazed the knuckles of my right hand. "Sorry, sorry. I forgot, let me see." I raised my arm and Caleb examined my bruised hand. "I'd hate to see the other guy," Caleb whispered, which made me smile. He looked at me with his hazel eyes, I was swimming in them. Accompanied by his long eyelashes and thick eyebrows, they were the most beautiful eyes I'd ever seen; more beautiful than any sunset, more beautiful than any rainbow or solar eclipse. His eyes were like a maze, I could get lost in them for hours.

"Caleb, I think it's burning," Parker called out.

"Oh, shit!" Caleb winced before shuffling back to the oven. I followed behind him to the edge of the kitchen. Caleb slipped on a pair of mitts and opened the oven door. He waved some smoke away before pulling out a sheet pan, placing it on the counter behind him. The garlic smell was emanating from the sliced baguette. "She's a little toasty," Caleb said. I moved closer. The edges of the bread were dark brown.

Parker popped into frame out of the corner of my eye. "That'll do donkey, that'll do," he said with a surprisingly good Scottish accent. Caleb and I laughed as Parker scooted off to grab the plates.

We sat at the small dining table and Parker told us about learning multiplication between each slurp of his saucy noodles. Caleb would throw out a random, simple equation, and Parker would use a finger technique to figure out the answer.

It wasn't often I had a home-cooked meal. My Dad ordered take-out for us most nights as he didn't have the time or patience to cook. The garlic bread was crunchy, and the butter on top was silky smooth, melted into all the nooks and crannies. The pasta was a thick spaghetti cooked al dente with a chunky red sauce that smelled like rosemary and thyme. I scarfed it all down and filled my stomach to the brim. We all did. Our plates were empty except for the smears of left-over sauce that decorated them like a first graders finger-painting.

I popped the last corner of garlic bread into my mouth. "So, where are your parents tonight?"

"Luke's not our Dad," Parker said with sauce all over his mouth. His words were sharp and I could feel the sting.

Caleb placed a napkin in front of Parker. "He knows that. Use a napkin, please." Parker did as he was told. Caleb looked at me. "They wanted a night away, so they're staying at a casino tonight. I'm sure they'll come home with a lot less than what they started with. That's usually the case." I could hear the frustration in Caleb's voice as he stood to collect our plates.

"Here, let me help," I said as I picked up the dirty napkins and remaining silverware.

Parker slouched in his chair with a fake frown. "Do I have to do the dishes tonight?"

"You know the rules," Caleb shouted from the kitchen. "I cook, you clean."

Parker rolled his eyes, peeling himself off his chair.

"I'll help you," I said to Parker, who perked up with a smile.

I washed and let Parker dry and put away the dishes. We flew through them with ease, telling bad knock-knock jokes to each other. We finished and joined Caleb on the couch. He had already popped in a DVD.

Parker jumped on the couch next to him "What're we watching?"

Caleb turned on the TV. "*The Lost World*, duh."

"Yes!"

I sat with Parker in between me and Caleb. "What's that?"

Parker glared at me. "The sequel to *Jurassic Park*!"

I sunk into the couch, embarrassed. "Oh, right."

I liked the sequel. It was exciting, especially one scene where two T-Rex's were attacking a trailer with people inside, trying to push it over a cliff. It was the most stressful thing I'd seen in a movie. During certain parts, Parker would look at me to see my reaction to what was happening on the screen.

Parker had fallen asleep twenty minutes before it ended. His head was in Caleb's lap and he'd stretched his legs out over mine. The credits rolled with the famous *Jurassic Park* theme song before Caleb clicked it off.

"What'd you think?"

I shrugged one shoulder, whispering, "It was good, but it can't beat the original."

Caleb smiled at me. "I knew I liked you." He petted Parker's sleeping head. "I'm gonna take him to bed."

I nodded. "Okay."

Caleb scooped Parker into his arms and his biceps didn't go unnoticed. Everything felt so peaceful in that trailer. I wondered how different it was when their mom and her boyfriend were around.

I heard Caleb's footsteps in the kitchen after a few minutes of silence.

"You want a beer?"

"Sure," I said. I didn't like the taste of beer, but I would've accepted anything Caleb offered at that point. I heard the hiss of the bottle as Caleb popped the cap off. It must've gone flying because I heard it hit the floor and topple away. Caleb swore under his breath as he chased after it. He popped a second bottle and sauntered over, holding it out for me to take. I grasped the bottom of the bottle, sending a chill up my arm as the frosty glass touched my palm. "I thought you weren't allowed to drink," I said with a smirk.

"In public," Caleb said. "But they can't monitor what I do in the privacy of my own home." Caleb plopped next to me and sipped from his bottle.

The beer was dark and bitter against my tongue, leaving a strong aftertaste of earthy flavor.

"Thanks for tonight. It was sweet, making dinner for me. Do you cook a lot?"

"Yeah," Caleb said as he pulled a leg up, leaning his back into the fluffy arm of the couch. "Parker would never eat otherwise."

"You don't think your mom would make sure he ate?"

"I don't know, she's selfish. They both are. It'd be very

different for Parker if I wasn't here." Caleb took another sip, and I focused on the way his lips kissed the edge of the bottle. "I'm trying to save up for a place, one for me and Parker. I'd love to get him out of here, but things are slow at Lucky's. I might have to look for something else but no one wants to hire me after a background check."

"I can't imagine how hard that must be."

"I thought about going back to school, get a degree in something to get a better job. Parker has always wanted a huge TV to feel like we were at the movies. He deserves that, ya know? I've avoided getting the court involved because I'm afraid they wouldn't let me be Parker's legal guardian now with my criminal record. It's tough, sometimes I feel like I'm raising Parker when I should be partying at some state school or something. I resent my mom because it shouldn't be my job. What twenty-one-year-old is raising a kid?" Caleb scratched his cheek and sighed. "God, that makes me sound like such a dick."

I sat up straight. "That doesn't make you a bad person. You didn't choose any of this. You're right, it shouldn't be your job. But Parker adores you, I'm sure he's grateful for you." I took another sip and forced the beer down, trying not to show my dislike for the taste.

"I'm sorry, I didn't mean for this to turn into another venting session. We can talk about something else." Caleb's eyes lit up. "Oh, hey, did you ever figure out who Michael Myers was at the party?"

I chuckled. "Yeah, it was Dan's brother, Chris."

Caleb choked on his beer. "Holy shit," he said with the liquid still in his mouth.

"But he said he was super drunk and didn't remember the party so; crisis averted I guess."

Caleb smirked. His T-shirt was riding up as he slouched into the corner of the couch. The golden skin of his hip was peeking out, and I felt like Gollum wanting to grab hold of his precious ring. I had to avert my eyes before he caught me staring. I caught a glimpse of a silver box sitting under the coffee table. It looked like an old tin lunch box. I pointed to it. "What's that?"

Caleb scooted to the edge of the couch and placed his beer on the table before reaching for the metal square. He set the box in his lap and unlocked the small hinges.

"This is where we keep pictures of our Dad. Parker and I were looking through them earlier," Caleb said, opening the top. It made a small squeak. I slid closer to Caleb as he reached for the photos. He flipped through them, explaining each one. "My Dad loved this motorcycle."

I focused on the picture. The colors were faded as if they had been exposed to sunlight too long. His Dad looked tall, with broad shoulders like Caleb's. His hair was wavy and pushed back, and he had a thin goatee. In the picture, he was standing next to a motorcycle, with grease stains painted down his arms. He was handsome in a classic literature kind of way.

"He let me work on it with him a couple of times," Caleb said. "I never understood what I was doing. I just enjoyed being around him." Caleb placed the picture at the back of the stack and flipped through a few more, stopping at one of his mom and Dad with their faces pushed together cheek to cheek. Caleb's mom took up most of the photo, only half of his Dad's face was present. But they both looked like they were having the night of their lives. They looked young too. His mom's hair was teased to the sky, with big hooped earrings on.

The box shifted in Caleb's lap, and I heard a clink of metal. I reached into the box, picking up a small key. "What's this?" It was a long brass key with the number 2443 carved into it.

"It's the only thing my Dad left behind. I found it on the floor next to his side of the bed. I tossed it in here in case I ever figured out what it went to."

I examined the key. It felt grainy between my fingertips. "Weird." I placed the key back in the box while Caleb stared at the motorcycle picture again.

"He got on that motorcycle and fled. I always think about where he could've gone. I know he has family back in Puerto Rico, so I always assume that's where he went." Caleb placed the pictures back in the lunchbox, hiding the single key underneath. "But who knows, maybe he's in Florida or Utah, or maybe he never left Texas. I wonder if I'd even recognize him if I saw him."

"I'm sure you would," I said, placing my hand on his thigh.

"When I was a kid, all I wanted to do was see him again, while we were out grocery shopping or on my walk to school. But now if I saw him, I don't even know what I'd say." Caleb reached for his beer. "I go back and forth between thinking I'd scream at him or just cry in his arms." Caleb paused without taking his eyes off the lunchbox. "I miss him a lot sometimes."

I knew how he felt. I would've given anything to talk to my mom one more time. I didn't feel her pain, but I felt the pain of her loss every day and it made me yearn for more time with her. She would have loved Caleb. Seeing the way he took care of Parker would've been enough for her to realize he was a good guy.

I attempted to wrap my arm around Caleb's shoulders just as he was taking a sip of his beer, accidentally whacking his arm. It caused him to spill his beer all over his shirt.

I slid away from him and stared. "Oh my god. I'm so sorry!"

"Don't be! It's okay, it was an accident," Caleb said as he waved it off. He placed the bottle on the table and reached for the bottom of his shirt, pulling it over his head and tossing it on the floor in front of him. My gaze lingered on his chest before I pulled my eyes away, knowing I'd be trapped there until he walked away; but he didn't, he stayed put. Caleb smiled at me, and said, "Were you trying to put your arm around me?"

I averted my eyes and whispered, "maybe."

"Smooth." Caleb smiled. "But I think that's against the rules."

I swallowed a lump in my throat. Something changed when Caleb was shirtless in front of me. I couldn't stop thinking about how badly I wanted to kiss him, and what I was willing to do to get it.

"I broke up with Lauren yesterday." The lie flew out of my mouth like a spitball from a straw.

"Wait," Caleb said, taken aback. "When?"

"Yesterday." The words formed before I could even think about the damage I was doing.

"Why didn't you tell me?"

"I hadn't found the right time I guess? That's why I agreed to come. I wanted to tell you all night, but it seemed weird to talk about it in front of Parker."

"Damn. Well, how did she take it?"

"She was upset, obviously didn't see it coming. But we talked for a while and she eventually understood why we couldn't stay together."

I was digging myself a grave that I wasn't sure I'd be able to escape from, but lust was a powerful monster that couldn't be stopped.

"So it's officially over?"

I nodded. "Officially over."

Caleb's smile was growing. "No more rules?"

"No more rules."

My brain was telling me to stop, but my eighteen-year-old hormones had already taken over, there was no going back.

"Come here," Caleb said as he reached for my arm, bringing me closer. He touched my chin with his thumb as his pointer finger wrapped underneath and gently pulled me into his lips. Caleb's hand moved to the side of my face as my tongue found its way to his. I placed my hand on his chest and followed the curves of his body down to his bare hip. I'd wondered what his skin felt like for so long that it was like I was in another dream. His skin was soft, void of a single divot or blemish. He leaned backward on the couch, pulling me down on top of him, and our kissing got more aggressive.

Caleb's hands explored my body, he sent his palms down my back and underneath my shirt before scaling back up. His hands felt warm against my skin. Caleb broke our kiss to pull my shirt over my head and tossed it on the coffee table before our lips relocked. My naked torso rubbed against his without an ounce of friction. His hands slid down my back again and pushed past the waistband of my underwear. My heart was beating so fast, I feared it would burst through my chest. Caleb's hands squeezed my ass, causing me to nibble his bottom lip.

Caleb whispered, "Is this okay?"

His breath warmed my upper lip. I was so nervous, but I didn't want any of it to stop. I looked at him in his perfect hazel eyes and nodded. He gave me another squeeze, and it sent a ripple of pleasure up my sides. I pushed myself against his leg, I'd never been as hard as I was at that moment.

Caleb's hands let go of me and instead reached between us, feeling the crotch of my jeans. We continued to kiss while he attempted to unbutton my pants. He struggled to get a good grip to remove the button from its hole. I could feel him smile under my kiss before I stood to take the pants off myself. Caleb did the same, still laying on the couch. He revealed blue boxer briefs that hugged him, leaving little to the imagination. I'd never seen anyone so beautiful. I let my jeans fall to my feet, stepping out of them, turning them inside out. Caleb tossed his jeans across the room and sat up onto his knees. I kneeled against the couch and kissed him again in our upright position. I let my hands explore him, allowing myself to linger on the dimples of his lower back before pushing my way into his underwear. My entire palm could fit around him, and I could feel the peach fuzz of his cheeks tickling my skin. I couldn't help but return the squeeze he had given me.

Caleb pressed his weight against me, laying me back against the fluffy cushions of the couch. He was on top of me and I could feel his excitement against my thigh. His lips explored the side of my neck and it sent a lightning bolt pulsing through me. My hips writhed against his. He continued to move his kisses down my chest and across one of my nipples, sending another shot of electricity to my groin. Caleb released his tongue and pressed it against my skin, letting it trickle down my stomach, swooping over every peak and valley of my abs until he reached my hip. He slowly peeled the top of my underwear down to expose my hip bone and he kissed it softly. I squirmed, letting out a chuckle as it sent a tickle of goosebumps up my arms. Caleb smiled as he peeled back the rest of my underwear, exposing me for the first time.

I lifted my waist to help him remove my boxers. I wanted him to see me naked; I wanted him to experience all of me the way no one else had. He touched me so delicately like I was an ancient Egyptian artifact dug up from a three-thousand-year-old tomb. Every time his lips connected against my skin, it sent another wave of pleasure over my entire existence. It wasn't until I felt his mouth around me I gripped a chunk of his hair in my fist. I pulled a bit to make him stop before I embarrassed myself.

Caleb leaned back on his knees and removed his underwear. I couldn't stop staring. I didn't want to blink because it meant I would miss a millisecond of enjoying his perfect body. I think he knew I was enjoying the sight of him because he looked down at me and ran his hands over his smooth skin, smiling the most devilish smile I'd ever seen.

Caleb crawled over me, and straddled my hips, grinding

against me before leaning down for another kiss. My hands had a mind of their own as they locked onto his hips. I pressed against Caleb's fuzz. As soon as I reached down and grasped Caleb in my hand, a moan escaped his lips. I had never felt someone else in my hand, but I had touched myself enough times to know what to do next.

I'd never felt that kind of ecstasy in my life. I was in a state of euphoria that I never wanted to escape from. It was better than any drug or any gulp of alcohol could've made me feel. Caleb made me a part of him that night, and I never wanted to go back to anything else. We were in our own intimate bubble and I'd never felt closer to another human. I wanted all of him and he wanted all of me.

Neither of us lasted long, our lust had escaped us, leaving us both gasping for air between each kiss. After it ended, I could still feel him on me and I'd never felt more sure. We stared at each other, unable to look away. All I could do was smile so big that my cheeks hurt. I ran my fingers through his hair; it was thick and silky.

Caleb closed his eyes. "I should shower," he whispered. "Wanna join me?"

I chuckled. "Can two people even fit in there?"

Caleb stared down at me. His hands were on either side of my head, holding his weight off of me. "I don't know, but we can find out."

Caleb hopped off and collected his clothes before running into the bathroom. I thought about how Parker could wake up at any second and find us, so I grabbed my clothes just as fast and joined Caleb.

Even in the shower, we couldn't stop kissing and smiling. Letting him lather me with soap felt so erotic and loving. He was getting to explore me all over again. I logged every touch, every kiss, every smile, and every inch of him into the Caleb file box in my mind. It was the best night I'd ever spent with anyone, and I didn't want to forget a single second of it.

My bike ride home wasn't as joyous. The guilt finally washed over me. I was a liar *and* a cheater, there was no way around it. I knew I'd have to break up with Lauren the next day, I couldn't put it off any longer no matter how hard it was going to be, even if a boulder sat in my stomach.

Grow some balls and do it, asshole.

THIRTY

The next morning I woke up in my bed feeling like an hourglass. My top half was full of guilt and my bottom half was still feeling the high from my night with Caleb. But the sand slowly dropped, filling me up. I entered the kitchen and scarfed down my cereal. I opened my phone before heading out the door, seeing a kissing emoji from Caleb. I couldn't stop thinking about him and everything that happened the night before.

I slid my backpack on before crossing the street, feeling a ping in my stomach as my brain switched from thinking about Caleb to thinking about Lauren. I had officially betrayed our relationship, and it was just evil to keep her in the dark. I had to tell her that day at school. My anxiety pushed through the roof just thinking about breaking the news to her.

The first warning bell rang as I walked down the entrance hall, spotting Steven at his locker. I was going to wave and head to my homeroom, but he reached out and pulled me through the crowd. I leaned my shoulder against the locker as he closed his.

"Spill it, bitch," Steven said, looking me up and down.

I tried not to grin. "Spill what?"

"The T-E-A, the tea! I need it!"

I stared at him with a crooked face.

Steven clapped his hands at me. "Oh my god, I'm talking about Caleb. How was Caleb's last night?!"

I shrugged.

Steven's jaw dropped. "I knew it, you guys did it, didn't you?"

"Does it matter?"

Steven punched me in the shoulder.

"Ow! What was that for?"

"For not waiting until you broke up with Lauren."

"I'm telling her today. I have to."

"Don't get me wrong," Steven said. "I'm glad you finally lost your V card, but you didn't need to drag Lauren through the mud while you were at it."

"Believe me, I feel like shit."

"Then why'd you do it?" Steven started to fix his hair in the reflection of his phone.

"I've been asking myself the same thing."

"Cheating is for straight boys. It's not a good look." Steven put his phone away and blew me a kiss before he walked off, not giving me much of a chance to say anything else.

Thanks.

I sat at my usual desk in my homeroom before pulling out my phone.

ME

You at school today?

CELEB

Yep, I'll be mopping the floors during the second period.

ME

Maybe I'll have to sneak out and come find you.

CALEB

Oh, please do. ;)

My stomach sank as a text from Lauren popped up.

LAUREN

Morning babe :)

ME

Hey, are you gonna be around later? I want to talk to you about something.

LAUREN

Of course, is everything okay?

ME

Yeah, just find me during lunch, maybe?

LAUREN

Me and Dan are going to the library to do some research during second period if you want to come talk then?

ME

I don't really want to talk around Dan.

LAUREN

We can sneak away :)

ME

Sure, I'll see if I can escape for a bit.

LAUREN

Okay <3

It was hard for me to focus during the first period. I was trying to find the right words to say to Lauren, a straightforward way to break the news. I had never broken up with anyone before. Hell, I'd never cheated on anyone either, and I knew it was going to make everything so much more difficult to say.

I glanced at Tommy Jacobs, who was sitting next to me, scribbling notes onto his spiraled pad. He and Tasha briefly dated during our junior year. The relationship lasted exactly seven days. I remember the entire break-up event happened outside the editing room where we put the monthly paper together. All of us gathered around a computer, pretending not to watch them through the open door.

We could all hear Tasha ending things. She pulled a small Tupperware out of her backpack and handed it to Tommy, saying, "I think we should break up, but I made you this cupcake." We had to stifle our laughter to not get caught eaves-dropping. Tommy opened the container and pulled out a purple frosted cupcake that looked like she ripped it from the pages of a fairytale. Tasha walked into the editing room and closed the door behind her without looking back. It was so easy for her to forget about Tommy. She looked content with her actions and went about her day as if nothing had happened. Poor Tommy looked depressed for the rest of the week every time I saw him until he started dating Becky Johnston soon after. I knew that a cupcake wouldn't get close to fixing the damage I had caused, I'd need a whole Mack truck full of them.

I walked to my second-period class, still racking my brain, but nothing was sticking. I hated not having anything planned to say. I was so bad at improv; I knew if I waited until I was face to face with Lauren I would freeze up and chicken out.

I stepped into Mrs. Donahue's class with my head down as I passed her desk.

"Landon," Mrs. Donahue said, stopping me mid-stride. "Are you all right?"

I was one of the last people to arrive. The bell rang, but I'd missed it entirely.

"Yeah," I said. "Just a lot on my mind, per usual." She smiled her warm smile and I noticed a *Madison Monthly* on her desk that had 'SPECIAL EDITION' printed at the top of it. I furrowed my brow, reaching for it. "What's this?"

"Just came out today." Mrs. Donahue leaned her elbows on the desk. "I have to say, your piece was the best you've written."

I picked up the paper, quickly flipping through the pages. "My piece?" I had no idea what she was talking about until I saw my name printed on the paper.

"Did you know this was coming out today?"

I racked my brain before remembering my hung-over conversation with Tasha in my room.

"Tasha mentioned it, but I didn't know it was today," I mumbled as I flipped through the pages.

"Well, really great work on this one."

"Tasha was the one that picked it. I..." My eyes caught my printed name and I started reading. "...wait."

"What's wrong?" Mrs. Donahue asked.

My heart stopped. "I have to find Tasha, I'm sorry I'll be right back." I turned and bolted out the door, still holding onto the paper. I power-walked through the empty halls frantically typing out a text.

Hey, where are you right now?

I stopped and waited for Tasha to respond but my patience was lacking. I paced back and forth with my eyes locked on my phone screen.

TASHA

Library, why?

I picked up speed again. Pushing through the swinging doors, I went straight for the front desk. Mrs. Fletcher, a short woman with white hair, was standing behind the desk, peering at her computer screen. My sudden voice startled her. "Have you seen Tasha?"

Mrs. Fletcher squinted, surveying the large room before pointing a wrinkled finger at the computer lab.

I looked behind me and spotted her, slapping my hands against the wood of the tall desk. "Thanks." The computer lab was a small room at the back of the library, secluded in a glass box. I weaved through the long tables and passed studying students. I pulled the heavy glass door open and approached Tasha, who was sitting in front of her laptop. I hovered over her chair like a vulture flying over a dying animal. "How did you get this?"

Tasha removed her headphones. "What?"

I slapped the paper down on her keyboard. "My college application story. How did you get it?"

Tasha pushed her chair from the desk and looked up at me, raising her hand in defense. "You said I could take whichever one I wanted."

"Yes, from my desktop."

"Landon, this story was on your desktop."

My eyes widened. "Are you sure?"

"Yes, I'm positive," she said. "What's the big deal?"

I slumped into a chair and gripped my forehead. "I'm such an idiot."

Tasha stared at me.

"I was so hungover, I wasn't even thinking," I said with a sigh.

"I'm not following here," Tasha said with raised eyebrows.

"That story was never meant for anyone to read. It was for my college applications."

"But it's so good."

"Yeah, but it isn't mine."

"What? You plagiarized it?"

"No. Not exactly," I said with a crack in my voice. "How many copies have gone out? Maybe we can reprint."

I stood and started pacing.

"All of them, during first period," Tasha said.

I flipped a plastic chair on its side and Tasha jumped to her feet in shock at my sudden outburst.

"Goddammit! This story wasn't meant for you or the paper."

"I'm sorry, Landon. If I had known..."

I looked at her. I could tell she felt awful.

"Shit, I'm sorry. This isn't your fault at all. It's mine." I picked up the chair and set it back at the table. "I'm sorry, I'm sorry. I gotta go."

I wanted to scream as loud as I could. Caleb flashed through my mind and I fled the room. I jogged back through the library, into the hallway, and pulled out my phone. I was typing a text to

Caleb until I heard his voice echo through the empty hall, hitting me like a forceful wind.

"What the fuck is this, Landon?"

I looked up from my phone, Caleb was approaching me with a powerful stride, holding the *Special Edition Monthly* in his hand.

"Caleb, I can explain. How did you even get one?"

"It's being passed out to everyone. And imagine my shock when I read it."

I stepped closer to him, trying to touch his chest but he pushed my hand away. "Please don't be mad, I-"

"Did you think this was okay?" Caleb said. "Everything I told you about my Dad... You knew how traumatized I was about the hat he gave me for Christmas and you turn it into a story for the school newspaper?"

I put my hands up, trying to explain. "No, it wasn't meant for-"

"I don't give a fuck, Landon. This is my life! This isn't one of your little made-up stories, this is real. You exploited me!" Caleb crumpled the newspaper and tossed it into a trash bin before walking away. I hurried to stop him, trying to grab his arm, but he pulled away and faced me again, pointing a finger at me.

"Don't touch me, Landon. I knew this was a mistake."

I stood in the middle of the empty hallway while he murdered me with his words.

"God, I feel so stupid! I knew when I saw you at Lucky's that day I shouldn't have started this with you," he said. "I should've trusted my gut when I said I couldn't do complicated. I trusted you, Landon! It's been really hard for me to get close to anyone since Andy. Do you realize what it took for me to have sex with you?" I watched his eyes focus on something behind me and his skin went pale. "Fuck," he whispered.

I spun around and discovered Dan and Lauren standing at

the library doors, frozen in place, staring at me. My stomach dropped out from under me like a trapdoor and my mouth went dry. Lauren and Dan had heard everything Caleb said. My entire world was crashing down on top of me and it was suffocating.

I ran to Lauren but Dan stepped in front of her and pushed me back.

"Dan, don't," she said.

I stared at her. My heart pounded through my chest.

"Lauren," I said.

She stepped to me and glanced at Caleb. "What is he talking about?"

"Can we just go somewhere and talk?"

Lauren's questioning continued. "Is it true? Did you have sex with him?"

"Please, let's go talk alone," I begged. I tried to grab her by the hand but she took a step back.

"I don't want to go anywhere with you. I want you to tell me the truth."

I glanced over my shoulder at Caleb who tilted his head at me with scrunched eyebrows. I was trapped between both of them with nowhere to go.

"Landon," Lauren said, pulling my gaze back to her. Lauren's face was flushed and her eyes welled up. "Are you gay?"

Caleb stepped closer to us, I heard his feet against the tiled floor. "You didn't actually tell her, did you?"

I spun around to face him. "Caleb, I can-"

"You lied to get me to have sex with you."

"It's not like that," I said. "I didn't mean-"

Caleb shook his head. "You're a manipulative asshole."

He turned to walk away. I tried to stop him with my voice. "Caleb!"

He turned to look at me one more time. His eyes were red

and puffy. "Don't call me, don't even text me. I don't wanna hear from you ever again. Seriously, fuck you, Landon."

I clenched my jaw. Caleb's words impaled me at the speed of light and I could feel it in my bones. I felt my hand start to shake as I turned back to Lauren. I was holding my breath trying to fight back tears.

"Lauren I swear to God I was gonna tell you. I didn't mean for it to go this-"

She slapped me across the face before I could finish my sentence. The sting of her hand snapped across my jaw. I couldn't look at her after that. I honestly should've seen it coming. I could hear her whimper and sniffle as she walked through the library doors.

Dan and I were left in the hallway alone. I expected him to punch me into the ground but it never came.

"Should've known you were a faggot," Dan said with fire in his eyes before disappearing into the Library.

I panted, grabbing my forehead; I had no idea what to do next. I paced, thinking Dan would tell everyone in the library about me. I felt a phantom pain in my stomach from the one-two punch I was just given. Both of my hands were shaking. I bent my knees, and leaned my hands on them, staring at the floor. I felt like I was hyperventilating.

Tasha appeared, pushing through the library doors. "Landon..."

I shook my head. "Don't." I could feel the anxiety reach my head, and it filled my eyes with tears. "Please, just don't." I couldn't look at Tasha. I just turned around, and walked back to Mrs. Donahue's class, feeling deflated and alone. I wiped the tears from my eyes before entering the room. I sat at my desk feeling empty. I zoned out, staring at the whiteboard. Lost in a daze, feeling as if I had just gone ten rounds in a boxing match where I didn't land a single punch.

I could tell the word was spreading every time I walked through the halls. People were staring at me and whispering as I passed by. I was on display, like a monkey in a zoo. I never expected to lose Lauren, and Caleb on the same day. It felt like I had a ton of bricks on my chest every time I thought about it.

I hoped the news wouldn't reach the teachers because then it might reach the principal, which meant it would then reach my Dad. I would've been okay going my whole life never telling him, even if it meant I had to hide someone from him. I just had a feeling that it would shatter him If I told him I was gay. I left school that day feeling drained. I could barely lift my feet to get myself home. Once I found my bed I didn't move for the rest of the night.

THIRTY-ONE

A week had gone by and every student at Madison High knew my deepest secret. Most mornings I'd be met with a new derogatory word printed out and taped to my locker. Fag. Fairy. Queer. Pansy. Steven eventually caught wind of it and started to come to school early to make sure my locker wasn't defaced before I got there. He was the only person in the entire school who'd known what I was going through. I appreciated all of his support, but when I tried to ask about Lauren, he'd change the subject. Lauren avoided me like I was an infectious disease. If she saw me walking toward her, she'd split down another hallway or duck into the bathroom. I wanted to talk to her and try to apologize, but it seemed she couldn't stand to look at me.

I caught her at her locker putting books away; she didn't see me coming.

"Hey," I said, leaning on the locker next to her. My voice made her jump.

Lauren rolled her eyes when she realized it was me.

"Look," I said. "I know you don't want to talk to me, but I just wanted to say that I'm really sorry."

"People keep asking me if I turned you gay," Lauren said as she slipped a textbook into her backpack. She slammed the locker shut and looked at me. "Do you know how embarrassing that is?"

"People are idiots."

"It still hurts."

"I'm so sorry, Lauren. You don't even know how bad it killed me keeping everything from you."

"I keep thinking about that night in your room and how it all makes sense now."

I nodded.

"How long have you known?" she asked.

"Not long, everything is still so new."

"Why didn't you tell me?"

"I was afraid of hurting you."

"So you thought cheating on me would be the better option? How could I ever forgive you for that?"

"I don't know if you can or even should. I fucked up, I know that. I'm saying I'm-"

"I can't do this right now I'm gonna be late." Lauren pushed by me and I watched her go, disappearing into the crowd.

———

Another week went by and I felt more alone than I ever had. Tasha and Steven were the only two who really spoke to me. They would switch off sitting with me at lunch every other day. When they weren't sitting with me, they were sitting with Lauren. It felt like I'd lost custody of them in a divorce.

Chris was the only guy from the team that would still talk to me. Everyone else was on Dan's side. It was an unspoken pact that no one could even look in my direction if Dan showed up to practice. They all took it out on me on the field, tackling me as hard as they could, not throwing the ball my way. Football was becoming harder and harder to enjoy.

I walked by Mrs. Donahue's room on my way to trig when I heard her call my name. I stepped back to pop my head through the open door. She was sitting at her desk in front of the white-board. It must have been her free period as no other students were in the room.

"Come in, talk to me," Mrs. Donahue said.

I nodded and walked in, sitting at a desk in the front row.

"I just wanted to check in. You haven't been taking part in class much lately."

"That's my fault, I can try talking more." I was about to get up to go, but she gave me a look that told me she wasn't done.

"Tasha told me you've been having a tough time recently."

"And you want to know if all the gossip is true?"

"It's not my business if it's true or not," Mrs. D said. "But I will say that I support you either way. I hope you know you can come talk to me if you need to."

I smirked. "I appreciate it."

"So that story was never meant to be published, huh?"

"Tasha really likes to talk doesn't she?"

She chuckled. "She told me you're still waiting to hear from NYU. With that story, I think you're a prime candidate.

"It wasn't mine to tell." I leaned on the desk, avoiding eye contact.

"You can't change the past, Landon. Everyone makes mistakes, I sure as hell have. A lot of them. But the beauty of making mistakes means we can learn from them and make ourselves better because of them."

"I'm learning the hard way."

"Have you thought about what you'll do if you get into NYU?"

I shifted in my seat, leaning against the chair and slouching.

"I don't know. I keep going back and forth, thinking about what my life would look like at UT versus NYU."

"And?"

"I'm afraid I won't feel any different at UT than I do now. I feel like I hate football more and more every day. I want to start fresh, somewhere where no one knows me. I want to be somewhere where I can be the real me."

Mrs. Donahue stood and walked around to the front of her desk. Leaning against it, she said, "The only person holding you back is yourself."

I looked at her in the eyes for the first time during that whole conversation because her words gave me chills. "My mom used to say that."

She smiled at me. "She sounds like a smart woman."

———

It was going on week three since Caleb broke it off with me and I left school eager to get home to shower. It had been one of the muggiest days of the year and my sweat-stained shirt proved it. I stepped into the kitchen. My Dad was standing at the island looking down at something. His hands were leaning on the countertop and his shoulders were tense. I closed the door behind me, dropping my backpack to the floor.

I had a moment of panic.

Word finally got to him. Maybe Coach found out and told him.

"Dad?" I stepped to the counter. He was reading a letter.

He didn't look up, just took a deep breath and sighed, saying, "Why didn't you tell me you'd applied to NYU?"

My eyes widened. "What is that?"

"Answer me."

"It was a late application that my guidance counselor gave

me. I just wanted another option because I didn't know if I was gonna get a scholarship. Why, what does it say?"

My Dad slid the letter toward me. My eyes scanned the words, I couldn't believe what I was reading.

"Holy shit," I whispered to myself. "I got in."

Dad looked at me and raised an eyebrow. "What the hell are you gonna do at NYU?"

"I wanna be a writer," I declared to him for the first time.

My Dad stroked his mustache and laughed. "Don't bullshit me, Landon. You're gonna play football at UT. You're not going to be a writer."

"That's what *you* want me to do," I said, trying to stay calm, but my emotions from the day were getting the better of me. "Have you ever considered what *I* want? My entire life you've pushed me to play football, but guess what? I'm done."

Dad crossed his arms against his chest, staring at me. "What do you mean you're done?"

"I'm done playing football," I said, staring him in the face.

I could see my Dad getting red, I could tell he wanted to raise his voice. "Landon, don't be an idiot. You have an amazing opportunity in front of you, you have a full scholarship."

"Fuck the scholarship, Dad! I don't want it. I want to go to New York!"

"Landon, I can't afford to send you to that school!"

I grabbed my backpack off the floor and slung it over my shoulder. "I'll figure it out then." I headed for the stairs.

"Landon, I-"

"You know," I said, cutting him off. "For so long I've been terrified of what other people think of me, including you. I didn't tell you about wanting to be a writer because I knew you wouldn't take me seriously. I need to think about myself and what makes *me* happy. Going to New York and getting out of this shitty town is about the only thought making me happy right now. So I'll figure it out, okay?"

My Dad stood there with his arms crossed, looking appalled by my words. I waited for him to respond, but all I got was silence. He eventually shook his head and walked through the living room, toward his office.

I slammed my bedroom door behind me, tossing my backpack on my bed. I sat at my desk as I read the acceptance letter over again. I'd felt so heavy for so long that I'd almost forgotten what it felt like to float. I wanted to show my mom so badly. I wanted to bust through her bedroom door and jump on her bed together, cheering and hollering.

I pulled out my phone. I wanted to text Caleb the good news, but recalled his voice saying the same thing I'd been playing over and over in my head; "Don't call me, don't even text me. I never want to hear from you again."

———

My life force was being drained, leaving me emptier than I was the day before. The first thing I would do every morning was check my phone, hoping that I'd see Caleb's name. My heart skipped a beat every time I felt the vibration in my pocket, only to be disappointed. After all that time of nothing, I'd assumed Caleb was entirely over me. I wondered if Parker ever asked about me, and if he did, I wondered what Caleb told him had happened between us.

For those three and a half weeks I never once spotted Caleb mopping any floors, cleaning graffiti off the walls, or even mowing the grass. It was like he'd walked off the face of the earth. I was alone in the dark, NYU seemed to be my only light at the end of the tunnel. It felt like the only good news was my Dad still had no clue, but even he barely spoke to me when we were home. The election was fast approaching, so he was laser-focused on his campaign.

Now that NYU had accepted me I'd decided to leave football behind. I went to the locker rooms as soon as school was over to talk to Coach. He was hunched over a playbook at his desk. I knocked on his door frame.

"Hey, Coach."

"Griffin, where the hell have you been? You missed two practices. I tried calling your Dad about it but he never picks up."

"His campaign team's been keeping him pretty busy. I'm sorry I missed them but that's kind of what I wanted to talk to you about."

"Come in. Shut the door."

I did as I was told and sat across from him.

"So, what the hell's going on?"

"I wanted to let you know that I declined the UT scholarship."

His eyes got wide and he closed the binder in front of him. "Why the hell would you do that?"

"Coach, my head hasn't been in the game for a while now and I know you can tell."

"We all have our slow weeks. That's all I chalked it up to be."

I chuckled. "It's a lot more than a slow week. I've been thinking about this for a long time. I just don't think football is my thing."

"You're not saying what I think you're saying, are you?"

"I'm sorry," I said.

"Oh come on, your Dad didn't raise you to be a quitter."

"Don't you want guys on your team that are passionate on the field?

Coach's face twisted. "You can't quit. You've been playing since you were a little kid."

"Sure I enjoyed it and I got good at it but I realized I wasn't doing it because it made me happy. I was doing it because it made my Dad happy."

It took a second for it to really sink in for him.

"Hell, I know the feelin'," Coach said. "But are you sure? Because the team needs you. At least play out the rest of the season."

I shook my head. "I'd just be wasting everyone's time."

Coach sighed, brushing a hand over his bald head. It took him a minute to let my decision sink in. "I don't like it, but I can't force you to do something you don't want to do. I just hope you don't regret it."

"I'll come to every game, I promise."

"Bet your ass you will, Griffin. Now go clean out your locker before everyone gets here. I'll tell the guys the news."

I nodded. "Thanks, Coach."

I folded my jersey, staring at my name printed on the fabric before placing it in my backpack. I tossed my pads into a big plastic bin and my helmet along with them. I was zipping up my bag when I heard the door swing open. I looked over my shoulder and saw Chris down the row. He placed his duffle bag on the bench in the middle of the aisle.

"You're here early," I said.

Chris pulled a pair of dirty shoes out of the bag and they slapped against the floor. "I know, I wanted to get some drills in before we started."

"Smart," I said with a nod.

"Team's not gonna be the same without you," Chris said as he stood, opening his locker.

"It's that obvious, huh?"

"We knew it was comin'. I told the guys to ease up but they don't listen to me like they listened to Dan. You quitting because of them?"

"Not fully, no." I said. "Football just isn't what I'm meant to do. But you guys will be fine, you don't need me." I smiled. "I'll be cheering you on at every game." I closed my locker and pulled my arms through the straps of my backpack.

"What about the scholarship?" Chris pulled off his T-shirt. He was wearing a tight Under Armour short sleeve underneath. He reached for his shoulder pads and slipped them over his head.

"It was a tough call, but I declined it, maybe they'll give it to Dan now."

Chris scoffed as he squeezed his big shoulder pads into his jersey. "Yeah right, he barely shows up for practice anymore."

"Has he gotten worse?"

"Most nights he doesn't come home at all."

"I'm sorry, Chris."

"It's not your fault," Chris grunted as he pulled on his knee pads. "He's choosing to do this. He doesn't even care about how worried our parents are."

I shook my head. "He's always been selfish. I should go before the other guys show up. I kind of want to avoid all the questions."

I started for the door, but Chris stopped me with his words.

"I lied before."

I looked at him as he was tying up his tight pants.

"I wasn't drunk at the party. I remember everything," Chris said.

"Oh." My jaw clenched. "Why didn't you say anything when I came to get my bike?"

Chris sat down on the bench, reaching for his shoes. "I don't know. I felt so awkward about it, and I didn't know what to say. I knew you were wasted. I didn't want to rehash it and make things more awkward."

"Just so you know, I thought you were someone else. I wasn't trying to hit on you."

"I know." He bent down, slipped on his shoes, and tied them up.

"Why didn't you tell anyone?"

Chris stopped tying and leaned his elbows on his knees, staring at me with a furrowed brow. "You're my friend, Landon. I wasn't gonna out you to the entire school."

A wave of relief washed over me and I smiled at Chris. It felt good to know he still considered me a friend.

"Thank you. You have no idea how much that means to me."

Chris smirked and nodded before going back to tying his shoes.

"I should go, but good luck tomorrow night," I said.

"Thanks, man," Chris said without looking up.

I walked out with my head held higher than it had been in a while.

The next night I walked out of my house and could already hear the excitement of a Friday night game. The school's parking lot was packed with cars. The lights of the football field made it look like it was the middle of the day. It was the first time in years I was watching the game instead of playing. I decided to grab some popcorn to snack on before heading to the stands.

I pulled on the hoodie I was carrying as the wind picked up. Standing in line at the concessions booth, I remembered seeing Caleb and Parker tossing popcorn into each other's mouths when they watched me play. I could hear their laughter and it made me miss them even more.

I spotted Steven's pink hair out of the corner of my eye. He was several feet away, talking to Lauren. Their eyes found me and I shot my gaze forward. I peeked over again and noticed Lauren was walking toward me. I slipped my hands into the pockets of my hoodie and pretended not to see her.

"Hey," Lauren whispered. It was the first time in weeks I'd heard her voice.

"Hey, hi," I said, avoiding eye contact until I saw she was smiling.

"Congrats on NYU. Steven told me."

"Yeah, thanks. Congrats to you too. Who would've thought we'd end up in the same city?" I chuckled awkwardly.

"I know, right?" Lauren smiled. "We should grab a coffee or something, like after we settle into our dorms and stuff."

I nodded. "Yeah, yeah, absolutely." I knew she was just being polite. I doubted we would ever actually get coffee after everything.

I stepped to the counter. The concessions stand was a little green hut just off the parking lot. Inside was a small popcorn maker, two coffee machines, and every popular candy bar splayed out. "Uh, can I just get a bag of popcorn please?" I looked over my shoulder at Lauren. "You want anything?"

"No thanks."

I passed a dollar bill to the small freshman boy who was standing in front of a silver money box before he scooped some popcorn into a paper bag and handed it to me. I gave him a nod and stepped to the side. Lauren was still lingering.

"I'm sorry we haven't talked much," she said as he pushed her hands into the pockets of her leather jacket.

"I get it, it's okay."

"I just needed time to like, process everything, you know? I felt like I cried for weeks." She pushed a strand of hair behind her ear that the wind had blown across her face.

"I feel awful about everything. I didn't mean for things to play out the way they did. I didn't want to hurt you, but It blew up in my face anyway, so."

"You were gonna hurt me no matter what. But I wish I'd heard it from you."

"Me too. I tried to tell you so many times but as time went on it just kept getting harder." I said, hanging my head.

"I should've gotten the hint when I found Grindr on your phone."

"Yeah, maybe."

We both chuckled, avoiding eye contact.

"So, did Steven force you to come talk to me?"

"Not exactly. He and Tasha have been there for me a lot. And while I can't say I fully forgive you, I do miss having you around."

I smiled. "You do?"

"Yeah. And I kinda had an idea."

"Oh god, what is Steven making you do?"

Lauren laughed. "It's something we've been talking about. Since prom is next week and my Dad went through all the trouble getting our outfits, maybe we could still go together? Not as a couple but with me and Steven."

Her offer stunned me; I thought she'd never want to talk to me again never mind take me to prom.

"Seriously?"

Lauren shrugged. "Yeah, we might as well use the clothes since we have them."

"Well shit, I'm down, yeah," I said with a smile. Lauren opened her arms, pulling me into a hug. I wrapped my arms around her, still gripping my bag of overflowing popcorn. "I'm so sorry," I whispered. "For everything."

Lauren squeezed me tight.

We were smacked into when Steven came running at us to add to our hug, causing the top layer of my popcorn to sprinkle the grass, becoming bird food. "Did we kiss and make up?"

Lauren and I laughed as Steven released us from his bear hug.

"Not exactly," Lauren said. "But we're good, for now."

I smiled at her, tossing pieces of popcorn at both of them.

"Hey don't waste that, I'm starving!" Steven said as he reached into the bag for a handful. I started throwing more at him as we all jogged over to the bleachers.

The three of us cheered and laughed the entire game. It was more exciting to watch than to worry about getting smashed to the ground at any second. I was searching for Dan's jersey, curious if he had shown up to play, but he was nowhere to be seen. Our team ended up losing by ten points, but everyone still seemed like they were in good spirits. Maybe Chris was right, maybe the team did need me. I'd had a lot of fun with Steven and Lauren. It was the first time in weeks I had forgotten about Caleb for a few hours.

Steven and I lingered at his car after Lauren had said her goodbyes. The moon glistened off the hood of Steven's white sedan. I could see a rainbow beaded necklace hanging from his rearview mirror.

"You still haven't heard from him at all?"

"Not in almost a month," I said as I zipped my hoodie.

"Have you tried texting him?"

I watched a black truck pulling out of its parking spot. "No, I've been too afraid, I don't want to make things worse."

"Girl, we need to get you out of this funk," Steven said as he reached into his pocket, pulling out a small pack of gum.

"What funk?"

Steven unwrapped a thin rectangle piece and popped it into his mouth, "I'm not blind. I've seen you moping around school every day for weeks, you eat by yourself at lunch, and you barely talk to anyone. Tonight was the first time I've seen light in your eyes since everything happened."

"Yeah, tonight was the first time in forever I've felt like myself."

"Maybe you just need a Grindr date. That always works for me."

I laughed and crossed my arms against my chest, leaning my butt against the hood of Steven's car. "Every guy that messaged me seemed like a creep. I deleted it anyway, so I'll pass."

"Oh my god!" Steven did a little hop and grabbed me by the arms. "I have an idea! I can set you up with my friend!"

I shivered away from him. "I don't know, I don't think I'm ready to get involved with someone else."

"No, that is exactly what you need!" Steven pulled out his phone and started typing. "You have to get back on the horse if you want to forget about Caleb." I stared at Steven with blank eyes. I didn't necessarily want to forget about Caleb, but every time I thought about him, it made me sad. I would wonder what he was doing during the day and if he was thinking about me at all. Steven was beaming with excitement, the brightness from his phone illuminated his smile. "My friend Blake is super cute. We used to do community theatre together." He held his bright screen in front of my face and it made my eyes squint. I had to allow my vision to adjust before I could see what he was showing me. It was an Instagram picture of a guy from the shoulders up. The blurry background looked like he could've been at the beach. He had blond hair shaved on the sides but fell into his eyes from the top. His eyes were the most piercing sky blue color I'd ever seen. "He's cute, right!?"

"I guess. I don't know. It feels too soon."

Steven looked down at his phone and I saw his thumbs move. "I'm texting him right now."

"Fine," I said, feeling exhausted. "I'm gonna go, I'll catch ya later." I slid my hands into my pockets and started for the street.

"I'm gonna send him your hottest insta pic!" Steven shouted. His voice ricocheted off the light posts that lit the parking lot.

"Whatever you say!" I yelled back over my shoulder. I

thought about Blake's picture as I walked up to my house. It felt strange to picture myself with another guy who wasn't Caleb.

It was two days before prom when I finally agreed to go on a date with Blake. Steven had been texting me daily, bugging me about him.

STEVEN

Blake thinks you're cute.

I want to set you guys up.

I think you'd really like him!

Blake asked about you again today.

Should I tell him to follow you on Instagram?

Do you have Twitter?

I'm gonna keep bugging you until you say yes.

You better not be thinking about Caleb!

Bitch if you don't answer me...

Blake has such a cute dog. Caleb doesn't have a dog. Red flag!

OMG Blake said he loves gingers, go out with him!I talked to Lauren, she thinks it's a good idea too.

kay, if I don't get back to him, he's gonna find someone else.

you're missing out, girl!

I'm just gonna tell him you're interested.

Jesus! FINE! I'll go on ONE date!

I let Steven set the whole thing up. He was ambitious about doing everything. I hadn't even spoken to Blake, I never texted him or even sent him a friend request as Steven suggested that it should be a blind date. It gave me anxiety meeting a person I didn't know. Luckily, I knew what Blake looked like so I could spot him in a crowd. Steven told me to meet Blake at Alvin's Coffee House in Madison's Downtown Square.

The square was cute at night. The small trees that lined the sidewalks were lit up by white string lights that were wrapped around their branches. The square had only been built in the last seven years. It was mostly filled with mom-and-pop shops, a few restaurants, and even a realty office.

Steven suggested Blake and I meet for Coffee and dessert first because it was less formal than dinner. If I didn't think things were going well, it's easier to walk away from coffee than it would be to sit through an entire meal. Steven was more experienced in the world of dating than I was, so I did what I was told.

I approached Alvin's and surveyed the few customers that were inside through the large pane windows. Even with the entrance door closed, The bitter smell of coffee filled the air. I didn't see any guys with blond hair in the shop, so I waited next to the fenced-off outside dining area.

I pulled out my phone. It was 8:10 p.m. Blake was already late, so I scrolled through Instagram. It was becoming a trend where everyone was posting their college acceptance letters. I typed in Dan's name, curious to see if he had posted anything recently, but everything I saw was from months ago.

"Landon?" A voice startled me. I looked up and saw Blake's familiar blond hair swooping across one eye.

"Yeah, hi," I said as I pushed my phone back in my pocket. Blake smiled and reached for a handshake.

"Sorry I'm late. Got caught up in a phone call," Blake said as he slicked back the falling strands of hair with his hand. I looked him up and down. He was wearing a gray suit, with a white button-up shirt under his blazer. He'd unbuttoned his shirt at the top and I could see the beginnings of his bare chest. He was also wearing a pair of clear, round-framed glasses. The lenses were thin and his eyes beamed brighter than the string of lights on the trees. A brown leather satchel dangled across his torso.

"It's totally fine. Though I feel a little underdressed," I said, pulling at the tank top I was wearing.

Blake waved me off. "You look great. Mind if we sit outside?" He had a faster way of talking than what I was used to, and I noticed his slight southern drawl on certain vowels.

"Yeah, that's fine."

"I come here all the time, it's great." Blake walked through the opening in the fence and sat at an empty table with two chairs, pulling his satchel over his head and placing it next to him. The table was made of dark wood and a mason jar sat atop it with a tea light inside. "You and Steven, y'all are close?"

"We've been friends for a while. He said you guys did theatre together?"

Blake chuckled. "I did one show after my family moved here from Alabama when I thought I wanted to be an actor. It was fun, but not something I want to do again." A woman walked up to our table wearing a T-shirt that had ALVIN's COFFEE HOUSE printed across her chest. Blake didn't wait for her to greet us. Instead, he spat out his order. "I'll have a caramel macchiato please, and a slice of cherry pie."

I smiled when I heard how he pronounced the word pie, with more of an 'ah' rather than an 'e' sound.

The server looked at me. "I'll have the same, thanks." I was nervous, the words just came out. I didn't want to struggle over any of the coffee names. The girl walked off after giving us a quick nod.

"So how old are you if you don't mind me asking, same age as Steven?"

"Yeah, eighteen. You?"

"Turn twenty next month," Blake said as he leaned his arms on the top of the table. His answer surprised me because his clothes made him look more distinguished and the fact that he mentioned an internship made me think he was much older than me. "Steven told me you play football."

"I did, yeah. I just quit the team though."

"Oh?"

I could tell by Blake's tone that he wanted me to explain, but the server interrupted us. "Turns out that we're out of the cherry pie," she said with a clenched jaw.

"Just the drinks are fine then," Blake blurted without asking me for my input. The server trotted back inside and I watched her grab two cups off the counter and slowly walk back to us. "So, what do you do now that you quit the team?"

"I guess I can focus more on my writing now."

"Oh, you're a writer. That's cute," Blake said before the server placed our drinks on the table.

My jaw tightened. Blake's words hit me like a condescending brick. My phone vibrated, and I checked it under the table. It was Steven texting me.

STEVEN

How's it going?

ME

I don't think I feel a spark...

Blake and I lifted our cups for a sip at the same time. I had no idea what to say next. I thought about the briefing Steven gave me the day before. He mentioned if the conversation gets stale, just ask about him because people love talking about themselves. I let my lips linger on the cup while I thought of a question. I could taste the sweet caramel syrup that was dripping over the edge of the mug.

My phone vibrated again, and I glanced at my lap where I left my phone face up and almost choked on my coffee. Caleb's name filled the screen. I put down my mug with a thud, causing some liquid to spill over the top. "Sorry I have to take this," I said, feeling short of breath. Blake nodded before I shot out of my seat and walked to the edge of the sidewalk.

I put the phone to my ear, "Hello?"

Caleb's voice cracked, "I need help."

THIRTY-TWO

"What's going on?"

"Luke hit Parker," Caleb blurted. My heart fell to my feet when I heard Caleb's voice. It sounded like he was speed walking. "I'm sorry I called, but no one else was answering."

"No, don't apologize. Go to my place, I'll be there soon," I said in a panic.

"Okay. thank you."

I hung up, rushing back to the table. Blake was looking at his phone.

"Hey, I'm sorry to cut this short, but something just came up, I gotta go."

Blake stood out of his chair. "Is everything okay?"

"I'm not sure. I just have to go."

"Well, let me drive you."

"No thanks, I have my bike."

"Okay," Blake said before wrapping me in a hug. Everything about it felt awkward.

I backed away and jogged to my parked bike, not bothering to leave any money for the coffee. Blake didn't exactly look like he was strapped for cash. I pedaled as fast as I could

Hearing Caleb sound so worried had me panicked, I hoped things hadn't gotten too out of control with him and Luke. The last thing Caleb needed was trouble with the cops again. I'd imagine they'd tack more time onto his probation if he were to get arrested. He sounded so winded; it made me worry that he was running from the cops.

I speeded down my street and could see Caleb sitting on the front steps of my house. Parker was in his lap, leaning his head on Caleb's shoulder. I dropped my bike in the grass and hurried to them. I kneeled and touched Parker's arm.

"Are you okay?"

Parker nodded his head. His eyes were red and puffy, and a bruise was forming on his jaw.

"He could use some ice," Caleb whispered.

"Let's go inside," I said before leading them to the side door. We stepped into the kitchen with Caleb carrying Parker. He plopped him down on a stool at the island. I clicked on the light and whispered. "We just have to be quiet. My Dad's in his room, not sure if he's asleep yet."

I grabbed a washcloth and opened the freezer, grabbing two ice cubes out of a small bucket. I twisted the cloth around the cubes and handed it to Caleb.

He touched the ice pack to Parker's face. "Just hold this here for a bit, okay?" Parker nodded as he held the ice. Caleb turned to me. "I'm sorry to make you do this. I hope I didn't pull you away from anything important."

"It wasn't." I resisted the urge to roll my eyes, thinking about Blake.

"I didn't want to bother you, but I was trying to call Miguel and the others, but no one answered."

"Caleb, it's fine, I don't mind at all. Let's go up to my room. You guys can stay there." They followed me up the stairs and it felt like the floors creaked with every step. I tried to tiptoe as to not alert my Dad. I could hear the TV on in his room, most nights he would fall asleep to the History channel. Caleb was holding Parkers hand and led him into my room. I pulled some folded blankets off of a hallway shelf and closed my door behind me. "So what the hell happened?"

Both Caleb and Parker were sitting on my bed. Parker slumped against Caleb's arm, looking exhausted. I laid some blankets on the floor between my desk and my bed.

"I should've known the piece of shit would do it eventually," Caleb said. "I was reading in our room and Parker was on the couch watching TV. Luke had been drinking all night, so I was staying away from him."

I grabbed a pillow off my bed and tossed it onto the small bed of blankets I'd created. Caleb led Parker over to the pile and gestured for him to lie down before he continued.

"I guess he wanted to take over the TV. He changed the channel, and Parker got mad at him. I heard Luke tell him to go to his room, but Parker refused."

I sat on my bed. Caleb took a seat next to me.

"The next thing I heard was Parker yelling my name," Caleb said. "I came flying into the living room and saw Luke yank Parker off the couch and punch him to the floor."

It shocked me a grown man could strike a kid over something so stupid. I shook my head. "What a fucking scumbag."

"I swear to god I wanted to kill him. I tackled him and just started punching, I didn't care where they were landing, I just lost it. And then my mom jumped on me, clawing and screaming for me to get off of him. She didn't seem to care that he'd just hit her son." Caleb looked over the bedpost at Parker, who had already fallen asleep. "When I stopped punching him, I just grabbed Parker, and we ran."

"Jesus," I said, grabbing his hand. I was nervous he would pull away from me, but he let me touch him.

"I'm not going back there, we can't. I can't put Parker through that again."

"You shouldn't have to," I said.

The room fell so quiet. All I could think about was how scared Parker must've been. Things could've gone a lot worse if Caleb hadn't been there.

Caleb looked me in the eyes for the first time that night. "Thanks for letting us crash here."

"Of course."

"With the way we left things, I didn't think you would answer either."

I scoffed. "I didn't think I'd hear from you again."

"I'm sorry I-"

"You have nothing to be sorry about. What I did was really fucked up. You didn't deserve that." Caleb looked down at my hand, still interlocked with his. I felt an awkward tinge in my stomach and stood, letting go of him. "You can sleep in my bed. I'll take the couch."

Caleb reached out, grabbing me by the wrist before I could walk away. "Stay with me."

I looked down at him, unable to say no to his puppy dog eyes. Sighing, I leaned to switch off the light before I got undressed. I could hear Caleb fiddling with his clothes before I slid my way under the covers. The sheets made me shiver. Caleb climbed in next to me and we shared a pillow. We flipped on our sides, staring at each other. He pulled the blanket up to our ribs. My eyes adjusted to the dark and I could faintly see him. The moonlight glistened over his bronze skin.

"What made you write the story, anyway?"

Our faces were so close I could feel his warm breath against my chin.

"It was for some late college applications." I reached my hand under the pillow, letting my arm rest against Caleb's bare chest. "No one was supposed to see it. I was just as surprised when I saw it in the paper."

"How'd it get there?"

"Miscommunication on my part. I told Tasha she could take a story off my desktop, I was so hungover when she asked me, I totally forgot the story was there."

"Rookie mistake." Caleb's hand touched my hip. He slowly ran his fingertips up my ribs. "I didn't mean to out you like that. I swear I didn't see Lauren and Dan standing there."

"Karma caught up with me, I guess," I said. "Now everyone at school knows."

"Did people care?"

"The guys on the team started treating me differently, making fun of me. Hitting me a little harder on the field."

"Seriously?"

"Yeah, I ended up quitting the team, not because of them, but because I realized football stopped being fun a long time ago."

"I'm sorry. None of that should've happened."

"Like I said, you have nothing to apologize for. It was bound to happen eventually."

"And what about Lauren?"

"We didn't talk for a while. She was the one that approached me at the game last week. I think we're okay now? I honestly didn't think we'd ever talk again."

Caleb smiled. "That's good."

He continued to stroke my skin. It felt nice to feel his touch again.

I pushed my fingers through his thick hair. "When I didn't see you at school, I was afraid you were gone for good."

"I was really angry. I knew I wouldn't be able to be around you. I didn't wanna keep seeing you in the hallway or something. So I asked to switch to another school district to finish my community service."

"Ouch," I said. I felt Caleb's stomach tighten as he held in his laugh.

"That doesn't mean I didn't think about you." Caleb pushed his head closer to mine. I let my hand slide to the back of his head, lightly stroking his hair. "Just promise me you won't lie to me again."

"I promise."

Caleb grazed my chin and lightly rubbed his thumb against my bottom lip.

"I missed you so much," I whispered.

He pulled me into his kiss. I gripped his hair as I let his tongue in my mouth. Caleb pressed his body against me and I let my hand trickle down his spine before sliding into the back of his underwear. He kissed me harder as he shoved his hips forward before he pulled his head away.

"I really want to," Caleb whispered. "But Parker's right there, we shouldn't."

"You're right." I kissed him gently. I'd craved his touch for so long that it was impossible to hide my excitement pressing against him. Caleb kissed my cheek and started pecking his way to my chin and then gave me a final kiss on the lips before flipping to his other side. He reached back and pulled my arm over, making him my little spoon. I laid my forehead against his back, realizing Caleb was my missing puzzle piece, I felt complete again.

My eyes popped open, waking me from a dream in which I had to pee, figuring out it was my body forcing me awake because I actually had a full bladder. Caleb and I hadn't moved from our positions, we were still cuddled together. I could see the sun was rising, and I slowly removed my arm from under Caleb's and flipped around. My clock read 6:44 am. I swung my legs off the bed and stood, peeking at Parker before stepping to the door. He looked so peaceful sleeping there on the bed of blankets, he'd tucked his knees close to his stomach and the washcloth was still damp from the melted ice.

I peeked my head into the hallway and saw my Dad's bedroom door was still closed. I crept through and closed the door behind me as gently as possible. As I entered the bathroom, I thought of ways I could get Parker and Caleb out of the house without my Dad finding out. My Dad didn't leave the house most days until 8:00 a.m., so I figured I could just keep them secluded in my room until he left for the day.

I tip-toed back across the hall, wearing nothing but my underwear while keeping a keen eye on my Dad's bedroom door. Shutting the door behind me, I heard the latch connect. I twisted the lock on my doorknob and stared. Seeing Caleb asleep in my bed made the butterflies rattle again. Never in a million years did I think I'd be sharing my bed with a boy, and definitely not one as impeccable as Caleb.

I lifted the covers, sliding back into my spot as if Caleb was the mold and I was the silicone being poured into it. I closed my eyes, taking in the smell of him, a mix of a warm summer breeze and clean laundry. My eyes got heavy again until I heard the latch of my door unhook. The butterflies in my stomach turned to ash.

"Hey, I heard you were up, so I-"

I let go of Caleb, springing out of the covers, and pressed my back against the headboard. I watched my Dad battle the shock of his discovery. His eyes moved from Parker's small sleeping body to my bed where he could see another shirtless boy asleep next to me.

My sudden movement had woken Caleb from a deep sleep and he rolled over, rubbing his eyes. Caleb's voice was groggy and hoarse. He said, "What's going on?" I didn't need to look at

Caleb to know he saw my Dad standing in the doorway because I felt his body go tense.

"Landon, get dressed and come downstairs, now," Dad said with a stern tone. If his words could control the temperature, my room would've frozen over. Like a statue, I sat there, unable to move until my Dad closed the door. I was already sweating, thinking up an excuse to give him. I jumped out of the bed and slipped on the clothes I was wearing the night before while mumbling every curse word I could think of under my breath.

"You didn't lock the door?"

"I keep forgetting it's fucking broken," I said.

Caleb got out of bed and dressed. "What should I do?"

"Just stay here," I said. "I'll go talk to him and figure it out."

I fled out the door and down the stairs. My Dad was sitting on the edge of his recliner with his elbows on his knees and his forehead in his hand. I sat on the couch and stared at him, unsure what to say.

He spoke first without looking at me. "What the hell is going on with you?" I didn't respond. I could see a strong vein across his forehead when his eyes caught mine. "What the hell is that boy doing in your bed?"

"Dad, he's not the bad guy you think he is."

"I've seen his record. I know just what kind of guy he is. I don't want you getting mixed up in that."

"Dad, please-"

"Did he make you do something? Did he force himself on you?"

"What? No!"

My Dad stood, towering over me. "Then why the hell is he in your bed, Landon!"

"Because I like him," I said.

My Dad bent over and looked me in the face. "I'm sorry, you what?"

"I like him," I said louder.

My words almost knocked him off his feet as he stumbled back and stared at me with his eyebrows raised. His jaw was slack. The gears were turning in his mind; he was putting all the pieces together. "The hell you do," he said with a scoff as he started. "You aren't like that. We didn't raise you like that."

"It doesn't-"

"You're with Lauren," he interjected.

I shook my head slowly. "Not anymore."

"Jesus, Landon. Why are you doing this? Do you have any idea what that'll do to my campaign?"

I shot to my feet. "This isn't about you!"

My Dad stared at me with a clenched jaw. I could hear him grinding his teeth. He started shaking his head. "No, you're too young to know what you want. It'll pass."

"Nothing will pass. This isn't a phase or whatever you think you want to call it. I like him. That's not changing," I said. I locked my feet in place and my legs were sturdy. My heart was pounding as I took a deep breath and squeezed my fists. I felt like an immovable mountain that couldn't be shaken. "I'm gay."

It was as if the word was my Dad's greatest fear. His face became void of any tightness and he went pale. He stood still and closed his eyes, wiping a hand down his face. "I can't look at you right now," he said as he pushed by me, grabbing his keys off the kitchen counter. I let myself slouch back onto the couch as I heard the side door slam, then the car engine roar.

He was gone.

I looked around the empty room, wondering where he was going and if he'd come back. I laid my head against the back of the couch, closing my eyes, feeling exhausted from the confrontation. I had no more secrets to be afraid of; it made my chest feel lighter.

Then I heard the creak of the stairs. I perked up on the

couch, I'd almost forgotten Caleb and Parker were still there. I turned. Caleb was standing at the foot of the stairs. Parker flanked him, holding his hand.

"We're gonna go," Caleb said with red eyes.

I stood, stepping closer to them. "What? No, you don't have to-"

"I've made your life complicated enough." Caleb rounded the corner and started for the front door.

"Caleb," I called out as I jogged after them.

Caleb gripped the doorknob and pulled it open. The sunlight spilled in like a tipped-over can of paint. "It'll be better for both of us if we stay out of each other lives."

"What're you talking about?"

"You realize I've pretty much caused every issue in your life since we met, right?"

"That's not true."

"I don't do complicated, remember?"

"So you're running then?"

Caleb's jaw tightened and his nostrils flared as he stared at me. The room was silent until he said, "I'm sorry for everything."

"Wait! Where are you gonna-"

I wanted to run for the door, but everything felt like slow motion. By the time I reached the threshold, Caleb had already slammed the door behind them. I pushed my forehead against the door, and my whole body became tight. I tried to fight back the tears.

"Goddammit!"

I smacked the door with the side of my fist and felt my arm vibrate with pain. I leaned back against the door and let myself slide down with a thud. My face fell into my hands. It felt like I'd lost everything.

THIRTY-THREE

The rest of my day felt like my head was filled with static. Getting Caleb back just to lose him again was giving me emotional whiplash. Luckily I had Steven and Tasha to vent to during lunch.

"So, he just walked out?" Steven sipped his bottle of water through a straw.

I took a bite of my burger and spoke with my mouth full. "Yeah, I assume he went to work, but I haven't heard from him all day."

"I can't believe he found Caleb in your bed," Tasha said. "That must've been terrifying."

"Girl, we've all been there," Steven said as he rolled his eyes.

I picked at my fries, drowning them in ketchup before popping them into my mouth.

"Watching Caleb walk out was the icing on the cake," I said. "Like, do I text him?"

"Maybe let him cool off for now," Tasha said, puncturing her mac and cheese with a plastic fork.

"The last time I did that, I didn't hear from him for a month."

Steven chuckled. "You could always text Blake."

Tasha slapped him on the arm.

"I'm sorry! I didn't realize how much of a douche he was," Steven said. "I haven't seen him in person since I was like thirteen!"

"Yeah, Blake and I didn't really click," I said, looking around the lunchroom. I wanted to see Caleb walking in to help the lunch ladies, or to take out the trash. Anything that reminded me he was okay and there with me.

I worried about Caleb and Parker for the rest of the day. I hoped they hadn't gone back home. I pictured Parker sleeping on a cot in the kitchen at Lucky's while Caleb worked the night shift, hoping that it'd never come to that.

I finished my homework for the night and sat to watch TV. Nothing was keeping my attention, I'd flip to a cooking show, then a 90s cartoon, and then over to an action movie that was already halfway through its runtime. I watched the screen as bullets blasted from a machine gun, shooting at an armored car that was speeding down the highway. I thought about something Caleb told me, "never watch a movie on TV," he'd said. "They censor it and cut it to shit. No film should ever be interrupted by a commercial. That should be illegal." I could hear his raspy voice in my head. It always got higher in pitch when talked about something he was passionate about.

I switched through the channels, ending on an infomercial about a mop when I heard a car pull into the driveway. I shot up and jogged to the side door, pushing back the thin curtain. My Dad stepped out of the car and walked down the driveway toward the street. I scurried over to the window above the sink. He continued through the courtyard and around the school.

What is he doing?

I wondered how his day had gone. If he had told anyone

about me at his office. Or if he'd confided in Grace at all. I pictured him researching conversion therapy online or pastors I could talk to. Recalling my dream in the church made me shiver. My Dad disappeared behind the school. I quickly grabbed my hoodie off the couch and slipped it over my head.

After jogging across the street and through the courtyard, I poked my head around the edge of the building. I couldn't see anyone in the distance. I walked across the parking lot toward the football field. The field wasn't as bright as it was on game night. The track was dimly lit by a few lamp posts. Stepping onto the turf, I felt my sneaker sink into the ground. I peered around the field until I noticed a figure sitting in the middle of the bleachers.

I climbed the steps, making my way to my dad, who was still in his full suit and tie look. I sat next to him on the bench and felt the cold metal through my jeans. My dad didn't look at me or say hi, he just stared out at the dark field. All I could hear was his breathing. We sat silent, letting the wind swim between us.

"I already miss seeing you out there," my dad finally said. His voice was low and gravelly. "You were ten when I brought you to your first try-out, remember that?"

"Yeah," I whispered, focusing on the green grass and freshly painted yard lines.

"You were so excited to put on all the pads. I swear you didn't take the helmet off for a week after you made the team," my dad said with a small laugh that tapered off into the air. "I couldn't stop thinking about you today." He scratched at his stubble. "I couldn't stop thinking about this one time when you were little, your mom and I were trying to get you to eat your broccoli, or maybe it was green beans. But I remember saying, 'don't you want to grow up to be big and strong?' And you looked up at me with your big eyes and mashed potato on your chin and said, 'I don't want to grow up, 'cause then I won't be Daddy's baby anymore.' I nearly fell off my chair. I looked up at your mom, she was practically in tears."

I looked at my dad. He had his feet up on the bench in front of us and was leaning against his legs

"I said to you, 'you're always gonna be my baby, no matter what'," he said. "Today I kept thinking, what kind of father would I be if I lied to that little guy's face?" Dad turned to me. His eyes were glistening even with the dark sky above us. "Every time I look at you, I see her face and it reminds me she's gone. Your mom had all the answers and I just feel like I've been swimming upstream. Where I got it wrong, she always got it right, and god damn I missed her today."

I spotted a few tears down his cheek and it brought a lump to my throat.

"I needed her more today than I ever have," he said. "But you know what? I kept hearing her voice in my head saying, 'you go home and you tell that boy you love him.'"

It was the first time I felt like my Dad truly saw me. I tried to choke back my emotions, but they were building higher in my throat before I finally busted into tears. My Dad pulled me in and my head fell against his shoulder as I wrapped my arms under his.

"I miss her so much," I said, trying to catch my breath.

"Me too, bud," Dad said. He wrapped his big hand around the back of my head and I felt his body convulsing from his sobs.

I pulled away from him, wiping my face on my sleeve. I'd turned into a complete mess and I could feel the dampness seep through to my arm. My Dad reached out and grabbed my shoulder.

"All I want is for you to be safe," he said with a sniffle. "And I want you to be happy. If *he* makes you happy and if writing makes you happy then that's enough for me." He wiped his cheek dry. "I can't pretend to know what you've been going through. And I know I'm going to screw up and make mistakes but I'm more than willing to listen and learn. You're all I have left. I can't lose you too. I just can't."

I nodded, unable to wipe my tears fast enough.

"I love you, son."

"Love you too, Dad."

Dad smiled at me. His tears had already stopped. "I did a lot of research on student loans today. I think we can make this work, especially if I get elected."

"Really?"

"Really."

We sat on the bleachers for almost two hours. Dad listened to what I had to say for the first time in years. I told him about Caleb and Parker. I told him about the stories I'd written and Ideas for what I wanted to write next. I told him about Steven, and how much he helped me when no one else could. I told him how excited I was about NYU and how crazy it would feel to live in a big city. Dad was a sponge, sopping up every word I said. It all felt familiar like I was talking to my mom again. It honestly felt like I'd gotten my best friend back.

———

I stared at myself in the mirror, I'd always felt ridiculous in nice clothes. I slipped on the black dress coat over my red vest and a white button-up shirt and reached for my red bow tie. I could hear Steven and Lauren chatting and laughing with my Dad downstairs. Red wasn't the best color to go with my ginger hair. I often got rosy in the cheeks, so I already knew I'd look like a ripe tomato during prom.

"We're gonna be late!" Lauren's voice boomed up the stairs.

"All right, I'm coming!" I did a quick check of my teeth before heading down. I gave my best dapper smile and buttoned my jacket as I entered the kitchen. I was met with over-the-top oooh's and ahhh's.

"You clean up nicely...for a jock," Stephen said as he walked over to hug me. He was wearing black skinny jeans with purple converse shoes and a matching purple blazer. He completed the look with a rainbow bowtie and glittery cheeks.

"Very handsome," Lauren said, strutting over to me.

"Look at you!" I said, gesturing to her with my mouth open in shock. She looked like a modern-day queen of hearts, her dress was strapless and cinched at the waist. Her hair was an array of ribbon-like buns, and she wore black high heels. "You're stunning," I said before taking her by the hand for a twirl.

"All right, let me get a picture," my Dad said from the living room. We all rushed in front of the fireplace and posed with Lauren in between Steven and me. The multiple flashes made me see purple and green dots floating around the room.

"We should get going," Lauren said as she reached for her purse. "Tasha texted me, she's just gonna meet us there."

My Dad pulled me off to the side. "Anything from Caleb?"

"Nothing," I said.

He frowned. "I have this charity dinner tonight so I'm not gonna be home until late," Dad said as he swiped through the pictures he'd taken. Steven and Lauren were practically out the door. I hugged my Dad and hurried to meet them. "Have fun, guys!" My Dad called out as we stepped outside. "And hey, no drinking and driving!"

We drove to prom in Lauren's Volkswagen bug while most people were taking limos, but we didn't see the point just being the three of us. Prom was being held at the Duncan Country Club and Golf Course, a forty-minute drive from Madison. I couldn't stop thinking about Caleb as I sat in the backseat watching the houses and trees whiz by. I wondered what it would feel like to slow dance with him in front of everyone. It was hard to fathom the idea of taking another boy to the prom. I looked at my phone, hoping to see Caleb's name, even though I didn't have any notifications.

He's gone for good this time.

My mind flashed back to looking at him lying in my bed. I could see him so clearly, wearing nothing but the moonlight. I hadn't realized I was studying him, memorizing every detail of his face in case he disappeared again.

We entered the lobby of the Country Club and collectively gasped. The theme of our prom was Winter Solstice, so everything was glistening with ice illusions and cool blue and white tones. A large Ice sculpture of a snowflake sat close to the ballroom's entrance. Strips of blue and white cloth decorated the walls, and large plastic snowflakes danced from the ceiling. There was a large square dance floor in the middle of the room surrounded by white-clothed tables set in semi-circles, each decorated with glittery snow. Living in Texas, it was the closest to a typical winter we could get.

We found our table and greeted Tasha with hugs. Her hair was tied up into three braided buns, mohawk style. I took in the sight of her black dress as I sat. It was a corset on top that blended into a ruffled skirt. I focused a little closer to see 'Black Lives Matter' printed in white letters all over the bottom of the fabric.

Everyone was taking selfies and posting Instagram stories while we waited for our food. We had to eat dinner before the dancing started. I ordered the fanciest steak I'd ever eaten and stuffed myself to the gills with mashed potatoes and asparagus. We had moved on to dessert when Jordan Palicki showed up at our table in a tux that looked much too small. He passed around a flask of mysterious alcohol. I was the only one at the table that didn't take a swig. The flashbacks from Dan's birthday party still haunted me.

The lights dimmed around us and the dance floor lit up with blue and purple lights and the voice of the DJ ripped through the room, "All right Madison High School are you ready to get this party started?!"

The whole senior class erupted into cheers and the music started blasting. Lauren and Steven screamed in each other's faces with excitement as the familiar sound of 80s pop drums thundered through us.

They started singing at each other. "Ooo baby, do you know what that's worth, ooo heaven is a place on earth!" They jumped out of their chairs and started dancing and scream-singing. I stared in amazement, laughing, not having heard the song before. Everyone flooded the dance-floor. They reached out, grabbed me by the sleeve of my suit jacket, and dragged me up. Both of them held me by one hand as they paved a way for us through the sea of dancing bodies, Tasha was close behind.

The colored lights flashed along with the drumbeats and spotlights circled the dance floor. We couldn't stop smiling at each other as we danced around like maniacs running wild at an insane asylum. I eventually caught on to the lyrics and shouted along, realizing it was the same words on repeat.

I felt my lower back getting sweaty as we reached the eighth song in a row, not slowing down our crazy dancing. Through the crowd I spotted Dan in a white tux, dancing with his shirt unbuttoned halfway down his torso, exposing his white tank top. I watched as he brought a hand up to his nose. He snorted something off his fist before throwing his head back, swaying chaotically. Dan didn't seem to be worried about getting noticed, it was obvious he was in his own world.

Another song started, but I needed a break. I trudged back to our table and took off my jacket, hanging it on my chair before rolling up my sleeves. My feet were already hurting, begging to be released from my tight shiny dress shoes. I sat and checked the blank screen of my phone, showing me nothing new. I glanced around the room, everyone looked so happy. In two weeks we'd be all be graduating and letting prom night become a memory. I'd probably never see Jordan Palicki again after graduation. I pictured him moving into a dorm at some state school and starting a successful weed business. I looked at the table next to me, Jessica Walters was sitting on Max Gibbons' lap. They'd become inseparable since she dared him to take the gum from her mouth at Dan's party. I pictured them going to the same college and promising each other they'd get married the day after graduation. I noticed all the different couples together, all straight couples who were smiling, taking pictures, kissing, grinding on each other on the dance floor. I felt an emptiness in my chest, suddenly feeling lonely.

Lauren, Tasha, and Steven popped up in front of me. They were out of breath and sweaty. Lauren looked down at me. "You okay?"

"I think so," I said, still staring at Jessica and Max. I could feel the jealousy forming in my stomach.

Steven smiled. "Do you guys want to tell him or should I?"

His words made my ears perk up. "Tell me what?"

"Well," Lauren said. "We wanted to do something special for you."

"Yeah, we were tired of seeing you sulk around everywhere, bringing the mood down," Steven said as he propped his arm on Lauren's shoulder.

I rolled my eyes. "What did you guys do?"

"Look for yourself," Lauren said, pointing behind me. My brow furrowed but followed her direction. I spun in my seat and saw Caleb standing awkwardly at the entrance of the ballroom. He was wearing a form-fitted navy blue suit with a black skinny tie, and his hair was perfectly pushed back from his forehead.

I shot out of my seat. "Oh my god!" I whipped my head back around and smiled, showing all my teeth. "How did you get him in?"

"I pulled some strings," Lauren said with a shrug, and Steven pantomimed a hair toss.

"I have so many questions," I said with a chuckle.

"It was actually Tasha's idea," Steven said. "She helped a lot."

I looked at Tasha with a smile. "Is this true?"

Tasha smirked. "I can't say I don't feel a little responsible for everything that happened after printing your story."

I stepped to her, taking her by the hands. "How'd you find him?"

Tasha looked at me with a raised eyebrow. "If someone's on social media, I can find them." We both laughed. "It was the least I could do, after everything."

"Tasha, you did nothing wrong, I promise. But thank you. You have no idea how much this means to me," I said. She smiled and I wrapped my arms around her in a tight squeeze.

"All right, go get that fine ass man before Jessica Walters sees him!" Tasha shouted over the music before giving me a playful shove. I gave her a salute and started through the tables with Caleb in my sights.

"Hey," I said with a head nod to Caleb.

"All right, let's slow things down," The DJ's voice echoed. "Let's get all the couples to the dance-floor. This is Slow Dance by AJ Mitchell."

It was the first slow song of the night. The crazy flashing lights transitioned into slow pulses. The song started with charming beats and plunks of a piano. The singer's high voice bounced off the walls, filling the room with ease.

I stood in front of Caleb with my hands in my pockets and smiled. "What're you doing here?"

Caleb cocked his head, "I guess I just can't get enough of you." He flashed his dimples as if he knew they were my kryptonite.

"Where's Parker?"

"I finally got a hold of Miguel after we left, so we've been staying with him."

"Oh, good, good." I nodded awkwardly.

Caleb offered me his hand. He was cool and relaxed. "Wanna go turn some heads?"

I took a deep breath, mentally preparing to come out to the entire room, teachers, chaperones, and any other student that hadn't heard the gossip before I placed my hand in his. We both smiled as he led me to the dance-floor. People caught on as we threaded through them. I imagined Caleb as a handsome prince leading me to our first dance in front of the King and Queen of the Winter Kingdom.

Caleb kept getting closer to the middle of the dance-floor and I was getting more nervous. He stopped in the center, turned to me, and wrapped his arms around my neck. "Is this okay?"

"Yeah, I think so," I whispered as I reached for his hips. My eyes darted left and right.

The dance-floor became a wave of swaying couples. I could see others were staring at us, but I tried to focus on Caleb's face.

"You look cute in a bow tie," Caleb said. It was as if he had a spell over me, I hung on to his every word.

"You're not too bad yourself."

"Miguel let me borrow the suit, though I'm not sure whose it is because he's way too short to wear this."

I grinned and shook my head.

We swayed as we spun in a slow circle. I could see people

whispering out of the corner of my eye. My jaw clenched as my anxiety built. Caleb was unfazed by the looks we were getting.

"Hey," He whispered, "Just focus on me."

I took a breath and asked him another question to focus on his lips. "What did Tasha say to get you here?"

"I've been sworn to secrecy," Caleb said. "But, I will say she reminded me how stupid I was for pushing you away. Life's gonna be complicated no matter what."

My anxiety began to ease as I noticed the detail in his eyes

"I can't believe you're here," I said before looking over to see Lauren and Steven dancing together, smiling at us. Steven started making kissing faces that made me smile. "I never thought this was how my prom would go."

I felt Caleb's thumbs stroke the back of my neck. "You mean you didn't picture yourself dancing with a guy in the middle of a bunch of straight couples while they stared at us?"

"Exactly," I said with a chuckle. Caleb pulled me in closer, making our bodies touch, and my stomach fluttered with excitement.

I let my hands rest on Caleb's tailbone and I focused on his lips, restraining myself from kissing him. "I just never pictured any of this. Since we lost my mom it's felt like I've been endlessly falling with nowhere to land."

Caleb slid his hands to the side of my neck. I felt his thumbs against my jaw. He looked me in the eye and said, "Well, I'm here now. You can land on me."

His words broke down all the walls I'd been building since the first day I saw him. Everyone's curious glances no longer mattered. I was all in with Caleb. Everyone else faded away until it was just the two of us swaying under the winter lights. Caleb was all I saw. I kissed him for the first time without an ounce of fear. There were no gasps from passersby, no words of discrimination thrown our way, no faces of disgust because none of it was important anymore. I was his, and he was mine. I felt protected by an invisible force field that our passion for each other had created.

Everything came back into focus when I pulled away from Caleb's lips. He pulled me close, and I rested my face against his shoulder. I looked up to see Dan glaring at us from the edge of the dance-floor. He was pulling at his nose before we locked eyes, and walked off.

The slow song transitioned into an upbeat pop tune that everyone cheered for. Lauren and Steven hopped closer to us and started singing and dancing along, even Tasha found her way over. I was finally able to introduce them to the boy that held my heart.

Another hour and a half of nonstop dancing had passed before I put my lips to Caleb's ear. "Wanna get outta here?"

"Are you sure? What about your friends?"

"They'll be fine without us," I shouted over the music. Caleb held up an 'okay' signal and nodded his head. I turned to the others and shouted, "we're gonna head out!" They all frowned but quickly transitioned into one hug after the other. I took Caleb by the hand, guiding him back to my table to collect my things.

We stepped outside. It was drizzling, making the ground slick.

"I'll get us an Uber," I said as I pulled my phone out.

"No need," Caleb said casually as he started toward the parked cars.

I jogged up behind him. "What do you mean?"

"Miguel let me borrow his car," Caleb said, stopping behind a Jeep.

"Caleb, you don't have a license."

He stepped in front of me and put his finger to my lips. "Sshhh. It was a special occasion." He snatched the keys from his pocket and tossed them to me. "But you should probably drive." I caught the keys against my chest and shook my head at him with a grin.

The whole drive back to my house, I couldn't stop thinking about getting Caleb out of his suit and into my bed. I wanted to feel his hands on me again. I craved the slightly salty taste of his skin. I gripped the steering wheel to help me focus on the road, but Caleb's hand on my thigh wasn't helping.

I parked in front of my house and glanced at the school, noting how creepy it looked at night. Caleb was quick to get out of the car and was already waiting at the side door.

I strutted up to him, thinking how lucky I was to be his. He was leaning against the house and I planted a kiss on his lips. His hands rested on my lower back, and I wanted him to take me right there on the asphalt of the driveway. Caleb let go of my kiss and stared at me, studying my face.

"What?"

Caleb smiled. "Tasha told me about NYU. Why didn't you tell me that the story got you in?"

I shrugged. "I didn't want to rehash it and risk pushing you away again."

"It made me realize I don't have a lot of time left with you now that you're gonna be a city boy. I want to spend every second with you that I can. That's what got me to come back."

"I think we can make it work," I said as I pushed my fingers through his hair. The usual soft strands had gone stiff from the hairspray holding it back.

"As your muse, I think it's my responsibility to stick around. Who knows, maybe you'll write a bestseller about me." I laughed before Caleb pulled me in for another kiss. I couldn't stop smiling against his face.

I heard faint footsteps against the dampened driveway. I quickly turned, and my heart jumped into my throat as I saw Dan standing there like a phantom in the shadows. Still wearing his white tux. The street was silent, the drizzling rain had stopped and Dan's heavy breaths filled the air. I noticed his shadow before I realized what was happening. Dan's arm was stiff and pointed. A nearby street light reflected off the bridge of the gun in his hand.

THIRTY-FOUR

y breath got short as I stared down the barrel of Dan's gun. I slowly raised my arms. I could feel Caleb close behind me. "Dan," I said. "What's going on?"

"Get inside," Dan said with a flat tone. "Hey!" Dan yelled, inching toward us, aiming the gun at Caleb. "Do not reach for your phone! Turn around slowly and get inside."

"Okay, okay," Caleb said with his hands up to his chest. I did as I was told, following Caleb through the side door, into the kitchen. My mind was racing. I glanced around for anything I could use as a weapon. The knives were too far away, but a stool was an option. Caleb and I stood pressed against the kitchen island. Dan closed the door behind him, not once looking away or pointing the gun elsewhere.

"Dan, just put the gun down. We can talk," I said with a voice crack. My heart was pounding through my chest.

"I don't want to talk!" Dan shouted, moving in front of us.

"Just, tell us what you want," Caleb said with a clenched jaw. "I have some money in my wallet, you can take it and go."

"I'm not going anywhere," Dan said with a sniffle. His eyes were wide and his pupils were large.

"Why are you doing this? I'm your friend," I said, my voice trembling.

"Faggots are not my fucking friends!" Dan yelled. A vein erupted from his neck. "You can't have everything."

"What're you talking about, Dan?" I said as calmly as I could.

"You've always been the fucking golden boy!" Dan said as he tightened his grip on the gun. "You get everything you want. The girls always wanted YOU! Fuck, even the guys want YOU! The scouts wanted YOU for the scholarship! Everything was so easy."

"You're high, man," Caleb said. "These are the drugs talking, not you."

Dan pointed the gun at Caleb. "FUCK YOU! You don't know me!"

"I do," I whispered. "This isn't you."

"Shut up, faggot!" Dan inched closer to me, pointing the gun at my chest. "You're so smart! You know everything, right golden boy?"

My jaw clenched as the tip of the gun touched my chest. My stomach swirled as I tried to think of anything to make him drop the gun.

"Say it again, see what happens," Dan said. "This isn't me? Say it again!"

Fear held my mouth shut.

"That's what I thought. Faggot golden boy doesn't have anything to say, does he?" Dan spat out a wad of saliva that hit my neck.

I closed my eyes, praying Dan wouldn't squeeze the trigger when I said, "I know what you're going through."

Dan took a step back, still aiming at me.

"Steven told me what happened," I said, opening my eyes once I didn't feel the gun against me. "And it's okay, you don't have to hide it anymore."

"Fuck you!" Dan spewed. "Whatever he told you was a fucking lie! I'm not a faggot. I don't need conversion therapy!"

"No one is saying you do," I said, keeping my voice low and calm.

"I'm gonna kill that queer next. I'll put this gun in his mouth for spreading lies about me!"

"Dan, please..." Caleb whispered.

"Shut up! Just shut up!" Dan rubbed his nose and shook his head. "You and him..." Dan said as he switched his aim to Caleb. "...make me sick!" Dan looked at us with his chin down and his eyes up with a furrowed brow. "Everything would be so much fucking better if you were dead."

I barely registered what Dan said before he pressed the gun to my head. I turned my neck out of instinct and crunched my eyes closed.

Caleb lunged for Dan's arm and a shot rang out next to my ear, sending a bullet through the window above the sink, sending shards of glass in every direction. I crouched away and grabbed the side of my head. All I could hear was a loud ringing that sent a bolt of pain down my neck. My hand felt wet and warm. I saw blood on my fingers, realizing the bullet had grazed my ear.

Still trying to wrestle the gun away from Dan, Caleb smashed him against the side door and the gun went off again, causing me to duck. Caleb sent a knee into Dan's stomach and the gun fumbled out of his grip, sliding under a stool.

Dan gained the upper hand, picking Caleb up into the air before slamming him down on the tiled floor. Dan was able to get a swift kick into Caleb's ribs as he tried to get back onto his feet. Caleb let out a gasping yelp, falling over on his back.

Dan stepped over Caleb's tussled body and pinned him down, sitting on his chest. I was totally frozen, still gripping my ear as Dan's fist came down hard, smacking against Caleb's face. Dan's fist shot into the air then down hard, again and again, each time splattering more blood across the white floor.

"Stop!" I cried.

Do something! I screamed in my head.

I jumped up, attempting to lock my arms around Dan's neck. It was as if he knew exactly what I was going to do because he swung his elbow back, connecting to my nose with a crack. My eyes went blurry with tears as I stumbled backward, smacking my back against the counter, knocking a stool over as I crumbled to the floor. The pain ricocheted across my face and I could feel the blood drip down my lip.

Through wavy vision, I could see Dan's arm swing again, hurling against Caleb's bloodied face. I was dizzy and tried to shake it off as I heard another wallop. I pushed myself on all fours and noticed a black blob on the floor that came into focus. I reached for the gun and gripped it firmly with both hands. I sat up on my knees, pointing the gun at Dan's back as he continued to hit Caleb four feet in front of me.

"DAN STOP! I'll fucking shoot you!" I screamed as tears poured from my eyes, but he didn't let up.

I squinted and squeezed the trigger, sending out a flare. The bullet ripped through the back of Dan's neck, sending a chunk of flesh spiraling to the floor. Crimson blood spat from the wound. Dan stopped punching and clumsily grabbed at his neck before he collapsed next to Caleb.

My ears rang. I'd heard gunshots in movies, but in real life, they are louder than you'd expect. My elbows locked and my arms shook. I wanted to drop the gun, but my entire body was frozen in place. All I could smell was the scent of hot metal emanating from the barrel of the weapon. My mouth was too dry to speak, and I could hardly swallow. I desperately wanted to reach out to make sure he was okay, but there was so much blood. It was so red, and it was coming out so quickly. I didn't want to shoot him but he wouldn't have stopped otherwise. Tears welled in my eyes. His blood was on my hands now.

I dropped the gun and crawled over to Caleb, crying. Dan was face down in a puddle of his own blood. I could hear him gurgling for a breath as his body jerked around before going still.

I pulled Caleb into my lap, out of the pooling red matter. I tried to wipe the mess from his face, but the blood was too thick. "It's gonna be okay," I whispered as I cried over him. I pulled out my phone, barely able to click the numbers because my hand was shaking so badly. I slapped the bloody screen to my ear, listening to it ring. "I need help!" I said through gritted teeth and sobs. "Me and my boyfriend were attacked and I can't tell if he's breathing. Please send someone!" I was panicked and almost forgot my own address when the dispatcher asked for it. I dropped the phone once the woman said an ambulance was on the way.

I gently stroked Caleb's matted hair, barely seeing through the blood and tears. I leaned over and whispered in his ear. "Please be okay, please be okay."

Two cops kicked through the front door and rushed their way to the kitchen with their guns drawn. I was huddled over Caleb's limp body before the officers pulled me away and two paramedics rushed to evaluate him. The officers held my arms behind my back as I watched one paramedic pump his hands against Caleb's chest, counting out loud in quick succession. The second paramedic checked Dan's limp body, searching his neck for any sign of life.

"He's gone," the second paramedic said, before moving away from Dan.

My entire body trembled as I sobbed. My legs felt weak, and the officers had to keep me from tumbling back to my knees.

Suddenly Caleb coughed up a spurt of blood.

"He's got a pulse," the first paramedic called out. "Get the stretcher."

I took a breath of relief and squirmed out of the officer's grip, kneeling next to Caleb. "Thank god," I said with a sigh. "I'm here, babe," I said, trying my best to wipe my tears away as they fell. Caleb slowly turned his head toward me, unable to open his eyes as they were already swollen shut. He started feeling around for me until he got hold of my hand. He used his finger to draw a circle on my palm. I let out a sob and interlocked my fingers with his. Bending over, I gently pressed my forehead against his before whispering, "I love you too, Caleb. I love you so much."

———

Red and blue lights filled the street. My Dad drove up to the house as Caleb's stretcher was being hoisted into the ambulance. He rushed toward me, but a pair of officers stopped him.

"That's my son!" he yelled at them. The officers eased their stance and let him through. He ran to me before I could jump in the back of the ambulance.

"Dad!"

He wrapped his big arms around me and I sobbed into his shoulder.

"Landon, what happened?"

I looked at him with my mess of a face. "Dan attacked us. He hurt Caleb pretty badly."

"Jesus." My Dad glanced at Caleb in the ambulance then back to me. "Go with him. I'll meet you at the hospital, we can talk there." He hugged me tightly before I hopped inside and the paramedics closed the door, leaving my Dad standing there looking scared.

Caleb was taken into surgery as soon as we reached the hospital. The doctors told me he had a broken rib and an orbital fracture around his left eye. I voiced my concerns about his vision but they said the break was clean, that his eye was swollen but they could fix everything with no risk to his vision.

I was getting my ear patched up when my Dad entered the room with two police officers. They made me recount the whole event from start to finish. I was so exhausted and worried that it felt like it took hours just to get all the words out.

The officers told us they'd removed Dan's body from our house and had notified his family. My stomach sank thinking about Chris and his parents. Prom had gone so perfectly. I never imagined the night would end the way it did.

"Are you in pain?" My Dad asked as the officers left the room.

I was still sitting on the hospital bed, with my legs hanging over the side. "A little. The doctors said the ringing should stop after a few hours, maybe a day at max."

My Dad wrapped me in a hug again before pulling back, keeping his hands on my shoulders. "Thank god you're okay. Did they tell you anything about Caleb?"

"He's in surgery now. They say he'll be all right." A wave of realization hit me. "Oh, my god. I have to tell his little brother."

"I can call his parents," Dad said.

"They've been staying with a friend. I have to call Miguel."

"Do you know his number?"

"They gave me Caleb's phone." I reached into my pocket and pulled it out. I opened the screen, but it had one of those pass-words where you have to draw a pattern. I sighed. "I don't know his password." I stared at the phone, trying to think of anything I could trace. I looked at my Dad again. "Miguel's car is at our house, though. He let Caleb drive it to the prom."

"Okay. Stay here. I'm gonna make some calls."

My Dad pulled out his phone as he left the room. I opened the screen of Caleb's phone again and stared. An idea popped into my head.

It can't be that easy. I traced out the letter A on Caleb's screen and his phone unlocked. My eyes widened. It actually worked. I could see a picture of him and Parker behind all the apps. I clicked through his contacts and hit the green button next to Miguel's name before touching the phone to my ear.

"Hey Miguel, it's Landon."

———

I was back in my kitchen, staring down the barrel of Dan's gun again. I was trying to tell Dan that everything would be okay, that he didn't have to hide anymore, but I couldn't hear my own words. My mouth was moving, but no sound was coming out. Dan was getting frustrated that I was moving my lips, but I wasn't talking. With no warning, Dan pointed the gun at Caleb and shot him in the chest. A rope of blood hit my face. I screamed as I watched Caleb crumble to the ground, or it felt like I was screaming, but again my voice couldn't be heard. I glanced at Dan just in time to see the gun erupt in my face with a loud bang.

My eyes popped open, and I quickly raised my head off of Caleb's bed to see Miguel and Parker walking into the room. I stood and Parker greeted me with a hug. "We have to be quiet," I whispered to Parker. "Caleb's still sleeping."

"Okay," Parker whispered back. He sat in my chair next to Caleb's hospital bed and reached to hold his brother's hand.

I stepped over to Miguel and hugged him. He handed me a small bag.

"I got you a coffee and a bagel."

"Thanks," I said.

"How're you holding up, sweetie?"

"I'm okay, I think." My wrist was still sore from the kickback of the gun. "Thanks for bringing Parker again."

"Of course. He's been an angel."

I glanced over to the bed. Caleb was waking up. They bandaged his head, covering his left eye, but he saw Parker and smiled.

"I need to make some work calls," Miguel said. "But when I'm done, I can stay here with Parker. You should go home and get some rest. You've been here for three days already."

"Yeah, you're probably right. Thank you."

Miguel smiled and reached for my hand, giving it a little squeeze. The jingle of all of his bracelets reminded me of the bell you hear when walking into Lucky's. Miguel closed the door behind him and I sauntered over to the bed, pulling up another chair on the other side of the bed.

"When are they gonna let you come home?" Parker's high voice had an impatient tone.

"In a few days, I hope." Caleb's voice was hoarse.

"But it's already been a week and two days," Parker said.

"The doctors just want to make sure I don't do too much before my body's ready."

"I'm gonna ask the doctor if we can go to the movies when you're out!" Parker said excitedly.

"I don't think they'll have a problem with that," I said with a chuckle.

Caleb smiled at me and turned his head to Parker again. "How's it been staying with Miguel?"

"It's been good," Parker said. "He sprays a lot of perfume, but other than that I like it there. He makes me a lot of sandwiches and lets me watch YouTube."

Caleb let out a small laugh followed by a grunt of pain. "Tell Landon about your loose tooth and the sandwich."

Parker's eyes lit up, and he looked over the bed at me. "This one time I was eating a ham sandwich, and I had a loose tooth, but when I finished the sandwich, my tooth was gone! I swallowed it!"

Caleb turned to me. "The whole day he begged me to call the tooth fairy to make sure he still got the dollar."

"And did you?" I asked Parker.

"It was under my pillow the next morning!"

We all laughed.

I held Caleb's hand before giving it a quick kiss. Seeing him smile again made my heart leap. Every day I got to hold Caleb's hand in that hospital bed, my love for him grew. I owed him my life, something I was sure I'd never be able to repay him for.

———

I stepped into the kitchen with a yawn. The sun was up, but I could barely keep my eyes open. I haphazardly reached for a bowl and a box of cereal. I grabbed the milk from the fridge and sat at the kitchen island. My line of sight connected with the floor where I could see Dan's lifeless body lying there in a pool of blood as if everything happened the day before. I was stuck there, staring, half expecting him to pick himself up and walk out the door.

"Morning, son," My Dad said. His voice pulling me from the trance.

I squeezed my eyes closed for a second and opened them. "Morning."

"I just got off the phone with Principal Jamison. He said you could take your final exams online if you wanted."

I watched my Dad pour himself a cup of coffee and join me at the island.

"Awesome, thanks."

"If you want that, of course. You can go back whenever you're ready."

"It might be good to be around my friends again," I said.

I poured my cereal and could smell the sugar from the box.

"Jamison told me they were having Dan's funeral today over at St. Matthews."

"Oh?" My stomach flipped when I looked at my cereal. I suddenly didn't have an appetite.

I thought about the funeral for the rest of the day. I thought about Chris and his parents and the pain they must've been going through. Lauren told me Chris hadn't returned to school. A part of me wanted to see him, but I was too scared to reach out.

I stepped into the living room to find my Dad watching TV.

"Can I use the car?"

He turned toward me, looking tired. "Sure. Going to see Caleb?"

"Maybe. Just kinda wanna clear my head."

"Want to talk about anything?"

"No, it's okay. I'm okay."

My Dad smirked. I didn't think he believed me.

"Keys are hanging up," he said.

"Thanks. Let me know if you need anything while I'm out."

.   .   .

I didn't want to clear my head. I knew where I was going. I didn't fully understand why I wanted to go to the church. Maybe I wanted to see how many people showed up. It wasn't until I pulled into a parking spot that I realized it was because I hoped to see Chris.

The parking lot was full of cars. I had a clear sightline to the entrance of the church. I'd guessed a lot of people from their congregation were there and extended family. I perked up when I saw Dan's Dad walking through the main doors. I hopped out of the car and leaned against the hood.

Chris and his mom were arm in arm, dressed in all black. He was so much taller than her. They stopped and greeted a few others coming in at the same time. A pit formed in my stomach when Chris spotted me. He hugged his mom and watched them go inside the church before he walked over to me.

"Hey," he said with his hands in his pockets.

I tried to swallow, but my mouth was dry. "Hey, man."

"What're you doing here?"

I stood up straight. "I wanted to see you, see if you were okay."

"I'm all right. My mom's a mess, but I'm trying to be with her as much as I can."

"Yeah, Lauren told me you haven't come back to school."

"We thought it was best. I've been doing everything online."

"Me too," I said, looking at the ground.

"If my parents see me talking to you they'll flip out, so I should get back."

He looked so drained like all the color was removed from his face. He turned away, but I didn't want him to leave.

"Wait," I stepped to him. "I'm so sorry, Chris."

His jaw tensed.

"I keep replaying everything in my head," I said. "Everything happened so fast. I can't sleep because I see him every time I close my eyes. I feel so fucking guilty." My eyes welled up. "I just... I wanted to make sure you knew I was sorry."

Chris suddenly pulled me into a tight hug, and I shattered in his arms, sobbing into his big shoulder.

"It's not your fault," Chris whispered. His voice sounded weak.

The guilt that had been building inside me for weeks released when I heard his words. Letting Chris hold me while I cried felt like the cleanse I'd needed.

Chris pushed away and looked at me with watery eyes. "Good luck in New York, okay?"

I nodded, wiping my wet face with my sleeve as I watched him walk away and disappear into the church. I stayed sitting in my car for another ten minutes before I could make myself stop crying.

———

"We fucking did it!" Steven cheered.

I was standing with him, Lauren, and Tasha in the front courtyard of the school. Graduation was being held on the football field. They had set up a small stage for the speakers and white chairs on the field for the graduating class. We were dressed in our red and white gowns.

"Are you sure you guys don't want to go naked under the gowns? There's still time," Steven said. We all laughed.

"Hell no," Lauren said.

Tasha pulled us all into a hug and said, "you guys are gonna come visit me in DC, right?"

"Hey," Steven said. "We have months together before we start booking trips to see each other." Steven reached into his pocket and pulled out his phone. "My mom's on the field, I'll see you guys over there!"

We all smiled as Steven jogged off.

Lauren turned to me. "You ready?"

"I'm ready for everything to be over," I said.

Lauren smirked, "Just think, in a few months we'll both be in New York, starting fresh."

"We all need to start fresh," Tasha said.

"Hey, there's Caleb," Lauren said.

I looked over my shoulder and saw Caleb walking over with Miguel and Parker.

Tasha nudged Lauren.

"We'll meet you on the field, okay?" Lauren said with a smile.

I turned back and nodded, giving them both a hug before they trotted off.

Parker ran into me, face first with a hug, and looked up at me. "Caleb said I should tell you congratulations."

I laughed. "Thanks, bud."

"Okay, come on," Miguel said, reaching a hand out to Parker let's go find a good seat." Parker let go of me and ran. "Congrats Landon,"

"Thank you!" I said to Miguel with a smile as he passed.

Caleb stood in front of me, straightened my red cap, and playfully dusted my face with the tassel. His smile felt so genuine, even though his cheek was still swollen and stitches ran through the middle of his left eyebrow.

"This is it," Caleb said, reaching for my hands. "You're finally free of high school. How does it feel?"

"It feels like it took forever. I just wish my mom was here to see it."

"She can see it, don't you worry," Caleb said, bringing my hand up to kiss it.

I smiled, thankful he was there. "How should we celebrate?"

Caleb chuckled. "Well, we have the whole summer before

you jet off to New York, so, we have plenty of time to figure it out."

"As long as I get to spend every day with you," I said, wrapping my arms around his neck. "I don't care what we do."

"Honestly..." Caleb held his arms around my waist and pulled me against him, giving me a gentle kiss. "... That sounds perfect."

Continue reading for a Sneak Peek of *Land On Him.*

NEW YORK CITY

EIGHT MONTHS LATER.

L auren and I picked at a chocolate croissant at The Ivory Den. The shop was overstuffed with college students taking shelter from the cold.

"I already have to write three papers by the end of the week," I said, licking the chocolate filling off my fingers.

"Not only do I have to write two papers, but I also have performances at the end of the week. So, two dance combos, two monologues, and a song from friggin' *Les Miz* to memorize."

"Jesus," I said before sipping from my cup. "Why are you even here?"

"I needed a break, believe me." Lauren ripped the end off the croissant. "These musical theater girls are bat shit."

I laughed.

"Has your roommate started to clean up after himself yet?"

I rolled my eyes, "Nope."

"Hey, I've seen your room at home. You aren't exactly Mr. Clean."

"Yeah, but this is next level," I said. "I've already used an entire bottle of Febreze since being back. And I have to wear headphones to bed because he stays up late on his computer."

"Doing what?"

"He's really into coding and hacking and stuff. He types so fast. I swear I can hear it in my dreams."

Lauren laughed, taking a sip from her cup. "How's your dad doing? He must be crazy busy since he got elected."

"Yeah, it seems pretty nuts. But you should hear what people suggest at council meetings," I said.

Lauren chewed, shaking her head. "Christmas break went by so fast. I feel like I barely got to see anyone."

"I know," I said, checking the time on my phone.

"Still nothing from Caleb?" Lauren asked before finishing her hot chocolate.

I sighed and crossed my arms. "I've texted and called him since I've been back, but he hasn't responded. He gave me a half-assed Happy Birthday when Parker called me, but that was it. I fucked everything up," I said, looking at my lap.

Lauren's voice got soft. "You both said shitty things. And you were drunk. He can't hold that against you forever."

Lauren unhooked her purse from the chair. "It's not like he hasn't gone dark before.

"It's different this time."

Lauren laid a hand over mine across the table. "He's being an asshole. Maybe I'll text him." She stood and slipped on her coat.

"I don't want to get you involved." I stared at my phone's dark screen.

"Okay, but I'll send him a text if you want me to."

"Thanks."

"I should stop procrastinating and get back to memorizing." She struggled to slip her backpack on so I stood to help her. "What're you up to for the rest of the day?" She wrapped her long scarf around her face.

"I have a writing session with Isaac, so I'm heading to his place next."

Lauren pushed the scarf under her chin and raised an eyebrow. "Who's Isaac?"

I shrugged, slipping my hands into my pockets. I could feel the chill whip in whenever someone walked out of the coffee shop. "This guy I met. He's a year ahead of me at NYU." I didn't want to spill all the beans about Isaac just yet.

"Is he cute?"

I smirked. "Yeah, I guess."

"Is he single?"

"Why? You want me to hook you up?"

"Hey, straight guys are hard to come by at my school. A girl has needs."

I laughed before pulling her into a hug. "He told me he had two boyfriends once, so I think you're out of luck."

"Two boyfriends? At the same time?" Lauren pulled back, leaving her arms around my waist.

I looked down at her. "They were a throuple, apparently?"

"Oh." I could tell the gears were turning in her head. Then she looked up at me with sincerity in her eyes. "Caleb will come around, okay?"

I nodded, forcing a smile. "I'll text you later."

Lauren flung open the shop's door, entering the human current along the sidewalk. Just as the door was about to close, I caught a glimpse of Dan standing in the middle of the sidewalk in his bloodied tuxedo, unnoticed by the people walking by, wrapped up in their winter garb. I scrunched my eyes closed and took a deep breath.

Fuck, not again.

———

Later that night, I sat at my desk, finishing a paper about plotting a story.

Josh popped his head out from the bathroom next to my desk. His dreadlocks swung in every direction. "Can I use your bar of soap? I'm all out."

I peered at him. "Sure," I said. He smiled and shut the door while I made a mental note to open a new bar of soap the next time I showered. Josh was cool, but co-existing with him in a small space wasn't ideal. I started typing again as I heard the squeak of the shower knob and the water hitting the porcelain.

I was on my last paragraph when a loud knock rocked my door, causing me to jump out of my skin. With a grunt, I pushed myself out of my chair, kicking a pair of Josh's boxers under his bed.

I opened the door, and my blood went cold when I saw Caleb wearing his tight jeans and leather jacket.

"Caleb..." I muttered, barely able to speak.

He held a backpack that looked like it'd been through a tornado. One strap was missing, and the fabric was torn and ruffled. He entered my room and tossed the backpack on my bed.

My tongue dried up. "How... How did you get through security?"

"I snuck in," Caleb said, sounding raspier than usual as he rifled through his bag.

"That's impossible. How?"

"Doesn't matter."

Caleb manically dug through the backpack.

I stepped closer with a huff. "What are you doing here? I've been calling you."

"Can't afford a new phone."

That's right, he smashed it on New Year's. "So you didn't hear my voicemail?"

"No."

I was relieved he hadn't heard of my mental break. "How did you get here?"

"Two buses. It was the cheapest way." Caleb finally pulled his hands from the backpack and opened them in front of me, revealing his numbered key. He looked at me, his eyes worn with bags. "He wanted me to find it," Caleb said.

"What?"

"The numbers. I figured it out."

"What about them?"

"I asked around some hardware stores, and one guy recognized it. Said someone came in asking to make a copy but said he couldn't because it was technically a federal key."

"What does that mean?" Staring Caleb in the face felt like a dream.

"He said it belonged to a safety deposit box. It took me a few days, but I finally found the bank it belonged to."

My jaw fell agape. "Holy shit."

"It gets weirder."

Caleb paced between the two beds in the room. My mind raced with questions. I hadn't been that close to Caleb in so long. I wanted to hug him and tell him I was sorry.

"The woman at the bank said I was the only person authorized to open the box. I had to show my ID," Caleb said.

"Why are you *here* then? It sounds like your dad might be in Texas."

"He isn't. There was a New York address in the box with some other stuff. I've been looking for it for almost two days, but without my phone, it's been hard to find."

"Caleb, you've been here for two days! Why didn't you come here first?" The thought of Caleb alone on the cold city streets shattered me.

"After—I thought I could do this alone, but I'm realizing I can't. I need you."

His words pierced my chest. I heard the shower turn off, and my eyes shot to the bathroom door.

"Landon," Caleb said with a whimper in his voice. My gaze went back to his hazel eyes. "I need to figure out what happened," Caleb said. "My dad is here somewhere. If I'm gonna find him, I need your help."

THANK YOU FOR READING MY BOOK!

As a new author, reviews can be such a huge help to get new eyes on the page! I'd love to see what you have to say about *Land On Me*. Please leave a review on Amazon and Goodreads!

To stay up to date with me and to get exclusives about my next book, please join my Newsletter at www.matthewrcorr.com and follow me across Social Media @matthewrcorr

ACKNOWLEDGMENTS

If you've read this far, first off, thank you! If you are someone who doesn't know me in real life or if you are someone who I didn't personally ask to read this book, I am forever grateful to you, a stranger, for giving a new author a chance. I hope I entertained you and I hope you took something away from this experience. This whole thing started as a short story I wrote on Tumblr years and years ago, so the fact that it's now in your hands as a full-fledged novel, it's almost hard to fathom. Just know that I am so appreciative that you spent your hard-earned money on a little gay indie book. Thank you, thank you, thank you!

There are a ton of people to thank that helped make this dream come true. My parents should be the first, you know, since I wouldn't be here without them. Mom, Dad, you've been nothing but supportive of me my entire life. You supported me when I came out, when I said I wanted to be a performer, when I moved to New York City to go to college, when I made it to the professional stages and the TV screens, and then when I said I wanted to write a book. But even when I made mistakes, and trust me there were plenty, you were both behind me 100% and I feel very lucky to have you. It sounds cliche, but I couldn't have asked for better parents. And of course, the rest of my family followed suit. To both my grandmas, Danny Martinez, Cheryl VanLuven, Kenny Dias, you all had a little something to do with this book. Whether it be throwing me a few dollars for an editor or promoting the book on social media, it all mattered to me. Thank you!

To my boyfriends, Ryan LaForest, and Kyle DePriest. Wow, where would I be without you? You've both been so patient with me throughout this entire process. I know I sacrificed a lot of time with you guys so that I could get this done, but you never faulted me for that. You both encouraged me to keep going, no matter what. I think I was even writing on Thanksgiving! Ryan, thank you for reading every version of this story and for celebrating me, and popping a bottle of champagne just for finishing my first draft. That feels like forever ago now. Kyle, without you I wouldn't have a title! Thank you for brainstorming with me and giving me your brilliant, mostly sarcastic ideas. This title means more to me than you know. Thank you for giving it to me.

To my amazing friends, you have been my life-force throughout all of this. To Katie Pickett, who was my original editor-in-chief, the only one who would read this thing...You gave me so much. I'm sorry it took years to finish, but I hope you're happy with the final product! To Will Wolz, who, besides Katie, was the first friend who actually read it when I asked, and it was only like ten chapters back then, thank you for your kind words! To Sarah McIntyre, who has read the first four chapters about five times and nothing else until I released the book, you actually had an enormous impact and even helped shape Landon's dad into who he is. Thank you. To Grayson Kilgo, who was my point man for strategy, you're so smart and intuitive. I value our friendship so much. And to Betsy Rinaldi, my ride or die, thank you for being my personal cheerleader since day one. Who knows where I'd be now without you? Thank you for always having my back through every life choice I've made over the past "90 years" of our lives. Now please move to New York City so we can be together forever!

I've been so lucky to have an amazing professional team of women by my side. To Quill Hawk Publishing and Amy M. Le, what started as a simple Facebook conversation turned into an amazing friendship. Without you, I would've gone into this business blind. Thank you for giving me the tools to grow as a writer and for helping me navigate this crazy landscape. To Dessiree Perez, my fantastic cover artist, I'm sorry I worked you to the bone, but damn did you deliver! Our collaboration and your talent means so much to me. Thank you for bringing my vision to life through every detail. To Alicia Dean, my editor who cleaned up this mess of a manuscript. You truly are a saint. Thank you for all of your positive light.

This story would be nothing without my team of Beta Readers. You all single-handedly shaped this story and made it a hell of a lot better. I had long conversations with all of you about these characters and their struggles. For that, I am indebted to you. Thank you Savvy Jones, Alyssa Venora, Christian Krenek, Justine Melvin, Jeremy Haig, Jesse Kramer, Dana Semmel, Brandy (Eva) Lovell, Emerald Ketope, Amanda Cusack, Chris Arceo, Karen Mann, and Jessica Osborne.

To my fellow queer authors who I've made friends with throughout my journey, you've all taken me under your wings and made me feel like I could truly achieve this. Thank you for constantly dealing with my annoying questions, especially Jeff Adams, Alex Blades, Jordon Greene, Jason June, and Robbie Couch. (Please go support these amazing authors!)

If I didn't mention you by name that doesn't mean you weren't an important part of bringing this book to life. If you read it, wrote a review, shared it, told a friend about it, bookstagrammed it, made a TikTok about it, tweeted it...you mean the world to me! Thank you for being part of *my* story!

ABOUT THE AUTHOR

Matthew Corr was born and raised in beautiful New England. Coming out as gay in high school in his small town fueled his big city dreams. Matthew moved to New York City, where he gained a degree in musical theatre. After countless performances on stages across the country, his passion for writing finally stepped into the spotlight. Matthew is a huge nerd for film and everything Marvel related. He currently lives in Brooklyn, NY. To learn more about Matthew, and the release of his next book, please visit www.matthewrcorr.com or @matthewrcorr

Made in the USA
Middletown, DE
20 June 2024

56104231R00272